REBEL DAUGHTER

REBEL DAUGHTER

L O R I   B A N O V   K A U F M A N N

DELACORTE PRESS

Text copyright © 2021 by Lori Banov Kaufmann
Historical note © 2021 by Jonathan J. Price

All rights reserved. Published in the United States by Delacorte Press,
an imprint of Random House Children's Books,
a division of Penguin Random House LLC, New York.

Delacorte Press is a registered trademark and the colophon is a trademark
of Penguin Random House LLC.

Visit us on the Web! GetUnderlined.com

Educators and librarians, for a variety of teaching tools,
visit us at RHTeachersLibrarians.com

Library of Congress Cataloging-in-Publication Data is available upon request.
ISBN 978-0-593-12581-6 (trade) — ISBN 978-0-593-12584-7 (lib. bdg.) —
ISBN 978-0-593-12582-3 (ebook)

The text of this book is set in 11.5-point Bulmer MT.
Interior design by Ken Crossland
Jacket photograph by Stephen Mulcahey/Arcangel Images Limited

Printed in Canada
10 9 8 7 6 5 4 3 2 1
First Edition

To my father, Dr. Charles Banov, who reads people like others

read books. He taught me that everyone has a story.

FOREWORD

In the first century, the Roman emperor ruled the lands from Britain and Europe all the way to Africa, controlling his empire with legions of well-trained and fearsome soldiers. The Romans boasted that they had brought lasting peace and security to the entire world; the seas were free of pirates, and trade flourished. Any hint of opposition to Rome's rule was crushed immediately, without mercy.

Yet in 66 CE, Jewish people in a small, remote province on the eastern edge of the empire rebelled and established their own state, with Jerusalem as its capital. The war of the Jews against the Romans, as the ancient historian Flavius Josephus called it, lasted four grueling, blood-soaked years. At stake was the survival of the Jewish people.

Rebel Daughter is based on the unlikely but true story of a woman and a man who lived through this momentous time. The woman's two-thousand-year-old gravestone, the earliest archaeological evidence of the Jewish captives brought to Italy after the war, was discovered near the Bay of Naples. In the epitaph, the man begs the living to take care of the remains of the woman he loved.

This was an era when war, torture, genocide, and famine were commonplace; when women were subjugated and slavery was ubiquitous; when knowledge about the natural world was limited and people sought answers in magic, spirits, and demons.

The beliefs and customs of that society were quite different from ours today—but in many ways, people were the same. They questioned how God could allow evil to flourish. They wanted to protect their families, to live their lives in freedom and with dignity, and to find love. Just like us.

PART ONE

Daughters of Jerusalem, if you find my beloved,
what will you tell him? Tell him I am faint
with love.

Song of Songs 5:8

CHAPTER I

ESTHER HELD HER BREATH AS THE PRIEST STROKED THE LAMB AND whispered into its ears. It was a moment in and out of time, between life and death, between creation and destruction. The fulfillment of God's sacred commandment.

Ever since she'd been little, Esther had climbed the staircase to the balcony above the Gates of Nicanor to watch the *Tamid* ceremony. From here, she had an unobstructed view of the bloodstained altar blackened with ash. The guard, a portly man with a large key dangling from his belt, was a friend of her father's, and he winked when he saw her. They both knew that at fourteen, she should have been down below with the crowd in the Temple courtyard.

Another priest raised his knife. The blade, honed to slice a single hair in midair, glinted in the rising sun. The lamb bleated and its legs twitched. Esther wondered if the lamb knew its fate. The day before, it had probably nuzzled its face in its mother's warm, soft belly. Now, with a smooth, swift stroke, the priest cut its throat.

Esther tucked unruly strands of her long hair under her scarf. Sometimes she wished she could tuck her whole self underneath it. Almost overnight, she had gone from being invisible to attracting attention she didn't want. Her sister-in-law Miriam said it was because of her eyes; they were even darker than her hair, the color of carob pods left out too long in the sun, with a ring of gold around her pupils.

But Miriam was wrong. Men weren't looking at her eyes, or even her face. It was her body they were looking at, a body with curves that she hardly recognized.

Esther immediately spotted her father, Hanan, in a line of priests carrying jugs of olive oil, pots of incense, and baskets of flour toward the altar. Each wore a white robe covered with a vest woven with purple, scarlet, and blue threads. Their heads were wrapped with silk turbans, and their feet were bare. He wouldn't look up—his every movement was prescribed—but he knew, of course, that she was there.

Even though she had three brothers, Esther was the one he'd asked to walk home with him and carry their share of meat left over from the offerings.

After the *Tamid,* Esther followed her father through the throng of people on the Temple Mount. He lifted the hem of his robe, side-stepping the sludge on the ground. She held the reed basket close to her chest, hoping the street dogs wouldn't smell the singed lamb necks inside.

People moved aside and bowed their heads when her father passed. Hanan was a senior priest with an office in the Royal Portico, where there were one hundred and sixty-two marble columns so large that even when Esther and her brothers joined hands, they couldn't encircle one.

Esther saw them first—Roman soldiers. One, with an iron helmet atop his head and a short red skirt, stuck out his foot. Hanan stumbled and fell to the ground. The soldier planted his muddy boot on her father's back and held him down as he struggled to get up.

"Look, the Jew is kneeling before us," he sneered. "Now you're in the correct position, holy man, to pay homage to the great Roman empire." He thrust a large wooden shield with a picture of a wild boar into her father's face. "Kiss it!"

Her father turned away. There was a gash on his forehead, and blood ran down his face.

"Kiss it! I command you!"

Hanan lay motionless. People averted their eyes and scurried away. Her father's white robe, woven from fine linen imported specially from Alexandria, was covered in filth and dung. His scrolls lay scattered, and his wax tablet had been smashed.

Esther's eyes widened as two soldiers grabbed her father under his arms and yanked him up. Still, he remained impassive and refused to look at them. They shouted, but he didn't respond.

"Dirty Jew! You and your scraggly beards and barbaric superstitions! You'd cut your son's cock, but you won't kill a pig? Is that right?"

"Let him go!" Esther demanded, dropping the basket and running toward her father. The soldiers laughed.

"Look at the little she-wolf who comes to the rescue!"

One stepped on a scroll while another snatched the basket. A soldier with feathers on his helmet pulled her arms behind her back.

"If he won't kiss the shield, make him kiss the ass of the ass!" another one said. Laughing, they pushed her father toward a donkey tied to a low branch of a nearby tree.

"You Jews don't like graven images?" the tall one asked. "You won't kiss it? Then kiss the real thing instead!"

Esther struggled to break free.

"Kiss the ass and we'll let her go."

She sucked in her breath. Kiss it? An unclean ass? Her father wouldn't do that! He was pure, a priest. God would intervene and strike down these vile tormenters. What was He waiting for?

The donkey, startled by the noise, flung his head back, flapped his large ears, and brayed.

"Stop screeching!" another soldier yelled as he brought the side of his *gladius* down on the donkey's neck. "You sound like a woman!"

The animal's hind leg shot straight back and grazed her father. The soldiers laughed again.

She looked at her father for reassurance, for a sign that this would soon end. She wanted him to stand straight, to break free, to be a warrior like Samson or Gideon and take her home. She willed him to look at her, but he wouldn't; it was as if he were trying to shield her from his shame.

"What are you waiting for, Jew?"

Esther's palms were wet with sweat. Hanan took a deep breath and stepped toward the donkey. He bent toward the beast, closed his eyes, and quickly touched his lips to the donkey's haunches.

The soldiers cheered and gave her a forceful shove. The entertainment was over, and they had already lost interest. Her father grabbed her hand. He limped but still moved so fast that she could hardly feel her feet on the road. She didn't dare look back to see if the soldiers were following them.

Her father pulled her into the dark alleyway under the arches, below the aqueduct. His face and beard were caked with clumps of mud and dried blood. She wanted him to bring her close and comfort her, but he closed his eyes, and his hands hung by his sides.

"We will forget this ever happened," he said.

Esther clenched her fists. She hated the Romans. Every last one.

CHAPTER II

AFTER THE INCIDENT WITH THE ROMAN SOLDIERS, HER FATHER seemed to age years. The cut on his face healed, but he now walked with a cane. Slow, tentative steps replaced his once-brisk stride. They used to learn together in the early evenings—her favorite part of the day—but no more. He was too tired, he'd say. She missed his small, dark study, its shelves stacked with rolled parchment scrolls, its smell of the wax tablets.

The lessons had started when Esther was a little girl. Initially Hanan had tried to teach her older brothers, Yehuda and Shimon, the words of the prophets and the law. Yehuda had quickly outgrown their father's teachings and gone to the study house to learn with Rabbi Yochanan Ben Zakkai, the renowned scholar. Shimon made shadow pictures on the wall every time Hanan bent over the scrolls. She couldn't understand how Shimon was bored by the same stories she found so exciting: Cain killing his brother, Abraham lifting the blade to his own son, and Joseph languishing in prison. Esther would sit on the floor in the corner, hugging her knees to her chest, hanging on to every word.

Sarah, her mother, would peer into the study and cast a disapproving glance. One eye, half-shaded by a drooping, pink eyelid, seemed to see right inside Esther. There was no hiding Esther's greed for learning; her mother knew everything.

"Why are you filling the girl's head with Torah stories?" her mother asked. "Will this help her suckle a child or knead dough? Will this teach her the laws of purity?"

"She thirsts for knowledge," Hanan explained. "And her mind is like a plastered cistern that doesn't lose a drop. Besides, what else should she be doing?"

Sarah placed her hands on her hips. "The Gamaliel girls are spinning flax on their roof. They're eking out the last little bit of moonlight to be productive."

Hanan shook his head. "Their mother is putting them on display so everyone will *think* they're hard workers. They're not spinning for yarn. They're spinning for husbands."

Despite Sarah's protests, Hanan never made Esther leave the study. One day, Shimon didn't show up. When he didn't come the next day, or the day after that, Esther moved from the floor to the bench. Hanan continued to tell her stories but balked when Esther said she wanted to learn to read Hebrew.

"Girls don't read," he said.

"What about Deborah? She was one of the Judges. She saved Israel from disasters."

He smiled indulgently. "You're going to save the Jewish people from disaster?"

"Maybe," she said. "Queen Esther did."

"Yes, she did."

"It even says in the *Megillah* that Queen Esther wrote a letter. So she must have known how to read too!"

Hanan sat back in his chair. Esther could tell he was trying not to smile.

"And besides," she added, eager to press her advantage, "I'll have to read my marriage contract, won't I?" With that, Esther knew she had won.

Tonight, for the first time since the attack, Hanan called her into his study. Esther bounded into his room and sat down. He walked to his desk with a laborious shuffle and lowered himself onto the chair. She hoped she still remembered the Greek letters he'd been teaching her. She had learned to read and write in Hebrew faster than he'd anticipated, and now they were starting on Greek.

Her father put the fingertips of each hand together, like a temple in the air. She reached for the abacus on his desk, moved the small beads up and down in their grooves, waiting for him to speak. The echoes of the click, click, click of bronze beads hovered in the air.

"I've always been a counter too," he said at last. "That's what I do. I count the columns in the portico, the shekels in the treasury, the hides to be sold, the jars of incense. I count the wages of the stonemasons and bricklayers and carpenters."

He sighed and sat back. "Even though Yom Kippur is past, I'm still making lists, counting all the good things I've done and all the bad."

"You don't have any bad deeds," Esther said.

"Everyone who has lived has erred. I've sinned against God. I'm angry with Him for giving life, then taking it away."

"What are you talking about? God isn't taking anything away."

"Not yet, but He will. I used to count how many days I lived; now I count how many I have left."

"I don't like when you talk like this."

"The truth often makes us uncomfortable," he said, then smiled sadly. "But the thing about the truth is that it doesn't go away if we ignore it. And the truth is that no one lives forever. I want to make sure you and the family will be safe when I'm gone. You know, most girls are betrothed by the time they're thirteen."

Esther knew the road she was supposed to take, but she didn't want to travel it—at least not yet. She wanted to see where the other roads went first.

"I can't get married now! If I'm married, I'll have to move to my husband's house, and we won't be able to continue my studies. Even if my husband lets me read, I won't have time."

Hanan sighed. "Maybe your mother was right about filling your head with learning." He sat up in the chair. "Esther, you need someone from a good family to be responsible for you."

"Why can't I be responsible for myself?"

"You're a woman. You need a man to protect you, especially now, with all the unrest."

Esther frowned. "There's always unrest. The Romans have tormented us for years."

"You're right. But now people want to fight back."

"Good. I hope we kill all of them."

"Esther!" he admonished. "How can you say that?"

"How can you *not* after what they did to you?"

A pained expression crossed his face. "I thought we had agreed not to talk about that." *The truth often makes us uncomfortable.* She bit her lip.

After a long pause, he said, "Those were a few soldiers having their sport. Yes, the Romans can be coarse and greedy, but they're not forbidding our prayers and customs. Besides, Judea is a small province with *no* army. How can we defeat the most powerful empire in the world?"

"Yehuda says we will." Her older brother claimed that it was written in the Holy Scripture: at the End of Days, the Jews will vanquish their enemy, and God will establish His kingdom on

Earth. "Yehuda said the prophets have already predicted our victory."

"I've read the prophecies of Daniel and Isaiah too. You can find anything in there."

Esther squirmed in her seat. She didn't want to talk about war . . . or marriage. "Can we learn now?" she asked.

"Maybe another time," he sighed. "It's late."

CHAPTER III

THE NEXT MORNING, ESTHER THREW MILLET SEEDS TO THE CHICKENS, who were jabbing their beaks in the dirt and making loud clucking sounds. Matti aimed a small slingshot.

"You're not going to help me feed them?" she asked, leaning against the coop.

"I *am* helping. I'm keeping the other birds away."

Esther smiled, amused by the six-year-old's determined expression.

"I think I hit one," he said in a trembling voice. "What if I hurt it?" He dropped the slingshot.

"Don't worry. You couldn't hit it even if you tried."

"Really?" He lowered his head. "I'm no good."

"But one day," she said brightly, "you'll be like King David. For now, though, I think the birds are safe."

"I need to practice," Matti said. "I need to be a good shooter."

"Why?"

"Because when I'm older than you, I have to protect you."

Esther tried not to smile. "I'm going to protect *you*. Always." From the minute he'd been born, Esther had felt like he was hers; she slept next to him at night and cleaned his bottom during the day. Even now, it was Esther who mended the holes in his clothes, picked lice out of his hair, and reminded him to bathe once a week. Like all little brothers, he could be annoying, especially when he insisted on bringing his smelly pet goat with him everywhere he went or begged her to tell him another story.

That night, Esther lay on her back on the grassy slope outside their home, her arms cradling her head. Spiky blades of grass tickled her neck as she looked up at the dark sky.

"I don't see any," she said to Miriam, her sister-in-law and first cousin. They were looking for angels.

"That doesn't mean they're not there," Miriam said. She was five years older than Esther, so she knew things like that.

They fell silent. The staccato song of cricket wings crackled in the air.

After a few moments, Miriam spoke. "I'd like to be invisible, like the angels."

Esther wasn't surprised. Miriam, married to Esther's middle brother, Shimon, wore the same dung-colored robe every day and hid her silky hair, the color of roasted chickpeas, under a scarf.

Esther turned to face her. "Me too, especially when Mother wants water from the well or dung for the oven."

"You're complaining? You stretch out under the fig tree instead of threading the loom, and spit pomegranate seeds until your mouth turns red—"

"I don't spit seeds!"

"But you could," Miriam said, her voice rising. "That's the thing, you *could*! What can a married woman do without everyone clicking their tongues and shaking their heads? Enjoy your freedom while you can." She pursed her lips. Two frown lines were etched on her face, from the corners of her lips to her bulbous nose. Her deep-set eyes gave her a permanently doleful look. "You'll be betrothed before the next harvest."

"Father said it's time, but I'm not ready yet. What if they marry me off to some thirty-year-old?"

"There are advantages to an old husband. The oil merchant's daughter married a man from Jericho with forty-three years. She lives in a big house on the east hill, and he buys her everything she wants. She has a copper mirror and alabaster bracelets."

"Father says I need someone wise like Solomon and humble like Moses." Esther twirled a blade of grass between her thumb and forefinger. "Mother says I should marry someone like Jacob . . . rich."

"And who do *you* want?"

"No one—at least, not yet. I'll die if I have to spend my whole life spinning, and making beds and babies."

Miriam was silent, then asked in a soft voice, "What's wrong with that?"

Esther wished she could put her words back. "How did you pick Shimon?" she asked, eager to change the subject.

"I didn't, but if anyone had asked me, I would have said yes. I was a child. How could I have gotten used to a new family?"

Esther remembered when Miriam had first come to live with them. She'd refused to come inside. She'd stood in the courtyard clutching her mother's hand and a doll with yellow hair made from flax.

Esther filled her lungs with the resinous air, heavy with pine. "The only thing I know is that my husband will be a Jew from a priestly family."

"That's obvious," Miriam said. "What else could he be—a Roman?"

Esther laughed at the thought. "I wonder when my father will find my 'perfect' man."

"Every man is perfect until he's your master." Miriam tore off the needlelike awns of the weeds. "Then you have to worry about pleasing him *and* his mother. You grind the flour, make his food, and wash his feet. You have to worry about bringing children into the world. What if you don't have any? He'll divorce you. . . . He can, you know, if you don't give him children."

Esther knew that Miriam prayed to God to fill her womb, and saved scraps of cloth in the bottom of a wooden chest to swaddle a baby.

"God will give you a child," Esther said.

Miriam got up. "Maybe, but what if it doesn't survive the journey from the womb? Or I'm split apart by birthing pains or give birth to a snake-child? Or maybe a miracle happens and you deliver a baby who is healthy and whole—and he falls down the stairs, or tumbles from the roof? Maybe the evil spirits will sink their teeth into his young flesh, or your husband dies and leaves you a widow—"

"Stop!" Esther put her hands over her ears. Why did Miriam always ruin everything with her constant worrying? "I don't feel like looking for angels anymore."

Miriam swatted at the leaves and the straw clinging to her tunic. "Me neither."

CHAPTER IV

IT WAS MORNING IN THE FIELDS; THE AIR WAS ALREADY WET AND SUF-focating. The grape harvest was disappointing this year, but Esther's family still needed all the hands they could get to bring it in, including tenant farmers and slaves. Her uncle said they couldn't do anything about the gangs roaming the countryside, the Romans sucking them dry, or the vine bugs and drought killing their crops, but at least they could make good wine.

Esther's robe stuck to her skin, but nothing could dampen her enthusiasm. She had waited for this day, when she would finally work in the fields with the grown-ups instead of carrying water to the field hands or clearing away rocks. Miriam held out the knife, and Esther took it. She was surprised by the heft of the sickle.

"It's time you did real work," Miriam said. "I've been working the fields since I was ten."

Esther wasn't sure Miriam was telling the truth. Sometimes Miriam seemed to remember things that had happened, and things that hadn't, with equal certainty.

Esther worked all morning, gathering the warm, ripe fruit. Soon, though, her back ached from stooping over the grapes, dropping the clusters into the birch basket, and dragging it behind her. The basket was overflowing and so heavy that she could move it only with great effort. She counted the remaining stakes. The work wasn't nearly as much fun as she'd expected.

She put the knife into the sack around her neck and picked a few grapes, careful to choose the plump ones that grew toward the sun. She closed her eyes and chewed, savoring their sweetness.

"Be careful what you eat; you may end up drunk."

Startled, she spun around.

"Once," the man continued in a deep, sonorous voice, "a robin ate so many fermented grapes from the vine that it began to dance. Then it fell from its perch."

"I don't believe you," she said.

"In this case, my story is true. I'm Joseph, by the way. And you are?"

She studied him curiously: his arch grin, thick black locks that curled around broad shoulders, and an azure robe. She had never seen a dye so vibrantly blue, not even on the robes of pilgrims from Phoenicia. He was a Jew; there were tzitzit—threaded tassels sewn onto the corners of his mantle.

"I'm Esther Bat Hanan," she said. "Where are you from?"

"Here."

Esther regarded him skeptically. "I don't recognize you."

"I've been away." He studied her with equal interest. "I remember you. . . . You used to follow your brothers around like a stray mutt."

He knew who she was, but she didn't know him. Joseph, Joseph . . . Suddenly she knew! He must have been the Mouth's son.

Alexa, whom Esther and Miriam had named "the Mouth," was forever bragging about her son, Joseph, the "brilliant scholar." Esther had pictured a slight, balding man who talked in a high nasal tone, like the Mouth herself. Not a man like *this*.

"Your mother is Alexa? Your family lives in the courtyard behind the dovecote?" she asked.

He nodded.

Esther's own mother couldn't stand the Mouth either. She

would say, *I don't know who makes more noise: Alexa with her incessant yapping or the rooster she lets run around in our courtyard.* Maybe, Esther thought, Joseph had really left to escape his mother, rather than what everyone said, which was that the Sanhedrin, the council of Jewish elders, had sent him on a mission to Rome.

He tilted his head and let his gaze roam slowly over her body. "A lot can change in two years."

She felt the heat rise to her cheeks. She shifted her weight from one foot to the other and moved the sack, readjusting the strap around her neck. He watched her carefully. She wanted to prolong the conversation, but her thoughts were hurtling too fast for her tongue to catch them. He smiled and went back to his work.

Esther continued to fill her sack, but time felt stuck, as though hovering in the thick air. It was hard to keep up with Miriam's pace.

"Quit daydreaming," Miriam said, nudging Esther in the ribs. "Why are you looking at him like that?"

"I'm not." But she had been staring, ever since Joseph had taken off his robe and displayed the sculpted muscles in his back as he'd hoisted a full basket onto a donkey.

Miriam narrowed her eyes. "What you think you know isn't always so. Joseph Ben Matityahu is a man of the world. He's interested in women, not girls."

"He was interested enough to speak with me," Esther said. Except for her brothers, no man had ever teased her before. Miriam could be so annoying. Joseph *had* looked at her in that way, with such intensity, as if he could see under her skin.

"I want to go to the treading tonight," Esther said. She'd never been to the end-of-harvest celebration—grown-up things went on there, and she knew she didn't belong. But now, she decided, she'd be there. She wanted to see him again.

Miriam gave Esther a sharp look. "What's wrong with you? You know your parents would never allow it."

"They don't have to know."

"You shouldn't see all those drunken men and wanton women," said Miriam.

"You said yourself that I'll soon be betrothed, so why does it matter?"

"It matters if you get caught."

"I won't."

Miriam frowned.

"Remember how I helped you track Shimon down in the pubs?" Esther asked. "And I helped you bring him home, even when he was so drunk, he couldn't stand? I know plenty about what wine does to a person."

Throwing her hands into the air, Miriam relented—as Esther had known she would.

CHAPTER V

ESTHER LAY IN BED, WITH MATTI BESIDE HER. EVERY MUSCLE IN HER body ached and her eyelids felt heavy, but she willed them to stay open so she could go to the treading. She was waiting for Matti to fall asleep so she could sneak out. He rolled back and leaned against her. She inhaled his tangy scent.

Esther remembered when he was born . . . and when he'd almost died. She could still picture her mother, rocking the tiny, limp baby against her chest.

"Who do you think you are?" her mother Sarah had shouted at the demon who'd invaded him. "You're nothing! A nothing-bastard of a fallen angel and a whore. Your horns are stalks of wheat. The other angels will destroy you. Raphael will bind you, Michael will burn you, and Gabriel will throw your ashes into the abyss."

Turning to Esther, she'd whispered, "You have to show them you're not afraid. I've buried three babies; I won't bury this one."

Night after night, they burned the mandrake root, applied herb compresses, and chanted King Solomon's ancient incantations. Finally Sarah's words caught the demon and pulled it out through Matti's ear. The exorcism worked, but the demon took the hearing in Matti's left ear on its way out.

When the exorcism was over, her mother warned her, "You must still be vigilant. The demon might return from his wanderings, and it could bring others too." For Matti's protection, Sarah sewed a tiny pocket in his swaddling cloth—and in every shirt he'd worn ever since—for the tooth of a fox.

Esther didn't know if she could fight the demons as her mother had. The world was teeming with unseen creatures—terrifying, menacing ones. Her mother wasn't afraid, but Esther was. Sometimes she felt the fear in every part of her body, from the tingling of her fingers to the stiffness in her toes. Some nights, she fell asleep with her fingers in her ears to block out the desperate howls of the jackals. Like the demons, you couldn't see the jackals, but they were there, waiting to rake their claws into their next victim. She was afraid of the beggars too, who sat around the Temple walls with their toothless grins, misshapen limbs, and open sores. Tonight, though, she would be brave. She would go to the treading, even though things happened between men and women that her parents wouldn't want her to see.

She rose ever so slowly, but Matti grabbed her arm; even though he couldn't hear well, he could always sense the slightest movements around him.

"Estie, tell me a story," he mumbled. Esther lay back down and looped her arm around him. Matti was the only person who called her "Estie." "Tell me about Samson, or David and Goliath."

Esther began, "A long, long time ago, there was a very brave Jew. . . ."

After a few minutes of going over the well-worn words with the same lilting cadence, she lifted her head to see if he was asleep. He stirred and brought a small woolen swatch to his nose. He wouldn't fall asleep unless he had the rough scrap from Esther's old robe. Once, after Mother had thrown it into the rag pile, he'd cried until Esther had fished it out and given it back to him.

Esther ran her open palm against the tuft of wispy tendrils on the top of his head. Her father wanted to teach her; her mother wanted to mold her; Miriam wanted to protect her. But Matti only wanted to love her. Just as she was. His love was like a mirror that reflected back a better version of herself.

At last, when the breath from his half-parted lips was heavy and deep, Esther slid silently off the bed.

Esther met Miriam in the hall. "Maybe you were right . . . ," Esther said, feeling decidedly less sanguine than she had earlier. "Maybe it's not a good idea."

"It's not," Miriam agreed. "But I'm going, so make up your mind."

What if her parents found out? Her mother would be furious. "The vineyard at night is no place for a priest's daughter," she'd say. Or "How will we find you a husband?" Her mother might slap her or, worse, make her sit inside for days and spin. Her wrists would hurt from holding the spindle, and her back would throb from sitting on the low stool. Her father wouldn't discipline her, but he'd give her one of his disappointed looks, and that would hurt even more.

But maybe she wouldn't get caught.

Miriam folded her arms and tapped her foot.

"If I'm old enough to pick the grapes," Esther said, squaring her shoulders, "I should be old enough to turn them into wine."

"You're not. And you're not old enough to drink it either." Miriam gave Esther a stern look. "If you're caught, remember, *I* didn't bring you."

CHAPTER VI

THEY WALKED DOWN THE STEEP TERRACES DOTTED WITH VINES. As they got closer, the shouts and laughter from the wine pit grew louder. Terra-cotta jars lined the path, and wooden barrels for the rest of the grapes were stacked in even piles.

Torches thrust into the ground lit up an unruly throng. Three men in the pit held on to an overhead pole, their tunics soaked with deep purple juice and sweat. They lifted their stained feet in tempo to the drums as a blue-black liquid flowed into an adjacent vat.

Miriam and Esther pushed their way through the crowd. One man lost his balance in the slippery mush. Shouting, he fell backward; the spectators cheered.

People were scattered across the field, some talking in groups, some pouring themselves drinks. A man lay under a tree, an overturned jug at his side. Esther didn't know where to look first. Men and women danced, pressed together. Miriam pulled her away.

Sapira, a friend of Miriam's, came toward them. While Sapira and Miriam talked and laughed, Esther studied Miriam, amazed at her transformation. Miriam rarely smiled; she said that the space between her front teeth was so big, a rat could run in. But tonight, Miriam seemed like a different person; she was happy, unfolding like a flowering caperbush. Miriam glared when she saw Esther staring, and turned her back.

Miriam and Sapira were talking about men; that's all they ever talked about. Miriam was always telling Esther to grow up, but how did Miriam expect her to know how, if Miriam wouldn't let her listen? Miriam was bossy and opinionated, and needed to be needed. But when Esther needed her—like now—Miriam ignored her.

Esther kicked the ground, then walked toward the amphorae, the large clay wine containers, at the end of the clearing. With their pointy ends dug into the ground, they looked like rows of soldiers standing at attention. Esther scampered behind them and hid in a nook between two large boulders.

From her hiding spot, Esther waited and watched, picking out one man after another, sure it was Joseph, only to be disappointed when the man turned around. She stifled a yawn.

Footsteps approached. She could see only hairy legs and mud-caked bare feet. She crouched, trying to make herself inconspicuous.

She heard a grunt. A burly man turned toward the shadows and pissed into the air—luckily, none landed on her. Then he hoisted an amphora and poured wine into a large jug, set the jug down on the boulder, and stopped. He saw her.

"What do we have here?" he said with a lecherous grin.

Esther scooted back on her hands and knees like a crab, then stood up. She ran, frantically searching for Miriam. People turned to look, so she slowed down; better not to call attention to herself.

Just as she felt her breath return to normal, a hand gripped her shoulder in a painful lock. An unmistakable odor assailed her—of the paste that Uncle Pinchas, Miriam's father, used to combat his baldness: goat fat and fenugreek.

"What are *you* doing here?" Uncle Pinchas bellowed. It was hard to believe this gruff man was the brother of her gentle father.

"I'm . . . I just came to—" She couldn't complete her thoughts because she had none, only panic.

"Get back to the house! Now!"

Esther raced off, desperate to put as much distance between them as possible. She looked back and saw him swaying. If he fell, he couldn't come after her.

After spotting an overturned barrel, she sat down and nervously rubbed the carnelian in her necklace. A gift from her father, it was her favorite possession and she never took it off, even though her mother said not to wear it at night because a demon might use it to strangle her. Miriam said it had magical properties because it looked hot, with its fiery-orange color, but was cool to the touch. It always made Esther feel better.

She kicked at the funnels, sieves, and stoppers scattered around her feet until the beating in her chest subsided. Joseph wasn't here. She might as well go back. She'd make Miriam take her home. The encounters with the man and her uncle had rattled her.

Esther sat for a while longer, then looked for Miriam. She was still huddled with Sapira.

"Go away," Sapira said when Esther approached. "It's married women's business."

They thought she was just a stupid girl.

Around women, she was a girl. Around men, she was a woman. With Jews from the Galilee or Jericho, she was a Jerusalemite. In the Lower Market, surrounded by peasants, she was the daughter of a priest, an aristocrat from the Upper City. With Romans, she was a Jew. But sometimes she wondered, who was she really?

Miriam was still ignoring her. Fine. Esther wouldn't stay where she wasn't wanted. And better to leave before her uncle spotted her again. She would walk quickly and chant the psalms to keep the evil spirits at bay. She started toward the path, but then stopped suddenly. Out of the shadows, two sharp eyes stared at her; it was the man from before. He stumbled toward her.

"Maybe I should take a sip from you," he said, putting his face so close that she could smell the sour drink on his breath. "Can you blame me for mistaking your narrow neck for an amphora?"

"Yes." The voice was familiar. Deep and authoritative. She looked back. Joseph was there.

The man, a head shorter than Joseph, raised his hands in mock surrender. "Seems I've picked the wrong one," he said, retreating into the shadows.

Joseph's hand rested on her shoulder. She felt his body press against her back. He put his other hand on her waist, and the heat of it burned through her dress. She turned to face him.

"Are you all right?" he asked. Joseph's eyes shone like stars. She had wanted to find him and watch him unobserved, not be rescued like a pathetic little girl.

"Of course I am," she said, trying to sound assured, relieved that he couldn't hear the blood throbbing through her veins.

"You don't belong here."

"I was just going over—over—there," she stammered.

"Over where?" He had a skeptical expression on his face, yet she noticed his mouth curving up ever so slightly.

She pointed to the grape pile. "I mean over there," she said, her shaky voice betraying her.

He feigned puzzlement as he looked around. "A priest's daughter is going to sit with the servants?"

"I'm . . . I'm making sure they pick off all the stems and leaves. Otherwise the stompers might cut their feet." She was pleased by her quick thinking.

"I see," Joseph said, rubbing his chin. Esther suspected that he was enjoying her discomfort. "Your parents permitted an innocent young girl to witness this debauchery?"

"I just wanted to see. I didn't drink."

"I should hope not. Plato says you shouldn't taste wine until you're eighteen, so as not to pour fire upon the body."

"He probably just wants more for himself. Is he here?" Esther asked, glad they were now talking about something else.

Joseph threw his head back and laughed. "Who? Plato?"

Her face reddened as she realized she'd made a mistake, even though she wasn't sure what it was.

"Be careful, and if you do drink some of this," he said, holding up a wine cup, "make sure you cut it with water. It's potent." He leaned down and whispered, his warm breath filling her ear, "It can lead your body to sin."

Esther swallowed hard.

"You'd better go now. This isn't a safe place for a young girl." He lowered his voice to a conspiratorial whisper. "Don't worry. You can trust me. I won't tell anyone you were here."

Trust me. That's what the salt-fish monger always said. The one who rested his pinky on the scale.

He reached out, grazing her lips with his finger. She raised her chin and looked him in the eyes. He ran his finger over her upturned chin and continued trailing it down her neck, then stopped at her collarbone. "You're an alluring spark . . . but don't light any fires you can't put out."

CHAPTER VII

ESTHER WOKE UP TIRED. ALL MORNING, SHE STOLE GLANCES AT HER mother, who was busy preparing dinner, bringing in produce and wine from the cellar, and shouting instructions to the slaves.

Sarah peered into a pot of lentil-chickpea stew simmering over the fire. Esther tiptoed past her. She wasn't ready to face her mother yet, especially since she didn't know if her Uncle Pinchas had said anything.

Esther had almost made it across the courtyard when Sarah called out, "Esther! Come!"

This is it, Esther thought. *She knows.*

Sarah lifted a spoon to taste the stew. Coriander and cumin suffused the air. "I need help with the stuffed grape leaves," Sarah said, licking her lips with satisfaction.

Esther's shoulders fell back into place as the tension in her body dissipated. Her mother couldn't know about last night. If she had known, she would have said something by now.

Under Sarah's watchful eye, Esther cut sheep tail fat into small cubes and tossed them into a hot pan sizzling with chopped onions, walnuts, and apricots. Adding mint, parsley, and cardamom, Esther stirred the mixture until her arm ached. She was relieved when her mother went inside the house. She always seemed to look at Esther like she was evaluating a gourd from the market—and deciding not to buy it.

When Esther finished cooking, she set the table. Yehuda came into the room. Ever since his wife and son had died the previous year, he'd seemed like a different person, angry and aloof. The playful brother who used to bite the back of her neck, calling her his pickled locust because she was "ugly to look at but tasty to eat," was gone.

"I won't eat from Roman plates, and neither should you," Yehuda said in stilted Hebrew.

"Why are you speaking the language of prayer?" Esther shot back in Aramaic.

"Why are *you* speaking the language of foreigners? What's wrong with our own tongue? Our holy books are in Hebrew, and God created the world in Hebrew." Yehuda's face reddened.

"You don't have to spit like a camel," Esther said, making a show of wiping her face with her fist.

He slammed his hand down on the table. "What's wrong with plates made in Judea by Jewish potters? I will not take my meal from a plate that was molded with enemy hands and fired in a Roman furnace. Where do you think it gets that color from? Maybe they mixed the clay with pig's blood."

Esther waited for him to tire himself out, but her silence only made him angrier.

"Don't you understand?" Yehuda shouted. "You're letting them dominate us—even in our own homes. We should eat off our own dishes." He grabbed the plate out of her hand.

"Give it back! I hate the Romans too, but a plate is a plate." The dishes from Rome were delicate, with a red glaze and geometric black borders. The chalk ones from the Lower Market were ugly and heavy.

Sarah came into the room. "What's going on?"

Yehuda stepped forward. "No Jew in Yodfat, Gamla, or even Capernaum would dare use Roman plates, but here in 'holy' Jerusalem, we embrace everything Roman."

"Must we reject everything Roman?" Sarah asked. Esther took advantage of the distraction and snatched the plate back.

"Nothing that is Roman is good," Yehuda said. "At least the Jews in the Galilee are patriots."

Sarah tsked. "Oh, those Galileans don't fool me, even if they fool everyone else. I've seen their paintings and fancy stucco moldings. Their houses are more Roman than the ones in Rome. They're not patriots; they're hypocrites. Now eat your food and stop arguing."

Yehuda struggled to find the right words in Hebrew, then switched back to Aramaic. "We need to return to our traditional, simple Jewish lifestyle!"

"Fine with me, but I'm not getting rid of my pan."

"If it's good, you can be sure our potters in the Hula Valley have already copied it," he said.

"Why should I buy a copy when I already own an original?"

Yehuda threw up his hands. "It's not ritually pure."

"A pot?" her mother said. "Purity this, purity that. It's all nonsense. The Jewish potters just want to control the market and prevent people from buying the imports. I don't want another heavy stone vessel that I can hardly lift, or one made from animal dung. Those are fine for storing wheat and lentils, but not for cooking." She gave him a sharp look. "Don't you have bigger foes than my dishes?"

Yehuda scowled, then stormed out of the room.

CHAPTER VIII

"DID YOU KNOW JOSEPH IS COMING FOR DINNER?" MIRIAM SAID. Esther's face broke into a wide grin.

"Oh, don't look so pleased. You can't go around talking to single men, and certainly not to a man like Joseph Ben Matityahu."

"Why not?" Esther asked. "He's not a copper smelter or tanner, and he's not too old either, only twenty-seven. Besides, he's been to faraway places. Don't you want to know what Rome is like? Do you think they really eat mice and owls? Or that their priests study pig guts?"

"You shouldn't listen to such tales."

"I've seen only Jerusalem. He's seen the world! He must know so much."

"What's so important for you to know?"

Esther put her finger to her chin and tilted her head. She considered the question. "I want to know the secrets of the stars and the moon, when time began, and the virtues of the roots so I can help Mother mix the medicines. I want to know if there are statues on every corner in Rome—"

"There can't be. It's a sin to make graven images, and it's probably a sin to talk about all this too. If you invite in evil thoughts, evil spirits will follow. Do you want the demons to come back?"

"*La li la li, la tahim ve la tahtim.*" Esther chanted the Aramaic incantation for protection. "What's evil about wanting to know things? If God didn't want me to ask questions, why did He make me curious?"

"You want to talk to Joseph; you want to talk to God. What else do you want?"

Esther shrugged. "I wake up, and there's something I want. I go to sleep, and there's something else. I want to know more and see more."

"I don't understand you," Miriam said. "First you said you don't want to get married, and now all you're talking about is Joseph."

Miriam was right. Esther didn't want to get married; she dreamed of adventure. But Joseph intrigued her. She imagined meeting him in the bed of violets near the cistern, the neighbor women watching as he took the heavy buckets from her hands. She imagined him standing behind her in the moonlight, one hand on her shoulder while he bent down to kiss her neck. She thought about his thick flowing hair, his strong back. How could she want everything and its opposite at the same time? No wonder Miriam didn't understand her. She didn't understand herself either. Sometimes she imagined that she was just an empty vessel for all the warring selves inside of her.

"I'm finished with my chores. Let's go to the forest," Esther suggested, suddenly eager to be elsewhere. "I want to bring Mother something special."

There was nothing Sarah loved more than ingredients for her medicines. She knew which plants cured which illnesses, and how to crush seeds, stems, and leaves to unlock the secrets inside. People came from all over the city to consult with her and buy her potions.

Miriam followed Esther down the slope. The midday sun washed the hills in a blue-gray light. Wild roses burst into view.

Rose hips! That's what she'd bring her mother.

The thorns nicked Esther's fingers and arms, but it would be worth it if they made her mother smile. Her mother used rose hips in her cough syrup, and used the ground leaves, mixed with zinc, honey, and wine, in her eye remedy. She also made an elixir from the shrub's roots. Sarah once told her that a Roman soldier had cured his rabies by eating the roots. But only women bought the elixir from her mother. They'd slip into the courtyard to see Sarah, hurriedly whisper something, and then hide the elixir under their cloaks before scurrying away. Esther knew that Miriam had some of the elixir too. So, obviously, the elixir cured more than rabies.

The rose hips weren't as special as some of Sarah's other ingredients, like the African barks, Arabian incense, or Indian spices, but Esther hoped that her mother would still be pleased.

Miriam rested while Esther picked the reddish-orange fruit, bigger than usual, with just the right amount of softness when squeezed. She couldn't wait to see her mother's reaction.

Esther put the rose hips into a small sack. Maybe, one day, her mother would teach her the healing secrets too. When Esther was little, Sarah used to let Esther watch her work. Her mother was a different person as she wrote on her wax tablet, her eyes focused in concentration, her touch loving as she arranged the glass bottles or held them up to the light. Sarah would stir the orange saffron, blend the silky talc powder, and fill the bottles with bitumen, clay, and sulfur. Esther wasn't allowed to touch anything. The ingredients were precious, Sarah had explained, gathered from up high in distant mountains, and transported in shimmering boats with golden oars. Once, though, her mother did let her peek at the lizard flesh and snake skins.

Esther heard a noise: the crunch of leaves. A gazelle with black eyes, fierce and fearful at the same time, halted and was stone-still. Pointy ears stood on an impossibly small head topped with lyre-shaped horns. In the time it took for Esther to draw a single breath, it bounded away.

"He looked right at me!" Esther exclaimed.

"It's a sign," Miriam said. "Animals don't appear out of thin air; the spirits send them to warn us. They're messengers."

Miriam closed her eyes and began chanting from the Song of Songs. *"Daughters of Jerusalem, I charge you by the gazelles and by the does of the field: 'Do not arouse or awaken love until it so desires.'"* She opened her eyes and gave Esther a penetrating look. "That's the warning: stay away from love."

"Why? Love isn't dangerous."

"Yes, but men are."

"Father says the Song of Songs is about God's love for His chosen people. It's not about men and women."

"So they say, but have you read it?"

Father had read parts of it to her, but Esther knew he'd skipped some of the verses. Now, she decided, she'd get hold of the scrolls herself.

Maybe Miriam was right, but the more Esther tried not to think about Joseph, the more she could think of nothing else.

They headed back home, up the slope to the Upper City, that spacious, green neighborhood filled with the mansions of the priests and aristocrats. Their stone house had two stories and a flat roof, where they often ate their meals in the summer. Their house towered over the one-story houses nearby. Esther liked to stand on the roof and look into the balconies and courtyards below.

She clutched the sack of rose hips as she entered the courtyard. "I brought you a present," she said to her mother. Just as Sarah reached for the sack, there was a loud noise. A wine amphora rolled off a cart and crashed to the ground.

Sarah ran toward the cart, shouting. She directed the servants to pick up the broken pieces. Then she went inside. Esther waited for her to come back. She waited . . . and waited. Her mother had forgotten about her. She didn't care enough to see what Esther had brought her. Esther let the rose hips fall to the ground. She smashed them into a pulpy mess. Her throat felt tight. *All those scratches for nothing.*

As Esther was walking toward the house, her mother called. "Esther, I need more leaves and branches for kindling." Esther groaned. She hated collecting the dry, sharp olive leaves that pricked her hands. "And when you're finished, I need you to move the spindle whorls behind the fleece bundles and then . . ."

Esther turned away. Her mother's snapping tone grew fainter with each step.

"Esther, do you hear me? Where are you going?"

Why did her mother seem to notice her only when she needed something done? Sarah was deferential to Esther's older brothers, maybe because one of them would, one day, be her guardian. Yehuda had an aloofness that kept people—even family—at a distance, and Shimon could do no wrong, at least according to Sarah. He could coax Esther's mother's scowl into a smile, charming her with impersonations of their neighbors; he was the only one who could make her laugh. Of course, Sarah didn't know that Shimon mimicked her sometimes too. And Matti was Sarah's precious baby, whom she had fought off demons for. Esther was just another set of hands.

Esther walked out of the gate to the orchard, her favorite place to think. It was hard to find the thoughts in her head when she was in the noisy courtyard with the chickens and goats, and her mother barking out commands.

Esther sat, drinking in the sweet smell of the fig and almond trees. Esther longed for her mother to take her in her arms. She longed to see her mother's face light up with a smile just for her, instead of the usual judgmental look. Maybe Sarah didn't know how to love a daughter, since her own mother, Esther's grandmother, had died in childbirth, or maybe Sarah was preparing herself for the day when Esther would leave to live with her husband's family. Or maybe Esther's mother's heart was so covered with the tough, hard scars from each buried child that it couldn't squeeze out any more tenderness and love for Esther.

"Where were you?" Sarah asked when Esther returned. "If Precious had lived, he would have brought the kindling without my asking. He would have—"

Another boy, whom her mother still called "my precious son," was the main competitor for Sarah's love. He had lived for a few months but died before Esther was born. Esther was used to hearing what Precious would have done. "He would have been a priest. He would have brought the water without my asking. He would have collected the eggs. He would have . . . He would have . . ." When Esther had been younger, she'd tried to anticipate what "Precious" would have done, so she could do it first. But it didn't seem to matter. Her mother still loved the dead boy best.

CHAPTER IX

ESTHER WAS EXCITED THAT JOSEPH WAS COMING FOR DINNER. SHE wanted to wear her yellow tunic for dinner, but surely her mother would notice. How could she explain why she was wearing her Shabbat dress when it wasn't the Sabbath? She couldn't even explain it to herself, but she knew Joseph must have meant *something* when he'd touched her at the treading.

Esther sat between Miriam and Matti on a low bench in the corner of the dining room, her hands resting on the small marble table. Esther cast surreptitious glances at Joseph. He seemed pleased to see her, but then again, he seemed pleased to see everyone. A silk shawl was draped over one shoulder and tucked into a leather strap tied around his waist. He wore two rings on each hand.

Esther put on her woman face: that coy, shy expression women donned when they wanted men to notice them, but pretended they didn't. She'd practiced for hours, trying to lower her head at just the right angle, while keeping her eyes up enough so she could still see. She tilted her chin to the side and put her lips together—a little smile, not too big. It was hard to follow the discussion when she had to concentrate on the pose.

Yehuda sat next to Joseph, gazing at him with unabashed admiration. "You've come back to a hero's welcome in Jerusalem. Everybody is talking about your success in Rome."

Joseph seemed pleased.

Yehuda continued, "When the Romans arrested our priests on

those ridiculous charges, we thought they were as good as dead. No Jew—and certainly not a Temple priest—walks out of a Roman jail. No one expected you to bring them back. It took two years, but you did it."

"Diplomacy—all of life, really—is a game," Joseph said. "You have to figure out the rules. For us, status is based on learning, but for the Romans, it's all about connections. They don't sit around studying holy texts. They make the rounds from morning to night, socializing and currying favors."

"But you didn't have any connections," Yehuda said.

"I made them." Joseph studied his long, elegant fingers as he spoke. Esther wished she could reach out and touch them. "I befriended a freedman who worked in the treasury. The Imperial Palace is overrun with ex-slaves; they know all the gossip. This freedman let slip some information that the emperor's wife, Poppaea, wished to keep secret." Joseph lips curled into a smug smile. "I used that information to . . . to . . ." He looked around as though he expected to find the right word floating in the air. "To *help* myself and the priests," he finally said. "Unfortunately for the freedman, he trusted me. But no matter; he was an ex-slave, and slaves are used to being used."

"You were in the palace of the Roman emperor Nero?" Esther asked, astounded.

"Yes. There was no point wasting time in the senate or anywhere else. The palace is where the power is. And what a place! Exotic birds, huge fish ponds in the garden, and enough gold and marble to blind you. Treasures flowed in from every corner of the earth, as well as people of every color. It was as if you could see the whole world in that one place."

Esther tried to imagine the splendor of it all.

"Is it true that prostitutes walk naked in the streets?" Shimon asked.

"Shimon!" Sarah's shrill tone sounded like the screech of the rusty cellar door. Everyone laughed. Esther laughed too, more from relief that her father hadn't even glanced in her direction, than at what Shimon had said. So, her father didn't know she'd gone to the treading either.

"Rome *is* the land of Esau," Joseph said. "The Romans are rich and powerful, but not so clever. They care too much about their pleasures, and finding the best chefs, the best women, and . . . the best boys."

Sarah cleared her throat and fanned herself.

Joseph continued, "The worst one is the emperor. He spends his time eating, drinking, and pretending to be a great singer."

"I wonder how such a degenerate can hold on to an empire," Yehuda said.

"He has good generals," Joseph answered.

Esther had so many questions she wanted to ask. "Do they worship the sun?" she asked.

Joseph held up his hand. "Wait, shouldn't *I* be the one with the questions? I'm the one who's been away for the last two years."

Shimon spoke up. "What do you want to know about? The Romans extorting us, or the bandits terrorizing us?"

"We can't do anything about the taxes," Joseph said. "The Romans were here long before we were born, and they'll be here long after we're gone. But those gangs terrorizing us are *Jews*!"

"Now that the Temple is finished," Yehuda said, "thousands of laborers and craftsmen are without work. A few lucky ones are paving the streets, but most are just wandering around."

"If there's no work," Joseph said, "there's no food."

Yehuda nodded. "I know these men. They'll steal if they're hungry, but if their children are hungry, they'll kill."

"It feels as though I've come back to a different place." Joseph shook his head. "Ever since I've been back, all I've heard about are gangs and rivalries, even priests fomenting revolt against the Romans!"

Yehuda looked down.

"It's true, we Jews are crazy," Pinchas said, pushing more stew into his mouth. "There's no kinship anymore. The Essenes hate everyone, the Pharisees hate the Sadducees, the Sadducees hate the followers of Christ, who—"

"Hate the Pharisees," Joseph chimed in. "We Jews hate each other, *and* we hate the Romans."

Sarah looked displeased. "Let's talk about something more pleasant. I heard it was quite a celebration last night."

"Maybe you should ask Esther," Uncle Pinchas said.

Esther startled. Her hand knocked over Miriam's wine, splattering both her dress and Miriam's.

Miriam jumped up. Hanan stopped chewing, and an angry flush crept up his face. Sarah drew a sharp breath. For a moment, no one spoke. Miriam grabbed Esther's shoulder and pinched her. Her mother squinted her eyes and cast her a scorching look.

"You try my patience," Sarah said. "I hope we survive until your father marries you off. Someone needs to keep you in line."

Then everyone spoke at once. Matti went to get a rag, and Miriam said something about her dress. Her mother dabbed at the spilled wine.

Joseph looked at her, and the corners of his mouth twitched up. He had noticed her after all . . . Oh, but the humiliation! Her cheeks flared and her eyes welled up. But she was determined not to cry. She squared her shoulders and looked straight ahead until dinner was at an end.

PART TWO

. . . and the daughters of Jerusalem went forth to dance in the vineyards. What were they saying: Young man, lift up your eyes and consider whom you choose to be your wife.

Mishnah, Ta'anit 4.8

CHAPTER X

THE SUMMER WAS ALMOST OVER. ESTHER WAS SURPRISED THAT HER parents had agreed to let her dance in the Virgin Circle, part of the annual Tu B'Av celebration—even if it was only so she could attract a husband. At first, Sarah had been adamant that a crowd of sweaty, drunken men was no place for the daughter of a senior priest. But her father had taken Esther's side.

"The Virgin Dance is a sacred duty," Hanan said, the crinkles in the corners of his eyes belying his serious tone. "Our people can't survive without marriage, just like the Temple can't function without wood. God *wants* the daughters of Jerusalem to be chosen as brides. And we want Esther settled."

Although her mother waved her hand in defeat, Sarah had, nevertheless, won one concession from Hanan: Shimon and Miriam would chaperone Esther at the dance.

Dressed in a white tunic, Esther paced up and down in front of the outside stairs, waiting for Shimon. Miriam tried to reassure her that he'd come. Esther retied her sash for the third time. The sheer linen cascaded in soft folds. She felt transformed tonight, grown-up and beautiful. She fiddled—once again—with the garland crowning her head. She hoped the pink and yellow mallows would stay in place.

After a few minutes, her brother sauntered up the road, whistling.

"Why are you both standing around?" he said, ignoring their

glares. "Let's get going, or we'll be late." He wobbled as he walked; he must have already been drinking.

Esther turned her attention to the boisterous rabble in the road, heading toward the vineyard. Young boys rolled jars of beer up the hill, and musicians clutched reed pipes and hand drums. They joined the men and women streaming into the fields. Shimon kept turning to look at the other girls.

"You're already married, you know," Esther whispered to him when Miriam wasn't looking.

Shimon ignored her, then disappeared into the crowd. Esther knew she wouldn't see him again for the rest of the night.

Esther and Miriam continued walking. Esther walked quickly, swinging her arms. The coin her father had given her to buy food was hot in the palm of her hand. She sensed that men were watching her, and for the first time, she felt powerful.

Esther stopped; the coin had flown out of her hand and disappeared. She looked around, used a broken branch to push back a tangled thicket of myrtle. Miriam helped her, searching behind a row of trees.

A glint of gold shone through the brush. Esther bent down, but it wasn't the bronze coin; it was an old flint blade.

Someone was walking toward her! A man with a beardless face and russet-colored cloak—a Roman.

Her heart hammered her ribs. She started to run, but tripped over an exposed root and went sprawling. He came closer until he was towering over her.

"I won't hurt you," he said in Greek. His voice had no malice. But he was a Roman, and Esther knew what they were capable of. She pushed herself back, all the while tracking him with her eyes.

His neck was a thick rope of muscle and sinew, and his shoulders were as wide as a plough. Bulging veins ran down his arms.

A colorful sheath decorated with intricate carvings cradled a silver *pugio*. The dagger sat at his waist, attached with brass rings to a wide belt cinching his tunic. He wasn't wearing the thick-soled boots of a soldier, only simple sandals with leather straps wrapped around sculpted calves. His eyes were the color of the wild lupines that blended into the sky in the Judean hills.

"Are you looking for this?" He held out the coin.

Esther stared in disgust at his outstretched hand, mottled with white and pink ridges of scarred flesh.

"Esther!" Miriam emerged from the trees. Esther exhaled. She wasn't alone.

"'Esther.' That's a beautiful name," the Roman said. "'*Aster*' in Greek. You're named after the stars."

"I'm named for the Jewish princess, the one who saved her people from *cruel oppressors*," Esther said, emphasizing the last words as Miriam tried to pull her away.

"Why do you people take everything as an insult? You're like these barbed, spiny plants," he said, pointing down. "But in between the thorns, there are some beautiful wildflowers. Pleased to make your acquaintance." He bowed in a mock salute. "My name is—"

"You don't have a name," Esther barked. "You're a Roman."

"My name is Tiberius Claudius Masculus."

Just then another Roman approached.

Tiberius pinched his thumb and fingers together in a gesture indicating for him to wait.

"There are plenty of other virgins," Tiberius's companion said. He looked Esther over. "Let's find one with a smaller mouth and bigger tits."

Esther flashed him an angry stare. They looked surprised that she'd understood. She didn't know Latin well, but she had picked up the street talk of the Roman merchants and soldiers wandering around the city. The Romans spoke Greek to the local population but Latin among themselves.

"You see," Tiberius said, addressing his companion. "Jews have a most rebellious nature, but they can't help it. Roman women pretend to be modest, but inside they're really scheming. Jewish women don't bother to hide their true feelings."

Esther glowered at him, even though she wasn't sure if his words were meant as an insult or a compliment. She wanted to get away, but she wanted the coin.

He offered it again.

She hesitated, thinking of Yehuda and wondering if the Roman's touch was enough to contaminate the coin. Then she took a deep breath and snatched it.

As she turned to leave, her robe caught on a thistle from a low nettle bush. She yanked at the thin cloth. Tiberius kneeled.

"Allow me," he said, carefully lifting the fabric hooked on the thorns. He stood up and made another exaggerated bow as he opened his arms. "By the powers vested in me by the Imperial Majesty Nero, I now pronounce you free." A smile softened his angular features.

"Of course I'm free," Esther snapped.

Miriam pulled her away. "Let's go."

Esther clasped her hands around the coin, trying to stop them from shaking.

"Your garland is loose and your hair is sticking out. Let me fix it," Miriam said, adjusting the crown of flowers. "You look like an urn with big side handles. We'd better get you fixed up, or you'll never find a husband."

Esther gave Miriam a grateful smile. Miriam was often exasperating, infuriating even, but sometimes, like now, Esther was glad she had her.

CHAPTER XI

THEY CONTINUED UP THE HILL, PAST THE VENDORS SELLING NUT cakes, past the sausage man, past a group of young men vaulting over barrels, and past the eager girls in their white robes.

When they reached the dancing, Esther joined in. She danced around the circle twice, scanning the crowd. After the third time, she spotted Joseph, so close that she could see his V-shaped hairline. She closed her eyes, swayed her long hair seductively, and smiled her most dazzling smile. She felt eyes on her: a tingling sensation on the back of her neck. The music tapered off, and she slowly lifted her gaze.

But it wasn't Joseph's face staring back at her; it was Lazar's, the silversmith, with beady eyes buried beneath thick eyebrows. He had a swarthy complexion and a stocky build. His hair was the color of mud. Flustered, Esther tried to get away, but he blocked her path.

"First you flirt, and then you flee?" he asked, leaning in so close that she smelled the wine on his breath.

She felt as if she had swallowed her own voice. *Where is Joseph?*

"You're . . . mistaken," she spit out.

"I don't think I am." His gaze traveled down her face until it rested on her chest, which rose and fell as she tried to catch her breath.

"I didn't mean to . . . for you to—" Esther fumbled for words, desperate to make him go away.

"I know you were dancing for me, Esther, daughter of Hanan."

"Not for you, for someone else," she insisted.

Lazar stiffened. "I know your father, and I know your older brothers. Didn't they tell you that girls shouldn't play women's games?"

"I'm not playing games."

"You are, but not very well. You can't be innocent and a Lilith at the same time."

Lilith was a demon who seduced men and spawned devil children. Esther hadn't even looked at Lazar!

"Perhaps," Lazar said, brazenly ogling her body, "I should speak to your father."

Esther turned away. She spotted Miriam in the crowd and ran toward her. "We need to leave. *Now!*"

CHAPTER XII

"I HAD AN INTERESTING VISIT TODAY," HER FATHER SAID. "FROM LAZAR and his father, Priest Kallos."

In spite of the end-of-summer heat, a chill rushed through her. *The silversmith?*

"We'd prefer for you to marry within the family, of course, but your cousins from Sepphoris are too young, and unfortunately, Pinchas has no sons. We've begun negotiations with the Kallos family."

"But you never asked me!" Esther said angrily.

"Lazar said you made eyes at him at the Tu B'Av dance. We thought you'd be pleased."

The dance had been only a few days before, and Lazar had already met with her father? "Lazar is a hairy ox with fat nostrils."

Her mother frowned. "He has a stall in the market. Besides, the family has property, and his father is an honest man."

"Who cares? I'm not marrying the father!" Esther paced around the room. "Anyway, I don't want to get married yet."

"A girl must get married when she becomes a woman," said Sarah. "You know what happens to bread flour if it's not used as soon as it's ground."

"Then at least let me choose!"

"This is the most crucial decision of your life," Sarah said. "Too important for you to make by yourself. You don't have experience; you're still a child."

"You just said I have to get married because I'm a woman. If I'm still a child, I don't have to get married!"

Sarah faced Esther. "So, who would you choose?"

Anyone would be better than Lazar, Esther thought. *Someone nice to look at, someone who's traveled and seen the world. Someone I could talk to and learn from.*

"Joseph Ben Matityahu," Esther said, surprising herself with how right it sounded as soon as she'd said his name. And while she hadn't really considered *marrying* Joseph, she was definitely intrigued by him. "He's a hero. He got our priests released from the Roman prison, and he's a scholar. Everyone says he's brilliant."

"Alexa's son?" Sarah shook her head angrily. "Some things don't go together. It would be like using a stone whorl to spin wool."

"You're only saying that because you can't stand his mother," Esther said.

Sarah crossed her arms over her chest. "Do you know how many needles she's borrowed and never returned? And she doesn't take the bone needles—oh no, she wants only the bronze ones! And what about the grain sifter she borrowed? She didn't even ask; she just took it from the cellar. That woman makes a fox look honest."

"Joseph isn't suitable because his mother borrowed a sifter?"

Her mother paced back and forth in the small room. "No. It's because we want your happiness that we're not considering Joseph. I watched him grow up. I saw things. He's not a kind man. He's not like your father."

"How do you know?"

"Your father told me that when the priests would gather for learning and include Joseph and his brother Matthias, he'd let Matthias answer first, then rip his answer to shreds. He always made sure to shine and make Matthias—his older brother, no less—look stupid."

"He was a child then." Esther was sure her mother didn't approve of Joseph because of Alexa. But to Esther, Alexa was quite harmless—even if she did talk too much.

Her mother would never change her mind. If a passerby accidentally shoved Sarah into the market, or a merchant shortchanged her by one *sestertius,* she'd remember. People's wrongs were etched in stone, their good deeds written on the wind. Luckily, Esther's mother didn't have the final word. Sarah had been opposed to Esther learning the holy texts too. But her father had prevailed. He let Sarah speak her mind, more than most men would allow, but ultimately, he made the decisions.

Hanan said, "I think your mother is right. Joseph is the kind of man who worries first about himself. We want someone who will think about his wife and family."

"You don't know him," Esther said, suddenly more determined than ever that Joseph was the right choice.

"And neither do you," Hanan said. Without waiting for a response, he took his walking stick, a gnarled olive branch, and pushed himself up.

Instinctively Esther reached for her necklace. Rubbing the stone's smooth surface with her thumb calmed her down when she was agitated. Any other girl would have been thrilled that her parents had found a good match. Why did she always want what she couldn't have?

She reassured herself that her father wouldn't marry her off without her consent. She'd make a plan. She *had* to find a way to stop the negotiations with the Kallos family.

CHAPTER XIII

"I won't marry Lazar," Esther said as she dumped a sack of almonds out onto the table.

Miriam took one, then bit into it. "Don't be ridiculous. He'll be a good husband."

"How do you know? Maybe he'll beat me."

"And maybe he'll give you a child and make you beautiful bracelets and rings from soft silver. Don't you want your own garden, a feather blanket . . . and a feast? Don't you want to be carried aloft on the bridal platform—"

"That's the wedding," Esther scoffed. "Getting married is not the same as *being* married. At least, that's what you always said."

"Don't worry. You have plenty of time before anything happens," Miriam said as she sliced the nuts. Then she dropped them into a bowl with olive oil. "The families haven't agreed on the bride-price yet. Your mother will bargain hard; she won't settle for a measly measure of wine and some raisin cake. She'll insist on heaps of gold. And then the Kallos family will present their demands. Your mother will offer only a few donkeys or cooking pots for your dowry. Believe me, it will take a long time before she parts with any land or coin, and then there's the feast. You won't be wed before Passover."

"No," Esther said, shaking her head. "Father said it needs to be sealed as soon as we can. He'll make sure the bargaining is swift.

It could be over by the winter solstice." She paused for a moment, then laughed bitterly. "Maybe I'll get lucky and the world will end before then."

"If the End of Days comes, then you'll have bigger problems to worry about than who to wed," Miriam said. "I've heard all of this talk about the End of Days too. It's ridiculous."

"Father says it is, but not Yehuda. Yehuda says the Romans will be crushed in three years and then the End will come."

"Don't wait for it."

"I don't have to. Marrying Lazar would be the end of my world." Esther paced the room. "I'd kill myself before I'd marry him."

"Don't be dramatic. It's a sin to talk like that."

"Then I'll kill *him* instead. If I have to marry anyone, at least it should be someone like Joseph. He's seen the world. He knows languages."

Miriam gave a knowing smirk. "You're interested in Joseph because he reads Greek?"

"He's smart . . . and handsome." Esther blushed, then said, "I have to stop the negotiations. Maybe I can write spells on pottery shards, or buy a charm."

"Just don't go to Siloam. The miracle-men there sell fake amulets. Go to Zahara's pub."

Esther knew where that was; it was the place where Shimon went to drink and gamble. "Remember that time when we dragged Shimon home last winter? You were so worried, and we found him sitting in the back tossing the wine lees onto the walls, so drunk that he couldn't walk home."

Miriam nodded, clearly not happy to be reminded. "Zahara's a harlot, but she knows men-magic."

"I'll go tomorrow," Esther said. "It's the seventh day of the month." An auspicious time for spells and magic, when the sun, moon, and stars were aligned.

Esther waited a full minute before knocking. What was she doing here? A daughter of a priest seeking advice from an innkeeper, a woman who spent her day in the company of men—Roman men—plying them with drink? Gathering her courage, she knocked, and a tiny peephole opened, then clicked shut. There was the screech of metal as the iron bolt on the inside slid through the rings on the back of the door, and the door cracked open.

Zahara, a buxom woman with strands of black hair falling out of a hairnet, peeked out. A scowl replaced her look of surprise. "He's not here," she said.

"I didn't come for Shimon." Esther stepped closer.

Zahara looked impatient. "I'm busy." She stepped back and started to close the heavy door, but Esther blocked it with her foot.

"Wait, please! I need . . . I'm to marry, but I—" A scraggly chicken ran toward her and brushed against her leg.

"Catch it!" Zahara screeched.

Esther grabbed a fistful of feathers and handed the squawking bird over. Zahara held it close and pulled Esther inside. She closed the door.

"Don't let my customers see you," Zahara ordered as she put the chicken on the floor. Esther felt her stomach churn. They were in a dark hall with a low ceiling. Laughter and noise emanated from a room in the back.

Zahara's features softened. "What do you need?"

"A potion," Esther mumbled.

"What kind?"

"The kind that will make someone not want to marry me."

"*Not* marry you? That's a new one." Zahara put one hand on her hip, which she thrust out. "It will cost you."

Esther pulled out the coins Miriam had given her.

"That's not enough for a sack of fava beans."

Esther reached for the small clay jar tucked in her belt. "I brought this too."

Zahara pulled off the cork stopper and raised it to her nose.

"It's face cream," Esther said. "My mother made it."

Zahara wrinkled her nose and thrust the jar back. "Get this greasy sheep shit away from me."

"*Please*, I need your help." She couldn't go back empty-handed.

"Why? Does he have another wife?"

"No . . ."

"Can he feed you?"

Esther nodded.

"Does he have scaly flesh that oozes pus?"

"No," she said softly.

"Then get out of here, child." As she spoke, her arms swished like they were tossing slops from a pail.

"But he's not the one I love."

"Love?" Zahara spat. "How do you know what love is? Real love is old and worn-out. It survives one hard, hungry day at a time . . . if it survives at all." Zahara looked up at the ceiling; she had a large mole under her chin. "If it survives the day your baby crawls into the puddle by the well and never comes out, or the day your beloved pokes his eye out with an awl . . . or the night your niece comes to his bed . . ."

Zahara regarded Esther, as though she were surprised to still see her. "You and your friends from the Upper City think you can buy love, but you can't. You can't just wear an amulet, or mix a potion."

"That's what you sell."

"Not to you. You don't have enough money for magic. You can afford only the truth."

Zahara shoved her out and slammed the door. Esther stumbled backward.

What now?

PART THREE

[The Sicarii] committed murders in broad daylight in the heart of the city. . . . They would mingle with the crowd, carrying short daggers concealed under their clothing, with which they stabbed their enemies. Then, when they fell, the murderers joined in the cries of indignation and through this plausible behavior, were never discovered.

Flavius Josephus, *The Jewish War* 2.255

CHAPTER XIV

ESTHER WAS IN THE TEMPLE COURTYARD, WAITING FOR HER FATHER TO finish the morning ceremony. Without his cane, Hanan looked as though he might stumble at any moment. His elbow was still bruised from a fall the week before. Fortunately, he had again drawn the lot to catch the blood. Gone were the days when he could wield a knife with precision, or heft a slack beast onto the hook after the slaughter. At least he could still cut a turtledove's throat with his fingernail.

Now, crouching under the lamb's head, Hanan held out a golden bowl to catch the dripping blood, grimacing in pain as he squatted. He stood up, one hand on his hip and one cradling the bowl filled to the brim with blood. She prayed that he would hold it steady. He walked toward the altar and poured some on each corner.

The slaughterer priest deftly slit the carcass and handed the fat and entrails to another priest. The fire crackled, eager to accept the sacrifice, and the smell of smoldering wood, sweat, and blood wafted through the air. It was so quiet that Esther heard the dull sawing of the knife through flesh.

And then shouts pierced the silence. Esther's fingers tightened around the railing of the balcony from where she looked down on the outside altar. People charged toward the gates of the courtyard. Abandoned sheep and goats stampeded in every direction. A man lay on the ground in a widening pool of gleaming, dark red blood. A small boy crouched beside him, screaming.

Despite the commotion, the ceremony continued. The priests

neither looked at the crowd nor changed so much as a single step in their choreographed routine. With each new offering, the fire sizzled and the flame flared higher. It was a windless day, and the smoke rose in a column to the sky.

Esther could hear her pulse in her ears. Where was her father? Did the priests *always* move so slowly?

People rushed out of the courtyard, trying to get away. A lanky figure elbowed his way through the melee, walking with that stiff gait of his that was all sharp angles. What was Yehuda doing here? Her brother was supposed to be at the study house.

The priests went inside the Temple, where wisps of fragrant smoke emerged from behind the curtain. After another seemingly interminable wait, they came out, raised their arms, and chanted, *"May God bless you and keep you. May God shine His face upon you and be gracious to you. May God grant you peace."*

No one was left to offer the usual hallelujahs and amens. The guard, gesturing wildly, approached her father, whose hand flew to his mouth.

Esther bounded down the steps and ran to the Kindling Gate, their agreed meeting spot.

When they met, Hanan, who usually launched his thoughts slowly and exactingly, blurted out, "They struck again. How dare they butcher a man in the Holy Temple!"

"How did they get in?" Esther said, still stunned. "Those Romans—"

"Not the Romans," he snapped, leaning unsteadily on his cane. "Jews." He shook his head in disgust. "Quick! We have to leave. They're going after everyone opposed to the revolt." He looked around frantically. "I might be next."

—⚏—

Yehuda was already home by the time Esther and Hanan arrived.

Hanan, his face sweaty and flushed, turned to him. "One of the Sicarii stabbed Haggai Ben Kessef in the Temple! He was still holding his son's hand when he fell to the ground. By the time people realized what had happened, the assassin was gone."

Esther watched Yehuda closely. His face betrayed no surprise.

"Ben Kessef must have been working with the Romans," her brother said. "A collaborator."

"Nonsense," Hanan said. "Ben Kessef was a grain trader. Maybe he did supply the Roman troops, but half of Jerusalem sells to the Romans, and the Romans sell to us. Someone had a private vendetta."

"What makes you so sure?" Yehuda asked.

"The Sicarii will kill anyone for a price."

Esther knew who the Sicarii were, even though her father usually dropped his voice when he talked about them. They were the most feared of the Jewish rebel groups, named for the small, curved knife they hid under their clothes and plunged into their victims, usually in broad daylight. Noted for their stealth, they blended back into the crowd before anyone noticed. Still, Esther never imagined that anyone—even the notorious Sicarii—would dare to defile the sacred ground of the Temple.

"Maybe you owe money," Hanan said, "or maybe you're mad at your neighbor because he threw his slops into your yard or his goat ate your bean plants. When a whisper is enough to condemn a man, no one is safe."

"No one is safe if he's a traitor," Yehuda said evenly. "The Sicarii kill only people who collaborate with our enemies."

"He wasn't a traitor!" Hanan said. "Even the priests trade with the Romans. Where would we be if the Romans didn't import the frankincense and myrrh for the sacrifices? The camels don't walk through Arabia by themselves."

"*Anyone* who sides with the Romans is a traitor. We must fight the Romans *and* the traitors."

Her father scowled. "What happens if we lose?"

"We won't," Yehuda insisted. "God is on our side."

"Which side? The side of the people who want peace, or the side of the terrorists?"

"The Sicarii aren't terrorists. They're fighting for our freedom! We must be free to practice our own religion and collect our own taxes."

Hanan narrowed his eyes and fixed Yehuda in a steady gaze. "Killing can be more intoxicating than wine. Many innocent people will die before the first Roman soldier leaves Jerusalem. You mark my words."

"And you be careful too, Father," Yehuda said, before he strode out.

Esther followed Yehuda. He went out back to the rain cisterns and dipped a rag into the water. Then he opened his cloak and pulled something out. Esther crept closer so she could see.

It was a small, curved dagger.

He wiped it off. The rag was red.

CHAPTER XV

"WHERE WERE YOU?" MIRIAM ASKED AS SHE SECURED THE THREADS AT the top of the loom. "Looking for Joseph again?"

Esther walked past Joseph's house almost every day, trying to meet him . . . by chance, of course. But today she hadn't been looking for Joseph.

"No." Esther shook her head. "I was in the orchard."

"Under your 'thinking tree'?" Miriam teased. "And what were you thinking about today?"

She couldn't tell Miriam. No one could know that her own brother was the mystery killer everyone in Jerusalem was talking about.

Esther watched Miriam's fingers dance along the edge of the loom. "How can you spend all day tying threads?"

"If you don't set it up properly," Miriam said, "then all the work you did before, and all the work you'll do afterward, is for naught. Don't you think it's worth spending one more day to make sure it turns out right?

Esther wasn't sure; one more day was a lot of time.

Miriam's fingers paused. "You're going to have this bed cloth for the rest of your life. I might as well make it as beautiful as I can."

"This is for *me*?" Esther asked.

Just then her mother walked toward them. "I've been looking all over for you," Sarah said, holding out a spindle. "If there's no yarn, there's no cloth. And if there's no cloth, you won't have a dowry."

Her dowry! It was all happening much too quickly. It felt like the yarn was being wrapped around her throat, instead of around the spindle. Still, she knew her parents hadn't finalized anything with the Kallos family yet. She had time—she hoped.

She didn't want the cloth or a dowry. She had learned to spin when she was nine, and had hated it ever since. She got bored; she got blisters on her fingers, and her back hurt. No matter how hard she tried, her thread was always loose and lumpy, not tight and smooth like Miriam's. Often the family courtyard was full of the neighborhood women gossiping while they spun, but they always stopped—to pick up a sniveling child, or to feed the oven—just when the stories got interesting. Miriam tried to entertain Esther by making up funny songs, but it didn't help.

Esther took the spindle and reluctantly sat down.

Miriam could spin twice as fast as anyone else, twisting the plant fibers without snapping them; Esther usually spent more time twisting the flax strands back together instead of spinning them. Miriam was even more skilled on the loom, weaving the madder- and saffron-dyed threads into elaborate geometric designs.

After a while, Esther took a break, shaking her shoulders and stretching her cramped fingers. When she looked up, she saw a man enter the courtyard. It was Joseph!

He walked through the courtyard gate, commanding the space around him as if unseen spirits were announcing his arrival. He looked regal, dressed in a pink robe tied with a crimson sash. A mantle with a brilliant blue border was draped over his broad shoulders and chest.

Why had she worn her old gray tunic? Esther hurried to the rain cistern behind the house and splashed water over her face, then scrubbed fiercely. Quickly she ran back toward him. She stood close enough to inhale his scent, like fresh leather and smoldering ashes.

"Ah, Esther," he said, smiling. "Is your father home?"

Her face grew warm. At the treading, Joseph had said she was "alluring," and he had touched her. He must have come to speak with Hanan about her. Even though her father had begun negotiations with the Kallos family, it wasn't too late.

Hanan came out of the house to greet him. Esther pretended to leave, then snuck behind a pile of unwashed wool.

"She's almost a woman," Joseph said to her father. "Are you negotiating yet?"

"We've just started."

Esther's limbs tingled; she felt like she could fly.

"I didn't invite you over for a social visit," Hanan said, his voice taking on an urgent tone. "We need to discuss something of the utmost importance."

Her marriage! Her father had listened to her after all. And Joseph was interested too! Esther clasped her hands in front of her mouth.

Hanan went on, "The murder in the Temple was a sight I never thought I'd see. This violence is spinning out of control. We have to do something."

Violence? Murder? That's what her father wanted to talk about? Her heart sunk. But still, she wanted to hear everything they said. She leaned in.

Hanan said, "Some of the priests—the young ones, of course— are pushing for a rebellion against Rome. Why is it always the hot-blooded young men who want war? I wish they'd listen to their fathers. I've heard that some even joined the Sicarii! Yehuda too is spouting slogans."

She wished that spouting slogans was all Yehuda was doing.

Joseph tugged at his perfectly trimmed beard. "Our relationship with Rome has never been good, but in the past, people accepted it.

Now they seem to think that God wants us to run the Romans out of Judea."

"And the young priests are to blame," Hanan said. "They're whipping up the masses with their tales of an upcoming apocalypse."

"Anyone, like me, who has seen Rome with all its power and wealth, knows that a rebellion is suicidal."

"Exactly!" said Hanan. "The young priests won't listen to people like me, the old guard, but maybe they'll listen to you. You just got back from Rome, and they respect you."

Joseph nodded slowly. "I know the Romans. It's better to work with them than against them. We've been through difficult times before."

"I agree," Hanan said. He hobbled over to the bench by the front door and sat down, resting his cane over his knees. "The Temple priests have partnered with the Romans for years. I buy incense from a trustworthy Roman whose goods are as pure as those from the Jewish suppliers—and are a third of the price."

"Who is this dependable gentile?" Joseph asked.

"A freedman named Tiberius Claudius."

That was the Roman who found my coin! He said he was a trader, but . . . no, it couldn't be the same man. Maybe "Tiberius" is a common Roman name.

Joseph scowled. "What's his family name?"

"Masculus."

"Tiberius Claudius Masculus is here?" Joseph asked, his voice rising.

"You know him?" Hanan looked surprised.

"Does he have a scar on his right hand?"

It *was* him!

"Yes," Hanan answered. "Tiberius told me that an oil lamp tipped over and scalded him as a child."

Joseph began pacing. "It can't be. I was told that he . . . I thought he was dead."

"He's very much alive, I can assure you," Hanan said, regarding Joseph curiously. Esther too had noticed the shift in Joseph's demeanor.

"He's the one I told you about at dinner," Joseph said. "The ex-slave. He may have come for me. To settle the score." He ran his hand through his hair. "I have to go."

Esther stomped back to the loom, grabbed a fistful of goat wool, and began pulling out the brambles. Maybe Joseph would have talked to her, or at least stayed longer, if he hadn't been distracted by the news that Tiberius Something Something was back in Jerusalem.

Oh how she hated the Romans. Every last one of them.

CHAPTER XVI

THE FAMILY WAS VISITING MIRIAM'S PARENTS, UNCLE PINCHAS AND Aunt Bruria, at their estate in the Judean Hills. The family always made sure to travel before the winter rains, when the trails would be muddy.

"Yuck!" Matti said. He spit out his milk. "The porridge is cold, their bread is gritty, and even their milk tastes strange."

"Because they have different goats," Esther said. "If you don't drink it, you'll be hungry. There's no more food until dinner."

He's right, she thought. Everything was different out here. She'd never felt truly at home in the fortresslike farmhouse on the estate, a rambling stone building with a tall tower in the middle. Slaves scurried around, going from the house to the ovens, to the storehouses, to the threshing floor and bathhouses. The estate reminded her of a giant anthill.

She and Matti didn't have their own rooms, or even proper beds. Aunt Bruria gave them straw mats. Sometimes they slept outside and sometimes in the wool room at the back of the main house. They rolled out the mats between the scale-weights and baskets of dyestuffs—pomegranate peels, dried safflower florets, and walnut husks. Overhead, newly colored skeins hung to dry. The room had a dank odor, but after a while they got used to it.

At home, Esther and Matti shared a soft bed stuffed with wool. When they woke, they ate warm bread smeared with sweet date nectar. Why, when she was home, did she want to be somewhere else—but as soon as she left, she missed her bed?

Shouts erupted in the distance.

"How dare you ask! I'm a farmer, not a moneylender."

Matti grabbed her arm and looked around. Without being able to hear with his left ear, he had a hard time telling which direction sounds came from.

It was Uncle Pinchas who was yelling.

Esther and Mattie walked toward the farmhouse and peered out from behind a cart. A short, wiry figure stood before their uncle, arms by his side, staring at the ground. Uncle Pinchas yelled at the slaves, but never at visitors. Pilgrims came to the estate to buy wine, sheep, or doves for their sacrifices. His words made people smile, even as they opened their purses and left with more than they had planned.

The tight muscles in the man's neck and forearms were at odds with his humble pose. A scrawny boy about Matti's age, in a torn, dirty tunic, stood next to him. Esther recognized the man as one of her uncle's tenant farmers.

Pinchas thrust his finger into the air. "You still owe two-thirds of the harvest. That's over eighty *seahs* of wheat! With back rent, your debt is more than two hundred *zuzim*. I sent my slave to collect, and he returned with nothing."

"How could I have any silver coins? I have nothing—no crops, no food, and certainly no *zuzim*. My family ate tree bark yesterday. My wife was on her hands and knees all day grubbing roots and looking for seeds. We managed to save a little of the barley after the leaf rust ran through the fields, but the wind scorched most of the wheat crop. I did everything I could, but I can't control the weather."

"Who do you think makes the weather, Ben Ya'acov? It sounds

like God isn't happy with you, and if God isn't happy, what can I do?"

"Give me an extension on my loan." He met Pinchas's stare. "It's not the weather, or God. First you took one-third of the harvest, then half, and now two-thirds."

"That's what all the landlords take. Those are the rates now."

"Not all landlords," the tenant said, balling his fist. "I can pay you back with the next harvest. I need more seed-corn, just enough to get me started."

"What about the loan from two seasons back and the fine for nonpayment? You're finished, Ben Ya'acov."

"I beg of you, I'll pay you when the barley comes in."

"Impossible."

The tenant clasped his hands in front of his chest. "Master, everyone has good years and bad years. I have worked your land for eight years!"

"You did, and you had a place to live and food to eat. I'm a reasonable man, but do you expect me to keep feeding you and your family indefinitely?"

"Our Book says 'every man under his vine and fig tree.' It doesn't say 'under his master's vine and fig tree,' yet I love this land as though it were my own. You'll get your money back, I swear."

Pinchas shook his head.

Ben Ya'acov kicked the dirt with his toe. "Your heart is like a stone. I'm a proud man, but if begging will save my family, I'll do it. I'll get down on my hands and knees and kiss your feet. Please . . . don't let us starve."

"No need to be so dramatic," Pinchas said. "If God wants, He can show you mercy. I can't afford to be so generous."

"Then I'll get the money from someone else. Somehow I'll get it. I'll rent myself out as a day laborer." The farmer's expression turned from desperation and supplication to fury as he looked down at his son and then back at Pinchas. "I have no choice; we must eat. You didn't even leave us the gleanings this year. You treat your goats better than your fellow man."

Pinchas's face reddened. "My goats earn their keep."

"Rent, debt, tax, and tithes! How can any honest man hope to survive? Everyone, Jews *and* Romans, take a piece of my family's hard labor until there's nothing left. My son is starving."

"Sell him as a debt-slave," Pinchas said. "At least he'll be fed. He'll get the Sabbath off and be free in seven years." Pinchas folded his arms in front of him and looked the boy up and down. "If you're lucky enough, someone will take him, even if he is Jewish."

Ben Ya'acov's eyes drilled into Esther's uncle. "You'll regret this one day," he said through clenched teeth.

The boy, stepping closer to his father, grabbed hold of his father's tunic and held it tight. Pinchas waved the farmer aside as if he were brushing a fly off his sleeve, and walked away.

The farmer put his hand on the boy's shoulder and whispered into his ear. Then the farmer left. The boy slipped off toward the kitchen hut just as Nonna, the old house slave, walked out of the hut, struggling under the weight of a stone bowl.

The boy crouched behind the water trough. When Nonna passed, he dashed inside the hut. A few seconds later, he ran out, clutching a dripping white ball.

"Thief! Thief!" Nonna yelled, waving her spindly arms. "He snatched the cheese from the draining jar!"

The boy scampered behind the oak tree.

Nonna turned to Esther and Matti. "Find him! He couldn't have gotten far."

Neither moved.

"Now!" Nonna snapped.

Esther ran toward the tree. A small silhouette was braced against its trunk.

Nonna looked behind the woodpile. "Is he there?"

The boy was so still that if Esther hadn't seen his shoulders move, she wouldn't have known he was even breathing. His bones looked as though they might break through his skin at any moment. He held the dripping curds against his chest.

Nonna called out, "Do you see the little maggot?"

Esther ran back to the clearing. Matti hadn't budged. Surely he had seen the boy too.

"Did you find him?" Nonna asked.

Esther looked first at Matti, then at Nonna. "No. He must have gotten away."

CHAPTER XVII

As soon as the family returned home, Esther went looking for Joseph. He was the only one who could save her from a future with Lazar. If Joseph wanted her for his wife, surely her father would have to acquiesce, no matter what her mother said. Her father wanted to see her in a good family, and Joseph's was one of the most distinguished in the city.

As she got closer to his house, she slowed her pace so it would look like she was just passing by. Joseph came out of his house with a large pouch slung over his shoulder.

"Esther, shalom!" Joseph called when he noticed her. "What a coincidence seeing you. Where are you going?"

"Oh, I'm just . . ." Her tongue seemed stuck to the roof of her mouth. *Why didn't I plan what to say?* "I'm delivering some medicines for my mother."

"Where are they?"

"Where are what?" Esther asked.

A small smile tugged at Joseph's lips. "The medicines?"

"Oh . . . ," she said, flustered. She realized she wasn't carrying anything. "I forgot them at home."

Two scrolls were sticking out of Joseph's pouch. "What are those?" she asked.

"The works of Thucydides."

"Who's he?"

"The greatest historian of all time. He understood better than anyone else why people do what they do."

She was burning with curiosity. "I'd like to read them too."

"They're in Greek."

"My father is teaching me Greek. I know all the letters."

He regarded her with raised eyebrows.

"My mother doesn't approve," she added. "She says women shouldn't learn."

"I respect wisdom and knowledge whenever I find it. Even our prophetess Huldah taught a king."

Esther beamed. Now she was more determined than ever to learn Greek, so she too could unlock the secrets of the world. "Where did you get them?"

"From the public library in Caesarea. I know the librarian there."

Caesarea, the bustling city Herod had built on the sea, was only a week's journey from Jerusalem, but so different. Although Jews lived there too, Greek culture prevailed. But they had a library! If she married Joseph, he could take her there.

She *had* to stop the negotiations. How could she marry a brute like Lazar instead of someone who loved learning as much as she did? If they were married, Joseph could bring scrolls home. They could read together and discuss what they read. "Is it true you know all the written Scripture and oral law by heart?" she asked.

"By the time I was your age, the sacred words were engraved on my soul."

Esther stared at him dreamily. *Engraved on my soul . . .* He even spoke like a poet.

CHAPTER XVIII

Esther's hands burned from the salty detergent as she scrubbed the bed linens and dunked them into the tin trough.

Her mother came over to inspect. "When you've hung them all up, take the figs and apricots that are drying on the roof to the cellar."

Esther didn't like going down the rickety wooden stairs into the cellar. It was dark and smelled of rotting onions. But she knew better than to argue.

When she finished storing the dried fruit, Esther rested on the bench in the courtyard. She hoped to get a few minutes alone before her mother spotted her and gave her yet more chores.

"Where are you?" her mother called.

Esther sighed.

Her mother motioned for her to follow. "Come with me to my workroom."

Her workroom? Esther jumped up, suddenly full of energy. It had been ages since her mother had allowed Esther to watch her work.

Rows of small glass bottles, ivory flasks, and clay jars lined the shelves. Thin metal and bone spatulas were arranged on the table next to a grinding slab. Esther looked around eagerly.

Sarah broke the seal on a small clay juglet. "It's balsam," she said, lifting it in her delicate vein-lined hands. Esther leaned in and closed her eyes. It had a sweet, woody fragrance, like the forest at dawn.

"This is the most exquisite perfume I have ever smelled," Esther said.

Her mother was watching. "You have a good nose."

Esther beamed.

"Balsam costs more than twice its weight in silver," her mother said, "but I didn't buy it for the scent. It's a miracle cure for many illnesses."

"That's why it's so expensive?" Esther asked.

"No, it's expensive because it's rare. Only a handful of people in the whole world know how to cultivate the trees and harvest the resin, and they all live in the oases of Jericho and Ein Gedi. It's the most carefully guarded secret in all of Judea—maybe even more than the formula for the Temple incense." She chuckled and added, "But *I* know it."

Esther gazed at her mother in admiration.

Her mother seemed like a different person as she patiently explained how an incision was made in the tree bark and the resin collected in a small horn. They were standing side by side, with their shoulders touching. Esther wanted to prolong this moment. She was afraid to say anything, lest she shatter the spell.

"Pour a few drops in here," Sarah said, squinting as she handed Esther a glass vial.

Her mother had entrusted her with a secret *and* her most costly ingredient! Esther held the vial steady as she poured. Finally her mother wanted to share her medical knowledge with her only daughter.

"Good," Sarah said. "I can't see so well anymore." She took the vial from Esther's hand and turned around. "Now you can leave."

Esther felt an almost physical blow to her gut. Her mother didn't want to teach her; she needed Esther's eyes because her own were failing. Esther was angry at herself for being disappointed; she should have known her mother just needed her for another chore.

PART FOUR

DECEMBER 65 CE

KISLEV 3826

When a woman has a discharge . . . being blood from her body, she shall remain in her impurity seven days.

Leviticus 15:19

CHAPTER XIX

ESTHER THOUGHT ABOUT JOSEPH CONSTANTLY. SHE THOUGHT ABOUT him so much that it hurt. Miriam once said that love hurt, but Esther hadn't understood what she meant until now. Esther felt different inside. She even checked in the mirror to see if she looked different. Parts of her body that she'd never before noticed now ached.

But this morning, she realized how wrong she'd been. There was a dried brown stain on the back of her robe. It wasn't love that had made her feel as if worms were gnawing at her gut; it was impurity. Esther had thought she knew all she needed to know about the blood, but now she had so many questions. How long would she be impure? What would happen if, by mistake, she touched the family's food? If she walked between two men? If she looked at the wine, would it change to vinegar right away, or only if she poured it?

She found Miriam in the courtyard, spinning furiously. "Miriam!"

Miriam stopped her frenzied manipulations, put the distaff in her lap, and laid the spindle down. "I don't know what to do. They came for Shimon."

"Who?"

"Thugs."

"So what? Somebody is always coming to collect from him."

"But this time the somebody is very dangerous. Thank God Shimon wasn't home. Who knows what they would have done to him?" Miriam sat back. With her creased brow and sallow complexion, she looked much older than her nineteen years.

The gambling had started two years before, when Shimon had begun distributing the family wine to the pubs and inns around town. Soon he'd been spending more time at the dice tables than at home. He claimed that he was building the business and that he'd sell more wine if he socialized with his customers.

Esther didn't want to talk about Shimon now. "There's something I have to tell you. . . ."

"First I need to tell you something," Miriam said. "I think I'm—"

"With child!" Esther said, delighted. So that was why Miriam looked so tired!

"No, it's not that," Miriam said, in a flat voice. "I'm barren."

"Are you sure? Did you have a dream?"

"Everyone else who's been married for five years has a babe in their arms and two or three more hanging on to their hems. I must have sinned. Otherwise why would I be without child for so long?"

Esther rested her hand on Miriam's arm. "God will answer your prayers yet."

"All day and night, I try to guess how I angered Him, and I still don't know. But my empty womb is proof of my sin." Miriam sighed and returned to her work. While her fingers guided the threads, she chanted psalms, *"Wash me thoroughly of my iniquity, and purify me of my sins; for I know I have sinned—"*

"You're not to blame," Esther said. "Everyone knows infertility is caused by a man being disrespectful to his wife."

"But Shimon isn't disrespectful. He just ignores me. It didn't used to be like this. When we were first married, we were always together. I've tried everything. I sprouted flax seeds, planted cucumbers, and put amulets under our bed, but he still won't come to me. He's hardly ever home. I want a son, more than anything."

"So Shimon will love you?"

Miriam wound and unwound the thread, pulling it taut with angry tugs. "So someone will."

"Don't despair; a baby will grow in your womb. Remember Sarah from the Torah."

"I can't wait until I'm ninety years old for a miracle."

Esther couldn't ask Miriam about the rag bucket now. It wasn't the right time to talk to Miriam about Esther's blood, a sign of her fertility. She'd ask her mother. She didn't want to—it would make her mother even more determined to marry her off quickly, and Joseph still hadn't asked for her hand—but she had no choice. She needed the rags.

"Mother, it's come. My blood."

"Blessed be God," Sarah said. Then she slapped Esther.

Esther held a hand to her stinging cheek as her eyes filled with tears. *What did I do wrong now?*

Sarah gingerly moved Esther's hand away from her reddened face. "See? Your lifeblood is already coming back. We mustn't let the death spirits feed on it. They try to take away too much blood, so we need to show them that we can get it back." Her mother smiled. "The rags are under the garlic braids hanging in the storeroom."

Despite her worries over Lazar, despite the stinging of her cheek, Esther was glad she had told her mother. Maybe they could be closer as women than as mother and daughter.

Yehuda grabbed Esther's arm as she came out of the storeroom. "Where did you get that?" he thundered.

"Get *what*?" Esther asked.

He snatched the rag with a force that surprised her, then pressed the tattered cloth to his face. "This was her headscarf," he whispered.

"I didn't know," she said gently. "It was in the rag pile."

Yehuda tucked the cloth into his belt. "When she comes back, she'll need it."

Esther hesitated, but couldn't stay silent. "She won't need it, Yehuda. She's dead."

"For now, yes. My beloved wife is asleep in the dust of the earth, but at the End of Days she'll wake up. That's why we need to save her headscarf, and that's why we'll need to gather her bones." He spoke wistfully, "Yes, very soon. She'll need them again when she rises."

Suddenly Esther understood. So that's why Yehuda had joined the Sicarii and supported the revolt. He wanted the end of *this* world so that his wife and son would come back to life in the next. He believed that defeating the Romans would hasten the End of Days, when the dead would rise again.

Esther also wished that her sister-in-law would return to life. Esther missed her. Tabitha would have helped her now and taught her how to fold the rag and fit it into her undergarment so it wouldn't ball up or slip out. Esther missed her warmth and her touch. Tabitha used to let Esther join her in the bath on winter days when the water was hot and steaming. Afterward, they'd lie together, running their fingernails lightly over each other's soft, downy backs. They'd huddle in the courtyard sharing toasted wheat kernels.

She remembered Tabitha's death as if it had happened yesterday. Her mother had run out of the birthing room, her body drenched in sweat. "If the baby doesn't come out soon," she said, "we're going to have to cut open her womb and pull it out—limb by limb. Esther, bring the smelling cures. Hurry!"

Esther ran outside for a fresh clod of earth. Her hands shook as she added mint, anise, and barley groats to the small basket. By the time she returned, Tabitha's savage screams had turned into feeble whimpers. Esther hovered outside the birthing room, hesitant to enter.

Finally, Miriam emerged holding a tin pail of blood-soaked rags in each hand. Sarah rushed after her, screaming for a knife to cut the baby out of the belly of the dead mother.

Yehuda, who had been waiting just outside the door, dropped to his knees. His wails of anguish rose as though from a bottomless pit.

The next morning, the family walked a half hour to their burial cave on the Mount of Olives. They were privileged to have a cave near the city. A month later, they heaved the heavy stone away from the entrance once more. They went down two steps to the large space carved out of the mountain. The baby was dead too.

Yehuda sobbed as he lay the small bundle, no bigger than a bird and wrapped in scented white strips of linen, next to his mother. "My dear son, you'll remain innocent and pure forever." Tiny purplish-gray toes peeked out. "All are from dust, and to dust all return."

The family had to pull him away. For months afterward, Yehuda slept outside the burial cave. When Esther asked him why, he said Tabitha wouldn't like being all alone in the cave, and he didn't want her to be afraid.

Now almost a year later, Tabitha's bones, along with her baby's, were waiting for their reburial in the ossuary, the bone box. The pink limestone box in Yehuda's room.

Yehuda pressed Tabitha's headscarf to his nose. Soon he would gather the bones that the decaying flesh had laid bare.

"The prophecies in Scripture are true," he said. "God will bring them back to me."

CHAPTER XX

IT WAS MIDMORNING WHEN ESTHER MADE HER WAY TOWARD THE southwestern corner of the Temple Mount. She was going to the ritual bath to purify herself after her period. The dusty air, thick with the familiar stench of animal excrement, human sweat, and smoke, greeted her, and a soft light bathed the area. The Temple stones radiated holiness and sanctity. Still, Jerusalem stank. The priests who blessed the city in their prayers and the workers who cleaned the streets couldn't sweep away its fetid odors.

Lazar's workshop was across the road. His signet rings, embossed with the image of the Temple, were a favorite souvenir for pilgrims. Esther pulled the veil over her face and raced down the street. She didn't want to see Lazar, or risk allowing him to see her. He might think she'd come to visit him.

Pack mules piled high with sacks of legumes, women balancing baskets of leafy greens on their heads, and beggars limping through the streets all competed for space on the road. Esther had always loved watching the parade of people in the city. They came from faraway lands such as Cappadocia and Pontus by the Black Sea, and from neighboring lands such as Cilicia and Cyprus.

The Syrians and Babylonians stood out the most with their multicolored robes and fringed sleeves. The Egyptians wore white linen garments with wide sashes and more jewelry than anyone else; gold bracelets adorned their arms and wrists. Jews from the west wore covered shoes, some made from wood, and they fastened their tunics in the front with large brooches. Some of the men from northern Europe even wore trousers. She couldn't stop staring whenever she saw them. The Jews from Italia wore toga-like garments with complicated folds of fabric that must have taken them—or their slaves—hours to arrange just so.

It was easy, though, to spot the locals. They always had on sandals, even in cold weather like now, when they'd pair them with socks.

Esther looked toward the Temple, its massive limestone walls and gold-topped columns towering over the city. She felt protected, knowing that God was close by. It wasn't only the Temple that made Esther feel secure. The north side of the city was protected by two walls, and a third one, not yet finished. The walls were more than twenty-five cubits high, with at least sixty guard towers. Once, she'd tried to count them, but there were so many that she'd soon given up.

Esther had grown up in the shadow of the majestic buildings. The Temple Mount and the Antonia Fortress, with their ornate towers, palatial plazas and porticoes, were part of her everyday landscape. She couldn't imagine Jerusalem without the Temple, although its completion had been recent. Her father had explained how the massive stones had been quarried, transported, and lifted into place. He'd shown her how the stones fit together perfectly. Most builders, he said, used plaster and cement to ensure that their buildings lasted for a lifetime. The Temple had neither, but even so, it would last for eternity.

Esther knew that the Temple could have been created only with God's help. She also knew that, like the Temple, she was meant to be here. Every living thing had a place where it thrived, and Jerusalem was her place. Just like the cedars had Lebanon, the rosebushes had Jericho, and the date palms had Ein Gedi—she had Jerusalem.

Esther raced down the dusty street, maneuvering around the customers at Jono's stall, with their salted fish rolls. She reached the staircase leading up to the Temple Mount. Sometimes she and Matti would sit at the base and watch the procession of people pulling their sacrificial animals up the stairs. She and Matti would lean against the smooth stones of the new Temple Mount wall and laugh at the recalcitrant goats who wouldn't follow their owners, as if the animals knew the fate awaiting them at the top. When Esther and Matti got tired of looking at the people, they would count the nesting swifts in the eaves and watch the brown-gray sparrows, swifts, and jackdaws darting under the arches.

The shops nestled at the base of the stairs were bustling. The pigeon seller always did a brisk business, especially with women after childbirth (who had to atone for their curses during labor) or people suffering from dysentery. It was the cheapest animal they could sacrifice. They could always offer grains but, everyone knew, a blood sacrifice was better.

Even from behind her veil, Esther's eyes burned from the strong rays reflecting off the plates of gold covering the Temple, and the smoke from the sacrificial offerings. The smell of burnt flesh hung in the air.

She entered the cavernous space, where a wide staircase led down to a pool of water, the *mikveh*. A red and orange mosaic floor, and floral frescoes on the walls, decorated the room. A brazier in the corner provided heat. Curls of steam twirled up to the vaulted ceiling.

This was not her first time here; she had come once with her mother and once with Miriam. Even though everyone had a *mikveh* in their own home—or at least everyone she knew—this ritual bath was for special occasions because of its proximity to the Holy of

Holies. For use before weddings, after childbirth, and, in Esther's case, after her first blood.

Women waited on the wide steps leading down to the pool, and more stood just outside the door. It was her turn. She nervously shed her garments and stood naked before the attendant, a wizened old woman. She motioned to Esther to descend the seven steps to the stone pool.

"Stand with your legs spread as though you're kneading dough and say the prayer," the attendant said. "Water cleanses the body, and prayer cleanses the soul."

"Blessed are You, Lord, our God, king of the universe, who has sanctified us with His commandments and commanded us to immerse."

Esther stepped into the pool, then immersed herself underwater to rid herself of impurities. She dunked again, to become holy. When she stood, she thought she'd feel different—pure and proud and womanly—but she felt the same as before, only cold and wet.

"Hurry, hurry," the attendant urged, waving a gnarled hand. "You're not the only one here."

Esther felt as if all eyes were on her. She fumbled with her loincloth, looping it carelessly between her legs and around her waist. Hastily she belted her striped wool robe. She should have asked Miriam to come with her. She hadn't realized how exposed she would feel.

Eager to escape the nosey stares of the other women, she dashed out of the room, holding the edge of her loincloth through her robe to keep it from falling down. She flew up the south stairs to her father's office, at the end of the long corridor, next to the office of the sacred donations. It was an oasis of calm in the midst of all the Temple's commotion. He wouldn't be back yet; he was inspecting the large, underground water cisterns and draining tunnels whose engineering plans he had brought home the previous evening.

She entered his chamber and closed the door. Her loincloth was slipping down her legs. She loosened her belt and placed her robe on the bench. Then she expertly wrapped the loincloth and tucked the end back under the now tight waistband.

The vases in the window shimmered. The tall, clear one caught the sun's rays and cast bright rainbows onto the floor and walls. When she'd been little, she had delighted in putting her hand in different positions to catch the colors.

She pulled her headscarf down to her shoulders and shook out her wet hair. Shivering, she turned around and reached for her robe.

A man—a *Roman,* the same one she had met before the Virgin Circle!—stood in the doorway. She snatched her robe and held it like a shield in front of her chest.

"What—what are you doing here?" she said, her voice unsteady. "The door was shut."

"I knocked," he said, his face turned pointedly to the window.

"I didn't hear you." Her face burned. She clutched her robe tighter to her chest.

"Aster, right? Aster with the fiery eyes, or was it the fiery tongue? I'm not looking. Get dressed."

She didn't move.

"Go on, unless you want to stand here like that all day."

Esther turned away and quickly slid her arms into the wide sleeves. Then she spun back around, watching him suspiciously.

Her hands shook as she adjusted her headscarf. Her fear turned to fury. "How dare you sneak in here?" She had been scared the first time she'd met him, but not now. She was safe here, in the Temple of God. It felt strange, almost euphoric, to throw off restraint and speak so freely.

"I don't 'sneak,'" he said. "I came to visit a Temple official, and you happened to be taking off your clothes in his office."

"This is my father's office, and I was getting dressed."

"Your father?" Tiberius looked surprised.

"Yes, my father. You Romans think you're masters of the whole world, but you don't rule here. Only God rules here. You will never rule the Temple, and you will never rule Jerusalem."

Tiberius ran his hand through his hair. "You may be right. This city reminds me of a beautiful and willful young woman who refuses to be tamed."

He was mocking her.

"Why don't you take a walk in the Inner Court?" she countered.

Tiberius laughed appreciatively. No one could miss the marble slab at the entrance to the compound, warning in large Greek and Latin letters that any gentiles who entered would be put to death. The mirth in his eyes was like kindling to the fire raging inside her.

"Your Roman dress and dagger do not allow you to violate my honor," Esther said hotly.

He raised his eyebrows but did not reply, simply leaning against the doorframe and folding his arms across his chest.

Under his gaze, Esther felt like an insect trapped in pine resin.

He looked amused and said, "The Jews will probably go the way of the Carthaginians, the Iberians, and the Gauls—all peoples stronger than you. At least, that seems to be the direction your stubborn nation is now headed. You have your own temple and are free to practice your own religion, yet you still protest. Rome was destined to rule."

She knew he wasn't arguing from conviction. Still, she could not resist having the last word.

"I accept nothing from you, a heathen," she said. "You were once a slave."

He seemed taken aback. "Yes, that's true. Who told you? Surely not your father."

"The man who told me knows the true nature of Romans. He's a priest, and his name is Joseph Ben Matityahu."

His face darkened; she'd hit her target. She felt powerful, as if she were brandishing a lit torch in his face.

"Hmm, so that treacherous snake has returned." He muttered under his breath, "*Vipera perfida.* I've been waiting for him." He narrowed his eyes. "He can't be trusted. You should stay away from him."

Esther laughed. "A Roman is warning me to stay away from a Jewish hero. *You* should stay away from me . . . and my father."

"I have something to give your father. Tell him I need to see him. It's urgent."

It was dangerous for her father to be seen with a Roman. There were spies everywhere; anyone could finger him as a collaborator. What if Yehuda found out? She didn't think he would turn in their own father, but she wasn't sure. She hadn't thought he would kill a man either.

Trembling, she pushed past Tiberius and ran through the Great Hall. It was difficult to navigate through the crowds, and she narrowly missed a man carrying cages filled with squawking pigeons and turtledoves. She stopped only when she'd arrived home.

Hanan was in his study. She stood by his door, about to tell him that Tiberius was looking for him, but then changed her mind. It was too dangerous. She had to protect Hanan from himself. It would be safer if there were no further contact between them.

She walked away.

CHAPTER XXI

A WEEK LATER, SARAH ASKED ESTHER TO DELIVER A POTION IN TOWN. Esther took the long route, past Joseph's house. She lingered outside for more than an hour, but no one came. Too bad, she thought. This time, she could have shown him that she really *was* delivering medicines for her mother.

When she returned home, an unnatural silence hung over the courtyard. Esther quickened her steps. A cold dread crept up her spine. It was the same feeling she'd had on the day Yehuda's son had died—as if normal life had stopped and was waiting for permission to resume.

Only Matti was in the courtyard. He raised a clenched fist with his little finger extended, a gesture indicating that a Roman was close, and tilted his head toward the house. She gulped, forcing herself to remain calm.

Something is wrong. What possible reason can a Roman have for entering our home?

Her mind tumbled over itself, images of her father prostate on the ground, blood running from a gash in his head, her mother pleading with the soldiers. But it was quiet and eerily still—no angry shouts, no anguished cries.

Through the side storage room door, Esther slipped inside. She made her way down the dimly lit hallway, every sense alert. The hair on her scalp and arms prickled. She tiptoed forward, softly placing the ball of one foot down, and then the other, until she heard voices.

She looked back, hoping Matti hadn't followed her inside. Hardly breathing, she concentrated on catching the sounds.

She braced herself for the screams that she expected to hear at any moment, but instead she heard only the easy rhythm of pleasant conversation punctuated by soft laughter.

Her father was *laughing*! Her fists unclenched and her breathing resumed, yet her relief was fleeting, and dissipated as quickly as it had come. *What if Yehuda comes back? A Roman is in our house!*

She peered into the room, and that was when she saw him—*Tiberius!* Had he come to threaten or blackmail her, maybe even tell her father that he had seen her disrobe? It was her fault he was here; she hadn't given her father the message. Maybe if she'd told her father that Tiberius wanted to give him something, her father could have sent a messenger. They would have been in contact, but at least Tiberius wouldn't have come to their house.

Hanan looked up. "Ah, here she is, my little queen. Esther, this is a friend of mine, Tiberius Claudius Masculus," he said, as casually as if he were introducing a neighbor.

Tiberius bowed his head ever so slightly. He had a polite yet impassive countenance, giving no hint that they had met before.

She felt a flush of heat, and hated that her face betrayed her. She forced herself to look at him, and then she knew: he wouldn't give anything away. But it was wrong to keep a secret with this man, whom she loathed, from her father, whom she loved. This made her despise the Roman even more.

Her throat tightened and she didn't trust herself to speak. She slowly took a step backward, out of the doorway. But she didn't leave.

What does he want to give my father?

She stood in the hall and peeked inside.

Tiberius was talking. ". . . and you weren't in your office."

"If you're worried about my side of the deal," Hanan said, "you needn't be. The shipment is almost ready; my people packed the crates last week and ordered the seals."

It sounded like they were exporting something together—that they were business partners! She covered her mouth with her hand. This was so much worse than she'd thought. She had assumed that Tiberius was simply one of the numerous Roman middlemen who supplied the Temple with incense and cloth. She'd never imagined that her father would be so reckless as to have a side deal with a Roman. Her father really *was* a collaborator!

Tiberius reached into his rucksack and pulled out an iron dagger. He held it by the bone hilt and set it down on the desk. "I brought this to your office, but you weren't there. I probably shouldn't have come here, but I want you to have it for protection. Things are getting rough."

Her father recoiled, staring at the dagger as if it might rise on its own. "Where did you get this?"

"I had it made in a weapons factory in Gaza. I work with smiths in Caesarea, but the ones in Gaza are better."

"You trade in weapons?"

"I supply whatever people buy, except slaves. I know you find it distasteful, but if people don't get the weapons from me, they'll get them from someone else. The swords will get bought, the *sestertii* will change hands, and a few coins will fall to the ground. Why shouldn't I be the one to pick them up?"

"Isn't it enough that we're selling spices and asphalt? Won't you have enough money from our deal?"

"Is it ever enough?" He paused. "Besides, ours is not a sure deal. The ship might sink, the rats might eat the spices, robbers might stop the caravans. There are hundreds of ways for our transport to fail. Yes, it could be profitable. Very profitable. But it could also be a loss. But swords, shields, javelins, missiles . . . those I can't supply fast enough."

"But they are used against our people . . . and yours too!"

"Your people? You should be glad I'm giving them weapons to protect themselves with. And used against my people?" Tiberius chuckled. "The Roman army? I'm not worried that the few weapons I supply your ragtag group of malcontents will topple the Roman empire. I'm sure Emperor Nero sleeps quite well at night. I'm a merchant. This is what merchants do: give people what they want, not necessarily what they need."

"I'm wondering," Hanan said, sitting back in his chair, a look of curiosity on his face, "how did you become such a successful trader?"

Tiberius sat back too, crossing one long leg over the other, as if he were settling in to tell a long story. "I'm from Britannia, the tribe of the Durotriges. When I was just a boy, I was brought to Rome as cargo, next to the really valuable freight—the copper, timber, and oysters. I used to help the soldiers count out the food rations—so I could pilfer a little for myself and my mother. Emperor Claudius took his share of the war captives to be royal slaves, and since I was known to be good with numbers, they sent me to the treasury. A freedman there, Marcus Antonius Pallas, took me under his wing and taught me everything I know."

Hanan stared intently at Tiberius.

"By the time Nero took the throne," Tiberius said, "Pallas was running the Imperial Treasury. Nero accused him of treason and had him executed. Pallas had become too powerful, I suspect."

"What happened to you?" Hanan asked.

"I was petrified," Tiberius said. "After all, I was Pallas's boy. Everyone knew we worked together. But then"—he paused and shook his head in wonder, as if he were still surprised—"I was promoted. I was one of the few people Pallas had trusted, so I knew the trail of money better than anyone else. I knew how to move Egyptian grain, Indian spices, Chinese silks, and Sodom salt. I knew that a donkey could haul three hundred drachmae of oil and a camel twice that. I knew each of the stations and ports in the eastern desert and the Red Sea. I knew the worth of every villa in Rome, Tuscany, and Campania, and, more important," he added, smiling, "I knew the private vices and debaucheries of their owners." His face turned serious. "I vowed that one day I would become rich and buy fine clothes and a house filled with my own slaves. Maybe even a villa, where I would grow vines and olives and live the life of a Roman aristocrat. Pallas had done it. He'd been born a slave too, and had died a rich man."

"It sounds like that's why he died; he was too rich."

"You're right," Tiberius said with a chuckle. "Still, I'd rather take my chances as a rich man than a poor one."

Esther, rooted to the spot, listened while her father and Tiberius went back to discussing the details of their shipment: routes, customs, and tariff payments. Then they rose. Tiberius's wooden chair made a screeching sound on the stone floor. Tiberius took a step toward the desk and slid the dagger into an ornate sheath. He pushed it toward Hanan.

"Use the knife if you must, and don't be so trusting," Tiberius said. "I know what I'm talking about; trusting a Jew almost killed me."

"Joseph Ben Matityahu said your paths crossed," Hanan said.

Tiberius smiled. "There are no secrets in this town."

"Joseph was surprised when I told him you were here."

"He shouldn't be. He knows we have unfinished business."

"Now it's my turn to give you some advice," Hanan said, leaning forward and placing a hand on Tiberius's arm. "I don't know what happened between you, but I do know that Joseph is not someone you want as an enemy. Revenge is an enticing temptress, but its path leads backward."

"Sometimes you have to go backward before you can go forward. Revenge is a temptress because it's sweeter than honey. The thought of confronting him is what kept me going when I was fleeing for my life." He dropped his voice, and Esther had to move in to hear.

"The worst was not the betrayal," Tiberius said, "or even that Joseph tried to get me killed. It was the humiliation. I hadn't felt that sense of helplessness since I'd been enslaved. For that, I'll never forgive him."

"What did he do?"

"He pretended to be my friend so he could get information. I worked in the emperor's finance bureau, a hornet's nest of intrigue. Most of the staff were freedmen, like me. People traded in secrets, but I was careful. Joseph was charming and daring, and gradually I let down my guard. It was nice to have a friend. We laughed and . . ." He seemed to be remembering as a wistful smile tugged at his lips. "Rome has some . . . ahem"—he cleared his throat—"brothels, actually. We enjoyed ourselves, and I thought he didn't want anything from me but *amiticia*, friendship."

Hanan leaned on his cane. He seemed embarrassed, but Tiberius kept going. "Clearly I was wrong. He was just using me to get information. I vowed to track him down, even to the ends of the empire."

Creases lined her father's forehead. "What are you going to do?"

"What he tried to do to me."

"Tiberius, you're courting trouble if you walk around with a hungry blade. This is his town, not Rome. He's well connected."

"Yes, but he's not a Roman citizen, and I have enough

information—or can make up enough—to have him hang from a cross. Remember what happened to Jesus, son of Joseph from Nazareth, and his brothers? You know that the Romans always get rid of troublemakers, just like those Galilean revolutionaries. I'll have to make up much less information than you think. There *is* some connection between Joseph and the rebels."

"There's a connection between every Jew and the rebels."

"All I have to do is hint to the Roman authorities that he's plotting revolution or working with the Sicarii."

There was a moment of silence.

"I will not be a party to this," Hanan said. "In spite of what he may or may not have done, he's a fellow Jew, and it's my duty to warn him."

"Please do. I want him to look behind his shoulder, to see me in the shadows, to hesitate before he opens a closed door, or walks down a dark alley. Besides, if he knows I'm here, then he already knows I'm looking for him."

"You sound like a Sicarius yourself, ready to carry out a personal vendetta with your hidden dagger."

"No, no, nothing so crude as that. He'll know it was me."

Esther felt her skin crawl. She had to warn Joseph! But Joseph wasn't the only one in danger; her father was too. She had to make sure that Yehuda didn't find out their father had a Roman business partner.

CHAPTER XXII

"You shouldn't be here," she hissed at Tiberius when he left her father's study and entered the courtyard. "My father could be murdered because of you! The Sicarii are killing collaborators."

"Everyone is killing everyone else," he said. "Your father is smart; he knows what to do."

"No, he doesn't!"

Tiberius seemed taken aback by her vehemence. "Is someone threatening your father? Tell me, and I'll have my people take care of him."

"Your people? You mean your Roman friends?"

"I have friends on both sides."

"So you're a traitor to your own cause too?"

"I'm a businessman. I'm loyal to my friends, not causes."

She couldn't tell him that the danger was in her own home, from her own brother.

Shimon's dog, a fawn-colored saluki with a narrow face, large gentle eyes, and droopy ears, jumped out at Tiberius, barking angrily. Shimon had brought him home when he'd been just a puppy, abandoned on a side street in the butchers' quarters.

Tiberius recoiled, sucking air through his teeth. Only when the dog lost interest and sniffed at the ground did Tiberius exhale. He rubbed the back of his neck.

Esther taunted, "An all-mighty Roman is afraid of a tethered house pet?"

"I don't like dogs."

"Looks like more than that to me," she said in a smug tone, folding her arms across her chest.

Tiberius opened his mouth to speak, then hesitated and rubbed his chin. After a pause, he spoke. "When I was a boy, there was a dog clenching something in its mouth. I wanted to see what the dog had, so I coaxed it toward me. . . . It was a baby's leg."

"You're lying. A dog can't snatch a babe from its mother's arms."

"Mother's arms?" He choked back a bitter laugh. "There was no mother, only an empty field littered with babies. Sometimes they got picked up by slave traders or brothel owners. Sometimes they died of thirst, and sometimes . . . they got torn to pieces by wild dogs."

"No mother—even a Roman mother—would leave her child in a field to die!"

"Romans and Jews are different."

A leather pouch fell from his belt, and a few sheaves of papyri floated to the ground. They both bent down. Esther picked one up, admiring the beautiful calligraphy of the Latin scrolls. She reached for another, then jerked her hand back as if she had touched fire. The charcoal marks on this papyrus didn't form letters, but rather a picture. A young girl, her hair wet, and her face unguarded with wide eyes and full lips. Esther felt the hair on the back of her neck stand up. She was staring at herself.

Tiberius shrugged. "I like to draw beautiful things."

She blushed, quickly turning her head. He thought *she* was beautiful? "It's a sin," she said. "It's forbidden to draw people." She didn't expect the earth to shake or the heavens to storm, but she wouldn't have been surprised if they had. Other than the image of the caesar on Roman coins, Esther had never seen a picture of a person. She snatched the picture and tried to tear it, but Tiberius grabbed it out of her hands. She glared at him, then stormed off. Let him have it. She didn't care what he did, or what he thought of her.

Her parents were arguing in the kitchen. Her mother stood in what Esther called her battle pose, as if she had a quiver of angry arrows set to fly. "I come home and find out that there was a Roman in the house!" Sarah said. "How dare you allow one of them to enter our home? Why did he come here?"

"Don't let your water boil," her father answered. "It's not as if we shared a meal. It was a business meeting."

"It doesn't matter. A Roman brought his heathen filth into our house!"

"He brought me a weapon and money."

"Money for what?" Mention of coin seemed to deflate her mother's wrath.

"The profit from our previous deal."

"Your *previous* deal?" Sarah repeated.

"We've been working together since he started selling incense to the Temple. We did a few import deals together—mostly spices—and then started exporting too. We began with dates but there were too many problems with spoilage. Now we're shipping tar from the Salt Sea."

"Why? There's no tar in Rome?"

"Ours is better. It's shiny and purple, not black like theirs. Good for waterproofing ships, and the best thing is, it's free! This new cargo was his idea. Now we don't have any more problems with pests during the voyage. And you know," he added, rubbing his chin, "he never tried to collect payment from me on those bad shipments we had together. He took on the losses like they were his own."

Sarah narrowed her eyes to sharp slits. "I don't care how he acts or how good a business this is. He shouldn't come to the house. I forbid it."

"Forbid it?" He spoke in a measured tone that belied an underlying fury. For the first time, Esther was afraid for her mother. "Sarah," her father said softly. "Remember yourself."

Her mother looked chastened, but only for a moment. She met his gaze defiantly. "I'm worried about Esther. What if the neighbors saw?" She dropped her voice to a whisper. "Do you think we could make a match for her if people knew that a Roman had been in our house?"

"So what if people know? I'm not afraid of what people may say."

Sarah said, "Things are different now. People are not just talking anymore. It's dangerous out there."

Esther could stay quiet no longer. "What if Yehuda finds out?"

"Yehuda lives in a world of his dreams," Hanan said dismissively. "He thinks the coins for his bread, his cloth, and his studies rain down from the heavens."

If her father wasn't worried, then he must not have suspected that Yehuda had joined the Sicarii. At least that was a relief.

"But how could you do business with a Roman after what they did to you?" Esther asked. As soon as the words left her lips, she wished she could put them back. She knew he didn't want to be reminded, but she couldn't help it. She could still taste the bile of helplessness in her mouth. She braced herself for his reaction—anger for bringing it up or anguish as he remembered the humiliation.

She waited, shifting her weight nervously from foot to foot. But he said nothing. He had a blank look on his face, as if he didn't know what she was talking about. *Maybe the past isn't only what you remember, but what you choose to forget.*

CHAPTER XXIII

THANKFULLY, YEHUDA HADN'T BEEN HOME WHEN TIBERIUS HAD VIS-
ited. But clearly her father didn't think he was doing anything wrong;
he spoke freely about their partnership. Surely Yehuda would soon
discover that their father had a Roman business partner.

During the Sabbath meal when they were all together, Esther's
stomach felt so twisted, she could hardly take a bite. Her father and
brother argued about the Romans and the rebels. Yet again.

She had to keep them apart—at least for now. It was too risky for
Yehuda to live at home. Maybe if she threatened to expose Yehuda's
secret, he would leave. He could sleep at the study house. Many of
his friends already boarded there since the lessons went late into the
night and prayers started at dawn.

She felt better now that she had a plan. She didn't want to force
Yehuda to leave home, but it was the only way to keep her father
safe. Yehuda could come back home as soon as the ship reached its
destination and the cargo was released. By then their father would
have his share of the profits, and the partnership would end. The
danger would be gone.

That evening, she spoke to Yehuda. She kept her voice low, for
fear her parents might overhear.

"I know you joined the Sicarii," she said, steeling herself for his
denial. He would be shocked, of course, that Esther knew.

"Yes, I did. We must be masters of our own fate! I can live under

God's mercy, but how can I live at the mercy of a bloodthirsty Rome?"

Now Esther was the one who was shocked.

"But you didn't join the Zealots, who just talk, or the other rebels who strut around like pretend soldiers. You joined the most fanatic of all the rebel groups, the ones who are murdering people in the street!"

She still hoped he would say that she was mistaken, that he had merely participated in a few meetings, that the knife she'd seen wasn't a *sica* dagger but rather a regular knife, the kind used to slaughter chickens. She hoped that he was still the same brother who used to sing funny rhyming songs to make her laugh.

He looked away with unseeing eyes. She recognized that distant expression of his; he was elsewhere.

"What if Father is on their list?" she finally asked, breaking the silence. "Which side would you choose?"

Yehuda met her gaze. "He won't be on their list because he's not working with the enemy. He's not a collaborator."

"Of course he's not a collaborator. But he did buy spices for the Temple from Roman traders. He said it himself."

"That was then."

Yehuda pushed past her to go into the courtyard.

This wasn't how she'd expected the conversation to go. She had to scare him. Otherwise he wouldn't move out—and then, surely, he *would* find out about their father's deal.

"What if I tell Father you're a Sicarius?" she called after him.

Slowly he turned around. After a pause, he said, "It's not what you think."

PART FIVE

MARCH 66 CE
NISAN 3826

Who can find a woman of valor? Her worth is far beyond that of rubies. Her husband has confidence in her and lacks nothing. She is good to him, never bad, all the days of her life.

Proverbs 31:10–12

CHAPTER XXIV

WHILE THE GOATS GRAZED, ESTHER SAT ON THE TERRACED HILLSIDE inhaling the fragrant scent of the crisp morning air and luxuriating in the sun's warmth. It had been three months since Tiberius's visit to their house. The deal was surely completed by now. Luckily, Yehuda had hardly been home since then. He spent most nights at the study house and maybe, she suspected, with the Sicarii too. It seemed that Yehuda wouldn't find out after all. As each day passed, she breathed a bit easier.

The hills were bursting with the pink and white blooms of the almond trees, their delicate petals the first sign of new life after the winter rains. The fields were carpeted with lilac cyclamens and red anemones. The world was waking up. She whistled as she walked into the house with a bag full of hyssop, sage, and lavender.

"Have you seen Shimon?" Hanan asked. "I hope he hasn't joined those rebels, like all the young men are doing."

Esther stifled a laugh. "Shimon? That's as likely as him going to a house of study. He doesn't care about politics."

Hanan smiled. "I have one son who prays for the redemption of the Jewish people, and the other for the green team's victory at the chariot races." Then he turned serious. "But now is not the time to be wandering the streets. You know Shimon. If there's trouble, he'll find it . . . or, it will find him."

She was tempted to say that Shimon wasn't the son he had to worry about, but she restrained herself. She took the herbs into the kitchen.

Her mother looked up. "Someone special is coming," she said with a grin. "Maybe you should put on your Shabbat dress." Sarah was cracking walnuts in her favorite glass bowl, and the table was set with their best dishes. Esther's heart sank.

More than six months earlier, Hanan had said that he'd begun negotiations with the Kalloses, but since then he hadn't spoken of it. Esther had assumed that the political situation, with its mounting tensions, had pushed the question of her future aside. She was relieved that nothing seemed imminent, since she hadn't spoken again with Joseph in months. She walked by his house every chance she got, but she hadn't seen him.

She realized now that she had been lulled into a false sense of security. Of course the negotiations had continued. Last week, she had overheard her parents talking about a pair of donkeys and folds of cloth. How could she not have realized they were discussing her dowry?

All afternoon she paced up and down the courtyard, stealing glances at the gate. In the early afternoon, Lazar arrived with his father. Hanan walked unsteadily, leaning on his cane as he came out the front door. He opened his arms in greeting, still holding the cane. Esther thought he might lose his balance. He embraced Priest Kallos, who thumped her father on his back, much too hard, Esther thought. Then Hanan, still grinning, clasped Lazar on the shoulder.

Turning to her, Hanan said, "Esther, welcome your husband-to-be."

She felt as if she were falling into one of the Salt Sea's gaping sinkholes.

"Esther," Hanan said, commanding her with his eyes.

She was drowning; there was no air.

Apologetically her father turned to Priest Kallos. "We didn't tell her you were coming today."

"No!" Esther shouted, wildly shaking her head. "No, no!" She took off. She didn't know where she was running to, only what she was running from: Lazar and his repulsive grin.

She ran all the way to the far corner of the back garden, a patchy riot of weeds and wild bushes. The prickly shrubs tore at her robe and scraped her calves, but she didn't notice. She leaned against the wall, panting.

"Esther! Where are you?" Sarah cried, swatting at the shrubs in her path. "What are you doing back here?"

Esther didn't look up.

"Lazar is a good Jew," Sarah said. "He already has his own business, and he's been helping his father with Temple duties."

"I don't care; I won't marry him. I don't love him."

Sarah put her hand on Esther's shoulder. "Not right away. First comes familiarity, then affection, and then—if you're lucky—love."

"But I told you, I'm going to marry Joseph."

"More nonsense about Joseph?"

"I don't understand why you're against him. His family is descended from the Maccabees, the greatest Jewish fighters of all time. He's learned, and his house is close to ours. They have three courtyards and a garden with pomegranate trees. They even have four ritual baths."

"I don't care if he's Judah Maccabee himself and if they have a hundred baths; you're not marrying into that family. And now I'm going back to our guests to apologize for your dreadful behavior." She wagged her finger. "You're making a mistake. How do you know Joseph is even interested? Did he say anything, or is this all in your childish imagination?"

"You don't care if I'm happy," Esther said. "You just want to marry me off."

Sarah sighed. "I wasn't happy about your father either when I married him. I didn't know him. In those days, no one asked for a girl's consent. I didn't have a mother to look out for me, like you do," Sarah said. "And I *am* doing what's best for you, even if it doesn't seem that way to you now." Her mother went back inside.

A few minutes later, Lazar approached her with icy eyes and a stony expression.

"First you tease me at the dance. Now you run away? When we're married, it will be different. The games will cease. When I call, you'll come. *I'll* decide when you'll be seen."

"I'm not going to marry you," she said through clenched teeth.

"You weren't my first choice either. I wanted to marry Elisheva, but her father only arranges the spices in the Temple storeroom. Your father hands out silver coins to suppliers and hundreds of workers. Your family is from the House of Seth, with eight high priests in your lineage. So there it is. We're stuck with each other. We both know this arrangement is not about us; it's about our families."

Esther looked at him in surprise. She felt a spark of sympathy at the revelation that he too was being forced to marry against his will. But it was quickly extinguished when he stepped closer, with breath that smelled like sour milk, and said, "You'll do as your father says, and soon you'll do as I say."

Esther took a step back.

Lazar kept talking. "You're still young and unformed, but I'll form you just like I take a lump of silver and fashion it to my wishes. I take hot fire and press the metal. I poke it, burn it, and in the end, it looks how I want it to look. I create objects of beauty and usefulness."

He appraised her, letting his gaze linger over her body. "You're beautiful, but not yet useful. Your father is right to give you to me. I will run a disciplined house."

CHAPTER XXV

A FEW DAYS LATER, SHIMON TOTTERED THROUGH THE FRONT GATE.

"You're back!" Sarah cried. Miriam dropped a tangle of dirty wool and bolted toward him.

"Why is everyone looking at me like that?" Shimon said, a rakish grin playing around his lips. "Why all the glum faces?"

"Where were you?" her mother demanded. "We haven't seen you for days."

"At the finish line, just outside the northern gate."

Miriam flung out her arms. "How can you leave and not tell anyone where you are? How can you race pigeons when it's so dangerous out there?"

"I never trust anyone. Only this!" He threw a sack of coins into the air and caught it with both hands. Then he knelt down on one knee and presented it to Miriam. His grin seemed as wide as his face.

Miriam beamed. He bent to rub his dog's neck, then pulled Miriam close and led her inside.

That night, Esther heard crying. Miriam was huddled in the corner of her room, her head on her knees. When Esther walked in, Miriam raised her head, flushed and tear-stained in the moonlight.

"He's gone again," Miriam said, choking back sobs. "He said his luck had finally returned so he has to follow it. He still doesn't have enough to pay off his debts. I wish he had never started selling the family wine, visiting all the pubs in town. Before this, he never gambled."

"Where did he go?" Esther asked.

"To stage his own cockfight, with the winnings from the pigeon race."

"He's buying chickens?"

"Not chickens, fighting cocks." Miriam wiped her dripping nose with her forearm.

Esther narrowed her eyes.

"You don't understand," Miriam said. "He has to do something. He has to pay it back, or they'll—"

Esther held out her hands, palms forward. She didn't want to hear. "Where will the fight be?"

"At Zahara's pub, where the Roman soldiers drink and gamble. Who knows what else goes on there? The soldiers have coins; they get paid three hundred *sestertii* every four months. They'll bet on anything. Zahara agreed to split the take."

"Doesn't he know what could happen?"

Miriam shook her head. "It'll be worse if he doesn't come up with the money. He owes money to a criminal named Xenon. Unless a stray ox that we can sell wanders into the courtyard, we have no way to pay back what Shimon owes." She balled her hands into fists and hit them together.

CHAPTER XXVI

ESTHER AND MIRIAM WERE IN THE KITCHEN CHANGING THE WATER IN the pickling jars. Out of habit, Esther's fingers reached for her necklace, to rub the stone. But all she felt was skin. "I still can't find my necklace. Are you sure you didn't see it?" Esther was sure she had left it on the small pine table next to her bed. She suspected that Shimon had taken it; he had been gone for a week now. The knowledge that he'd do something like that sat like a leaden weight in her gut.

Miriam wouldn't meet her eyes.

"Shimon took it, didn't he?" Esther said.

Miriam shook her head.

"Then who?"

"Me," Miriam said in a shaky voice. "I didn't know what else to do. I had to give him something."

"Who?"

"Xenon. His slave came for the hundred denarii Shimon owes."

Esther drew in a sharp breath. "One hundred denarii? How could he owe so much?"

"He has until the end of Nisan to pay, or . . ." Miriam hesitated. "They'll be back."

"You gave him *my* necklace?"

"I had no choice. And it's not worth even close to what Shimon owes. Do you know why they call Xenon the 'tree'? It's not because he's tall and has muscles like oak boughs. He hangs his victims over his shoulders. He wraps a rope around their necks, slings them onto his back, and lets them down only when they've stopped kicking."

Esther shuddered. "But why did you have to take my necklace? Mother has a pouch in the workroom where she hides coins from her sales."

Miriam's face clouded over. "That's long gone."

"He stole mother's money too?"

"He borrowed it. He'll return it from the winnings. He said he had magic birds; there's no way he lost. He'll buy you a new necklace too."

Esther felt her voice rising. "You shouldn't have given Xenon anything!"

"You haven't heard the stories about him. He gouged out the butcher's left eye just for looking at him the wrong way. At least your necklace bought us a little time."

"What if Shimon didn't win? Father can get the money. If he doesn't have it, he can get a loan from the Temple."

"Shimon would be furious if I told your father."

"Furious is better than dead. Besides, don't you think they already know he's in trouble? Do you think Mother hasn't noticed her money is missing?"

Miriam shrugged, looking more distraught than Esther ever remembered seeing her. "I don't know anything anymore except that I need to find him.

"He's probably drinking away his winnings."

"He told me he couldn't lose, but—"

"If he lost, he would have come home right away."

"I don't know," Miriam said uneasily. "I have a bad feeling."

"He knows how to take care of himself," Esther said, trying to reassure her.

Shimon was maddening—irresponsible and reckless—but Esther

still adored him. One of her first memories was of Shimon shoving his food onto her plate when her mother's back was turned. Her mother always served Father and her brothers first.

"I'll go with you to look for him," Esther said. "I want to go back to Zahara's anyway. I didn't bring enough money last time."

It had been ten days since Lazar's visit, and Esther still didn't have a plan. She always felt better if she had a plan.

"It would be suspicious if we're both gone," Miriam said.

"Then I'll go by myself," Esther said.

Miriam was silent, thinking. "Tell your mother you're going to pick garlic."

Esther mulled it over. It could work. "But I don't have any money."

Miriam returned a few minutes later with two bronze coins, which she pressed into Esther's hand. "I found these in the bottom of my drawer. Shimon must have missed them."

Esther turned the coins over in her palm. The atmosphere in the market was increasingly tense. The Sicarii were getting more daring in their attacks, and there were assassinations almost every day. People were wary of walking too close to anyone else, lest an innocent-looking passerby have a dagger hidden beneath his cloak. That beggar on the corner might be a spy; the empty storeroom might be a meeting place for rebels. Still, no one would bother a woman; Esther would be safe. And she had to try; her future depended on it.

"All right," Esther said. "I'll go."

"When you're there, would you go to the Pharmaka stall and get some holy water—the kind that brings babies? I need some magic too."

CHAPTER XXVII

"You're hurting me," Matti said as they made their way down the dirt path. Esther loosened her grip but still held him firmly.

"If you'd walk faster, I wouldn't need to pull you." She was irritated with him. When she'd told Sarah that she was going to pick garlic, Matti had insisted on coming along. She didn't want to take him, but it would have been suspicious if she'd refused.

"I'm looking for chariots," he said, slowing down to look at the hippodrome.

"You shouldn't. That place is for pagans."

"Shimon goes there."

Esther was surprised Matti knew about that, but she didn't comment.

Esther didn't want to see anyone they knew, so they continued down the side paths, avoiding King's Road. Just thinking about what her mother would do if she found out that Esther had lied and snuck off to the market—with Matti!—made Esther sweat.

"Ugh," Matti said, scrunching up his nose. "It stinks!"

The stench reached them before the vats of the fuller's laundry came into view.

"We're almost there," Esther said, sidestepping around the donkey droppings on the ground.

When they got to Zahara's, Esther pointed to a spot by the door. "Sit here." Matti sat cross-legged and reached out to pat a scrawny kitten wobbling by. "And don't move."

"Have you seen Shimon?" Esther asked Zahara when she opened the door.

"Not since the cockfight."

"What happened?"

"He didn't buy the right birds. He should have checked their beaks instead of their tail feathers."

Miriam would be disappointed. Now there was no chance Shimon could pay off his debts.

"If he had strapped points to their spurs, he might have had a chance," Zahara added.

"Where is he?"

"How should I know?" The innkeeper stepped back and closed the door. Esther knocked again, but there was no answer. She pounded and pounded, but there was still no answer.

She hung her head for a moment. If Zahara wouldn't sell Esther any magic, she'd make her own. She'd get some shards at the potter's, write her own spells, and bury the shards in Lazar's garden. Anyway, it was later than she'd thought. Time to get Matti and go home. If they hurried, they'd be back before the goats' afternoon milking. She might even have time to finish pressing the dates into cakes.

Where was Matti? She had been standing right next to him. Where could he have gone? Esther's eyes scanned every direction. A creeping dread wrapped around her so tightly, she could hardly breathe.

She ran to the corner, called his name, and then ran back. Still no sign of him. *Which way?* Her mind was racing, but her limbs were paralyzed.

After what felt like forever, she heard a noise. A shuffling sound, something moving between two buildings where the wood pillars had warped and cracked. A head of tousled black hair emerged from a small opening.

"Matti!" Esther ran toward him. "You scared me." She crouched down to help him crawl out. "Don't ever scare me like that again."

He was covered in dirt but had a smile on his face. "I followed the kitten to her house. That is where she lives."

"Come," Esther said in a tremulous voice. She seized his hand. "We're going home.

CHAPTER XXVIII

As they walked home, Esther felt a growing uneasiness. Something seemed different about the market; the air was heavy with tension. A young mother with two boys walked rapidly, scolding the little one when he couldn't keep up. A peddler pulling a donkey laden with crates of onions pelted the ragged beast with blows and urged him on. Women in the houses lining the streets slammed the wooden shutters and hastily gathered up the blankets and rugs airing out on their balconies. The blind beggar, who usually sat on the steps of the Temple, walked quickly, navigating the puddles and avoiding stray dogs; Esther had always suspected that he wasn't really blind. Everyone, it seemed, was in a rush. Shopkeepers huddled together and glanced furtively at the Roman soldiers stationed at the major intersections.

People were furious with the Roman governor Florus, appointed by Emperor Nero to rule Judea. Florus had allowed the Greeks in Caesarea to desecrate the synagogue there. The Greeks had put a chamber pot at the entrance and then sacrificed birds on it. What angered people was not so much what the Greeks had done but that the local Jews had paid Florus eight silver talents to ensure that incidents like that wouldn't occur. Even their protection money couldn't protect them anymore. And only yesterday Florus had stolen seventeen talents from the Temple treasury, an enormous sum.

Esther and Matti came upon a crowd in the middle of the street. Lazar's younger brother, Natan, was at the center. She recognized him at once. Natan and a few other young men were prancing around, imitating the Roman governor. "Please . . . more coppers for a poor starveling," Natan shouted, facing the cheering mob with a shallow basket. He nodded encouragement to those who booed. "What's a poor governor to do if there's no money?" he asked theatrically. "I'll have to take from the Temple treasury so I can pay the actors and dancers in my court and buy finery for my lovely dear wife. Oh, pitiful me, the poorest governor of the Roman empire!"

Natan clownishly clasped his hands together. "Thank you, thank you, dear citizens!" he yelled. "Please give money to me, Gessius Florus, your poor governor. We all know how much a banquet costs!"

An older man in the front playfully kicked Natan in the backside and yelled, "Free us from Florus!" More people jeered, and the banter quickly turned into a menacing roar of shouts and curses.

"Impure feet have trampled our holy ground!"

"Florus stole our gold!"

"Whoever robs the Temple robs God!"

The crowd chanted, "Free us from Florus! Free us from Florus!"

Natan punched his fists into the air, encouraging the frenzy. Esther had seen enough. Natan was courting danger by making fun of the Roman governor. Words that people would never utter alone flowed freely, each person emboldened by the next. And the Roman soldiers were near.

Esther took Matti's hand. "Let's go."

As Esther led Matti back toward the main market street, she heard a low rumble followed by a chilling high-pitched scream.

"What's happ—happening?" Matti grabbed her arm and looked around frantically, trying to tell where the noise was coming from.

The racket intensified with the crash of carts and overturned tables, the neighing of stampeding horses, and the howling of people trying to get away. Fear nailed Esther to the ground.

A woman, her face contorted in terror, flailed her arms as she ran toward them. The wild cries of Roman soldiers shook Esther out of her daze.

"Come!" she yelled. She grabbed Matti and ran. When they reached the corner, more people flooded by. The ground shook. Where had all these people come from?

From the roofs, women pelted broken tiles down on the soldiers. A horse reared up and kicked its forelegs high in the air. The soldier astride it tried to hold on, but slid off. Another rider bared his teeth like a crazed animal and stormed through the crowd, reins in one hand and a long sword in the other. The iron blade glinted as he brought it down on a man's head. Blood splattered onto Esther's face.

She wiped the blood out of her eyes, letting go of Matti's hand, just for an instant. But it was enough; he was swept away. She swung around, but the surging crowd locked her in.

"Matti!" Her cry was lost in the thunderous uproar.

More soldiers, on foot, brandishing daggers and clubs, streamed into the market from every direction. It was impossible to turn around; bodies pressed against her from all sides. She pushed her way toward the stores and crawled under some wooden planks nailed across an empty stall. She lay on the ground, panting. The noise was overwhelming as the crowd roared past. Esther was face-down on the hard dirt, her arms outstretched and palms raked with scratches. She needed to find Matti! Each second she lay there took him farther away.

The stall was littered with broken melons and squashed pomegranates. She struggled to push herself up, stumbled to the back, and kicked open a half door leading to a passageway only a bit wider than herself. The sulfuric smell of rotten eggs and rancid meat made her gag. She waded through the muck until she reached another back alley. Walking as quickly as she could—it hurt to run—she turned at the bakery. She'd made a loop and was close to the same spot where she and Matti had started out. Zahara's pub wasn't too far. Maybe he'd gone back there.

Esther pounded on the door. No answer.

"Let me in!" she yelled. "Help me!" She pounded again and again, leaving marks in blood, until the peephole slid open. Zahara yanked her inside, then slammed the heavy door and bolted it.

"I have to find him," Esther said, breathing heavily. Blood was splattered over her face, and her robe was dirty and torn. "I lost Matti. Is he here?"

"My God, what happened?" Zahara said, her eyes widening.

"The soldiers . . . they're killing people in the streets." She turned back toward the door.

"Stop! Aster . . ."

Aster? Esther swung around. Only one person called her that. She shouldn't have been surprised he was here; Zahara's pub was crawling with Romans.

"You could be killed if you go," Tiberius said, approaching. "The soldiers will leave this place alone. It's the safest place to be."

"My little brother is out there!"

Tiberius cursed in Latin. "At least stay here until the soldiers have satisfied their bloodlust." He said something about the stupid Jews falling into their trap, but she couldn't concentrate. She pulled the iron ring dangling from the door's crossbar, but it wouldn't budge.

"You can't go out there," he said, blocking the door.

Esther tried to push him away. "Let me out!"

"I won't allow it," he said, seizing her.

"I don't take orders from you." She broke free.

"I'm a friend of your father's, and I help my friends."

"Let me out!" Esther shouted, trying to wedge herself behind him, to open the door.

"*I'll* look for him. You stay here," he commanded. He steered her away from the door but this time more gently.

Esther faced him. "You have to find him!"

"I'll keep looking until I do."

"He *has* to be safe." Her lips trembled.

Tiberius turned to Zahara. "Don't let her leave. Tie her to a chair or lock her in the cellar if you have to, but don't let her out of your sight."

Zahara nodded, her previous bravado gone. She led Esther away. "Come, let's get you cleaned up."

Two Roman soldiers from the back room rushed past. Esther drew a sharp breath, but the soldiers didn't even glance her way.

"It's all right," Zahara said soothingly. "Here, they're just men. They only turn into barbarians when they leave."

When Zahara relaxed her grip, Esther broke free and stumbled outside. The Roman soldiers must have left the door open. She limped down the street yelling Matti's name. A stab of pain shot through her right knee.

Tiberius ran after her. "What are you doing?"

"Matti doesn't know you. He'll be frightened. And even if he's not, he may not be able to tell where you are, because of his bad ear."

He saw her determined expression, and nodded. "Stay close to me."

Walking quickly, they scoured alley after alley, shouting Matti's name. Esther stayed close to Tiberius, stepping over the figures strewn on the ground, their limbs angled in unnatural poses.

Tiberius spotted something and ran ahead. The body of a small boy was lying facedown, his legs splayed out. Esther tried to quell the bile rising in her belly as she willed her legs to move faster.

Please, please let it not be him.

Tiberius turned the boy over. It wasn't Matti. Her body convulsed and seemed to separate from her soul. She felt faint and gasped for air. The corpse had been a laughing, innocent child before the sun had risen and brought with it this murderous day. When her retching subsided, they continued walking. For almost two hours, they combed the streets and back alleys.

In silence, they surveyed the scene of the massacre: dead bodies strewn in the road, buzzards already circling overhead.

"So many people . . . ," Esther said, shaking her head. She looked at the carnage. "Why?" She mumbled to herself, not really expecting an answer.

"They didn't pay the proper respect to the emperor," Tiberius said. "Or they were chanting revolutionary slogans. Or maybe they were just buying vegetables at the wrong time." He shook his head. "To the Romans, no Jew is innocent."

"But why do they kill children?"

"The sword of a Roman soldier is like a ravenous cyclops. It devours everything in its path."

Esther swallowed. Her mouth was dry and her eyes stung.

"I'm taking you home," he said. Esther started to protest, but Tiberius held up his hand. "I'll come back and keep looking. It's better this way. I can go faster without you."

She wanted to stay, but she knew Tiberius was right. Besides, she had to let her parents know what had happened. Father would know what to do. He would organize a search party; he would find Matti.

She forced herself to keep walking, to keep moving, away from this field of death. Vaguely conscious of Tiberius's presence beside her, she walked as if she were in a trance, concentrating on putting her feet on the ground. She told herself to breathe, and above all, to not look at the bodies.

At last, she found herself at the staircase leading up to the familiar gate of her home. It was as if she had returned from a long sea voyage where she had been buffeted by storm after storm. It didn't seem possible that she and Matti had left their house only this morning, on this very same day, in this very same lifetime.

"Go on," Tiberius said gently. Esther usually bounded up the staircase to their house so quickly that she hardly felt her feet touch the stones. But today, the steps seemed insurmountable. She concentrated on the stone stairs, anything but what awaited her at the top.

If only it were still yesterday, when Matti was playing in the courtyard. Why had she taken him with her to the market? Her parents would never forgive her. She'd never forgive herself.

I'll never tell another Samson story. I'll never tickle my palm on the soft tuft of hair on the top of his head. Why didn't God take me instead?

He didn't want me.

I don't blame Him.

She reached the top of the steps.

"Estie!"

She staggered forward. The boy flew into her arms as she gasped for breath.

"Matti, Matti." She couldn't stop saying his name, touching his face, rubbing her hands over his cheeks. He was safe! She squeezed him so hard that he shouted. The tears she'd fought back broke loose, and she was swept up in a wave of relief so powerful that she had no choice but to surrender to it.

They stayed locked together, rocking back and forth. Then Esther's gaze shifted. Tiberius was still at the base of the staircase, watching. She mouthed a silent "thank you" while she clung to Matti. Tiberius gave a slight nod, then left.

"I looked for you everywhere," Esther told Matti.

"I waited," he said, his words muffled by their embrace. "But you didn't come. A priest who knew Father found us and brought us home."

Esther wiped her eyes. "Us?"

"Me and the kitten. We hid in her hole. I made her be quiet so the soldiers wouldn't find us. I was like Samson, right, Estie? Just like when he escaped from the Philistines!"

"Yes, you *are* very brave, just like Samson." She tousled his hair and cupped his face in her hands.

Her parents and Miriam crowded around her. Esther looked into Miriam's eyes and shook her head. She hadn't found Shimon. Miriam's hand flew to her mouth.

"What in God's name were you doing there?" her mother demanded.

She couldn't tell her parents what she'd seen.

Sarah's eyes were red and swollen. "You said you were gathering garlic, and you ended up in the market! What were you thinking?"

"Sarah, let her rest," Hanan said, putting his hand on his wife's arm. "We'll have time to find out everything tomorrow."

"She has a lot of explaining to do. The one person I can count on disappears with her little brother."

Her mother's words broke through her fog. *The one person I can count on?* Sarah put her face close to Esther's cheek and kissed her, then stayed there for a few seconds. Esther wanted to say "I love you," but the words wouldn't come. She couldn't say it because she was afraid that her mother wouldn't say it back. But the feel of her mother's face pressed against her own was enough.

CHAPTER XXIX

ESTHER USUALLY WOKE WITH THE ROOSTERS, BUT THE SUN WAS already high and hot when she opened her eyes. The dawn was a betrayal. How could the sun rise as though it were just another ordinary day?

She walked toward the kitchen. She braced herself for a confrontation with her mother. The night before, she had felt a rare sensation, snug in her mother's embrace. Surely it would be gone as soon as her mother learned the truth: that she had tried to thwart their plans for her betrothal, that she had lied to them about where she was going, and that she had risked Matti's life. She paused by the doorway, trying to summon the courage to enter.

Her mother called. "Shimon? Is that you?"

"It's me," Esther said, walking in.

Usually so careful about her dress, Sarah was wearing a stained, wrinkled robe, and her headscarf was coming undone. Long, loose gray hairs fell from her hairnet.

"I know you went to look for him," her mother said. "Miriam told us she sent you. When you didn't come home, she broke down and told us everything."

Sarah didn't blame Esther; she blamed Miriam. Esther felt guilty. It had been her idea as much as Miriam's.

"Of course it was her fault," Mother said, "but you shouldn't have gone. You see how dangerous it was."

This mild rebuke was not what Esther had expected. "It wasn't

Miriam's fault. I wanted to go," Esther said. "I wanted to buy a potion."

"A priest's daughter should not be speaking to an innkeeper. It's not done."

That's what her mother was concerned about? People had been killed—she and Matti could have been killed—and she was worried about social proprieties?

"Where's Matti's tooth?" Sarah asked.

"He didn't lose a tooth," Esther said, confused.

"Not *his* tooth. The fox's tooth I sewed into his shirt to protect him. It's gone."

"It must have fallen out," Esther said. "Anyway, it obviously didn't help the fox."

"But it helped Matti. He came home, didn't he? I just wish Shimon had one too."

Hanan and Yehuda were in the dining room. Hanan said, "Florus *wants* us to revolt so he can tell Emperor Nero that he had no choice but to use violence. We shouldn't fall into his trap. We should do what he demands and turn over the troublemakers who mocked him—"

"Florus doesn't need an excuse for his savagery," Yehuda said. "Turning over the boys won't appease him. He'll just kill them and then kill others too."

"I wonder who was stupid enough to provoke the Romans," Hanan said. "They gambled with the lives of innocent people!" He stopped and looked at Esther. "You were there. Did you see who they were?"

In her mind, she saw Natan's face contort as he punched his fist into the air. Her mouth was dry.

Yehuda's voice shook her from her stupor. "Esther, what did you see?"

She had an idea; her future was finally in her own hands. She whispered, "Laza—"

"Lazar?" Yehuda asked.

"Impossible," Hanan said quickly. "Lazar's a solid man and not drawn to trouble. It was probably his brother; they look alike. His father said he'd joined the rebels."

"I'm not sure," Esther said. "They were too far away. I couldn't see." She balled her fists, digging them into her thighs. She was disgusted with herself.

Her father sighed, closing his eyes as he leaned back in his chair. He looked pale. She wished she could blame it on the chaos of the riot, but in truth he hadn't seemed well in a long time. He may have been determined to forget the Roman soldiers' attack, but it seemed his body held on to the memory nonetheless. And there had been so much more violence, more blood since that day. When would it end?

Later that day, Miriam found Esther in the courtyard.

"You and Matti were almost killed because of me."

"It wasn't because of you," Esther said. "I wanted to go."

"I should have told you not to."

"No one could have known that the soldiers would attack."

"I was so scared when you didn't come home. We heard what was going on in the market."

The images of the bodies in the street returned, unbidden, but Esther shook her head hard, as if to dislodge them.

"What took you so long? When Matti came home alone, we thought . . ." Miriam looked away, wiping her tears.

"We were looking for him," Esther said. "We couldn't leave if there was a chance he was still there."

"We?"

"Me. It was just me."

Nothing made sense anymore. She'd had to run for her life in her own city, and it was a Roman who had come to her rescue.

PART SIX

MAY 66 CE

IYAR 3826

A woman is acquired through money, through a document, or through sexual intercourse.

Mishnah, *Kiddushin* 1.1

CHAPTER XXX

AFTER THE RIOTS, THE ROMANS HAD HOISTED ROWS OF CROSSES IN front of the palace, to punish the Jews. "Maybe the Romans crucified him along with the protestors," Miriam said. "Maybe Shimon was there and we didn't know." She paced the room. "Maybe they caught him. Maybe he's—"

"No," Yehuda said quickly. "After the riot, we looked everywhere, and asked everyone. He wasn't there." His face paled. "The soldiers played the horn and passed around jugs. For them, it was a carnival. Our women came with sacks of coins, begging the soldiers to cut down their husbands and sons. After the soldiers had their fun and left, the priests ordered everyone to take down the bodies."

Miriam said, "I told him you can't dance on the edge of the well and think you won't fall. I tried to warn him, but he didn't listen. Maybe someone accused *him* of being a collaborator."

"No one would believe that," Esther said. "He's been away before, and he always comes back." Her brother was like a chameleon, darting around walls and under rocks. It didn't seem possible that someone could have caught him. But then, why hadn't he at least sent them a message?

Miriam didn't look convinced. "But it's been more than six weeks and he's not back yet, is he?"

CHAPTER XXXI

ESTHER AND MIRIAM WERE IN THE SMALL GARDEN, AN OVERGROWN patch behind the water cistern. Rue, mint, and oregano grew on one side, and wild mustard and dill on the other.

"Your eyes are red," Miriam said.

Esther didn't know what—or who—she was crying for, only that since the riot, she'd found herself breaking into tears for no apparent reason. She was worried about Shimon, and her father's failing health. She was worried about her seemingly inevitable marriage. She thought a lot about Joseph, putting her fantasies into a precious box that only she could see.

Sitting cross-legged, Esther scraped the small rosemary leaves from their tough stems. She brought them to her nose and closed her eyes. The woodsy scent transported her to the sun-soaked open fields and shady hillside forests beyond. She imagined she was there, instead of stuck within the stone walls of the courtyard, waiting for her fate to be sealed. If she didn't talk to Joseph before her father concluded the negotiations with the Kallos family, it would be too late.

"I love Shimon," Miriam said as she snipped the rue and put the sprigs into a basket. "But he doesn't love me back, at least not in the same way. He doesn't bring me spiced wine, he never rubs my body with lemongrass oil, and he never sings to me."

Esther blushed. She didn't know husbands did that.

"We used to laugh a lot, when we were children," Miriam continued. "I lived from harvest to harvest counting the days until he came to visit with your family. He chased me through the vineyards."

She smiled wistfully. "We had our own secret hiding place, in the shed behind the olive press."

Esther wasn't used to hearing Miriam talk like this.

"Sometimes," Miriam said, "I wonder who this man is that I married." She looked up at the sky, squinting as if the answer were there, in the clouds. "Maybe it's the boy I still love, and not the man."

Esther was perplexed. What went on between a man and a woman was a mystery to her, but how could it be a mystery to people who were already married?

"If he's d—" Miriam stopped herself. The unutterable dangled in the air. "If . . . if he doesn't come back, I'll be all alone."

"You won't be alone," Esther said reassuringly.

"You're right; they'll make me marry Yehuda."

"Shimon will come through the courtyard gates soon, like he always does. I know he will."

CHAPTER XXXII

At dawn the next day, Hanan stood by the east window, facing the Temple. His tallit was draped over his head. The leather strap of his tefillin was wrapped around his upper arm, hand, and fingers, and the two small leather boxes were on his arm and forehead. He rocked back and forth as he chanted the Shema and other prayers.

Esther wished she could burn his image into her memory. What if she forgot his face? For once, she envied the Romans who were allowed to make graven images and draw pictures of people. Maybe that Roman Tiberius had drawn her father too. Even though she couldn't look at it, she would like to know it was there. In her mind, her father's face would fade, but it would stay on the papyrus forever. Could that truly be a sin?

She was sure her father hadn't noticed her. When he was in his daily conversation with God, a jar could crash down next to him, and he wouldn't flinch. Today, though, in the middle of his prayers, he motioned her over. She walked tentatively toward him, and he lifted his arm to bring her under the tent of his tallit. She could feel his warmth as she stood next to him. She inhaled, wanting to imprint on her memory his scent of old wax, from the tablets he worked on all day, and the minty cardamom that he chewed to calm his gut.

When Hanan finished chanting his prayers, he looked at her with a question in his eyes. She knew what he was asking. Would she give her consent? Would she marry Lazar? Esther wanted to do as he asked, and she knew she should be grateful that he was seeking her opinion at all. But she would never love Lazar. Never.

The sun streamed through the small window near the ceiling and illuminated the specks of dust floating in a narrow beam of light. Hanan followed her gaze.

"All are from dust, and to dust all return," he said. "Did you ever notice that you can see the motes of dust suspended in the air only when the room is dark and there's just a sliver of light?"

She looked up toward the shaft of light.

"I have just a sliver of light left," he said. "That's why I can see things you can't. My mother, my father, and the sons I've buried are waiting for me, just like I'll be waiting for you."

"I don't want you to wait for me there," Esther said. "I want you to stay with me here." Tears blurred her vision; her father seemed to be disappearing already.

CHAPTER XXXIII

MIRIAM SEEMED LISTLESS AND HEAVY AS THE DAYS DRAGGED ON AND Shimon still didn't return. She moved with an uncharacteristic awkwardness and barely spoke. Esther sat next to her on the wooden bench in the courtyard and spun. Miriam, whose fingers were usually nimble and quick as she pulled the raw bushy wool, fumbled with the thread.

"He'll come back, Miriam. You'll see," Esther said, in what she hoped was a reassuring tone. Esther was furious at Shimon for making them worry. Yet her anger at Shimon's recklessness was tempered by her memories of him bringing her dried apricots from the market and whirling her around in the air.

Shimon's dog wandered aimlessly. The black skin around its gums was set in a frown. She fondled the dog's ears and looked into its eyes, wondering what it knew.

"Things are happening, bad things," Miriam whispered. "A heifer gave birth to a lamb in the Outer Court."

Esther looked up in alarm.

"And that's not all. . . . The bronze gate of the Inner Court opened by itself! That gate is so heavy that it takes twenty men to open it, *and* it's fastened with iron bars and secured by bolts."

"I wonder what it all means," Esther said.

"Maybe it means that God will open the Temple to our enemies," Miriam said. She stood up slowly. "There's something else too."

Esther didn't want to hear more omens. She lay her spindle on the ground and waited.

"I'm with child," Miriam said flatly.

Esther jumped up to embrace her cousin, but Miriam remained motionless. Esther wanted to share this moment of much needed joy that Miriam's prayers had finally been answered. God hadn't abandoned them after all. But she saw a sadness in Miriam's eyes so deep that it left Esther speechless.

Miriam took a step backward. "God gave me a child but took away my husband."

"Not everything is a sign. Sometimes things just happen."

Esther knew that Miriam didn't believe that. Esther didn't know if she believed it herself.

"I can't do this alone," Miriam said.

"You're *not* alone. I'm here." Esther reached out and held Miriam close, rubbing her back in slow circles. "You'll never be alone."

CHAPTER XXXIV

HANAN AND ESTHER WERE ON THEIR WAY TO THE TEMPLE, TO SEE IF anyone had news of Shimon. Esther was glad to leave the house, where she'd been confined ever since the riot ten days ago. But her smile faded as soon as she witnessed the destruction in the market: rubble everywhere; broken doors; smashed lintels; and crusty, dried blood still on the pavement stones. Her throat was suddenly so dry that she could barely breathe.

In some streets, people carried away debris. Other streets were deserted, shops boarded up or ransacked, tables overturned. Rotten fruit littered the ground. Hanan and Esther walked slowly, Hanan stopping every few minutes to rest. What was usually a ten-minute walk took almost an hour. It was a different city than the one she'd known. The devastation had not only changed the face of Jerusalem; it had covered the city with soot, like a veil of mourning.

They arrived at the Temple Mount to see tens of priests, shouting and gesticulating. Yehuda was in the middle . . . and Joseph too! Esther and Hanan made their way over to the group.

"What's going on?" Hanan asked Yehuda.

"We voted to stop the sacrifice for the emperor!" Yehuda said.

Hanan's face went ashen. "Stopping the sacrifice is a declaration of war! The Romans will use that as an excuse to punish us—again."

Joseph stepped forward. "I begged them to be reasonable and think of the consequences, but they wouldn't listen." He looked at Yehuda as he spoke. "I know the Romans better than anyone else here. I'm the only one who's lived there and gained entry into Nero's court. The Romans let us live as Jews; they're not making us go to the baths or to the hippodrome. We have religious freedom. Rome recognizes the sanctity of our Temple."

Yehuda looked directly at Joseph. "Do the Romans really recognize the sanctity of the Temple—or just the size of our treasury? Why should we offer two lambs and a bull every day for the emperor? Let the Romans make their own sacrifices!"

Esther turned to Yehuda. "How dare you undermine our father! He's one of the priests who make the sacrifice! He does his sacred duty."

"His duty?" Yehuda asked, looking straight at Hanan while he spoke. "Is his duty to the emperor, or to the Jewish people?"

Esther felt the heat rising to her face. "Remember the fifth commandment," she told him.

"And you remember the first," Yehuda replied. "There is only one God."

Her father lifted his cane, pointing it at Yehuda. "Once you break the dam, you can't put the water back. This isn't the time to inflame passions. It's time to calm things down."

Yehuda and Joseph kept arguing.

Hanan said, "Who would believe that our own flesh and blood are working against us?"

Esther looked away.

After a few more minutes of fierce debate, the priests quieted. The younger men, in favor of the revolt, looked exhilarated. The older ones looked frightened and pale. They began to disperse. Her father asked everyone if they had information about Shimon, but no one answered.

"Joseph." Esther ran after him when the group broke up. "Wait!"

A look of annoyance flitted across his face. "Not now, Esther. I'm in a rush."

I hate him for not wanting me as much as I want him, Esther thought as she watched him go down the steps. It felt confusing, a surge of emotion that roared and changed its shape. As soon as she felt something solid, it twisted into something else—from control to chaos, from joy to despair.

CHAPTER XXXV

THE NEXT DAY, YEHUDA BURST INTO THE DINING ROOM. HE HAD NEWS.

"Shimon is alive!"

"Praise God!" Sarah said, reaching for Hanan's arm.

Yehuda held up his hand. "It's too early to give thanks."

Esther's heart raced. "Where is he?"

"He's with the rebels."

"Shimon hates them!" Esther said. "It doesn't make any sense. Why would he join them?"

"He didn't. He's their prisoner."

"I'll offer myself in his stead," Hanan said.

Yehuda shook his head. "They don't want you. Shimon swindled them out of a lot of money. He sold them weapons he didn't have."

"Weapons?" Sarah echoed, baffled.

"Apparently Shimon heard about a shipment of weapons that was being delivered to the Sicarii. He tried to divert the shipment and sell it to a different rebel group."

"Which one?" Hanan asked.

"I don't know. I only know that they're unemployed croppers and laborers who pillaged the countryside for months before coming to Jerusalem. Their leader is ruthless, a tenant farmer who lost his land."

"Who's their leader?"

"Ben Ya'acov."

"Wasn't he one of Pinchas's tenants . . ." Hanan's voice trailed off.

Esther shuddered. Ben Ya'acov! The man who'd pleaded with Uncle Pinchas for an extension on his loan.

"We have to tell him who Shimon is," Miriam said, looking more alive than she had in weeks. "Ben Ya'acov will let Shimon go once he finds out. My father supported him all these years. I'll talk to Ben Ya'acov."

Esther wrung her hands. Her uncle had shown Ben Ya'acov and his family no mercy. She wanted to say something, but when she saw Miriam's face filled with hope, Esther faltered. Her mouth felt as though it were full of gravel.

"*I'll* talk to Ben Ya'acov," Hanan said.

"We have no idea where the rebels are," Yehuda said. "Only that they're somewhere inside the Third Wall. But you can't go; it's too dangerous. They could take you prisoner too."

Hanan rubbed his chin. "Maybe Joseph can get a message to them. He makes it his business to know everything and everyone. We have to make sure that Ben Ya'acov knows who Shimon is."

"No!" Esther blurted out. Everyone looked at her. "Ben Ya'acov hates our family. If he knows Shimon is Uncle Pinchas's nephew, he'll . . ." Esther couldn't finish the thought. She could still see the tenant farmer's face as he swore revenge.

"What are you talking about?" Miriam said. "Mother and I brought them greens and soup bones after his wife gave birth."

"He won't spare Shimon's life because you brought them table scraps," Yehuda said sharply.

"I was always kind to him," Miriam shot back. She put her hands on her hips. "I knew he filched oil from the olive press, and I never told anyone."

Hanan turned toward Esther. "How do you know?"

"I overheard him talking with Uncle Pinchas during the grape harvest. He asked for an extension on his loan, but your father refused," she said to Miriam. "Ben Ya'acov pleaded with him. He said his family was starving."

"You don't know what really happened!" Miriam said, practically shouting. "You don't know what my father said."

"Yes, I do," said Esther quietly. "He told Ben Ya'acov to sell his son."

That night, Joseph came over. "I hear you've been looking for me," he said to Hanan. "Everyone knows about Shimon."

"Knows what?" Hanan asked.

"That Ben Ya'acov announced his trial."

"A trial?" Esther's father gripped his cane so tightly that his knuckles turned white. "When?"

"Next week."

Esther's throat closed. At least Shimon was still alive. "What will happen if they find him guilty?" she asked.

"They'll probably want to make an example out of him and use the trial to show their power."

Hanan swayed, and Esther gripped his arm to steady him.

"I'll pay whatever they ask," Hanan said. "I'll borrow from the treasury."

Joseph shook his head. "They want weapons, not coins. The blacksmiths and shield makers are working day and night, and still they can't meet the demand."

"Even if I could get my hands on some weapons," Hanan said, "I wouldn't give them to those bandits. They'd only use them to kill more Jews."

"They'll get them anyway," Esther said.

"Esther is right," Joseph said. "Your only chance to save Shimon is to give the rebels what they want: swords, shields, knives, bows, and arrows."

Sweat glistened on Hanan's forehead. After a long pause, he spoke. "I know someone who can get them."

Joseph looked skeptical. "Who?"

"A Roman trader," Hanan said quickly. "Will you negotiate with the rebels if I get the weapons?"

"If I were sure you could get them, I would," said Joseph. "But it's impossible."

"It's not. You know him too. Tiberius Claudius Masculus."

Joseph flinched. His eyes narrowed, and the ropy muscles in his neck hardened. "I'm not having anything to do with that ex-slave, and neither should you."

"I trust him."

"I don't." Joseph turned to Hanan. "I've done what I can."

"Please, don't go," Esther pleaded. "You have to help us."

Joseph stood and looked from Esther to Hanan. He seemed to be thinking. "All right," he said, finally. "I'll do it. I'll talk to Ben Ya'acov. But stay away from Tiberius! Do you know what they'll do to Shimon if they think he's connected to the Romans?"

"No one has to know where the weapons come from," Hanan said. "And you said you can't negotiate without them."

"Forget Tiberius," Joseph said. "I'll get the weapons myself. I still have a few contacts. Just stay away from him!"

The thick desert wind cloaked Jerusalem in a gritty haze, slowing everything down. The minutes seemed to creep by as the family waited for news from Joseph. Sarah tried to calm Hanan. She brought him tea and made him lie on the couch. His leg hurt, and he had trouble breathing, but he continued to rant about the political upheavals that had turned the social order upside down.

By the next afternoon, he'd fallen into a deep sleep. His head fell back and his jaw moved up and down in his sleep, as though he were still talking.

Esther walked outside to the back garden. Miriam was sitting in the corner, her face in her hands. She looked up, bleary-eyed. "I'm so worried," she whispered.

Esther tried to be optimistic. "Joseph must have talked to Ben Ya'acov by now."

"I don't have as much confidence in your *beloved* as you do," Miriam said, digging her tongue into the word.

Esther winced. Miriam was still dismissive of Esther's passions, but maybe Miriam was right. Could someone be your beloved if they didn't love you back? Maybe Esther was more like Miriam than she wanted to admit.

"Joseph promised he'd talk to Ben Ya'acov and negotiate his release. He knows everyone. Father says he knows how to get information out of people while at the same time they think he's helping them." As soon as the words left her lips, Esther realized that Father might not have meant them as a compliment. But she had to trust that Joseph would bring Shimon home. There was no other choice.

CHAPTER XXXVI

ESTHER WAS SWEEPING THE COURTYARD WHEN YEHUDA AND JOSEPH walked in. It had been a week since Joseph had promised to negotiate Shimon's release. Her smile faded when she saw their grim expressions. Yehuda refused to meet her gaze. His lips disappeared into a thin line. Joseph walked a step behind him, his eyes fixed in a glassy stare.

Esther covered her mouth with her hand. *No, it couldn't be.* Shimon had flitted in and out of trouble his whole life, but he'd always found his way back to safety.

Sarah covered her ears. "Don't tell me! Don't say it," she said as she walked in circles, her hands clutching her head.

Joseph spoke. "The women are preparing the body for its final journey. It will be here soon."

"The *body*?" Hanan said. "You mean my son?" He collapsed into Yehuda's arms. "My boy! Where's my boy?"

"You must have made a mistake," Esther insisted. "Did you see him?"

Yehuda's face clouded. His drawn eyes and sagging shoulders suggested a man much older than twenty-six.

Miriam, returning from the rain cistern, saw everyone and froze. She dropped the jug of water and looked from one person to another. Her eyes grew larger as she scanned their faces.

"No," she mouthed. She continued to say "no," each time louder and louder until she was screaming. "I want Shimon! I want my husband!" She ran to Yehuda and grabbed him by the shoulders. "Where is he?" she demanded. His gaze remained lowered.

She ran to Joseph. "You know where he is," she shouted. "You're hiding him from me! You're trying to trick me!"

Miriam wobbled. Esther rushed over and held her steady. Matti covered his face.

Two slaves, their faces red and dripping with sweat, walked into the courtyard carrying a wooden bier on their shoulders. As they put it down, the corpse almost slid off. Miriam screamed when she saw the shrouded form.

Shimon's body was wrapped in linen. Esther detected the scent of myrrh and aloe. In the presence of death, her senses were more alive than ever before. She could see everything around her in the finest detail: the dirt on the slaves' feet, the oil stains on the shroud, the brown spots on her mother's hands. She could hear Matti's quiet sobs, her mother's incoherent babbling, and Miriam's howls. She could even hear that which was not spoken: Shimon begging Esther to comfort Miriam, to take care of his dog, to forgive him. Time slowed.

Miriam tried to unwrap the cloth covering the body. Joseph and Yehuda grabbed her, but she swung her arms wildly, fighting back. "Let me go!"

"At least we have his body," Yehuda said in the smooth, soft tone one would use to calm a nervous colt. "If he had been lost at sea or burned in a fire, he couldn't be resurrected. But now he can. His flesh will melt and his sins will dissolve. We'll have his bones, and he will live again. Just like my wife and son."

Esther was sure Miriam hadn't heard a word Yehuda had said, but she seemed calmed, nevertheless, by the soft rhythm of his words. She slumped to the ground with a dull look in her eyes.

Esther bounded up the ladder to her room. She paced around

the small space, then sat on the bed. She wanted to scream, but bit her knuckles instead. She opened the drawer in her night table and frantically rummaged through it. *Where is it?* She pushed bird feathers, an old scarf, and Matti's baby teeth to the side. Finally she found what she was looking for and clasped it in her fist. Mewling like a wounded animal, Esther rocked back and forth, the precious object pressed to her chest. She needed to move, to get away from the emotions threatening to overwhelm her. She jumped, flinging herself up and down until her legs ached and her lungs burned and she collapsed on the floor. She banged the floor with her other hand, pounding until it stung. Then, finally, she lay still, panting. The storm passed and she was spent.

When she unclenched her hand, a small clay tile fell to the floor. Shimon's ticket to the hippodrome with his seat number etched on the front. He had given it to her, solemnly and with much ceremony, one night after he'd returned from the chariot races. Flush, happy, and with coins in his pouch, he'd said he wanted to share his luck with her.

CHAPTER XXXVII

DURING THE SHIVA, THE SEVEN-DAY MOURNING PERIOD AFTER THE burial, Joseph approached and offered the traditional words of comfort.

Esther glared, surprising herself with the venom in her voice. "You said you'd get him back."

Joseph looked surprised and, for the first time that Esther could remember, at a loss for words. "I said . . . I'd try, but there was nothing I could do. Ben Ya'acov and his gang aren't real revolutionaries. They hate us more than they hate the Romans."

"Us?" Esther asked.

"People like us: the priests, the leaders of the people, the keepers of the wealth. Ben Ya'acov's a criminal. You can't talk to him; he has no respect for the old order."

"But you did talk to him, didn't you?"

"This really isn't the right time," he said, then looked away.

"It's the right time for me!" she said, furious. "You promised you'd negotiate, but you didn't, did you? We were waiting and waiting, and you didn't even talk to Ben Ya'acov!"

"It wouldn't have made a difference. We had no bargaining power. What could I offer him? Besides, Tiberius didn't get the weapons."

"You said *you* would get them. You told us not to involve Tiberius."

"You misunderstood," he said brusquely. "How could I get my hands on weapons when there are none to be had?"

He spoke with such certainty that Esther began to doubt her memory. Was it possible she *had* misunderstood?

"It's not my fault," Joseph said. "Your brother wasn't as clever as he needed to be in the game he chose to play." The corners of his lips tightened. "There was nothing anyone could have done. Do you know how many people wanted to finish your brother off? The gangsters he cheated, the gambling buddies he owed money, even the Roman authorities. All troublemakers are alike to the Romans—thieves or idealistic rebels with swords in their hands—and they all deserve the same fate."

As if a window had opened in a dark room, she now saw what had always been there: Joseph's true nature. *What you think you know isn't always so.* She stared at him—this man she'd once thought she loved—and realized that she didn't know him at all. It wasn't he who had betrayed her, but rather her naïveté.

She ran inside to Yehuda and reported her encounter with Joseph.

"You're upset," Yehuda said evenly. "Joseph is a good Pharisee and a respectable priest. He did everything he could."

"No, he didn't! He never even talked to Ben Ya'acov. He never tried to get the weapons. He—"

"What difference does it make? Will it bring Shimon back?"

"Don't you want to know what happened?" Esther demanded.

"I know," Yehuda said. "A friend from the study house told me. Ben Ya'acov's gang never had a trial. He ordered his men to stone Shimon as soon as he was captured. The first stone smashed his skull. Ben Ya'acov was furious that Shimon died so quickly. He wanted him to die a slow, cruel death. He said he wanted him to suffer, like his own son had."

Esther crumpled over.

"Esther," Yehuda said, placing his hand on her shoulder. "There was no way Shimon would have gotten out of this alive. From the minute he double-crossed the Sicarii, he was doomed. He tried to sell weapons to Ben Ya'acov that the Sicarii had already paid for. If Ben Ya'acov hadn't killed him first, the Sicarii would have."

She wanted to scream at Shimon, to shake him.

How could you have been so stupid?

Why didn't you ask us for help?

She hadn't known she could be this angry at someone who was already dead.

CHAPTER XXXVIII

"WE CAN'T WAIT ANY LONGER FOR THE BETROTHAL," HER FATHER SAID one morning, only eight weeks after Shimon's death. Esther had thought her parents' grief would make them forget about Lazar, at least for a while.

He continued, "It's only a matter of time before the Romans punish us for stopping the sacrifice, and then . . ." He paused and looked upward. "God help us."

Esther scrambled for a response. "But I told you, I don't love Lazar! I don't even know him."

"Love has nothing to do with making children and keeping a Jewish home. You need a good man from a good family. Marriage is your only protection—not only from the Romans but also from our own fanatics."

"How do you know he's a good man?"

"I checked his pedigree in the Temple archives. The Kallos line doesn't go back to the Babylonian exile like ours, but it's pure."

"That's not what I meant." Her parents said love didn't matter. Maybe they were right. They had been right about Joseph; maybe they were right about Lazar too. She was tired of fighting.

For days, she alternated between absolute certainty that marrying Lazar was the right decision and absolute certainty that it wasn't. Her thoughts were like a maze she couldn't escape. She would marry him; she wouldn't. She had to; she couldn't. Finally she accepted that she had to go through with it.

It was late in the day and the sun was going down. Her mother spread the orange cloth over the table. Esther couldn't remember her ever using it before; it had been stored in the bottom of the chest in the corner of the wool room with the family's other fine fabrics. Esther and Miriam used to peek into the chest when Sarah wasn't home, secretly caressing the luxurious fabrics and admiring their vibrantly colored threads.

"You're using those?" Esther asked when she saw her mother set out the beeswax candles. They were even costlier than the tallow ones.

"This is a special day," Sarah said, clearing away the everyday oil lamps. Her father took out his favorite wine from the cellar.

"I don't love him," Esther said in a resigned tone, even though she knew it was too late.

Sarah didn't look up as she arranged the honey cakes, dates, and nuts on the table. "Today isn't about your childish dreams," she said. "It's about money and land, about how many chickens, sheep, and goats you'll fetch, which spices, what kind of bed."

In other words, it's about what I'm worth.

Esther sat down and put her head in her hands. Had the Virgin Dance been only one year before? Where was the confident girl who'd danced for Joseph? She still got a queasy, sick feeling whenever she thought about him.

Lazar arrived with his parents. No one greeted her. They disappeared into the study to finalize the details of the dowry and set the date for the wedding. Her mother had already explained that she would live at home until then, but from this day onward, she would be legally bound to Lazar.

She went outside and sat against the wall of the house, not caring if her robe got soiled. If love didn't matter, then a dirty robe didn't matter either. She picked up a twig and drew in the dirt. At first, her hand shook as she made a circle for a face and two small eyes and a nose. It was a sin to draw people. Esther quickly smoothed over the dirt and wiped out the image. She waited for something to happen. If the drawing had upset the cosmic order, wouldn't she know it?

"Why are you out here?" Lazar asked, startling her.

She dropped the twig.

"And your hair isn't covered."

"I'm at home."

"When we're married, you'll be modest. Even in our home, you'll cover your hair."

She stood up. Lazar took her hands in his and turned them over. He studied them. "No calluses. Don't you spin?"

Esther quickly withdrew them.

He continued, "Idle hands are dangerous; women need to be occupied. When we're married, I'll make sure to keep you busy."

The words cut like a knife. "Maybe we should wait," Esther said. "This isn't the right time. Shimon is dead. People are still mourning the victims from the riot. Who knows what will happen next? Maybe war will break out. Everyone's talking about it."

"Of course war is imminent," he said with a grin. "That's why we *can't* wait."

"How can you be happy about war?"

"Because God is our general. The Romans have a mighty army, but God is stronger. Victory will be swift; you'll see." He had that same feverish look on his face that Yehuda had when he spoke about the End of Days.

"I have something for you." Lazar held out a small bag. She untied the pouch and looked inside. There was an engraved bracelet with a miniature relief of the temple framed by a delicate rope design. It fit her slim wrist perfectly. She rotated her arm, admiring the fine detail. How could such a coarse man have created such beauty?

Esther had a fleeting thought of throwing it back at him. She didn't want to wear it, knowing it would feel more like a slave cuff than an ornament. On the other hand, it was made of heavy silver. She'd never owned anything so precious. If it had been a gift from anyone else, she would have treasured it.

"I hope you like it," he said, and looked down shyly. Esther was taken aback. Was this the same person so filled with bluster just a few minutes earlier? Maybe there was another side to him. Maybe he was just acting the way he thought a husband should. Gently he took the bracelet off her arm. "I have to give it to you during the engagement ceremony. But I thought you might like to see it."

Soon the house filled with guests. Since this was a match between two priestly families, most of the guests were priests themselves. Esther knew all of them. Only ten men were needed to say the blessings and ensure that the betrothal was legal, but, just to be sure, her father had invited twelve. Some came straight from the Temple; their clothes reeked of smoke, balsam, and clove.

Lazar read the betrothal contract.

"By this bracelet you are sanctified to me. When you enter my house, you will be my wife according to the religion of Moses and Israel.

"If you are taken captive, I promise to redeem you and take you back as my wife . . ."

He continued reading, but Esther's thoughts drifted. She was filled with an increasing sense of dread and powerlessness.

She kept her head down to avoid meeting Lazar's gaze. She

knew he was watching her. She wondered if the contract was less binding since it was written in Aramaic and not the holy tongue.

Lazar turned to Hanan. "Will I be able to stay with Esther unsupervised until the wedding?"

The guests chuckled. Esther drew in a quick breath. She wasn't ready for *that*. She didn't know if she'd ever be.

Hanan must have seen her distress. "You will always be welcome in the house for meals, but in the coming months of Elul and Tishrei and the arrival of the pilgrims, there won't be any spare beds. You'll have to wait until the wedding."

Esther exhaled.

Lazar, her father, and the witnesses signed the contract. Her mother poured wine, but Esther remained seated, motionless and numb. She watched as the men toasted Lazar.

Smiling, he walked toward her and put the bracelet on her wrist. And just like that, her fate was sealed.

PART SEVEN

The Jews continued the pursuit [of the Roman army]
as far as Antipatris, and then, failing to overtake
the Romans, turned and carried off the machines,
plundered the corpses, collected the booty which had
been left on the route, and, with songs of triumph,
retraced their steps to the capitol.

Flavius Josephus, *The Jewish War* 2.554

Man is born for mutual help; anger for mutual
destruction. The one desires union, the other
disunion; the one to help, the other to harm. . . .

Seneca, *On Anger* 1.5.2

CHAPTER XXXIX

Hanan called Esther into his study. "I'm worried," he said as she sat down.

"You're always worried," Esther said. "But now—of all times!—shouldn't you be celebrating? The rebels have chased the Romans out of Jerusalem!" Even Esther couldn't help being caught up in the euphoria. For the past eight days, there had been skirmishes between the rebels and the Romans. Yehuda had been with the group who'd attacked the Antonia Fortress, the Roman headquarters. He'd told the family that the Roman governor Florus, along with almost all his soldiers, had fled Jerusalem. Only a few dozen soldiers hadn't managed to escape in time.

Hanan said, "But the fighting isn't over. This is just the beginning. The Romans will be back; mark my words. And the rebels aren't finished either. Now they're going after the Jews who opposed the revolt, like me!"

"No one would harm you. They wouldn't dare." She felt the metallic taste of the lie on her tongue.

"Even if the Jewish rebels don't get me," he said, "the Romans or the Angel of Death will. We need to prepare. Listen to me! There's food in the cellar, and I've already hidden some of our valuables for safekeeping."

"Where?"

"In the safest place in the world, where God stands guard."

The Temple, then. "In your office?"

"Under it. When the workers dug a new drainage tunnel a few months ago, I pulled out some stones before the mortar dried." He pushed two scrolls toward her. "We need to put these in the cache for safekeeping. This one is your betrothal contract—"

"It would be safer in the kitchen fire," she mumbled under her breath.

"It's security," he said firmly, and reached for the second scroll. "And this one is my contract with Tiberius."

Esther grabbed it and sprung up. "Don't you know how dangerous this is?" she said furiously, waving the scroll in the air. "I was sure the ship had already arrived. What if Yehuda finds out?"

There was a shuffle at the door. Esther turned around.

"Finds out what?" It was Yehuda.

Esther went rigid. He never came home at this hour, if at all. He had practically moved into the study house. She held his gaze steadily while slowly moving her arms behind her back, to hide the contract.

"What's that?" he asked suspiciously, stepping into the room.

Esther took a step backward. He reached for the contract, but Esther tried to swing it out of his reach. Yehuda snatched it in midair.

"Stop!" Hanan said, pushing himself up. "Both of you, stop!"

They turned to look at him.

"Yehuda, that is my contract with a Roman trader. For an export deal that will provide this family with financial security in the uncertain times to come."

Esther braced herself for Yehuda's reaction.

Hanan went on, "Even the rebels know you can't fill an empty belly with slogans about freedom. Everyone respects silver."

A sudden hush fell over the room. For a long moment, they

stood in place, as if any movement would unleash forces they could never rein back in.

Finally Yehuda spoke. "It's not me you should be worrying about. It's the Sicarii. This," he said in a quiet tone, holding up the scroll, "is a death contract."

"Are you sure we shouldn't be worrying about you?" Esther asked pointedly, unable to stomach her brother's lies for any longer.

Hanan's mouth opened wide. "What's going on? You're not . . . one of *them,* are you?"

Yehuda tugged nervously at his beard. He looked from his father to Esther, as if deciding how to start. "At first," he said, "I did believe in their mission. But I soon realized that they were just power-hungry thugs."

Hanan drew in a long breath and let it out.

Yehuda had done more than merely "believe in their mission." She had seen the knife in his hands. "I don't believe you," she said.

"After the riot in the market," Yehuda said, "when you and Matti were almost killed, I realized that Rome was the enemy, not other Jews. I knew the Sicarii were frauds even before that, but I pretended to be loyal so I could protect Father."

"Protect me? How?" Hanan asked.

"By making sure you didn't get on their list—or if you did, by warning you in time. You opposed revolt, so you were a rebel target—even before your deal with Tiberius."

The color had drained from her father's face.

"Let him rest," Esther said, taking the contract from Yehuda and placing it on the desk. She helped her father sit, then motioned to Yehuda to come with her.

Esther led Yehuda into the hall, then faced him. "You knew about the deal?"

"Of course I did," Yehuda said. "Father didn't keep it a secret, and neither did Tiberius. I heard that he even came to the house."

"I was there!" Esther said. "I was worried that you'd turn Father in if you knew."

"How could you think I would do something like that?"

There was silence, and then she said, "Because you killed a man."

"I never killed anyone," he said.

"I was at the Temple the day the grain merchant was stabbed. He was holding his son's hand! I saw you clean the *sica*."

"It wasn't me. The Sicarius who stabbed him dropped the knife into a fruit basket, which he passed to someone else. The knife got passed around six times before it ended up with me. That's how they do it."

"You should have told me."

He looked down, smoothing the unruly hairs of his eyebrows with his index finger, like he did when he was unsettled.

"I knew you suspected," he said. "I didn't lie to you. I didn't deny it, but I didn't want to involve you. You might have told Father, and who knew what he would have done? It would have been dangerous to bring attention to me, or to him."

He seemed to retreat into himself. She was used to his long silences.

She too was quiet, as she tried to rearrange the fragments of her memory to tell a different story.

Yehuda broke the silence first. "You really thought I would turn Father over to those murderers? Or kill a Jew?"

What you think you know isn't always so.

She was filled with a lightness she hadn't felt in a long time. She had never been so happy to be wrong.

CHAPTER XL

A WEEK LATER, YEHUDA BURST INTO THE HOUSE WITH A TRIUMPHANT grin. "The Sicarii are gone! They won't terrorize us anymore."

"What happened?" Hanan asked.

"Their leader, Menachem, came to the Temple yesterday garbed like the Messiah, with a flowing white robe and silk turban. The other rebel groups, including the Zealots, tried to capture him, but he fled to the hills of Ophel and hid in the water tunnel. Some rebels dragged him out, and an angry mob finished him off. The rest of the Sicarii fled, probably to Masada."

"Jews killing Jews," Hanan muttered, visibly shaken. "When will it all end?"

"Father, this is good news," Yehuda insisted, taking his hand. "Don't you see? It will be easier to defeat the Romans without the Sicarii."

Esther didn't know what was good news anymore. There were so many different factions fighting the Romans, and each other, that it was hard for her to tell them apart.

On Shabbat, Esther and her father walked slowly toward the Temple. Esther clasped his arm, her fingers pressing into the loose, papery skin above his elbow as she guided him around the holes in the road. The heat from the stone pavement radiated through the thin soles of her sandals.

As they neared the palace, they heard shouting and stones crashing to the ground. Esther was apprehensive as they quickened their pace. One of the palace's three towers lay in ruins. Chunks of the collapsed structure were strewn on the ground, and flames shot out from the palace itself.

Armed rebels, most wearing the white robes of the Zealots, swarmed the plaza. Eleazar, the leader of the Zealot faction, stood on a massive pile of rubble shouting orders, waving his hands, directing his men to various positions and admonishing the surging crowd to stay back. Next to him stood a tall, gaunt figure.

"Yehuda!" Esther yelled. The noise of the crowd drowned her out. They pushed through the mob to reach him. She called again.

Yehuda came down slowly, taking small steps and holding his arms out by his sides for balance. His face and hair were dusted with white chalk, like an old man.

"What are *you* doing here?" Esther asked, surveying the scene of destruction and the frantic crowd. There must have been over a hundred people. "Now you've joined the Zealots?"

"I told you I want to fight the Romans, and that's what I'm doing," he said proudly.

"What's happening here?" she asked.

"Some Roman soldiers have been trapped in the palace, and they're running out of food and water. Their commander asked for safe passage for his men. We sent a delegation to tell them we'll let them go if they surrender their arms."

"You sent *our* people up there?" their father asked. "They could be taken hostage or killed!"

"Three Jewish merchants escorted a Roman arms trader who's got the trust of both sides. I think you may know him," Yehuda said, with a knowing look in his eye. Esther exchanged an uneasy look with her father; it must have been Tiberius.

At that moment, Joseph approached. How he always seemed to be in the center of the action was a mystery to Esther. He greeted her father and Yehuda but did not so much as glance in her direction. Her girlish infatuation was over, yet she found herself disappointed that he hadn't acknowledged her. She was angry at herself for caring.

Along with the rest of the growing and impatient crowd, Esther and her father waited for Tiberius and the merchants to return. After almost two hours, they came down. Tiberius squinted as he walked outside, raising a hand to shield his eyes from the sun. The rebels cheered, apparently mistaking his raised hand and lowered head for a salute.

"We relayed your offer," Tiberius said to Eleazar. "We told the Roman commander that his men would be spared if they surrendered their arms. He asked if you could be trusted." Tiberius paused and gave Eleazar a piercing stare. "I told him yes, that you were a priest of God and you were giving your word."

Eleazar appeared pleased. Tiberius looked around, seemingly surprised by the large crowd. He saw Esther and her father. Then he saw Joseph.

Tiberius and Joseph locked eyes.

Joseph's face contorted into a forced grin. "At last, we meet again, my friend." His voice seemed to unleash something in Tiberius, who lunged toward him.

Hanan shouted "No!" and positioned himself between the men. Esther gasped. Tiberius released Joseph's robe, pushing him away with a violent shove.

"How dare you call me your friend?" Tiberius said, in a voice filled with venom. "You tried to have me killed."

"If I had acted any other way, our priests were the ones who would have been killed. I put my loyalty to my people over our friendship." Joseph smoothed his robe and continued. "God has designs that we can't always see. A man whose name I share was sold as a slave and became extremely powerful in Egypt, second only to the pharaoh. Look how his destiny changed. And look how yours did—for the better, I might add—after you met me. This is proof that it must be God's will that we meet again."

"It's not your God's will," Tiberius said through a clenched jaw. "It's *my* will. I came to Jerusalem to track you down. I know the Roman governor, Florus, quite well. One word to him, and you'll be hanging from a cross."

"Unfortunately for you, the governor isn't here anymore. Do you really think you can touch me? A freed slave is no match for a Jewish hero. I have royal blood coursing through my veins. You have no one. Even your own country spit you out." Joseph regarded him coldly. "You're quite alive, from what I can tell, and splendidly living off my country's riches. You should be grateful that I got you out of Nero's brothel."

"You didn't get me out of anywhere. I ran for my life because of your lies."

"And whether or not you admit it," Joseph continued, as if Tiberius hadn't spoken, "I did you a favor. What future would you have had in Rome? You couldn't have built your little trading empire if you'd stayed a lowly clerk. Now you'll return as a rich man."

"You left me for dead in Rome. You used me as a tool for your needs and then cast me aside like a broken lamp."

"Oh, that's it, isn't it? You were *offended*?" Joseph said. "But it was Aristotle who said that slaves are living tools, not me." Joseph's lips inched up into a half smile. "And now you, my dear friend, are returning the favor. I know that you've spread lies to get me arrested. Isn't that what you really want, to even the score? To humiliate me?

You don't really want me dead. If you did, you could have paid someone to stab me in my sleep."

Tiberius's eyes twitched. He reached for the dagger hanging from the side of his belt, but before he could pull it out of its sheath, a loud roar emanated from the crowd. The Roman soldiers were coming down from the tower.

One by one, the Romans, wearing the standard red military cloaks, sandals with leather leg bindings up to their calves, and wide belts from which hung leather strips like aprons, came out of the tower and laid their swords on the ground. Eleazar's men quickly snatched them away.

A centurion who Esther guessed was the commander gave the order to march, and the soldiers walked in formation, their heads held high, trying to ignore the jeering onlookers.

A cry of *"Kadima!"*—Charge!—erupted from someone in the crowd. Suddenly men surged forward on all sides. The collective will of the crowd was unmistakable: *death to the Romans!* The rabble attacked in a savage frenzy. The air was thick with gleeful bloodthirsty cries. The Romans stumbled and looked around in confusion. Some tried to run.

The centurion yelled that the Jews had made an oath: *"Fides! Sacramentum!"*

Yehuda and some others looked around, as if waiting for a command. They didn't know whether to shield the Roman soldiers or join the crowd attacking them. Hanan and two other priests tried to stop the onslaught.

One of the priests yelled, "We promised them safe passage!"

"This is murder!" Hanan shouted. "We can't desecrate God's name!"

"We're doing holy work," Eleazar answered in a cold, measured tone.

Hanan grabbed Eleazar's arm. "Holy work? These people are defenseless, and you're breaking an oath that you made on God's name. On the Holy Sabbath, no less!"

"They are Roman soldiers," Eleazar said defiantly. "Enemies. Oaths to them and by them are worthless. We're saving Jewish lives by wiping them out."

Eleazar turned his back on Hanan. Joseph looked discomfited and, for once, powerless. He tried to speak with Eleazar, but Eleazar ignored him too and joined the mob.

A Roman soldier stood in the middle of the crowd pleading for his life. He was young, no more than eighteen. Esther could see the fear in his eyes. He took a few steps backward, and the circle closed in on him.

She told herself that he wasn't a boy; he was a Roman soldier. Still, she felt a repugnance beyond anything she'd ever felt before as the crowd savagely taunted him.

The scene took her back to that day with her father, when she'd tasted the same fear. Since then, that fear had turned into rage, at first slow-burning and then into a thirst for vengeance. But now she was loath to take it.

Eleazar brought down his sword with full force against the Roman boy-soldier. He swayed, then fell backward, throwing his hands into the air. Blood gushed from his shattered skull and spurted from his mouth, nose, and eyes. But the crowd didn't relent; men continued to maul the body, kicking the now lifeless lump of flesh and bone, lifting it up only to throw it down again.

Esther looked to her father. His shoulders sagged. "Let's go home," he said with a ragged breath. "The rebels are drunk with blood. They'll swarm to the Temple after this."

As Esther walked alongside her father, she looked back. Ti-berius stood, seemingly rooted to the spot, transfixed by the massacre. She didn't understand why he was still there. Didn't he see the mob moving like a pack of wolves? He could be their next target.

Why did she care? He had helped her look for Matti—and for that she was grateful—but he was still *one of them.*

And yet . . .

Go! she pleaded to him in her heart. *Get out of here!*

CHAPTER XLI

AFTER THE LONG, HOT SUMMER, THERE WERE ONCE AGAIN CLOUDS IN the sky and there was a bite to the air. Esther pulled her shawl tightly around her shoulders and looked around in amazement at what she didn't see: Roman soldiers. There was a sense of liberation in the air since the slaughter at the palace the week before. For the first time in more than a hundred years, there were no Roman soldiers patrolling the Outer Court of the Temple, occupying the Antonia Fortress, or stationed on street corners and at the city gates. Now it was the rebels who paraded around the city with swords and daggers swinging from their wide leather belts. Esther couldn't take her eyes off the rebels, drawn to their swagger and raw masculinity. Their muscular bodies—and even their weapons—mesmerized her.

Esther and her mother had come to the market to buy thread for her wedding dress. Esther didn't want either the dress or the wedding, but at least the sewing kept her mother busy and out of her way. The market, always busy on Friday, seemed even more packed than usual with people stocking up on food, oil, and wine in anticipation of what they all believed was an inevitable Roman return. The rebel attack was only the first strike; no one thought the Romans were gone for good.

Esther and Sarah narrowly dodged a group of boys with wooden swords playing Jews and Romans. Then Sarah entered the shop. While Esther waited for her mother outside, she stared at a rebel polishing his sword on the side of the road. Her thoughts took her away; she was with the rebels, in one of the mansions they had requisitioned for their headquarters, pouring the handsome young men wine while they admired her smooth skin and shapely arms.

Stop!

She tried to focus on the thread for her wedding dress, that it shouldn't be too thick or too yellow, but instead she stole another glance at the rebel.

The rebel put down his sword and smiled broadly. Her face burned, and she ran into the shop.

What is wrong with me?

As they walked home, Esther found her thoughts drifting again; this time, to someone else—Tiberius. She hadn't stopped thinking about him since she'd seen him at the palace. She doubted that he was still in the city. All the Romans had left. But would he have abandoned his lucrative business supplying arms to the Jewish militants? Maybe he'd gone to the blacksmiths in the hills outside of Jerusalem to buy more weapons to trade. She wondered if he had a family to go home to.

She didn't care, of course, but he owed her father money, and . . . that way he looked at her, with his sorrowful eyes. That blue—the color of flax flowers, the color of the upper wings of the small butterfly she'd seen the day before in the garden. He was a Roman, but he was kind. She shook her head hard, as if to shake out the thought.

Joseph had called him a friend. What had really happened between them? All she knew was that they had been together in Rome, and that Joseph had betrayed Tiberius. Joseph had fooled her too. So she and Tiberius had something in common after all.

CHAPTER XLII

HANAN TAPPED HIS FINGERS NERVOUSLY ON THE DESK. "WHAT DID THE rebels think? That they would run the Romans out of town and there would be no repercussions? The Romans have to control their territories. If they don't put down this little rebellion, they'll soon be dealing with uprisings from Syria to the Black Sea. The Britannians, Cyrenians, and other conquered nations might be tempted to follow our lead."

"Where are the Romans now?" Esther asked.

"Their army is already on the way back to Jerusalem with more soldiers. They've swept through the Galilee and down the coast, decimating every town on the way, yet no one in Jerusalem seems to care." He shook his head. "I don't understand it."

He was right, Esther thought. People didn't seem worried; they were excited. They even seemed to talk louder, no longer afraid that they'd be overheard by the Romans or the Romans' local informants. Shofars from the horns of newly sacrificed rams were for sale all over the city, and every few minutes, a blast would sound. She wasn't sure if people were practicing for the moment when God would establish His kingdom on Earth, or were just trying to hurry Him along.

Her father leaned over the desk and spoke in an urgent tone. "I told you before. We have to hide the contracts. The rebels are looting private houses as we speak. Time is running out."

Esther had hoped her father would forget about the contracts—

one that bound her to a man she didn't love, and one that proved her father was a collaborator—but he never forgot anything.

It had been years since she'd been in the Temple's dark, dank warren of underground passages, accompanying her father on his inspection of a new storeroom. He had held her small hand and a torch as he'd guided her through the labyrinths with their slimy walls, as if the stones themselves had broken out in a cold sweat. But he hadn't seen what she had: the rat eyes glowering in the blackness, the demon squeezing her chest. She still remembered the walls closing in on her as she gulped for air.

She didn't want to go back down. It would be darker than pitch.

"I'd do it myself," he said, "but I can't make it down those steps anymore. They're too steep and slippery."

She knew how much the admission cost him. Still, she wished someone else could go instead of her, but there was no one else. She suspected that her father didn't completely trust Yehuda. Perhaps, her father suspected, he would give the money to the cause.

She looked at him, her now frail father, still trying to protect his family as his own walls closed in. He hadn't given in to fear, and neither would she.

"I'll go," she said. She saw the relief in his face. "I promise."

The scrolls were tucked under her robe. Esther would hide them after the morning service.

Twelve Levites walked up the steps to the Temple carrying lyres of different sizes, with horn-shaped side arms and strings of sheep gut. No matter how many times Esther witnessed the daily sacrifice, it never failed to send a frisson of excitement through her.

The Levites sang, *"O God of vengeance, Lord, O God of vengeance, shine forth. . . . The wicked crush thy people, they slay the widow and the stranger, and murder the fatherless."* She used to cover her ears when she heard those words, a litany of horrors she could barely imagine. But now she didn't flinch. The year before, she'd danced in the vineyard; this year she'd stepped over dead bodies in the street.

The plaintive song, accompanied by the lush tones of the harp, cried out: *"How long shall the wicked triumph? Who will stand up for me against the workers of iniquity?"*

She found comfort in the Hebrew words that used to terrify her; she closed her eyes and swayed, letting the music wash over her. The pure, sweet notes of the lyres and the bright chiming of the bronze cymbals answered the Levite's cry:

"The Lord will not cast off His people, neither will He forsake his inheritance. . . . God is my rock of refuge."

When the choir finished, Esther opened her eyes. She wiped her wet cheeks. So much had changed, but at least this place would always be the same.

After the ceremony, a buzz went through the crowd. The Romans were back! They were just outside the city walls! Esther was swept up by the surge of people, running toward the Antonia Fortress to see the Roman forces. She clambered up the twenty steps on the wall and managed to squeeze through the people standing two and three deep. She looked down.

Thousands of Roman soldiers, with swords, breastplates, and helmets adorned with wolf skins and feathers, stood in orderly rows. The Jews on the wall shouted curses and insults across the valley. Horsemen and archers, camel riders and horn blowers waited below. Hundreds of supply carts and mounds of ammunition—piles of spears, lead balls, and stone ballistae—dotted the slope. And more soldiers kept coming.

Esther brought her hand to her breastbone, splaying out her

fingers as if she needed to feel her pulse, to reassure herself that she was still there. She rubbed the soft spot at the base of her neck where the carnelian used to hang.

Her father was right; time was running out.

Trumpets sounded. The Roman army was stirring. Messengers ran through the troops, and officers shouted orders. The soldiers rolled the battering rams closer to the walls. Horses whinnied.

She scrambled down the wall, sweat running down her back.

Until she'd seen the Roman army with her own eyes, she hadn't really visualized what war would mean. The revolt had been mostly talking about fighting the Romans, rather than actually fighting them. War had been a mere story—an exciting and thrilling story, but a story nonetheless, set somewhere in the distant future. But it was a story no longer.

Esther ran home, not stopping until she reached the bridge, where she slowed to catch her breath. The courtyard was quiet. She burst into the house and told them what she'd seen.

Her mother was livid. "An unaccompanied girl mixing with the riffraff? I tremble to think what could have happened to you. Shame!"

"This is what you care about?" Esther shot back. "That I was unchaperoned? Didn't you hear anything I said? The Romans are here! They're back!"

Esther waited for her father to reassure her—to say how God wouldn't let anything happen to His Temple or to His people; to tell her how thick the walls were, and how brave the rebel fighters were. But he said nothing.

She tossed the contracts under her bed. She'd have to hide them another time.

CHAPTER XLIII

FOR THE NEXT WEEK, THE ARMY STAYED OUTSIDE THE WALLS, WAITING, it seemed, for more legions to arrive. Four days later, Neshra, their neighbor, banged on the door. "The Romans hopped over the northern wall foundations like goats. They're in Bezetha!"

Sarah and Hanan sat, immobile. Esther scurried up to the roof to see for herself. A massive dust cloud on the horizon masked where the Roman army had been. Within the city gates were more plumes of smoke and flames than Esther could count. The huts and stalls of the timber market were on fire!

Esther came back down but didn't know what to do. Everyone was busy except for her. Matti was filling water buckets; Miriam was locking the outer courtyard gate.

"Where's Yehuda?" Sarah cried. Hanan shook his head. He was pale, and his breathing was quick and shallow. Yehuda had been home the day before, but he'd returned to the Zealot headquarters on the Temple Mount. Esther didn't want to tell them that he'd gone to fight. "You know Yehuda. He's probably bent over some scroll in the study house," she said.

They barricaded the front door with a wooden beam and huddled inside.

On the second day of the Roman attack, Esther again ventured up to the roof. The Romans were marching toward the Temple with interlocked shields over their heads. The clanking hooves of their horses and the clatter of their hobnailed boots made it sound as if the entire Roman army were moving past their house.

People pelted rocks and arrows from their rooftops, but the missiles bounced harmlessly off the Roman shields. Esther couldn't see the soldiers, only row after row of shields decorated with pictures of a wild boar. Seeing that unclean animal in her holy city was almost as disturbing as the presence of the soldiers themselves. The Romans seemed invincible. How could the Jews' inexperienced forces ever defeat them?

An earsplitting noise filled the air, followed by an incessant pounding as if the earth itself were grinding and moving. The house shook.

"Esther!" her mother screamed. "Come down here at once!"

In the corner, her father prayed, *"Heavenly Father, protect Your people and Your Temple . . ."*

Her mother marched around the dining area as if she were a soldier herself. She muttered spells under her breath, appealing first to God's good angels—Gabriel, Uriel, Michael, and Raphael. When she'd finished with them, she cursed the troublemakers—Mastema, Samael, Belial, and Satan.

Matti stood alone, clutching his small bow and a few arrows. Esther motioned him over. She lifted him onto her lap and began to sing one of his favorite songs:

"Pharaoh's chariots drowned in the sea, drowned
    in the sea.
They sank to the bottom like a stone, like a stone.
The Lord dashed the enemy to pieces, to pieces."

He asked, "If God could drown the Egyptians, He can get rid of the Romans too, right?"

"Of course," Esther said. But how would the sea reach them all the way in Jerusalem?

As the day turned into night and the night into day, the din intensified: the shrieks of men, the clang of metal, and the smashing of stone. The sounds of the shofar pierced the air. Its short, angry blasts and long wails spoke for the desperate Jews, expressing all that they could not.

Matti curled up next to Esther and buried his face in her chest. She stroked his back. It gave her something to do with her hands to keep them from shaking.

During the fighting, the neighbors ran back and forth, trading information. Someone had ventured onto the roof; someone else's son had returned home from fighting. Whispers, rumors, and speculations flew through the air as quickly as the arrows whizzing by.

For five days they stayed inside. There was no lull in the battle, even during Shabbat. Esther did her best to keep Matti distracted; she sang about David and Goliath and told him about the heroic victories of their Hasmonean ancestors. Matti jumped with each boom and clung to Esther. Her parents and Miriam sat quietly, having run out of tears and prayers.

Early on the sixth day, Esther could hear the rebels shout:

"Impure!"

"Roman swine!"

She could hear the Romans too, shouting orders that she didn't understand. Neshra said the Roman catapults were striking the Temple walls, and that the Romans were about to break through and enter the Holy Sanctuary. It looked as if the unthinkable would happen. Hanan buried his head in the scroll of Jonah.

Hours later, the Roman soldiers were still battering the walls of the Temple Mount. Reports from the neighbors trickled in that the Romans were suffering almost no injuries, sheltered under their pig shields, and the rebels were retreating. Her mother went from the kitchen, where she'd been busying herself shelling beans, to the dining room, pacing back and forth. Esther felt herself nodding off, but she jerked up her head. Sleep gave her something to fight. If she could stay awake, nothing bad would happen. She would be in control.

Toward midday, the sounds of war abruptly stopped, as if the whole city were holding its breath. The unexpected silence felt premonitory, and she braced herself for the reverberations of more destruction. But instead, cheers of joy—in Hebrew!—rose into the air. Esther's family looked at one another, stunned; triumphant shouts in the holy tongue were the last thing they'd expected to hear. Unable to contain her curiosity, Esther ran up to the roof, ignoring her mother's cries of warning.

From the rooftop, she saw a sea of color and metal surge by; Roman soldiers with their swords and shields dangling by their sides. And they were running *away* from the Temple. Many stumbled and fell. The iron studs of their boots, useful in gripping the rough terrain in the hills, proved treacherous on the smooth stones of the city. Jews—including women and children—emerged from their houses and pounced on the fallen soldiers with swords and even kitchen knives.

A Roman trumpeter blew his horn, trying to restore order, but the soldiers continued to run pell-mell through the narrow winding streets. Esther watched but still couldn't quite comprehend what was happening. The Roman troops had broken through the defensive walls of Jerusalem. They'd successfully fought their way through the crowded streets of the market and Upper City. They'd reached the Temple . . . and then they'd turned around?

It made no sense.

Maybe miracles never did.

A few hours later, the Romans were gone. Euphoric men, women, and children shouted hallelujahs and rushed into the streets. Many looked to the sky, for a sign from God. Others looked to the Mount of Olives, certain that the Messiah would soon appear, riding His white donkey.

In the early evening, Yehuda returned home, flushed with the thrill of victory. His eyes were bloodshot and his voice was so raspy that he could hardly speak. He hadn't slept for days.

He was the happiest Esther had ever seen him.

CHAPTER XLIV

Esther awoke to an unfamiliar hush. After the chaos of the previous week, the city was now eerily quiet. It was the first time she'd slept through the night since the fighting had begun. She felt groggy and disoriented. She got out of bed slowly and tentatively, as if she were testing the ground beneath her.

When she came downstairs, her father told her that the rebels, together with almost all the other men in the city, had left to give chase to the defeated Romans and collect their discarded weapons.

"You must hide the documents today," he said. "Everyone's gone, so the Temple will be empty. No one will see you go down to the cache." He pushed himself up with his cane and limped toward the wooden chest in the corner of the room.

Hanan unlocked the chest and lifted its heavy top. Esther craned her neck to see inside. She'd always wondered what was in there. Once, he'd told her there were gold coins from a Phoenician pirate ship, and another time, precious gems from an Egyptian temple. Her mother said there were just old building plans from the Temple. Her mother had been right—no treasures. He sifted through a jumble of scrolls and pulled out a thick bundle wrapped in strips of yellow linen. She recognized the fabric: scraps from the wedding dress her mother was sewing. He peeled off the strips one by one until a dagger, nestled in an intricately engraved silver sheath, lay on the desk. He gripped the bone hilt and pulled, slowly revealing a leaf-shaped blade with a deep groove down the middle.

It was the dagger Tiberius had given her father. Hanan pushed it toward her. The only time she'd used a knife this big was during the grape harvest. God help her if she really had to use it.

"Remember to go down the southern stairwell, like I told you. The one between the last two columns of the portico. Look for the unfinished drainage ditch parallel to the main water tunnel, and count fifty paces after the second torchlight on the left side. There you'll see a stone sticking out. The cache is behind the stone."

Drainage tunnel, second light. . . . He had told her all of this before, and she hadn't remembered. "Father—I'm not sure. I—" she stammered.

"Go now," he said firmly. He dropped his voice, "And make sure no one follows you."

Esther took a breath to steady herself. She had no choice. She had to do it.

She walked the familiar streets, now littered with the detritus of battle: stones, arrowheads, splintered clubs, smashed shields, and slick pools of oil and blood. When she rounded the corner of an alley near the Gennath Gate, she saw a Roman soldier lying, lifeless, in the gutter. His fingers were bent as if he'd clutched at the earth in his last moments, not wanting to leave it.

Esther was still trying to understand how the rebels had bested the famed and feared Roman legionaries. The rebels didn't have proper armor, uniforms, or helmets. Their tunics were dirty and torn. Some of the fighters had sandals, some boots, and others went barefoot. Yet this disorganized and disheveled group of farmers, craftsmen, shepherds, and scholars, armed only with stones and clubs, had routed the most disciplined and best-equipped army in the world. Yehuda was right; their victory had to be proof of God's favor. There was no other explanation.

She quickened her steps. It was cold and drizzling, the first rain of the season. A few older priests were milling around the staircase leading to the Huldah Gates. None paid her any attention. The Royal Portico, normally packed with pilgrims purchasing sacrifices, was empty. Esther's footsteps echoed in the deserted hall. She looked down at the ornate mosaic floor, which was usually hidden beneath hundreds of sandaled feet. The pattern on the tiles—stars and diamonds cut from pink, white, and blue marble—was dazzling. She had never noticed it before.

Behind the last column was a small door that led down to the subterranean level, where a maze of water tunnels, sewage channels, cisterns, and storage chambers were carved into the bedrock. Pushing open the wooden door, Esther stared into the forbidding blackness. Bats screeched, fluttering overhead. Her hands trembled as she took out a candle and the fragments of steel and flint she had tucked into her robe. She struck the steel with the flint and guided the sparks toward the wick. The small, flickering flame lit the way down the narrow steps. The sludge on the ground, the slime of the mineral deposits, and the algae on the walls came into view. The walls were so close—just wider than her shoulders. She filled her chest with air, trying to will her heart into a slower cadence, but it didn't help. She felt like she was suffocating.

Don't stop, don't stop, don't stop.

The long tail of a rat swished over her foot. She froze, too frightened to move.

Don't stop, don't stop.

She pushed herself to keep going. When she reached the ditch parallel to the main water tunnel, she began counting, but she didn't know if she was supposed to take big steps or little ones. Flummoxed, she lost count. If she didn't find it, she'd have to turn around and start over. She held the candle close to the wall, looking for the niche her father had described, but all the stones looked the same. She looked again, and then she saw: around a small bend, a stone protruded. She pushed the stone, and it moved. She'd found it! The stone was smaller than the surrounding ones, and its corners were smooth. It was not set into the wall with mortar but simply placed in a niche. Esther rested the candle on the ground and grabbed the stone. It was heavy, but she found she could drag it forward bit by bit.

She bent down and peered inside the cache. There was a ceramic jar, its opening sealed with gypsum and burlap. With a small, sharp rock, she smashed the seal, and yanked out the linen scraps stuffed into the mouth of the jar. Then she jammed the scrolls in.

She had fulfilled her promise; she could return to the light.

CHAPTER XLV

Yehuda was home, eagerly describing the Roman retreat. "We chased them all the way back to Beth Horon. The Romans were trapped between the crags above and the ravines below. We picked them off like chickens in a pen! Their swords couldn't reach us, and their heavy weapons got stuck in the mud."

Matti reached out to touch the dagger strapped to Yehuda's waist. Yehuda took it out. "A gift from the Romans," he said, chuckling, showing it to Matti. "They called upon their heathen gods, but only our God is in the heavens. He's the one who made the heavens!"

Miriam, Matti, Esther, and Yehuda went up to the roof to watch the rebels returning.

Even Sarah climbed the rickety staircase to see. Some rode atop stolen Roman wagons, while others led oxen hauling the other spoils of battle: siege engines, catapults, and battering rams. Children sat astride donkeys and mules. People danced around the returning fighters, accompanying them on their victory march home.

"Look at the wealth God delivered into our hands," Yehuda said as they watched the procession.

Esther found her father in his study with a faraway look in his eyes. She felt terrible, knowing it had been quite some time since Hanan had been able to easily make his way up the stairs to the roof.

"Father," Esther said gently, "I know you wanted to go up and see for yourself, but you can't be sad today, not when we've had such a victory."

"It's not that," he said. "It's because we won."

Because we won? She didn't understand.

Hanan said, "People are celebrating, as if King David had returned to Jerusalem after defeating the Philistines. But this isn't the end, despite what Yehuda thinks. Like I told you before, this is just the beginning. Now we'll truly feel Rome's wrath."

"But the Romans retreated. Our victory is proof that God is on our side, like Yehuda says!"

"I don't know if God takes sides, but I do know that the Romans will be back to avenge this humiliating defeat, and next time, they'll bring an even bigger force. Nero will send his best generals and troops." The crease lines on Hanan's face deepened. "I probably won't be here when they come back. You'll be on your own." The noise of the celebration outside made it hard for Esther to hear him.

He pinched the bridge of his nose and rocked back and forth in his chair. "Have I done everything I can to protect my family?"

Esther knew that the question wasn't for her ears. He continued to rock back and forth while he said, over and over, "Have I done everything? Have I done everything I can?"

CHAPTER XLVI

THE CITY WAS CRACKLING WITH EXCITEMENT AND PULSING WITH preparations for another battle. Rebel troops, shouting in unison, marched through the streets. Men and women who only a few weeks before had huddled in their homes, trembling with fear, now walked jauntily through the streets. They'd defeated the Romans before; they'd do it again.

A continual clamor of metal against metal filled the air: the hammering of nails, the forging of shields, the pounding of swords on anvils, and the sharpening of blades on the grinding rocks. Thick smoke, laced with the stench of molten iron, billowed out from the metalworking shops.

Yehuda returned from a meeting at the Temple with the news that all of the different rebel groups had joined forces. "We have a unity government," he told the family. "We're all Jews now."

For so long, the rebels had been united only by their mutual hatred. When they fought each other, they identified themselves as Sicarii or Zealots, followers of Eleazer or Ben Ya'acov. But when they fought the Romans, they were all Jews.

"Don't tell me that the Zealots joined forces with Shimon's murderers," Hanan said, shaking his head.

"There's no choice, Father. The gangs have all the Roman spoils. Besides, they're the only ones who know how to fight. Where are we going to find experienced soldiers without blood on their hands?"

"It's your brother's blood." Hanan turned away.

"Wait!" Yehuda said, talking to his father's back. "Don't you want to hear what else happened at the meeting? Joseph was appointed general of the Galilee."

Esther dropped her jaw. Joseph a general? What did he know about soldiering?

Hanan swung around. "The Galilee is the first line of defense. That's the most important post after Jerusalem. The last I heard, he wasn't even in favor of the revolt."

"He changed his mind," Yehuda said. "After our victory, he realized that God wants us to fight."

"Only prophets know God's will," Hanan said, "and Joseph is no prophet, even though he may think he is."

"You're wrong about him," Yehuda said. "He's the one who united the factions, and he's the only one who can control them. He has the touch of Midas."

"Why are you, who only wants to speak the holy tongue, quoting Greek nonsense?" asked Esther.

Hanan nodded. "Don't forget what happened to Midas. He was killed by his own gift."

Hanan faded in and out at dinner. He fought to keep his eyelids open; they would droop, and the life seemed to slip out of him for a few seconds. Then he'd open them with a startled, agitated expression and sit back up. After a while, his eyes stayed closed.

"I'm going with Joseph to the Galilee," Yehuda said to Esther, after their mother had finally helped Hanan to bed for the night and Miriam and Matti were upstairs.

His words were like a punch to her gut. "You can't leave us!"

"The best way to protect you is to stop the Romans at the front."

"You're going to stop the Romans? You're not a soldier. You're as thin as a reed. Your neck is barely strong enough to hold up your head, which is heavier each day from all the crazy thoughts you're putting into it."

"My faith is strong. It doesn't matter how strong my body is."

"It matters when you're facing a trained Roman soldier!"

"God will bring me back on eagle's wings for the final redemption, and then we'll all be together again—Tabitha and my baby boy. Shimon too."

"I know you want to see them again, but your duty is to the family that's still alive! Who will bring the tithes home, or teach Matti Torah? What will we live on? We need you more than Joseph does."

"I'll be back soon, I promise. I trust Joseph."

"I don't!"

Yehuda looked away, and Esther realized that nothing she could say would stop him. He had made up his mind. "When are you going?" she asked.

"Tonight." He rubbed his hands nervously. "I can't tell Father; he'd try to stop me. You'll have to tell him."

"Tell him what? That you're abandoning us?"

"Tell him I have to go, that I'm willing to die for our freedom."

"You think you're brave because you're willing to face death? Knowing what you'll die for is easy. Don't you have anything to live for?"

Yehuda's eyes radiated a vehemence that frightened her. "As long as Rome threatens us, there's nothing worth living for."

"That's not what our Book says. God commanded us to choose life." Esther felt anger burning through her—anger at Yehuda, at Joseph, at Lazar, at the Romans, at all the stupid men in the world and their stupid wars.

That night in bed, she pressed up next to Matti's warm body and draped her arm around him. He stirred in his sleep and leaned back into her, his head nestled under her chin.

She had lost another brother, but at least she still had Matti.

I'll always have him. He'll never leave me, and I'll never leave him.

PART EIGHT

Many of them that sleep in the dust of the earth shall awake, some to everlasting life and some to reproach and everlasting abhorrence.

Daniel 12:2

CHAPTER XLVII

WHEN HANAN FOUND OUT THAT YEHUDA WAS GONE, HIS KNEES BUCK-led and he fell into a dead faint on the floor. They moved him to his bed, where he swung back and forth between delirium and lucid-ity. Esther stayed by his side while Sarah scuttled in and out of the room, giving him tea made from horehound leaves. His chest rose and fell with each raspy gulp of air.

On the third day, he opened his eyes and fixed Esther with an unwavering gaze. "I'm ready," he murmured.

"How could you be ready to leave us?" she whispered.

"It's time." He reached for her with a limp, cold hand. "But how did it happen so quickly? That's what I don't understand."

"It's not time."

"I see my mother and father. They're waiting for me at the Shab-bat table."

"You're not with your parents." Esther tried to pull him back with her words. "You're still with me. Me, Esther!"

He gripped her hand with an unexpected burst of strength.

"I can't . . . do it . . . without you," Esther said, her voice catching in her throat.

"You don't have a choice. That will make you strong."

He slipped into a restless unconsciousness, then jerked awake. "Esther, come—come closer," he sputtered.

"Fluid in the lungs," Sarah said, shaking her head. *How can she stay so calm?* It was harder and harder for her father to speak. He was drowning from the inside.

Tell me, Father, how can I live in a world without you?

But he didn't offer answers. Instead he gave her a list of things to do: give his shoes to the beggars on the bridge, take the wax seal and the vases from his office in the Temple, make sure the rain cisterns were plastered before the spring. Her father told her that Uncle Pinchas had recently taken some of their valuables to store at the estate. She should go to him if the family needed anything.

He closed his eyes and, in a barely audible whisper, said, "Make sure you order my ossuary. Avram, the stonemason, is making Shimon's. A beautiful box for my beautiful boy. Rosettes on the front."

She didn't want to talk about ossuaries, the boxes where the bones would lie until the resurrection.

"Rest, save your strength," she said, patting his arm.

He held on for another day but said no more. Esther told him how much she loved him and how scared she was, that she hoped he forgave her for not wanting to marry Lazar.

Soon there would be no one to tell her about the runaway animals in the Temple, the bumbling priest who couldn't remember the order of the service, or the treasures buried in secret places. There would be no one to call her "my little queen." She wished she could sit in the corner in his study and watch him work, hunched over his scrolls, but those days were far behind them both. She would be strong, when her father couldn't.

"You can go now," she whispered into his ear. "I'll be all right. I won't let anything happen to Matti. Miriam and I will help Mother."

He opened his filmy eyes and looked toward the afternoon rays streaming into the room, the dust motes dancing in the narrow shaft of light. His head leaned to one side, and the color left his face.

Time had stalled, waiting patiently with them for the Angel of Death, but now it rushed by at a dizzying speed. There were people to tell, arrangements to make, burial spices to grind, a shroud to find. The neighbors descended on the house and embraced her mother. The keening began and the sounds of mourning filled the air.

Esther stumbled outside and fell into a heap, slumping against the wool pile. She began to laugh—a hard, sharp laugh—wielding it like a knife, slashing at the world around her. It turned into deep, guttural sobs, then shallow whimpers. No one paid attention. Everyone was busy.

That night, she and Matti lay in bed, their heads resting on their father's tallit, his prayer shawl. They breathed in its spicy anise smell.

"I didn't know it would happen," Matti said accusingly.

"I told you he was dying."

"You didn't say I wouldn't see him again. I didn't get to say goodbye."

"You can still say it."

"Where is he?"

"What do you mean?"

"How can I talk to him if he's not here?"

"He's in heaven."

She felt swallowed up by the sadness. Unlike Matti, she had known this moment would come. But she wasn't ready either. Her father was the one who paid the grain merchant and scheduled the deliveries. He was the one who brought home the white bread for the festivals. He knew what blessings to say before eating which foods, and when they were supposed to fast. He worried so she didn't have to.

She fell into a restless sleep but woke as the black night grew light. The sun rose and the moon disappeared. The moon would be back, but her father wouldn't.

The next day, Esther asked her mother what she should do, but her mother waved her away. Sarah was lethargic, staring vacantly at the front door. Miriam, sick from her pregnancy, was too weak to leave the house. Esther would have to take charge. The pain would come, but for now she was too busy. She went over the list of chores her father had given her. If she forgot something, would he know?

There was no frankincense in the market, but she managed to purchase a few drops of myrrh instead, some old cinnamon bark—which, she discovered when she got home, had lost its smell—and a bundle of cassia strips. The cassia had been bulked up with ordinary cherry bark, but she'd bought it anyway. It wouldn't be enough to scent the scraps of linen for her father's shroud, or even scent the air in the burial cave, but what could she do?

It seemed like yesterday that the family had last walked to the cave to bury Shimon. This time, Esther had to pay porters to transport her father's body, because there were no men in her family left to help. The neighbors found a rickety cart that made a loud creaking sound when the wheels turned. There were rotten vegetables rolling around in it, but she was lucky to find it. The rebels had taken everything else.

She was furious at the porters. They handled her father like a sack of grain and left his feet sticking out. But she couldn't dismiss them. She needed strong men—Jews—to roll back the heavy entrance stone, and they were almost all away with the rebels, training.

Her mother, Matti, and a few neighbors entered the cave and lay the corpse in the sunken groove in the ground. Despite the cloth

Esther held close to her nose, the stench was overpowering. She looked at the corpse next to her father, a mound of putrid flesh covered with mites and maggots. Could this really have been her brother?

Esther rushed through the prayers while batting away a swarm of flies. Then she walked out into the bright, harsh sunlight. Ravens and hawks circled the sky.

Matti was outside. Esther stood next to him.

"I'm looking for Father," he said, looking up.

"We just put him in the cave."

"I'm looking to see where his soul went." He pointed to the sky. "He's there. I know it. I'm going to check every night, since that's where he'll come back from."

Esther looked, but all she saw was a vast swath of nothing.

CHAPTER XLVIII

ESTHER WAS RELIEVED THAT IT WAS THE LAST DAY OF SHIVA. THE sharp stench of body odor assaulted her as she entered the cramped room. Mourners were prohibited from bathing during shiva.

The house was full of people who'd come to pay their respects: priests, neighbors, and even shopkeepers. Her father would have been pleased, even though he probably would have pretended not to care. She looked around. A mirror was covered and the couches turned over; platters of food were arranged on tables; and rows of wine jars lined the walls. Her mother sat on the floor, with a torn robe, symbolizing her torn heart. Her face looked like the bottom of a dry riverbed.

Lazar had come every day. He'd brought her water and made sure the servants continued their duties while the family mourned. She still didn't want to marry him, but she felt some of her antipathy dissipating. Maybe her father was right; it was helpful to have a man around.

That afternoon, Matti whispered into Esther's ear. Someone was here. She got up from the floor, where the family had to sit during shiva, and went outside to look. Halfway down the steps, she paused. She almost didn't recognize him. He wore a tunic and sandals, and had a beard. He looked like a Jew. Until she saw his eyes—that blue was unmistakable.

"I thought you'd be gone by now," she said when she reached

him. "You saw what they did to the soldiers at the palace. I wasn't sure you'd make it out of there alive."

"Nor I." A sardonic smile crossed his face.

"Why did you come?"

"He was my friend," Tiberius said. "Your father was . . ." He didn't finish the sentence. His eyes watered.

He'd loved him too, Esther realized. *A Roman loved my father.* "How did you know he died?"

"Jerusalem is a small place. Priest Katros, who used to order spices, told me."

"The spices you imported with my father?" she asked in a biting tone, crossing her arms. She knew she was being spiteful, but she couldn't help herself. She was mad at everyone lately, even at her father for dying and leaving her to take care of everything.

She wanted to go back to how it was before, when there was an order to the world, when there were rules and everyone knew them. She thought about Tiberius occasionally, the kind of thoughts she used to have about Joseph: imagining him touching her, imagining them together. She was drawn to him; she couldn't deny it. To his strength and to his concern for her family—and it terrified her. Anger was easier than fear.

"This isn't a business visit," he said. "I came to pay my respects. And to see how you were coping. I know you must miss him terribly."

That surprised Esther. In the flood of mourners, had anyone singled her out, or asked how she was doing? Tiberius was always surprising her. But that didn't matter right now.

"Pay the money you owe me instead."

"There is no money."

"What about the shipments? I know about the shipments with my father. I have the contract to prove it."

"Do you think anyone is buying spices now? People only want weapons."

"What about the tar from the Salt Sea?"

"The ship hasn't made it to Ostia yet."

She raised her eyebrows. "You talked to my father about that deal last winter. You must have the money by now."

He shook his head. "We had to wait until the spring to collect the tar. It took another month to have it hauled up to the port of Caesarea. Once there, we had to find the right ship and wait for the right winds. And then—even though it only takes a month to sail to Ostia—it takes another month or more to find out if the ship actually made it. I'm still waiting to find out. Maybe it sank or was delayed."

"You're lying."

He bristled at the accusation. It was a mean thing to say, and she didn't even believe it herself.

"I'll give you as much money as you want," he said.

"I don't need your charity. I only want what you owe us."

"When I get the money, I'll keep it for you. Whatever happens, I'll honor my agreement with your father. If you ever need me, leave word with Zahara."

"I won't need you."

He sighed and ran his hand through his hair. "The Romans will avenge their defeat. They'll be back."

It was exactly what her father had said.

He continued, "And when they come, promise me you'll leave immediately. The Romans will surround the city and destroy it. They'll kill or enslave everyone—anyone who hasn't starved first."

"*They?* You speak like you're not one of them. If you really cared for my father," she said, her voice shaking, "then stay away. Don't come anywhere near me or my family."

He nodded slowly, resignation tinged with sadness in his eyes.

"Be safe," he said.

As she watched him leave, she tried to convince herself that she had done the right thing. Everyone knew that Romans couldn't be trusted, and it would be dangerous for her and her family if their connection were ever discovered.

Why, then, was it so hard to believe it?

CHAPTER XLIX

IT HAD BEEN SIX WEEKS SINCE HER FATHER HAD DIED, YET ESTHER still expected to see him wrapped in his tallit reciting his morning prayers. Without a man, the house felt lifeless. They moved in a heavyhearted languor, silence edging out their feeble attempts at conversation. Her mother sat for hours in her father's chair in the dining room. Wrapped in her old brown shawl, she looked small and forlorn, like a lone sparrow waiting for her mate.

The winter was raw and bleak, and Esther's fingers and toes were stiff. Unless she huddled in front of the brazier, she felt the chill in her bones. The house was damp, the floors were caked with mud, and darkness shortened the days. She continuously checked for fungus creeping up the walls; the last thing she needed now was house leprosy, requiring an elaborate purification ritual by a priest.

Sarah used to run the house, but no more. Esther couldn't remember the last time her mother had counted the sacks of beans, salted the meat, preserved the fruit, or gone to the market. Now she just sat, running her fingertips around and around the rim of her father's wineglass. Listening to the low thrum. The shelves were emptying.

"You're a child," her mother said, looking at Esther in a dull stare. "Your parents are supposed to die. I'm the one who's a widow. Now I have nothing."

Nothing? Esther waited for her mother to continue, to say she didn't mean it like that, that she still had Esther and Matti and

Yehuda. To say they were all grieving. Esther waited . . . but her mother said no more.

Matti tugged on Esther's robe. "I'm hungry and I can't find Ezzi. Someone left the gate open, and Miriam won't help me because her feet are so big and red that she can hardly stand, and the white-legged hen won't go broody. She left her nest again."

"Why can't everybody just leave me alone?" Esther shouted, putting her hands on her head.

Matti's lower lip quivered, and Esther was ashamed of her outburst. It wasn't his fault.

"I'm sorry," she said quickly. "Come, let's go find Ezzi."

Esther hadn't forgotten her promise to her father about the bone box. Her vow sat like a tiny pebble in her shoe. Until now, though, she had been so overwhelmed with the demands of everyone who needed to be fed, cleaned, and comforted, that she hadn't gotten around to ordering it. Today she would do it.

The stonemason was in Bezetha, in the northern part of the city, next to the quarry. As she made her way north, the roads were clogged with people fleeing the Galilee and coming to Jerusalem for safety. Whenever she could, Esther asked the refugees if they had seen or heard from her brother. No one had. A few knew about Joseph, though. One man said Joseph was building up an army for his personal power. Another defended him and claimed he was beset by danger all around. Esther assumed that Yehuda was still by his side, helping him train soldiers and fortify the cities up north: Gamla, Yodfat, Jamnia, and Migdal. And, she reasoned, if something had happened to Yehuda, surely Joseph would have sent word. He owed her family that much.

By the time she reached Bezetha, the crowd had thinned. Lathes, paving stones, small columns, and half-finished tables were strewn outside next to the workshops. Esther spotted a few unfinished ossuaries. The stone boxes were recognizable by their size: the length of a femur, the longest bone in the body.

Esther located the stonemason, who was not in his workshop but close by, at the site of the city's new wall. Avram, a short, slight man with a drawn face, was shouting commands in a husky voice to a cadre of workers. Men twice his size heaved bags of dirt and stone. Slaves, in rags that barely covered their muscular bodies, mixed lime with sand and water to make a thick slurry mortar. Avram stood next to the wall, which reached his knees.

She watched the workers toss the roughly finished ashlars and misshapen field stones into place. Even to her untrained eye, the work seemed hasty and sloppy. Apparently it was more important to finish the wall before the Romans returned than to make it straight. She hoped it would be strong enough to withstand a Roman assault.

Avram, handing out hammers, chisels, and pry bars to the workers, ignored her for almost five minutes.

Finally he turned to her. "What do *you* want, girl?"

"An ossuary."

"No one is making ossuaries anymore. Every mason in the city has been drafted to work on the wall."

Esther's face fell.

Avram said, "Who's thinking about the next life now? We need to worry about this one."

"But what about the bones?" Esther asked.

"There will be even more bones if we don't finish this wall."

"But my father already ordered one for my brother. And now I need another one. Please."

Avram squinted at her. "Who's your father?"

"Hanan Ben Shimon."

Avram rubbed his chin. "He made a partial payment, but he never came back."

Esther hesitated, then looked down. "He died. That's why I need another one."

Avram's face softened. "He was a good man, and a good customer." He picked up a pail. "All right," he said. "I'll finish the ossuary that your father ordered for your brother. It's almost done anyway. But I can't make another for him. Put the bones together."

They hadn't gotten along in life. How could they lie together in death?

She started to protest, but Avram held up his hand. "All right, all right," he said wearily. "How can I refuse? I can work on them only now, while the crew is near my workshop. Once we finish this section of the wall, it will be too late. The wall will go around Bezetha, and I have to go with it. Pay me now, so I can buy the stone."

Her father had said that each ossuary cost ten shekels. She had fifteen shekels with her, five for the balance of Shimon's and full payment for her father's.

"Don't expect anything fancy," he added. "This is no time for artistry."

She bit her lip. Her father *had* wanted one with an arched lid, decorative rosettes, and a red wash.

"You'll use hard limestone, right?" Esther asked.

He scowled.

"Soft chalk crumbles," she said.

"Who cares? How long does it have to last? The End of Days will be here soon. And besides, you can scratch the inscription with your fingernail. I don't have time for engravings."

She knew not to argue. She counted out the fifteen shekels and handed it to him.

"This isn't enough," he said. "It's thirty-five. I'll honor the price

I gave your father for the one he already ordered, but another one will cost twenty-five."

"Twenty-five? That's more than ten sin sacrifices!"

"What can I do? Prices are inflated all over."

"But I have only fifteen shekels with me—"

"I need at least twenty-five to buy the stone," he said, turning back toward the wall.

"Wait! I'll get the rest!" she called after him.

He turned around slowly. "And I take only *our* silver now. No pagan money."

She nodded. She didn't have enough money at home; she'd have to go to the cache, where her father had hidden the family valuables. Her family was wealthy and her parents had been prudent. For that at least, she was grateful.

CHAPTER L

MATTI WAS HAMMERING A STAKE INTO THE GROUND.

"What are you doing?" Esther asked.

"Fixing the fence. Ezzi chewed it."

"That goat of yours is more trouble than she's worth," Esther said, even though she didn't mean it. She was relieved he was busy again. After their father's death, Matti had moped around, not leaving her side. Ever since she'd said that he was now the man of the family, Matti had abandoned his cart, hoops, and bladder balls and started helping more.

She went to the milking shed and was greeted by the musky scent of the goats. She sat on the stool. Shifting her weight, she clasped the goat's teat.

"Shh, shh . . . ," she said, slowly massaging the delicate pink udder. A few drops squirted out, and she began. She was grateful for the mindless work; it was soothing. As she squeezed and pulled, she thought about how she had taken her old life for granted, even the most ordinary of days—the days that used to unroll on their own as she and Matti rose with the sun, milked and fed the animals, and slept with the moon. Now the days seemed to stall, screech, and grate with friction. She was tired of being the one who had to coax the household back to life.

When she finished the milking, she saw Miriam standing in the doorway. Her belly was so big that she seemed to totter on her feet. But at least she felt well enough to come outside, and for the first time in weeks, she was wearing a clean robe. Miriam pointed to the pail. "It's too full."

Esther smiled. That comment was straight from her old life.

"What's so funny?" Miriam asked.

"Nothing. I'm just glad to see you feeling better."

"And," Miriam said, rubbing her belly as she spoke, "you left too much grit in the flour."

Esther laughed. "Actually, I'm not so glad."

Maybe, Esther thought, it'll be all right. Soon there would be a new baby in the house. A new life.

CHAPTER LI

LATER THAT AFTERNOON, MATTI SAT BY ESTHER'S SIDE AS SHE scraped the mold from the last round of cheese. They discussed ways to get the hen to sit on her eggs.

A piercing scream shattered the calm. Esther dropped the knife and ran to Miriam's room. Matti followed her.

Miriam flailed her arms as she looked down. A rose of blood was blooming on her tunic and pooling at her feet.

"Get Mother!" Esther screamed. Matti stood rooted to the spot. "Go, *go!*" she urged. His eyes widened in fear.

For the past week, Miriam had been saying that she didn't feel the stirring anymore and that her belly had sunk to one side like a load of lead. Esther had tried to comfort her; she'd said that the baby must have been sleeping. Now she stood, helpless as Miriam screamed . . . and screamed.

She couldn't do this; she didn't know what to do.

She was immobilized, staring at the blood.

Oh God. . . . Oh God. . . . Where is Mother?

After a few minutes that seemed like hours, Sarah came. She threw off her shawl and pushed up her sleeves. She yelled at Matti, "Get Shifra, the midwife who lives behind the bee man. Tell her it's Miriam's time!"

She ordered Miriam to lie down on the bed, and told Esther to bring olive oil, warm water, and wool. Relief washed over Esther; her mother was in charge. At last, Sarah had shaken off the chains of her grief.

Esther went outside to the wool pile and found a bundle of washed and carded fleece. She grabbed it and went back inside. Miriam was on the bed, and her mother was pressing on her belly.

"It's dead. I know it's dead," Miriam cried, turning her head from side to side.

"You're not God. You don't know that. And you're going to have to deliver it either way," Sarah said. Her brow knitted in concentration, she put her hand between Miriam's legs. "The skin at the neck of the womb is so thin that when I touched it, the water broke." She brought her fingers to her nose. "It's clear. No death smell."

She instructed Esther to make a compress to stop the bleeding. Boiled pomegranate peel and pine bark, if Esther could find them. If not, a bag of warm ground grains. The stomach of a calf or lamb would have been better, Sarah added, but there was no time for that now.

Esther worked quickly, glad to have an excuse to leave the room and catch her breath. If Miriam died . . . Esther shook her head as if to dismiss the unthinkable. She couldn't lose Miriam too. She had never considered the possibility that Miriam could end up next to Yehuda's wife, Tabitha. Since Shimon's death, Miriam had withdrawn into herself. But now Esther realized how much she needed Miriam's constancy; it was a refuge from her mother's brittle and sporadic love.

When Esther returned, she massaged Miriam's belly with warm olive oil and held her hand. Shifra came with the birthing chair, a low stool with a crescent-shaped hollow bottom and two angled planks of wood for the feet.

Miriam's eyes bulged when she saw the chair. "Get *Ema*! I want my mother." Her wan face was streaked with tears.

"I'll send a messenger to bring your parents tomorrow, or the next day, at the latest," Esther told her. She wanted Aunt Bruria to come too; she could cook and help take care of Miriam and the baby. Surprisingly, she found that she wanted Uncle Pinchas too. He was gruff, but he would see the state of the house and take charge.

Esther changed the bloody fleece under Miriam's legs and stroked her brow. Miriam moaned and dozed off. When she awoke writhing in pain, Esther gave her sips of spelt water. Her mother chanted psalms and tied an herb of savory around Miriam's belly. The labor began. Esther helped Miriam onto the stool, unpinned her hairnet, and loosened her hair. Esther covered Miriam's feet with a blanket and massaged her shoulders. Their neighbor Neshra gripped one side of the stool with her bony arms, and Sarah held the other. Esther stood in the back to make sure Miriam didn't rock backward and fall.

"Drive your breath into your flanks and don't scream," Shifra said. "That's good. That's good. . . . Breathe. . . . Push. . . . Breathe. . . . Push."

Esther stroked Miriam's hair and whispered into her ear, "You'll be fine. You'll be fine. The baby will be fine. Everything is fine," even though Esther suspected it wasn't, from the looks Shifra and her mother exchanged.

Hours later, the baby was born. His bones and ribs were visible through translucent white skin, and his head was misshapen. Shifra laid the baby on a pillow and cut the cord. Esther's mother put a finger on his tiny chest, slick with blood. She shook her head. Miriam opened her eyes but refused to look at the baby, even when they brought him to her.

But only when it was all over—when Miriam was still and almost lifeless herself, and they'd bound her breasts to stop the milk—did Esther run out of the room, fighting back the bile surging up inside her.

CHAPTER LII

MIRIAM'S PARENTS HADN'T ARRIVED YET. BUT IT HAD BEEN ONLY FOUR days since the baby had died, so, Esther told herself, they'd come soon. They must have had arrangements to make and supplies to pack.

"Lazar's here!" Matti shouted from the courtyard. Esther sighed and went outside. Lazar was down on one knee, tying a rope around the neck of Matti's goat. Matti beamed. "Lazar fixed Ezzi's leash!"

Since Esther's father's death, Lazar had come each week, always carrying baskets of food. At first, Esther wouldn't take anything, but Sarah would snatch the baskets out of his hands, apologizing for Esther's behavior. Afterward, her mother had scolded her. *Don't be ungrateful,* she'd said. *You can't eat pride.* Esther had explained that she didn't want to be beholden to him; they could buy their own food. Still, she was glad to see him now. It was nice to have some help, especially after all that had happened.

Lazar stood up and brushed the dirt off his tunic. He looked at her shyly.

Esther hesitated. She didn't want to let him into the house, or her heart.

But she was so tired of doing everything by herself.

The messenger returned the following day. Alone.

Esther's uncle and aunt, Miriam's parents, were dead, he said.

The family estate in the Judean Hills, where Miriam had grown up, was gone. Burned to the ground—not a building, tree, or even a radish left. The Roman troops had destroyed all the farms on the march back to Jerusalem, taking not only food and supplies for the soldiers, but lives too. There would be no mercy after their last defeat.

Esther shook her head. "It can't be. We just got a caravan of produce from there." But as soon as she'd said the words, she realized that it *had* been quite some time. "Maybe they escaped. How do you know for sure?" she asked the messenger.

"The house servant said the soldiers murdered the master because he wouldn't tell them where the valuables were. When the mistress tried to stop them, they chopped off her arms."

Esther felt light-headed.

"How did—how did the servant escape?" she stammered.

"They let him live because he spoke their dialect and gave them wine."

She waited until the room stopped spinning, then put her face into her icy hands and gripped it tightly, as if to keep it from shattering into a million pieces. How would she tell Miriam?

PART NINE

DECEMBER 66 CE
TEVET 3827

Who knows whether you have come to the kingdom for such a time as this?

Esther 4:14

CHAPTER LIII

"Don't you know the sun's up?" Esther said, standing over Miriam's bed. Miriam had hardly left her room in the previous two weeks, since the stillbirth. She said she wanted to be with her baby and her parents.

"The only thing I know is that God is angry with me," Miriam said, staring at the walls and rubbing her slack belly.

"I'm angry too. Get out of bed!" Esther flung the blanket to the floor.

"What for?" Miriam pulled the blanket back over her legs. "No one needs me."

"I do! Mother hardly talks, Matti is scared . . . and . . . and I'm scared too." She sat down on the bed and took Miriam's hands in hers. "I thought you were going to die," Esther said softly, "that you would leave me too."

"You'd manage; you always do," Miriam said, but she allowed Esther to help her out of bed. It was a start.

Esther wanted to surrender to the sorrow too, but her father's words echoed in her head: *You don't have a choice. That will make you strong.* She missed him so much. She wanted to tell him that he had been wrong; she wasn't strong at all. It took every ounce of her being to not sink into a sadness so deep that she couldn't feel anything at all. But someone had to gather the eggs and milk the goats, check the wood pile and fetch the water. Not having a choice didn't make her strong. It made her tired.

She'd been so busy that she hadn't had time to pay the stone-mason. At least that's what she told herself. But deep down she knew that she hadn't wanted to go back to the underground cache to get the money. The tunnels still terrified her. But she had to pay Avram, before he changed his mind.

Now that Miriam was up, Esther had no more excuses. She'd go today.

A few hours later Esther entered the Temple Mount. Three rebels—unwashed young men with unkempt hair—were carving their names into a column. Thank God her father couldn't witness this desecration. More rebels strutted in and out of the gate, brandishing their newly acquired weapons.

Catapults lined the Outer Court of the Temple Mount, along with piles of bows and arrows, lances and javelins, and stones of different sizes. Shields of all kinds were propped up against the walls. The rebels had marked their newfound property in crude Aramaic letters: *Stolen from a Roman pig. Property of Jacob.*

She made her way to the staircase leading to the underground level, but stopped in front of her father's old office. No one was there, but it was clear that someone had taken it over, probably some petty rebel officer. She swiped the oil lamp off the desk and ran out.

At the bottom of the stairs Esther lit the lamp's wick from a torch in the wall, hoping the light would keep the rats away. Her breath curled in steam in front of her face. She tried to breathe evenly.

Keep walking, one foot in front of the other. Breathe. Don't look around.

She counted her steps. The stone protruded from the wall in the same place. This time, she had located the cache easily. A good sign. She'd have to pull the jar out, since she needed to reach the coins at the bottom. Grabbing the jar's lip, she pulled as hard as she could, her grunts echoing in the empty tunnel. She yanked out the tattered burlap and linen scraps she'd stuffed into the opening the last time. Reaching through the broken seal of straw and wax, she removed the papyri, one by one.

Her betrothal contract was tied with a red cord. She tossed it to the side, not caring if it landed in the mud. Then she reached for another scroll. It looked old: aged brown papyrus with edges that crumbled when she touched it. Unrolling it, she scanned the Aramaic text. It was her mother's *ketubah,* her marriage contract.

Next Esther noticed a cream-colored scroll, clearly new, since the stringy fibers of the papyrus plant were still visible. Curious, Esther opened it and read the words *Last Will and Testament.* Her hands trembled. Her father had left the family's share in the estate to Yehuda, along with detailed instructions about caring for their mother. Esther received a date grove in Jericho and the revenues from the partnership with Tiberius. Of course, the actual contract with Tiberius was there too. She'd put it into the cache herself. She'd never bothered to read it before, but now she was curious. It was written on a thicker papyrus than the others, and in Greek instead of Hebrew. It spelled out that they'd split the profits from the sale of the Salt Sea tar they'd exported together—after the ship reached its destination and the middlemen were paid. Tiberius had said the same thing when he'd visited after her father's funeral. He'd promised he would keep her share of the profits for her.

When she saw the last scroll, she smiled. It was the leather *Megillah,* the family heirloom her father had read to them every year on the holiday of Purim, and on her birthday. He had commissioned the scroll with its beautiful script and colorful borders from a famous scribe in Sepphoris and had been very proud of it; not many families possessed their very own copy. She clasped the scroll to her chest and felt a tightness in her throat. She swallowed and blinked as she remembered sitting on her father's lap as he read the story of brave Queen Esther, the most exciting story she had ever heard. She stuffed the *Megillah* into her bag; Purim was soon, and she wouldn't make another trip here just to get the scroll.

Now it was time to get the money and leave. She peered into the jar, looking for the coins and the jewels her father had said he'd hidden. But there was nothing—except a small package wrapped in linen and tied with string. Inside was a letter with her name on it, closed with his seal. She ran her finger over the raised wax, tracing her father's emblem. He was the last person who'd touched it, and her name, written in his slanted, distinctive handwriting, made her feel like he was here. She was grateful to be told what to do, to hand back the burden of being in charge, if only temporarily, and experience his love one last time. Esther could picture him at his desk holding the stylus and making each mark slowly and carefully—for her. The contracts had all been written by scribes, but her father had written this letter himself.

She broke the seal and with a fluttering heart read: *If you've found this, I'm with my fathers and I knew you'd come.*

The letter instructed her to take the family to the estate if the Romans returned. *On his last visit, Pinchas took all of our jewelry and money to the estate for safekeeping. They may lay siege to Jerusalem, and even though there is plenty of food and water in the city, the Romans are mighty foes.*

To the estate? There was no estate, not anymore. She felt smothered in a heavy fog. She couldn't think.

What will happen to us now?

CHAPTER LIV

SHE DIDN'T TELL HER MOTHER OR MIRIAM ABOUT THEIR PRECARIOUS financial situation, for fear it would push them into another spiral of despair. Panicked, Esther went over and over what her father had written, trying to understand what it all meant.

They had enough food—for now. They had milk and cheese from the goats, eggs from the chickens, and vegetables from the kitchen garden. But they had only a few coins left to buy wheat and barley, and she still needed to pay the stonemason. If she didn't pay him soon, he might not finish the work. He might change his mind or get so busy with the construction of the wall that he wouldn't have time. She couldn't take a chance; her father's and Shimon's eternal life depended on having a resting place for their bones.

The family had some valuable possessions—her father's vases, the ones that used to cast rainbows on the walls in his office; the Purim scroll; and their silver candelabra—but who would buy them now? And her mother would know if those things were missing. Esther could sell Lazar's bracelet; she didn't know how much it was worth, but it was silver and it was heavy. It would fetch a good price, but how would she explain its disappearance to Lazar? Maybe she could tell him it fell off her wrist or that it was stolen from her in the market. Or she could track Tiberius down, through Zahara, and claim what was legally hers.

But now that her father was dead and the Roman administration, with its courts and clerks, had evacuated, maybe Tiberius had decided to keep the money. With no one to enforce the contract, it was worthless. She could never bring it before a Jewish court, since it proved her father was a collaborator.

Still, her father had trusted Tiberius. And she trusted her father. She would leave word for him with Zahara, like Tiberius had told her to do.

Esther dreaded going back to Zahara's pub. The memories of the riot were still vivid, too vivid. The street looked the same. The hole in the wall where Matti had hidden with the kitten was still there.

Esther knocked. No answer. She knocked again. Then, a click of the peephole, and the squeak of the hinges. Finally the door cracked open. Zahara had the same wild hair, the same mole on her chin, and the same all-seeing eyes.

The place was empty and quiet, so different from the last time. But this time, Zahara seemed eager for the company, and stepped aside to let Esther in.

"Do you want me to read your fortune?" Zahara offered, seemingly not surprised to see her.

"I don't have any money," Esther said.

"My treat." She motioned for Esther to sit and told her to pour some oil from a jug into a glass beaker. Zahara studied the oil as it spread out on the surface and then broke up into little drops.

"What do you see?" Esther asked.

Zahara looked at the beaker again and pronounced, "You need a man."

"I need money."

"Isn't it the same thing?"

"I'm betrothed," said Esther, "and that's already one too many."

"There are different kinds of olives," Zahara said slowly, as though she were talking to a small child. "Some you eat fresh, some are dried, some are salted, and some you have to pound to get rid of the bitterness. You have to work them before they're useful, but we can't live without them."

"You do. You're free."

Zahara shook her head. "No woman is free. Only men buy my drink and rent my rooms. No Jerusalem matron would dirty her soles on my doorstep, except . . . ," she said, fixing Esther with her shrewd stare, "someone very desperate. Women want my help but hate me for giving it to them."

Esther shifted uneasily.

Zahara sat back in her chair. "So, what's wrong with your betrothed? Is he a rebel?"

"He's making the coins for the new government."

"Then he's perfect," she laughed, "even though he's a rebel. They're worse than the Romans. Romans are corrupt and incompetent, but the rebels . . . well, they're just mad. Still, your man will always have money, and that's no small thing."

"He gave me a bracelet. I'll sell it if I can't get my money from Tiberius."

Zahara sat up. "Tiberius?"

"He owed my father money from a shipment. But now that my father's dead, Tiberius owes me the money instead. I need it to pay for the ossuaries."

"I heard about Shimon. I'm sorry," Zahara said, suddenly solemn. She muttered the Hebrew words of comfort: *May you know no more sorrow.*

Esther inclined her head slightly, in a gesture of gratitude.

"If Tiberius owes you money," Zahara said, "you'll get it. But I heard he went to Alexandria for business. I don't know when he's coming back."

"He said you could get a message to him."

She nodded. "Sometimes. His agent brings me food."

"The stonemason wants his payment, and I don't have it."

She opened a drawer and pulled out a small bronze disc with a hole in the middle. "This will protect you."

"I don't need protection; I need money."

"We always need protection."

Esther realized that her words might have sounded ungrateful. "Thank you," she said, spinning the disc on her fingertip. She didn't know why she had been so apprehensive about coming; Zahara was nice, even if she was just an innkeeper.

"What will it protect me from?"

"Disease, evil spirits—both flying and resting—and miscarriage."

"Miscarriage? I don't plan on having a baby—at least not yet."

"We don't plan on a lot of things that happen," Zahara said. "I didn't plan on being an innkeeper in Jerusalem. And yet, here I am."

"Because your husband died?"

"That's what I tell people. It's simpler that way. Otherwise, they gossip—say that I'm the daughter of a slave, the illegitimate daughter of a priest, or a whore. No one seems to know, but they're sure anyway that there are sins in my skirt."

Esther regarded her with a newfound curiosity. "You're not a widow?"

"I wish. That would mean the old bastard's dead. But no such luck. He's still where I left him, on our farm near Gamla."

They lapsed into a comfortable silence. Esther waited for her to continue.

"He tried to get rid of me when I refused him a second wife. He accused me of adultery—me! After he bedded every woman in the village . . ." She wrinkled her nose and pursed her lips as though she'd just bitten into an unripe fig.

"Where did you get the money to open the inn?" Esther asked.

"Aaah . . . ," Zahara said, leaning back again in the chair. "Now, that's *another* story. I rented a room in a house with an old man. One night, I had a dream that I would find a buried treasure in his garden, under the oak tree. So the next day, I dug—and found a box full of gold coins with Emperor Augustus's image."

Esther frowned.

"What's the matter?" Zahara asked.

"I thought you were telling me the truth."

"I am." Zahara smiled and ran her fingers through her hair. "But it's a different truth. The old man died, and I found his savings. What does it matter? He couldn't take it with him."

As Esther stood up to leave, she noticed the graffiti and drawings on the walls. "Aren't you scared to have pictures on your wall? It's a sin."

"I have bigger sins to worry about," Zahara said, waving her hand dismissively.

Esther stared at the wall, almost completely covered with lewd sayings and sticklike images. She drew a sharp breath when she noticed a detailed portrait in the top corner: a nude girl in front of a window.

"It's forbidden to draw people," Esther said quickly, looking away. She didn't want Zahara to know she recognized herself.

"Not for a Roman." Zahara wore a knowing smile. "Tiberius talked about you. He was worried. He's one of the good ones," Zahara said, "the kind you don't have to pound."

CHAPTER LV

ESTHER COULDN'T WAIT FOR TIBERIUS TO RETURN FROM ALEXANDRIA; she didn't know if he'd come back at all. The only thing she did know was that if Avram didn't get the money soon, he wouldn't make the ossuaries.

She'd have to ask Lazar. There was no other choice. Legally he was her betrothed. And, she reasoned, she could always pay him back if Tiberius came through.

Esther felt the blast of heat even before she crossed the threshold of Lazar's workshop, and the noise was almost deafening. Where before there had been a display of souvenir trinkets and jewelry, there was now a large table. Two workers stood behind a wooden anvil. One, stripped to the waist, his chest glistening with sweat, placed a hot metal disc on the anvil. The other worker struck it to impress the design of the coin onto the disk. The first worker removed the coin with large iron tongs and dropped it onto the table. They worked in tandem, placing, striking, and lifting, in a finely coordinated dance of swift arm movements. The pounding reverberated in her ears. There were enough coins right there, Esther thought, to pay for the ossuaries.

"What do you think of the new government's mint?" Lazar asked.

Esther was startled. She hadn't seen Lazar come up behind her, so mesmerized had she been by the growing pile of coins. "It's . . . hot," she said.

"The furnaces are working full-time," he explained, the pride in his voice unmistakable. "We're making thirty coins a minute."

"Where do you get the silver?"

"From the Temple treasury. Come, I'll show you."

Lazar led her to a back room where men at long benches poured molten silver into wooden trays filled with sand. They pressed the sand into discs the size of the coins.

The heat was so stifling that Esther turned back toward the door. "But you're an artisan. You make jewelry," she said.

"Our people need money more than jewelry. I design the coins and I make the dies. The skill is in the engraving. Striking the coins is the easy part."

It didn't look easy to her.

He handed her a coin. It had a chalice on one side with the inscription *Shekel of Israel* and on the other, pomegranates and the words *Jerusalem the Holy.*

"They're beautiful," she said, and she meant it. Surprisingly, the shiny coin with its Jewish symbols filled her with pride too. They had their *own* coins now; no more pictures of Caesar and Latin writing. Reluctantly she handed it back.

"I need some," she said. "A loan."

"That's why you came?" Hurt flickered across his face. "To get money from me? I don't have any."

"That's impossible. There's money everywhere. You're making it!" Esther softened her tone. "I need to pay for ossuaries. For my father and brother."

"It's not my money; it's the government's. A committee checks everything—the raw metal, the silver content of the coins, and even that the denominations are true to weight. I have to submit my designs for approval. Everything about this revolt is disorganized except for this mint."

"It's just a loan," Esther insisted, hating the pleading tone in her voice. "Someone owes my father money, and as soon as I get it, I'll pay you back."

"I could be killed if money is missing."

"I need twenty shekels. I know you have that."

"Your family should pay for the ossuaries."

"There's no money. My father sent our money to the estate for safekeeping. The Romans took it all and burned the estate to the ground." She paused. "My uncle and aunt are dead."

He frowned, then reached into a pouch tied to his belt.

"Here," he said, putting some coins into her hand.

Her heart sank as she counted to ten. It wouldn't be enough to pay for the ossuaries in full, but at least it would get Avram started.

"I can't give you more." He turned toward his workers.

Esther wanted to throw the coins into his face. He had more; if not here, then at home. "Then give me the bride-price back! That will pay for the ossuaries. I'm not marrying you anyway."

"Your father signed a contract."

"My father is dead."

"Contracts don't die."

"Who will you find to enforce it?" Esther shouted. "Are you going to petition the Sanhedrin? The priests in the court have either fled or are hiding in their houses. Anyway, it's just a piece of parchment. I can burn it."

With his hard eyes and flared nostrils, he looked like a goat about to butt. "You have to marry me!"

"Never!" Esther said.

Lazar raised his hand in a blur of motion. Esther hunched over, covering her face with her hands, bracing herself for the blow. . . .

Nothing happened.

She opened her eyes and peered through her fingers. Lazar's hand was down and his body was slumped, as if in defeat. Luckily for her, she thought, his better nature had prevailed.

Esther ran out, fury propelling her steps. But by the time she reached home, her anger was gone. She felt pity, and no small measure of guilt, in its place. She'd gone to get money, and he'd thought she wanted to see him.

Esther waited until the next day, trying to decide what to do. She still couldn't pay Avram in full. But with Lazar's coins, she had enough for Avram to start. And when he finished? Well, she'd worry about that later.

The stonemason was in the same spot as yesterday, but the wall was higher. It now reached his waist.

"I have the money," she said, breathless from walking so quickly.

He looked puzzled. "He already paid me. Not all, but enough for me to buy the stone. You can pay me the balance when I finish."

So Lazar had given Avram the down payment. She was so surprised that it felt as if the smallest gust of wind could knock her over. Lazar must have felt guilty about losing his temper. Or maybe he was worried that she really would burn their contract. He must have come right after she'd left the mint.

CHAPTER LVI

IT WAS THE FIRST PURIM WITHOUT HER FATHER. HIS EMPTY CHAIR, HIS cane leaning in the corner, and the darkness of his study made his absence so vivid that it hurt to look.

Every year her father would make a small pile of sesame candies, one for each of her years, counting very solemnly as though he were counting the most important thing in the world. And every year the pile would grow a little bigger. She wondered whether he would have done it this year; sixteen was too old for childish rituals.

Her father should have been the one to read the *Megillah,* the story of how Queen Esther saved the Jews. It was the story they read every Purim. Esther handed the precious scroll to her mother, but she refused to take it. Esther offered it to Miriam, but she shook her head too.

So, Esther began reading. Matti was smiling. With a pang she remembered her father's lessons, and was grateful that his teachings could still bring some joy to their life.

Reading the ancient text, Esther felt as if the young queen were sending her a message: that she had to act. When Queen Esther had been faced with the looming destruction of her people, she hadn't waited for someone to rescue her. She'd made a plan. The biblical heroine had had to depend on a man she didn't love. She'd had to win the king's heart and get him to save her, her family, and her people.

She looked at Miriam and her mother, their faces softened by the glow from the flickering lamp, and she felt a deep gratitude. They still had each other. The idea of losing them—of being all alone in this world—was too terrifying to think about.

The Roman army was on its way back. People seemed confident of another Jewish victory, but she hadn't forgotten her father's warnings. She hadn't forgotten the dizzying fear she had felt during the first attack.

She would be a fool to think that three women and a boy could manage alone in another assault. They needed a man. Maybe she had been wrong about Lazar, just as she had been wrong about Joseph. After all, Lazar had brought them food after her father had died, and he'd paid Avram. And there were no more coins in her father's chest. How much longer could they survive without help?

Perhaps like Queen Esther, she too had been born for such a time as this. If Queen Esther could save the Jewish people, couldn't Esther save what was left of her own family?

PART TEN

The custom was that when a bridegroom and a bride were led in a procession, a rooster and a hen were carried before them, as though to say, "Be fruitful and multiply like fowl."

Babylonian Talmud, Gittin 57a

CHAPTER LVII

"IT'S YOUR WEDDING DAY. YOU SHOULD ENJOY IT," MIRIAM SAID, down on her knees draping Esther's dress.

"How can I enjoy the wedding when I know what's going to happen tonight?" Esther said.

Miriam stopped fussing with Esther's dress and stood up. "I always thought it was best to expect the worst. That way, I'd be prepared if something bad happened, and if nothing did . . . well, I could be pleasantly surprised. But then Shimon was killed and I wasn't prepared at all. I missed out on enjoying so many things because I was so busy worrying."

Miriam wasn't finished. "It turns out bad luck is just as fickle as good, and you can't count on either one. I soured everything with my poisonous thoughts. I still grieve for all the happy moments I let pass me by—and we did share some, you know. I just wish he were here, now that I know that."

Miriam's words didn't help. Esther's gut spasmed when she thought of her marriage bed. She had bathed; she was wearing the finest dress she'd ever worn; her skin was soft and fragrant, massaged with expensive fragrances and lotions; and her hair was loose. Yet all she felt was angst. The thought of being intimate with Lazar left her weak-kneed. On her last night as an unmarried woman, Matti had clung to her as they'd both cried themselves to sleep. She'd promised him he could visit her every day.

Miriam turned Esther around, examining the folds of the dress from all angles. Esther had barely glanced at it, though her mother had been working on it ever since the betrothal ceremony seven months before.

"Stand still. I don't want to prick you." Miriam pinned a brooch to the neckline of the dress.

Esther's gaze caught on a crack in the ceiling, the one that always made her think of a lizard with a long tail. Once, she'd seen a rat clamp its mouth onto a lizard and bite off its tail. The tail had writhed and wiggled, distracting the rat while the lizard escaped. Now she felt like the lizard: sacrificing a part of herself to save her family.

She had to remember: *the tail will grow back.*

It was dusk, and the procession to Lazar's house, her new home, began. Legally Esther already belonged to Lazar, but tonight they would consummate the marriage.

Matti handed out roasted corn for the well-wishers to toss. Esther rode sidesaddle on a neighbor's old horse instead of being carried atop a litter, as was the usual custom. There weren't any litters or carriages available for hire; they had all been requisitioned for the building of the Third Wall. At least Miriam had laid a white blanket on the horse. Sarah had cajoled some of Hanan's old colleagues, Levites from the Temple, to bring their instruments and accompany the pipers. Sarah let a hen and rooster run loose in front of the procession for good luck. Esther couldn't take her eyes off the poor hen, led to the slaughter while the rooster crowed.

As she rode through the streets, Esther looked at the fruit and wine distributed to the spectators and could think only of the extravagance of it all. Didn't they know Jerusalem was preparing for a siege?

The procession stopped when it reached the Kallos house. Lazar, dressed in a fine linen tunic, helped her down from the horse. He carried her into the house and seated her in a chair covered with gold cloth, raised onto two planks like a throne. She avoided his eyes.

The house was packed with guests, and the wine flowed. Tables, laden with plates of steaming food, lined every wall, and all the dishes were reputed to promote a night of sexual bliss: lamb meat smothered in garlic, spicy lentils over fish, beets cooked in cinnamon and wine. The aromas tickled her nose, and her stomach rumbled; she hadn't eaten since the night before. She'd been too nervous.

People surrounded her, clapping their hands and singing:

"Blessed art Thou, O Lord our God, king of the universe, who hath created joy and gladness, bridegroom and bride, mirth and exultation, pleasure and delight, love and brotherhood, peace and friendship. Blessed art Thou, O Lord, who gives the bridegroom joy in his bride."

Esther forced a smile. She felt hollow inside.

The celebration seemed like it would never end. Her family and friends had left hours before. Lazar's friends and family were unfamiliar. His friends were craftsmen with rough hands, not scholars like her father's circle. Like Lazar, they were much older too. Lazar was in the middle of the crowd, drinking and singing. He seemed to be enjoying himself more and more as the evening progressed and his cup emptied . . . over and over. The hymns and psalms turned into ribald verses, and their chants kept time with the thumping of the hand drums. Esther closed her eyes. She felt empty, surrounded by people she didn't recognize, in a house she didn't know, with a man she didn't love. Her heart was gone, no longer transporting her breath and blood. It had left her body and was now in the throbbing beat of the drums. She had never felt more alone.

By the early hours of the morning, most of the guests had left, except for a few who had drunk too much and were now sprawled out on the couches.

"Come, my bride," Lazar said, picking her up once more and carrying her toward the wedding chamber. The room, saturated with a woody, balsamic fragrance, was festooned with cedar leaves. But she wasn't fooled. This wouldn't be a sweet night of love under the branches. It was a test of her virginity, and there would be no legal or physical transfer of property until her groom had proof.

He laid her down on the bed, then lay down beside her. Her breath quickened and her palms were sweaty. She felt paralyzed. When she summoned enough courage to face him, she saw that he was asleep, with his mouth open.

"Wake up," she said, nudging him.

"What?" He looked at her in confusion, as though he were surprised to see her there.

"We have to do it," she said, glad she hadn't eaten anything. Her stomach was already churning.

"I'm not in haste to brush the bloom from the fruit," he said as he ran his fingers over her bodice. "It might taste bland once it's no longer forbidden."

She didn't know what he was talking about. She just knew that she wanted to get it over with. She had heard stories of girls who hadn't bled on their wedding night, and as much as she dreaded this marriage, she dreaded even more the idea of not being declared a virgin. Not only would it mean public embarrassment and a legal disaster, but also a ruined future, for her and her family. Thankfully, during the negotiations, her father had convinced Lazar to waive the custom that someone be appointed from each family to wait next to the door, listen, and check for genuine virginal blood. But still, Lazar would need proof.

The feeling of his face so close to hers and his breath mingling with hers was worse than the actual consummation of their marriage. Quickly she sat up and searched for the blood. Lazar was already asleep.

She scooted closer to her side of the bed and looked at the sheets. Nothing. Miriam had told her to prick her finger or her gums with the brooch on her dress if she didn't find any. She stood up and pulled at the fabric of her dress behind her. There was a dab of blood—just a dab, but it was enough. The dress her mother had worked on for so long was now wrinkled, dirty, moist, and stained with blood. Her mother would be pleased; it had served its purpose. A warm, sticky trickle ran down her legs. She wiped herself with the dress, hoping to make the bloodstain even bigger. Then she crawled back into bed and curled herself into a ball, as small as possible, with her back to Lazar.

Esther wanted to go home. But this was her home now. She was no longer a daughter. She was a wife.

CHAPTER LVIII

LAZAR CAME HOME LATE. HE PACED THE SMALL KITCHEN, OPENING AND then slamming the cupboards shut. After only two months of marriage, Esther could read his moods.

"What's wrong?" she asked as she picked up a handful of beans and let them run through her hand, checking for stones.

He pounded his fist into the palm of his other hand. "My brother is dead."

"Natan, dead?" she repeated in shock. "How do you know?"

"His commander came to the mint today. They were together at the battle of Ascalon. Five months ago!" Lazar shook his head. "And I found out only now. . . ." He lowered himself onto a stool.

Esther was stunned. She'd heard about the battles. Two different rebel groups had attacked the Romans, and both had been defeated. The unexpected defeat had sent the population scurrying to hoard even more food as the myth of Jewish invincibility began to crumble.

"He said Natan was speared on the battlefield by Roman cavalry, stabbed through the gut." He looked at her. "I'm going."

"But you just said he was killed months ago."

"The bodies are still in the field. I've got to get what's left of him. I'm his older brother; I have to."

The pained look on his face made Esther want to comfort him. But she still felt awkward around him. "I know how important it is to collect the bones," she said gently, "but you can't leave Jerusalem now. It's too dangerous. You've heard what they're saying. The Roman army is coming back. Besides, you won't be able to recognize his body . . . by now."

"I have to try, don't I?" he asked, his voice trembling with emotion. "I'm the big brother, the one who is supposed to take care of him."

She understood his fierce protectiveness. She would go after Matti too.

"When we were little," he said, "I was the one who made the sword, and he was the one who wielded it. No one ever said how beautiful the sword was, how smooth the wood was, or how delicate the carvings in the handle were. They only said how skillfully Natan used it." Lazar's unguarded face revealed a vulnerability she had never seen in him before. "But still, I always fixed it when it broke. I guess this will be the last time I'm the fixer."

The next day, he showed Esther where he had stored tightly sealed jars of dates, figs, dried grains, and nuts in the cellar. Food that wouldn't spoil, that would keep for a while. He had buried more jars in the garden, under the stones next to the back gate. He'd even put some in the bottom of the rain cistern. She hadn't noticed him preparing or hiding them.

Next he led her into the dining room and moved the table. When he pushed down on the edge of one of the corner floor tiles, the opposite edge popped up. He lifted it and showed her where he had buried a large pouch, filled with money, in the sand underneath.

After he replaced the tile, she looked into his eyes. They were good eyes. She was grateful for his trust. Her father had been right. Lazar was a decent man and a good provider. He took his obligations seriously; he protected her and he let her take food to her family. He let Matti visit her every day. He even let Matti bring Ezzi into the house. And mostly, he left her alone at night. She was impure for almost two weeks a month, and she usually waited an extra day or two before going to the *mikveh,* the ritual bath. All in all, her marriage hadn't been as bad as she had feared.

She understood that Lazar was a man who tried to do the right thing, and that his admonitions to her—what to wear and how to act—came from that. He spoke sternly, but he had never hit her, even though he had come close a few times. His anger and arrogance toward her before their wedding had been born of hurt, a hurt she herself had inflicted by making no secret of her feelings. She had scorned and rejected him.

Before he rode off, she grabbed his hand and kissed it. "Be safe," she said in an urgent whisper. "Come back soon."

He looked surprised.

She was too.

CHAPTER LIX

The following week, Esther moved the table and counted out ten shekels, to pay the balance on the ossuaries. Lazar would be gone for a while. When he came back, she would tell him that she'd spent the money on food. Prices had increased so much lately, even for simple grains. Besides, the pouch was still heavy with the remaining coins.

She set off in the direction of Bezetha, with a lightness to her step. She would fulfill her promise to her father. The family would be able to bury the bones. Her father and brother would rise from the dead, and one day they'd all be together again.

"I was waiting for you," Avram said when he saw her. "I didn't know where to deliver them."

"Them? You finished both ossuaries?"

"Of course. He paid the balance."

Esther felt guilty for having taken the coins from Lazar's pouch when he must have taken care of things before he left. And he hadn't even told her.

"I told you I wouldn't accept pagan money," Avram said, "but this time, I made an exception. Besides, any coin is worth the value of its metal."

"He gave you denarii?" That didn't make any sense. Lazar had refused to touch Roman money ever since the mint had become operational.

"What else would a Roman use?"

"A Roman?"

"Well, he didn't come himself, of course. He sent a messenger."

Esther was dumbfounded. He must have gotten her message from Zahara after all. Tiberius was not yet done surprising her.

CHAPTER LX

"LAZAR SHOULD HAVE BEEN BACK BY NOW," ESTHER SAID TO MIRIAM. "It's been two months since he left."

"Maybe he joined one of the rebel groups in the countryside," Miriam said.

Impossible, Esther thought. Lazar had always said he was a silversmith, not a fighter, and that he could contribute more to the war effort by running the mint. She fought off thoughts about what could have happened. If she didn't think about it, it wouldn't be real. He wouldn't have been attacked by robbers, Romans, or a gang of feral dogs. His decomposing body wouldn't be on the side of an abandoned road.

Nor did she want to think about what would happen to her if Lazar didn't come back. That she'd be an agunah, bound to a dead marriage. If there was no witness to his death, she would never be able to marry again. If she had children, they'd be *mamzers,* bastards forbidden to marry other Jews.

Every day she went back and forth from Lazar's house to her own. Finally, after another week with no news, she moved back to her mother's home for good. Lazar's parents tried to convince her to stay. She felt bad about leaving them, but her own family needed her more. She promised to move back as soon as Lazar returned. Before leaving, she lifted the floor tile once again and took the pouch. She found a small chest Lazar had left her too, with silver candlesticks and two bracelets. She packed those in her bag. Silver was valuable and could always be melted down.

Esther poured the dried barley into a jar while Miriam held the jar steady. "We have to seal the jars with gypsum so the weevils don't get to them first," Esther said.

Miriam groaned.

"We're not done yet," Esther said. "There are two more sacks."

Miriam straightened up and stretched backward, her hands on her lower back. "Don't we have enough?"

Esther looked around the cellar. "No, we have a few baskets of salted fish, garlic braids, and some preserves. I don't know what you and Mother have been doing while everyone else has been stockpiling food."

"The priests stored food in warehouses all over the city, and there's enough water from the Gihon Spring. They won't let us starve. Besides, the walls will protect us."

"How can you be so sure?" Esther asked.

"Someone heard a voice in the Temple—"

"I don't believe in voices," Esther scoffed. "I believe in a full cellar."

"Me too, but where are we going to get more food? You've been to the market; there's nothing but fava beans and greens." Miriam sat on a barrel. "Remember when we used to go to the market to look at the amber and touch the silks from the East?"

"I can't think about the past right now." Esther counted the jars of food again. "We don't have nearly enough. If there really is a siege, how long do you think this will last us? Not very long." She wiped her forehead. "Maybe we should leave before the Romans come back." In the last few weeks, hordes of residents had fled the city, including Lazar's parents.

Miriam crossed her arms over her chest. "And go where? The estate is gone, razed to the ground. We can't go to the family in Sepphoris either—unless you want to move to a city already filled with Roman troops. Besides, it's too dangerous to travel now. The roads are filled with desperate refugees and bandits."

Esther sighed and continued to work. They finished storing the barley, then soaked date kernels for animal feed. Esther looked around the cellar. "It's better," she said, "but we still have two empty shelves. I'm going to the market."

"It's a waste of time. Every time I go, prices have doubled," Miriam said.

"So I better go quickly, before they double again."

CHAPTER LXI

A FEW HOURS LATER, ESTHER CAME RUSHING BACK FROM THE MARKET.
"Joseph has been captured. He's in the Roman camp!"

Sarah and Miriam, washing clothes in the courtyard, looked up
in alarm.

"Yodfat fell," Esther said, breathless. "Everyone's talking about
it in the market."

Sarah twisted the tunic in her hands, squeezing out the water
so hard that her face turned red. "Yodfat was the last holdout up
north."

"What did they expect, with Joseph in charge?" Esther said dismissively. She lowered her voice. "People in the market said there
were no survivors. You know what that means."

Her mother flung the tunic back into the tub. "No, I don't! If
Joseph is alive, then Yehuda could be too."

Esther wished she were as hopeful as her mother. She felt like
termites were eating her from within; it was the same feeling she got
whenever she thought about Lazar.

*When will God finally pick up a sword Himself? Can't He just
slay the evil Romans and be done with it?*

Two weeks later, a tall man entered the courtyard pushing a wheel-
barrow with a wounded fighter inside. The fighter's head hung, loll-
ing on his chest. One eye was swollen shut. He moaned.

"We found him on the side of the road, near Nazareth," the man said.

Esther stared. Was that Yehuda? Was he *alive*?

Miriam screamed. Matti scooted to hide behind the loom but peered out. Sarah came running out of the house.

"Bring him inside! Quick!" Esther motioned for the man to follow. "Thank you. It was kind of you to bring him home."

The man dumped Yehuda on the sofa, then stood and looked around the room, making no motion to leave.

Trying to keep her voice steady, she repeated, "I said thank you."

He snarled, "I was expecting something for my trouble."

Miriam came into the room and knelt beside Yehuda.

"Miriam," Esther said. "Tell the *men* that Yehuda is home. Lazar is in the chicken coop and Shimon is out back."

Miriam looked puzzled, but as soon as she opened her mouth, Esther gave her a stern look and said, "Go get them!"

Esther turned back to the man. "I'll give you a reward now, before my husband and brother come. They might not be so generous."

The man stood in place, a suspicious expression on his face.

"Wait outside. If you don't leave, I can't get the money," she said firmly, knowing that she could show no fear.

He looked around once more, then walked slowly back to the courtyard. Esther ran to the study and took a few coins from the pouch at the bottom of the chest.

"Now get out of here!" she hissed at him. "Show respect for my family and my brother."

The man examined the coins in his dirty palm, frowned, and looked up. Panic shallowed her breath, but she placed her hand on her hips, planted her feet shoulder-width apart, and stared without blinking until the man was compelled to look down.

"Lazar! Father!" Esther shouted over his head. "Yehuda's back!"

She prayed he would believe there were really men around and not just two women and a boy.

The man seemed reluctant to leave but finally did. Esther's muscles went slack as she watched him go.

For two days Yehuda slept. Esther put her ear to his mouth to make sure he was breathing. Sarah sponged him down and cleaned his wounds.

Grunting in pain, he tried to lift his head. "Where's Father?"

Esther said nothing, but he read the answer in her eyes.

"I'm glad he can't see me like this," Yehuda murmured.

"Who did this to you?" Esther asked.

"Joseph and I were taken to a Roman camp, and the soldiers tortured me."

"And Joseph? He's alive?"

"Oh, he's alive and doing well. He eats with the Roman general Vespasian." Yehuda closed his eyes again and dozed once more.

His breathing was labored. Then he found the strength. "The Romans broke through the wall. There were only forty of us in a cave in the side of the mountain. We argued about whether it was better to die free than be taken captive. Joseph said that even if we survived, we'd be sent to the mines in Africa or be torn apart by wild beasts in the arena. After a long night of debate—and prayer—we vowed to kill each other. We wrote our names and drew lots: who would be first, who would kill whom. Each man forgave his friend before offering his throat to be slit. I only realized—afterward—that Joseph had manipulated the lots so that he and I would be the last two alive. Then, when we were standing in so much blood that it covered our feet, Joseph said that God had sent him a message that we had to live.

"I was shocked, of course. But part of me still believed in him. Maybe the part that wanted to live. So we came out of the cave and surrendered to the Romans." He rested for a few minutes, then continued. "Joseph put on quite a performance, claiming he had the gift of prophecy and that Vespasian himself would be crowned Emperor! I played along, confirming everything Joseph said."

How could Joseph have dined with the general while the Roman soldiers tortured her brother? She tried to imagine all the ways she could kill him; she could stab him, set him on fire, strangle him, drown him. Now she understood what Tiberius had meant when he'd said he couldn't let go and that he had to avenge Joseph's betrayal.

Esther stayed by Yehuda's bedside.

"Where's Lazar?" Yehuda mumbled.

"He went to find the remains of his brother. Natan was killed in battle. That was almost two months ago and he hasn't come back."

He grimaced. "Whatever God decides will be."

"But what if God isn't deciding?" Esther asked. "What if things just happen, like a rock that rolls down the hill and dislodges another one, and then that one hits another . . . and another?"

For a long while, Yehuda didn't say anything. "Maybe Shimon was right. I always said that the world was proof that there's a God, but Shimon said the world was proof that there wasn't. Maybe my fears were just masquerading as faith."

Esther and her mother took turns feeding Yehuda soup and wiping his brow with a warm cloth.

Yehuda had a far-off look in his eyes. The same distant look Father had had before he died. Esther grabbed Yehuda's hand and stroked it. Her tears fell.

"Don't be sad," he whispered. He closed his eyes and didn't open them again.

At least her brother couldn't feel his pain anymore.

PART ELEVEN

---

*The City became a desolate no man's land where they
flung themselves at each other's throats, and almost
all the grain—enough to support them through many
years of siege—went up in flames. It was hunger
that defeated them, a thing that could never have
happened if they had not brought it upon themselves.*
Flavius Josephus, *The Jewish War* 5.33

*They are not recognized in the streets; their skin has
shriveled on their bones.*

Lamentations 4:8

CHAPTER LXII

ESTHER AND MIRIAM WERE IN THE GARDEN. "IF THE ROMANS WAIT long enough," Esther said, "they won't have to lift a finger to defeat us. We'll all be dead by the time they come back, thanks to the rebels."

"Maybe that's their plan," Miriam replied.

"They've left us alone only because they've been busy with their own war," Esther said. "They'll be back."

Ever since Emperor Nero had committed suicide and civil war had erupted in Rome two years before, the Romans had abandoned their fight against the Jews. News had trickled back to Jerusalem that General Vespasian, whom Nero had appointed to crush the Jewish revolt, had returned to Rome to claim the throne for himself. Joseph's prediction, that Vespasian would become emperor, had come true after all.

Esther closed her eyes and sniffed the air. "I smell something, like baking bread."

"It's not bread. It's the smell of hunger to come," Miriam said. "The rebels must have found another grain warehouse—*for the people!* We had enough food to feed Jerusalem for years. Now there's probably nothing left. How could they burn our own food?"

"If a rival gang controls the warehouse, it's fair game. They don't care about the people. It's Jews against Jews, the same as it was before the Romans ever left."

"All the rebels do is drink and kill," Miriam said.

"No, that's not all. They also kidnap and torture, they melt down the sacred vessels in the Temple, and they dump corpses into the street. I hate the rebels as much as I hate the Romans. They're the ones who turned the city into a battlefield."

Miriam planted herself on the bench next to Esther and said, "What difference does it make who kills us?"

Esther nodded. "We're like the doves watching the crows and buzzards spar. It doesn't matter who wins; we'll get eaten either way."

Miriam interlaced her fingers. Esther still wasn't used to seeing her without a spindle, even though there hadn't been any wool to spin for more than a year. There was nothing to keep them occupied—hardly any animals to take care of, no spinning, no olives to pound, nor beans to shell.

Esther took Miriam's hand in hers and rubbed it between her own. They sat like that for a while, neither speaking.

"I'm eighteen," Esther said at last, staring into the distance. "I was always sure that by this age, I would be mistress of my own house, with two or three children playing in the courtyard. I pictured myself walking through the market, buying fish and cakes for dinner. I'd have a husband—"

"You have a husband."

"I'm an agunah," Esther said. "I'll never be able to remarry or have children. . . ." She bit her bottom lip. "This wasn't how it was supposed to be."

Miriam squeezed Esther's hand. "It never is."

CHAPTER LXIII

"Where's Ezzi?" Matti shouted, running through the courtyard. "I've looked everywhere. She's not in the shed, she's not in—"

"Maybe she made another hole in the fence and got out," Esther said. She checked the back garden. Suddenly she stopped and sniffed. A distinctive smell wafted out from Neshra's house: the gamy odor of goat flesh.

Matti, panting, had followed her. He stopped, and his eyes grew big as the realization of what had happened sank in. Shrieking, he ran to the fence and banged his head against the wooden post. He kept hitting his head until Esther grabbed his shoulders and pulled him back. He fought her as his body shook, racked by coughs. Matti collapsed in her arms, gasping for air. Neshra would deny it, of course.

How dare she take our goat?

But very quickly Esther realized that she was angrier at herself for not thinking of it first. They were hungry too.

Ezzi had been the last of their goats. They'd already eaten the other ones—and the chickens too. They'd had no choice; there had been no more hay or fodder to feed the animals with. There was hardly any produce either; it was a sabbatical year as prescribed in the Bible, a *Sh'nat Shmita,* and nothing had been planted or harvested since the previous fall. For weeks, no food had entered the city. And since the rebels had burned the city's food warehouses, there had been no more grain distributions. People were relying on what little food they'd managed to squirrel away and what edible plants they could find.

Esther had already slipped out of the city a few times to forage for food. Last time, she'd seen a few mulberries. By now, there would be more. There was also a field of amaranth not too far from the gate; they could make bread from the ground seeds. Or rather, what they now called bread. Esther decided she'd go the next day.

"The gates are locked. The rebels won't let you out," Miriam said, "unless you're a slave or a beggar."

"I'll tell the guard I'll split whatever I gather," Esther said. "It worked last time."

"No one's getting out anymore."

"Rabbi Ben Zakkai did."

"That was two weeks ago," Miriam said. "And his students smuggled him out in a coffin."

"If I don't get us more food, we won't have to pretend to be dead."

Miriam drummed her fingers on the table. "Even if you get out, the Romans could find you. And if they do, they'll cut off your hands . . . or worse."

"Where are you going?" her mother asked. For months now, Sarah had been muddled and distracted; she'd go into the courtyard with a basket, stop, and then look around as though she'd forgotten why she was there.

"To get food," Esther said. Sarah threw back her head and cackled, a shrill sound that made Esther shiver.

Esther smiled flirtatiously at the guard and promised to bring him back some mulberries. He opened the gate.

On the way back, she had a full bag of dandelions and sorrels.

They could boil the roots and eat the leaves. She hadn't found the mulberries, but it didn't matter. There was a different guard stationed at the gate. She followed a group of rebels returning from a raid, staying close. The guard barely glanced at her, so she didn't have to share her pickings.

That night, Esther looked for Matti. She looked in every room in the house and shouted his name. At last, she found him outside, sitting behind the unused loom.

"What's wrong?" Esther asked when she saw his tear-streaked face. He was biting his lips. Esther sat next to him.

"I found some honey in the bottom of a jar and ate it all. I'm sorry. I shouldn't have."

Esther draped her arms around his shoulders and pulled him closer. Burying her nose in his hair, she pretended to take a bite out of his head. "You're even sweeter from all that honey. How about a story?"

"But not about Ezzi."

She wished she could think of something to whisk him away from all of this—and her too—to another world, even if it was only a pretend one.

"Tell me the story about the Passover seder," he said, through sniffles, "when you ate so much that your stomach hurt. . . . No, tell me the one about the wedding, when the boy reached into a bag of corn and grabbed a rat's tail." She told him that story, and then another and another. Every time she tried to stop, he said, "Don't stop, Estie. Tell me more."

CHAPTER LXIV

SIX MONTHS PASSED. AT TIMES, THE HOUSE WAS SO COLD THAT THE water froze in the pitchers. They saved any bugs trapped in the ice and ate those too. Knowing that people would steal from their garden, Esther planted radishes in pots on the roof. They grew quickly and helped stave off starvation.

Every so often, Esther would find herself daydreaming, planning an escape—by herself. She would map out a route to the desert in the south, or to Sepphoris in the north. She even thought about surrendering to the Romans in Caesarea. But she knew she would never abandon her family.

During those long, dark months, Esther hardly left the courtyard. She couldn't bear to see what had become of her city. The dead were piled up in abandoned houses, or had been thrown over the walls. Those still alive shuffled through the streets like walking corpses.

During Hanukkah, one rebel group distributed small quantities of oil from the Temple supplies. Another group staged a pageant, with speeches about the coming defeat of the Romans. They promised a new Jerusalem. She didn't want a new Jerusalem. She wanted the old one, the one the rebels had destroyed.

Just when it seemed that spring would never come, it did. The blue of the sky and the gold of the sun poured into the day. It was the first night of Passover.

Esther and Miriam were foraging for herbs in the field behind the launderers' quarter, or rather, what used to be the launderers' quarter. It had been a long time since anyone had cared about bleaching their wool clothes. The area didn't even stink anymore.

"It's hard to believe this is our fourth Passover since the war started," Esther said.

Miriam nodded. "Remember last year, when we scraped together enough money to buy a neck, and it cost as much as the whole lamb used to?"

"And now, we couldn't get that—even if we had bags of gold."

On the way home, they stopped to look at the thousands of Roman soldiers camped on the Mount of Olives and on Mount Scopus. After a hiatus of more than two years the Romans had finally returned, but this time with a new general. Vespasian, who had commanded the Roman troops at the start of the revolt, was now emperor, so he'd sent his son Titus to finish what he'd started. Titus had arrived with four legions to defeat the Jewish rebels once and for all and to restore Roman control over Judea.

The rebels shot arrows at the Roman siege towers positioned just outside the city walls, but the arrows caromed harmlessly off the massive iron-plated structures, like drops of water in a hot pan. Two rebels, so young that their chins were smooth, struggled to set up a catapult launcher, captured from the Romans years before. It was obvious to Esther that the boys had no idea how to operate the machine.

Mule-pulled wagons distributed skins of water to the Roman soldiers training in full view of the Jews on the wall. The soldiers shot at targets, practiced with drawn swords, and marched in tortoise formations with overlapping shields above their heads. Centurions barked out commands. The Jews shouted curses at the Romans, reminding Esther of the last time she'd seen the Roman army outside the wall, four years before. The Jews had taunted the Romans then too, but with much more confidence. Now they knew better.

As Esther and Miriam passed the house of Simeon the physician, Miriam slowed down, crept closer, and peered into a half-covered pot in the garden. She pulled out a small sack, probably something the family had hidden from the rebels. Miriam looked at Esther, but before Esther could respond, Miriam thrust it under her robe. They tore off, and ran the whole way home.

When they reached the courtyard, Miriam opened the sack. It was flour, rancid, with a sharp sour smell and a crumbly texture. She wrinkled her nose. Esther tried to block out what her father would have said about stealing.

That afternoon, Miriam mixed the flour with water and made matzo, the ritual flatbread. Esther set the table with their holiday dishes. The plates, once piled high with sweet dates and apples, carrots with cumin, and succulent roasted lamb, were now empty. Indeed, this night *would* be different from all other nights.

"We're lucky," Esther said, surveying the table.

Miriam wrinkled her brow. "Lucky?"

"Well, maybe not lucky," Esther said, "but still better off than a lot of people." It was true. Many had nothing. Some people had bartered their entire possessions for whatever food they could find—a scattering of moldy grains or a fistful of figs.

Peering into the cooking pot, Matti scrunched up his nose. "What is it? Hay soup?" The pot was filled with water and a few brown flakes that floated to the top. Esther had made a thin soup from an old turnip and some chaff they'd found in an abandoned stable.

"It's lamb stew," Esther said. "You just can't see the lamb."

"Or the stew," added Matti.

"What's for dessert?" Miriam asked. "Nut cakes with no almonds?"

"No, that's for tomorrow." Esther forced a smile, mostly for Matti's sake. She tried to keep his spirits up, but it was hard. She tried to remember the holidays of years past, when their plates had been full and the city had been noisy and joyous.

"I don't remember if I used to be happy," Esther said. "I only remember that I was always worried, but now I don't know why. I had a full belly and parents who worried for me."

That night, the city was silent. People huddled in their houses, fearful of the future. Esther couldn't get the picture of the Roman army out of her mind. Maybe this was how the Israelites had felt the night before they'd fled from Egypt. The Israelite dwellings had been marked with blood, and theirs would be too, once the Romans attacked. They read the story from Deuteronomy, but Esther couldn't bring herself to utter the biblical words "You shall remember that you were a slave in the land of Egypt." She didn't want to think about slavery, about what could happen to her and her family when those battering rams started to pound the walls and the Roman soldiers began fighting for real.

Instead she focused her thoughts on a different part of the story: how Miriam, Moses's sister, cared for him. She looked over at Matti, seemingly content as he sucked on the hard, dried matzo, and she vowed to protect her little brother.

Eight days later, just as the Passover holiday drew to a close, the assault began. The warring rebel factions banded together again, as if they hadn't spent the previous two years tearing the city apart with their fighting. The Romans showered the top of the new wall with arrows and catapulted huge stones into the city. One broke through the roof of a house, and another landed on a woman in her garden, crushing her to death.

The Roman battering rams emerged from the siege towers and began to pummel the wall. The ground shook as if it were splitting apart, and the din was as loud as thunder. The rebels laid wooden boards reinforced with metal over the wall to absorb the impact of the blows, but even that didn't help. The relentless clamor of the battering rams seemed to penetrate the marrow in Esther's bones.

For fifteen days, the tumult continued. On the seventh of Iyar, the earth convulsed as the wall crumbled. Matti flew into Esther's arms.

"What happened?" he cried.

"The Romans broke through the new wall," Esther said. "But it doesn't matter. There are two more."

"Are we going to die?" Matti asked in a small voice.

She hugged him close. "I'm here. I'm here with you." It was all she could say.

Nine days later, the second wall collapsed. A sinister silence followed. Now there was only one wall left, the city's last line of defense.

The clamor had stopped, but the ringing in Esther's ears continued. At least she could talk again without shouting, but she knew it wouldn't be for much longer. If the last wall fell, the only thing left between them and the Romans would be the Temple Mount. All she could do was hope for another miracle.

CHAPTER LXV

AFTER THE SECOND WALL FELL, THERE WAS A LULL IN THE FIGHTING. No one knew how long it would last. There were small skirmishes every day as the rebels attacked the Romans at night, but no fighting within the city.

There was a knock on the door. Esther was surprised to see Zahara, thin and shrunken, a shadow of her former self. Esther was even more surprised when Zahara handed over a small package and said, "It's from Tiberius. He bribed one of the Jewish sentries to bring it in."

She hadn't seen either Zahara or Tiberius for three years.

"He's a sutler in the Roman camp now," Zahara said, "supplying their troops with grain."

Esther eyed the package in her hands. "You didn't keep it for yourself."

"I was tempted, but I'm an honorable person," Zahara said with a raised chin. "Even if no one else thinks so."

As soon as she left, Esther ripped the package open. Inside was a letter, along with figs and almonds. Tiberius would meet her with food at the Serpent's Pool, next to the old aqueduct. She knew that spot, right outside the wall, where she and Miriam used to pick wildflowers.

He wrote that she should tie a scarf to the broken turret, the fourth from the southwest corner, near the Gate of the Essenes, to alert him that she was coming. He'd leave a sign when he was there: a dagger in a crevice of the boulder opposite the gate.

Esther climbed the wall. When no one was looking, she knotted her red scarf around the stone, like Rahab had. God had helped the harlot from Jericho; maybe He'd help Esther too.

An hour later, something flashed in the sun. Squinting, she leaned on the parapet to get a better view. The dagger. He'd seen her scarf! She quickly untied it and flew down the steps toward the gate.

People crowded around, pushing and shouting. When the guard opened the gate to let out a cart loaded with corpses, Esther slipped into the group behind it. Once out, she turned off the road and ran down the rocky slope, scratching her legs on the brambles. Her arms flung out by her sides as she struggled to keep her balance.

I am descending into hell.

When they'd been young, Shimon had threatened to throw Esther here, into the Hinnom Valley, when he wanted to scare her. The weavers used to work here, stirring their boiling, odoriferous vats of dye. The ghosts of children, sacrificed on the fire by ancient pagans, supposedly roamed the valley at night. But she wasn't afraid of ghosts anymore. How could anything be worse than what she'd already seen?

Tiberius stepped out from behind a tree. She recognized him, of course, but he looked different—older. His hair was thinner, and there were more lines and planes on his face. But those eyes—the color of the sea and sky—were the same. She squirmed under his intense gaze.

He held out a water skin, and she took a big swig, and then another. Their eyes met, but they didn't talk. When he offered her bread, she snatched it out of his hands and stuffed it into her mouth. Immediately her gut felt as though it were turning inside out. Putting a fist into her mouth, she waited until the nausea passed. Tiberius placed a hand on her shoulder. She stiffened, before moving away.

Esther was the first to speak. "If you wanted to help, why didn't you come earlier?"

"I was in Alexandria. I left Jerusalem when I couldn't route my shipments through the port of Caesarea anymore. I ended up staying, working with the same Roman businessmen and Nabataean middlemen I'd worked with before. It was the only way to keep the expensive perfumes and spices flowing to Rome from the East. This war hasn't stopped trade. Besides, you told me to stay away, remember?

"I needed money. I found the contract for your shipping deal with my father. Why didn't you give me the proceeds from the deal?"

"What good is money now, when one date costs fifty shekels?"

"How do *you* know that?" she asked.

"I have sources inside. And besides, if I wanted your money, I wouldn't be here trying to keep you alive." He reached into a sack and pulled out a leather pouch. "Here."

She opened the pouch. Inside were shiny bronze coins, newly minted. She held one up and examined the inscription: *Redemption of Zion.*

Redemption. She scowled. The coins from the first year of the revolt had proclaimed *Freedom of Zion.* Evidently the leaders had given up on the dream of freedom. All they had to offer now was redemption, as if the revolt were out of their hands and only God could save them.

She pulled the strings taut, closing the pouch. "This isn't all."

"No, but any more could be dangerous. If people think you have money, they'll kill you—and your family—for it. This is more valuable." He unwrapped a package of dried fruit and nuts, salted fish, and hard cheese.

She stared. So much food. She'd have to make sure they ate it slowly so their stomachs could adjust. Her mouth watered and she reached for a fig, then closed her eyes so she could concentrate on the sweet chewiness and the crunch of the seeds. She was convinced she'd never eaten anything so delicious in her whole life.

"Come with me," he said. "Most of the merchants and traders have women with them. If you're with me, you'll be safe."

"Where?"

"The Roman camp. I'm running the grain caravans."

Esther stared at him incredulously. "You want me to abandon my family and come with you to the *Roman* camp?"

"If you go back inside, you're dead," he said. "Until now, your brave leaders have been bartering with us and smuggling supplies in for themselves. Soon that's going to end and there won't be any food in the city."

"There's already no food. That's why I have to bring them this," she said, pointing to the packages of food on the ground.

"I can try to get them out. I still have contacts. I'll bribe the rebels."

Esther shook her head. "Mother can hardly walk; she'd never make it. How could we leave her?"

Tiberius looked exasperated. "You'll all die if you stay! If you're lucky enough to survive, you'll be taken away in chains. If you knew what slavery was, you wouldn't go back. You'd understand."

"If you knew what family was, you'd understand."

For a minute, neither spoke. "I do understand," he said, in a sad voice. "The day the Romans came, I was seven. I remember it was a beautiful day—I was catching butterflies. My father had already gone off to fight, and soldiers came to our farmhouse. I hid in the trees, but I heard the screams. My mother and sister . . . She was ten." He covered his ears. "My sister didn't survive; she died a few days later. My mother and I were shipped, with all the rest of the captives, to Rome." He squeezed his eyes tightly, as though he were trying not to cry.

She knew he was sharing a part of himself that had been buried deep, beneath the scars. Maybe he did understand, after all.

Tiberius hung his head, then said, "I'll watch you go as far as the gate, in case there are any soldiers lurking around, but I can't go with you. The rebels might be watching."

She took another look at the delicacies arrayed on the ground. "I'll have to hide this. Otherwise the guards will take it." She stood up and stuffed as many of the nuts and dates into her undergarments as would fit. She wrapped the dried fig cakes around her thigh.

"I'll take the rest back," Tiberius said, picking up what she couldn't take.

"No!" Esther's forcefulness seemed to surprise them both. "Hide it here, behind the rocks. I'll come back later."

Tiberius nodded. "All right, and remember, if you need me, leave a sign. I'll meet you here with more food."

Esther started up the hill, clumsy and staggering because of the food tied to her legs. She prayed nothing would fall out. After a few ungainly steps, she turned around. There was still something she wanted to say. "You paid for the ossuaries, didn't you?"

Tiberius gave a slight shrug. "Your father was my friend. A true one."

"Thank you," she whispered.

CHAPTER LXVI

THE FOOD TIBERIUS HAD GIVEN HER TWO WEEKS BEFORE WAS GONE. They were down to two jars of "stinkies"—dried sardines that had already started to decay—and some old vegetables. Matti hunted grasshoppers and picked the wild mallow growing around the city. But it was hardly enough for four people, even though Sarah barely ate. For the previous ten days, she had been delirious and bed-ridden.

Esther tossed a few weeds and their last dried mushroom into a boiling pot of water.

"We'll starve if we don't get more food," Esther said. "I'll try to make contact with Tiberius again."

Miriam shook her head. "The rebels have closed all the gates. No one can get out anymore."

"I'll go through the tunnels," Esther said with a confidence she didn't feel. She shuddered at the thought of the tunnels, teeming with sewage and rats the size of cats. But the tunnels drained out of the city and were now her only exit.

Esther tied her scarf to the turret, but after two days, there was still no sign from Tiberius. She couldn't wait any longer. Even if the food he'd hidden for her was gone, she could still scout the fruit of the thistles, the sour berries of the thorn bushes, and the nuts of the tumbleweeds. She'd take the knife Tiberius had given to her father.

The public *mikvehs* near the Ophel connected to the drainage

274

ditches under the Temple Mount. From the baths, Esther found the steps leading to the lower level. She entered a narrow passage carved in the rock and ran alongside the wet walls, then came out of a small hole that she had to bend down to squeeze through. She blinked as she came out of the tunnel into the sunlight and took a deep breath.

The tightness in her chest faded. The warmth of the sun on her skin reminded her of those long-ago days when she'd scoured the hills for crocuses, following the goats and singing with the wind. Now she reveled in the hushed sounds: the rustling of the leaves and the trill of the birds.

But as she looked around, an uneasy feeling crept through her. The majestic pine trees that used to pierce the clouds were gone. The tamarisks and oaks were gone. The towering sycamore with its twisted trunk and intertwined branches that had spread out like a mythical sea creature—the one she and Matti had loved to climb— was gone. The Romans had stripped the land bare for its timber.

Thankfully, the patch of wild sorghum was still there. She walked toward the bronze spikelets waving in the wind. She had once collected these grains for animal feed. Now they would make a feast for her family. She continued picking until she looked up and spotted two figures approaching. White-hot fear filled her lungs and mouth, leaving her breathless. The sun, so warm and enveloping just minutes before, now blinded her with a menacing glare.

Roman soldiers. What were they doing here in the southwest corner of the city? The Roman camp was far away, and all the Roman attacks were directed against the city's northern walls. No Roman soldiers had ever been stationed here, or even regularly patrolled this steep and treacherous valley. Perhaps Titus had sent patrols around the entire city to catch any Jews trying to escape. She swallowed and slowly, cautiously, took a step backward, trying to maintain her balance even though she felt light-headed. A prickling sensation in her hands spread to her arms and legs, as if her blood had been replaced by ice.

She dropped her bag, and the grain scattered, and was then blown away by the wind. The soldiers came closer. One was tall, with hair the color of a rusty plow blade, and the other was stocky with dark curls. Each of them had the soldier's skirt, and a knife strapped to his waist.

She ran. She didn't feel the ground or the thorns and bristles scraping her legs. When the shorter one lunged at her, she fell to the ground. He pinned her down, his eyes gleaming with the excitement of a hunter who has nabbed his prey.

"What have we here, sweet fruit for the picking?"

The other soldier, a piece of straw dangling from his mouth, sauntered closer. He muttered something she couldn't understand. They both laughed.

"I have money. I know a Roman trader. He'll pay you," Esther said, her voice coming out in a high-pitched, breathless squeak. "His name is Tiberius. He's in your camp."

She writhed and tried to push the soldier off her. It was happening so fast, she could only comprehend in glimpses. She saw the blister on the bottom of the soldier's lip, heard the whoops of the second soldier, and felt the roughness of the ground beneath her. She spit at him, and he looked stunned, momentarily. He covered her mouth; she couldn't breathe. She bit his hand, and he hit her so hard that her ear rang. The coppery taste of blood filled her mouth. She had never been struck like this before, and the pain brought everything into sharp focus.

Looking up into his leering face, she willed herself to calm down, to think. She scrunched the fabric of her tunic until she could feel the knife tied to her thigh; she wrapped her hand around it. With a snarl like a wild dog, she raised the knife, then shoved it into his back. The soldier screamed and rolled off. The other one stopped laughing and quickly came to see. When he pulled out the knife, Esther sprung up and fled, stumbling over the rocky ground, gulping for air. She looked back. The soldier was coming after her!

Another figure loomed ahead. A man with his feet planted in a wide stance and his hands on his hips.

"Halt!" he thundered at the soldier. "What are you doing here?" *Tiberius!*

The soldier slowed. He regarded Tiberius warily, perhaps studying his civilian garb.

"I am on General Titus's staff," Tiberius said in an imperious tone. "You're supposed to be patrolling the walls, not hunting. Now get back to your station, or I'll have you strung up and flogged!"

The soldier looked unsure. Then he lowered his head and mumbled something that Esther couldn't hear.

"Now!" thundered Tiberius.

The soldier looked back at his companion bleeding and writhing on the ground.

Tiberius followed the soldier's eyes, then said, "Go to the camp and call the medics to tend to this man. Hurry!"

The soldier took off.

Tiberius ran to Esther. Sobs tore through her as she clutched his tunic, crushing her face into his chest. He held her tight as she cried until she was limp and exhausted.

"Did they . . . hurt you?" Tiberius asked as he tilted her face up, rubbing his thumb on her wet cheek.

She shook her head. She wanted to tell him what had happened, but her lips seemed soldered together.

He continued to hold her close. "I was gone for a few days, supervising a delivery. I came as soon as I saw the scarf."

A shaky smile slid onto her face. "I guess you were busy with General Titus . . . now that you're on his staff, that is."

He managed a weak grin back. "I'm not surprised the soldier believed me. If you speak forcefully enough, people will listen . . . everyone except you." He looked into her eyes. "Aster, you *must* come with me," he said, his voice laced with urgency.

She put a hand on his chest and took a step back. "I can't leave my family."

"The siege wall is going up. Haven't you seen the carts filled with wood and stones? Once the wall is finished, nothing and no one will go in or go out. The Romans will completely surround the city. The Fifteenth, Twelfth, and Fifth legions are on their way. The Tenth is already east of the city on the Mount of Olives. That's more than sixty thousand men! In addition to the Roman legions, there are auxiliary forces from Syria and reinforcements from provinces nearby."

"Our fighters—"

"Your *fighters*?" Tiberius interrupted. "The only experience you Jews have is fighting each other. Your *fighters* don't have any professional training and don't even have standard weapons, except for the few they captured from the Romans or the ones I sold them."

"But God is on our side," she said, hating the doubt in her voice.

Tiberius waved his arms dismissively and leaned in, placing his hands on her shoulders. "Aster, listen to me. No one walks back into a Roman siege."

"I'd rather die with my family than abandon them."

He started to say something, then shook his head, defeated. His face was lined with worry, and something else too, something that made her look away. But it couldn't be anything more than pity.

CHAPTER LXVII

ESTHER WIPED HER MOTHER'S BROW WITH A COOL CLOTH. THE HEAT of the day had receded, but Sarah's bedroom was filled with thick, sticky air.

"I forgive you," Sarah whispered. Her once hawk-like eyes looked like dabs of mud.

"For what?" Esther asked.

"For killing Precious."

Esther continued stroking her mother's brow. For months, Sarah had been mumbling to herself and saying strange things.

"He died before I was born," Esther said softly. "How could I have killed him?" She dipped the cloth in water and wrung it out.

"You lodged yourself in my womb so soon after I birthed him that my milk dried up. I was so weak, I couldn't pick him up."

Her mother touched Esther's face. "I blamed you, but it wasn't your fault. I always loved you. Maybe I even loved you the best, because you were like me. But I gave you a different kind of love. I didn't want you to get used to the easy kind, the kind you might not have gotten later on. See, you were always soft. Too soft. Soft women don't survive."

For the first time in her nineteen years, she understood her mother. And she felt compassion too for this weak old woman who still managed to surprise her. Esther lifted Sarah's hand. Her skin was so thin, it was like holding bones. Her finger joints were swollen and misshapen, and a web of blue veins protruded. This hand, which had expertly poured and mixed medicines, had picked Esther up when she'd fallen, cleaned her cuts, and fed her, was now lifeless and limp.

"I love you," Esther said, marveling at the ease with which she could now say the words that had been stuck for so long.

Sarah smiled weakly, revealing bloody gums and black teeth. She closed her eyes.

They would not open again.

At least her mother would be spared what was to come. The Roman siege wall was up. Tiberius had been right; it was now too late to escape. They were trapped.

PART TWELVE

The Romans piled the dead bodies in heaps in the streets. The flow of blood was so great that in many places it extinguished the fire. Toward evening the killing stopped. But the fire prevailed all that night.

And on 8 Elul, morning broke on Jerusalem ablaze.

Flavius Josephus,
The Jewish War 6.406–407

They will besiege all your towns until your high, fortified walls, in which you trusted, collapse everywhere in your land, which the Lord your God gave you. Then, because of the severity of the siege and distress that your enemies are inflicting on you, you will eat the offspring of your own body, the flesh of your own sons and daughters, whom the Lord your God has given you.

Deuteronomy 28:52–53

CHAPTER LXVIII

ON THE NINTH OF AV, THE INEVITABLE HAPPENED: THE ROMANS BROKE through. The wall's monstrous stones crashed to the ground. *This is it. The End of Days. Is this the earthquake that's supposed to be the sign of the Messiah?*

The thunderous booms that shook the house were followed by a momentary silence. Then came the cries, like birds of prey shrieking; the sounds from men so exhausted from hunger that they could hardly lift a sword.

Esther raced up to the roof. The scene was utter pandemonium: everyone trying to outrun the Romans, some climbing over a still-standing section of the wall to get out of the city, and others running in the opposite direction, toward the Temple.

"We have to go!" Esther shouted as she bounded down the steps.

The Romans were flooding in, their bloodcurdling cries getting louder every minute. Esther, Miriam, and Matti ran down to the street, and were immediately swept up in the swarm of people rushing toward the Temple Mount. Mothers screamed as they lost sight of their children. Others fell and were trampled underfoot.

As they neared the bridge, Esther saw the Roman troops coming toward them.

"Quick, this way!" she yelled, pulling Miriam and Matti with her. They turned off the road and clambered down the rocky slope.

At the bottom, they merged with a throng of people rushing toward the Huldah Gates. Some carried cooking pots and blankets;

others, fine clothes. Apparently no one knew what they'd need when the Messiah came. Esther shuddered. When these people reached the Temple, it wouldn't be the Messiah waiting for them, but Roman soldiers ready to slaughter them like innocent lambs.

Esther stopped when they reached Huldah's tomb, just below the stairs to the Temple Mount. The crowd continued to surge past.

"Why did you stop?" Miriam screamed. "The sanctuary is up here!"

"We're going to the tunnels," Esther said. If they could get down there, they had a chance.

"No!" Miriam shook her head, wild-eyed. "The kingdom of God will begin in the Temple. Our Book says the Messiah will save us in the sanctuary."

"He can find us in the tunnels too!"

"I'm not going." Miriam looked toward the Royal Stoa on the southern edge of the Temple Mount. "The prophet Daniel said the End of Days will be in God's house—"

"Miriam, it's suicide to run *toward* the Roman soldiers! We can go through the Kidron Valley, hide in one of the tombs or caves. We'll climb over the Roman siege wall at night and make our way to the desert—"

"Everyone's going to the Temple," Miriam said. "Come on!" She grabbed Matti's hand and turned to join the frantic horde.

For a split second, Esther hesitated. Then she followed them up the steps.

We have to stay together.

CHAPTER LXIX

THEY REACHED THE TEMPLE COMPOUND AS HUNDREDS OF ROMAN soldiers flooded in from the other side with drawn swords and lit torches. A fusillade of javelins rained down from the sky. Confusion and terror on their faces, people fled in every direction.

Esther, Miriam, and Matti dashed through the columns of the Royal Portico, dodging pieces of burning wood falling from the ceiling. The crowd fell one by one, pierced by arrows and stabbed by swords, knees buckling and arms flailing. Some of the soldiers slipped in the blood, their armor clanging as they hit the ground. The moans and groans of the mangled and the half dead filled the air.

A wall of fire burst out of the Temple, spewing live ash and thick black smoke. The gold on the doors dripped downward, exposing the wood beneath and sending vapors of molten metal into the air. The earth spasmed as if its core were boiling over. Some people yelled *"Shema Yisrael!"* and dove into the flames. The End of Days had arrived.

Corpses piled up near the altar, and blood poured down the sanctuary steps. There was so much blood, it looked as if the Temple itself were bleeding. A side door blew open and an explosion shook the ground. A plume of ash and debris billowed in the sky. Esther stopped short, barely missing a ball of flames reeking of burning oil. She looked back in horror to find Miriam caught in the flames. Yellow and red waves shot down her back, devouring her tunic and flesh. Miriam shrieked as she ran, trying to rip off her tunic. She staggered and fell.

The flames sizzled in the blood on the ground and were extinguished.

Esther collapsed on her knees next to Miriam.

"Run!" Miriam gasped.

"I'm not leaving you!"

"Go!" Miriam said. "Save yourself and Matti!"

A sound louder than she'd ever heard hammered Esther's ears. Pieces of the ceiling came crashing down, chunks of plaster and stone smashed to the floor, and columns collapsed. Seeing soldiers approaching, Esther seized Matti's hand. He was covered in ash and was bleeding. Esther pulled him away, but after a few steps, she turned around. She couldn't see Miriam anymore, only a pile of tangled limbs. The bodies on top slithered down, as if the dead were moving.

People leapt from the walls and from the top of the portico, their arms outstretched as they fell through the sky. Their screams were drowned out in the clashing inferno amplified by the hollowed hall.

Esther's eyes stung; the air was thick with smoke and an acrid smell of burnt flesh. Everywhere was a sight more horrific than the last: A soldier raised his sword and brought it down on an old man trying to crawl away. The man's severed head hung on the front part of his neck, but he was still moving. The soldier kicked him. A woman with an arrow buried in her head ran past with a lifeless child in her arms.

Please, God, save us!

Why was she praying? There was no God here.

Someone grabbed her by the hair. Yowling, she twisted and

flailed her arms, trying to escape. "Matti!" she screamed, as he was lost to the chaos.

She bit and kicked. The soldier uttered incomprehensible threats in Latin. She couldn't think; there was only instinct and fear. But the instinct was to live; it was stronger than the fire, stronger even than her body, which was coughing, sputtering, and aching.

CHAPTER LXX

ESTHER, ALONG WITH HUNDREDS OF OTHER CAPTIVES, WAS TAKEN TO A field lit with torches. The red flames illuminated the faces of the Roman soldiers. She stared at the barren night sky, now a gray expanse filled with clouds of noxious smoke. The stars were gone.

The Romans have wiped out the heavens too.

A girl lying next to her alternated between guttural groans and high-pitched shrieks. The skin on her calves was black and charred, so burned away that muscle and bone were exposed.

All around, the survivors whimpered and coughed. Esther put her head on her knees, trying not to think about the terror Matti must have felt when they'd been separated. Maybe he was moaning like that girl; maybe his leg was burned down to the bone too; maybe he was calling her name. Was he waiting for her to find him? Or was his body lying in a mound of corpses rotting in the heat?

Esther dozed, but then woke with a start, feeling like she was drowning in a cauldron of heat. Closing her eyes, she concentrated on swallowing and breathing, anything to stop the spasm of coughs that pounded her sternum.

She drifted back into a fitful sleep, but was awakened by trumpet blasts and a changing of the guard. A procession of Roman soldiers filed past, their arms filled with spoils from the Temple. The laughing soldiers dumped the loot onto the ground: gold tables, jeweled bowls, and bolts of cloth. More soldiers hauled a cart with the seven-branched golden menorah. The menorah, as tall as a man, was down on its side, and its light, which was supposed to burn eternally, was now extinguished and shamed. The sight stunned all the prisoners into silence.

How could God have allowed this?

The sun rose, and it was hot. Esther's eyes were puffy and dry, and her throat felt as if it were filled with shards of glass. The girl next to her, whose eyelids were so swollen that her face was a grotesque mask of agony, called for her mother. Esther wanted her mother too. She felt herself choking, now on guilt. She had lost Matti and Miriam. She should have had a plan; she should have protected them. Why was she the one still alive?

She looked around. More captives were here than had been last night. The sight of so many survivors gave her a sliver of hope. Maybe her brother had survived. A group approached: six soldiers and three men on horseback. The middle rider looked like Joseph, but he was dressed like a Roman, talking to a Roman centurion.

It was him. There was no mistaking that black wavy hair and those flinty eyes. A surge of life coursed through her, and she scrambled to her feet, waving her arms. She tried calling his name, but she could manage only a raspy growl before convulsing into coughs. She swallowed and tried again. She stepped over and around people, trying to get closer. The group moved farther away, but she ran after them, screaming his name.

He stopped.

Joseph pointed at her, then turned away before she had a chance to say anything more. He acted like he was in a hurry, riding through the survivors, picking people out. Two of the soldiers came for her.

"Where are you taking me?" she cried as she walked, struggling to keep up with the soldiers as they half dragged her away. They didn't answer.

The soldiers led her to another field. She looked around,

searching desperately for Matti. Her legs were wobbly, and she stumbled a few times. Each time, the soldiers yanked her up and ordered her to keep going. Finally they reached another group, smaller than the first. She recognized almost everyone—all priests or their families. People from the Upper City. And there was Matthias, Joseph's older brother! Surely Joseph wouldn't let any harm come to his own brother.

"Have you seen Matti?" she asked whomever she could, but no one had. She didn't ask about Miriam. The only way Miriam could still be alive was if the soldiers had carried her.

Toward afternoon, soldiers herded the group together. No one knew where they were going, but at last there was hope, especially once Joseph joined them, riding in front on a white mare.

As Esther walked, another group of captives entered the camp. Most of them were bloodied and burned, and could barely walk. She saw a small, gaunt silhouette dragging behind, trying to keep up with the group. She squinted as the figure retreated in the hazy vista. It was . . . Could it be . . .

Esther stopped. "Matti!" She was sure, even though she was still far away and the boy didn't lift his head. She broke away from the group, shrieking his name while she ran.

A soldier grabbed her by the waist and held her back. She kicked him and hit his face. He cursed at her and yelled something to the soldiers in front. Joseph turned on his horse, and his eyes locked with Esther's.

He came closer and motioned for the soldier to release her.

"Joseph, Matti is right there!"

"I'm Flavius Josephus now."

"That's a Roman name! You're a Jew!"

"I'm a Jew, and now a Roman too. Don't look so surprised. I'm not the only one; Titus's chief of staff is a Jew. And King Agrippa—"

"I don't care," Esther shouted. "Please, Matti! Joseph—Josephus—please! I have to get my little brother!"

"Esther!" he said sharply, pronouncing her name like a command. "I convinced Titus to let me spare my family and a few of my friends. That's all. I chose you because of your father and Yehuda—"

"Who is dead because of you! At least save his brother!"

Joseph's mouth twisted in annoyance. He gathered his reins.

"I'm not leaving without Matti," she shouted. "I have money. I can buy him! I have a contract with Tiberius."

Joseph smirked. "Even if you had the contract, it would be worthless. No Roman court will honor a contract between an ex-slave and the daughter of a dead Jew, now a slave herself. Besides, your brother isn't mine to sell. He belongs to the new emperor Vespasian now, like all the captives."

"But you know the emperor; you could talk to him," Esther pleaded.

"You should be thankful that you'll live. General Titus said I could save fifty, and not one more."

"Then now you have forty-nine." She glared at Joseph. He shrugged his shoulders, and Esther ran toward the other group, screaming her brother's name.

CHAPTER LXXI

MATTI'S HAIR WAS SINGED AND HIS FACE WAS FILTHY. HIS NECK COULD barely hold up his head. Esther pulled him close, feeling his protruding ribs and the knobs of his vertebrae. His arms hung limply by his side. She cupped his face in her hands and looked into his eyes. They were empty, registering neither surprise nor joy at seeing her. She'd found him, but he wasn't there. She dropped her arms, not sure what to do. But when she looked away, he clutched her wrist and wouldn't let go.

They were marched with the other captives in a column almost a mile long, six in a row, with Roman soldiers on each side. The air was grainy and thick. She breathed deeply, wanting to inhale the smoke and ash, filling herself with the charred remains of Jerusalem. It was all she'd have, those particles of dust. The muscles in her chest and abdomen contracted, and she coughed, expelling the last bits of what had once been her home. Even her own body refused to let her take anything with her.

She wanted to turn around for one last look at the still smoldering city, but she didn't want to remember it like this: a city with its heart gouged out. The desolation would be forever seared in her memory. The place where heaven had once met earth had now turned into hell. She felt as if her angels were warning her not to look, like they had warned Lot's wife. But she had to bear witness.

She'd already said goodbye so many times, to so many things—

to eating hot bread smeared with honey, to searching for saffron in the hills, to ambling through the spice market, to listening to the Levites' songs. To her mother and father. To Shimon, Yehuda, and Miriam. To her dreams. To her past.

Don't look! Keep your eyes down, at the rocks, the dirt, the weeds, and the trees. They're the lucky ones. They get to stay where they are. The game board etched on the street near the dove mart, the olive trees rooted to the earth, and the hillside dotted with sprigs of green—they all stay.

Look! This is your last chance. Soon we'll descend into the valley and it will be too late.

Don't look!

Look!

She turned around, slowly. Shafts of sunlight shot through the clouds. Opalescent rays descended from the heavens to the blistered earth, forming a canopy of light over the empty space on the horizon where the Temple had once stood. She blinked, still not believing that it was really, *truly* gone; that the Temple—God's house—had now been reduced to a rubble of stone and ash, painted with blood and festooned with corpses. Only the wall on the western side of the Temple Mount still stood, gleaming white. She looked to the Upper City, where her house had been. The neighborhood was leveled too.

Vultures soared high above the trees. Once, the sight would have thrilled her. She loved watching birds fly, seemingly still, yet soaring through the air, in perfect formation. But now their flight riveted her with fear. She stood in place, unable to move until Matti's insistent tugs on her hand pierced her consciousness. She forced herself to keep going. She had to keep going, if only for him.

Mile after mile, they trudged alongside hundreds of other prisoners under a glaring, unrelenting sun, their backs to Jerusalem.

Matti hardly spoke. Even though her mouth was parched and her throat still in terrible pain, Esther tried to tell him stories and even sing to him. Her voice was the only thing she had.

When people fell to the ground, from hunger, heat, or exhaustion, the other prisoners walked around them. Whoever stopped would be clubbed. The soldiers would kick the fallen bodies to see if they were still alive. Sometimes they'd be thrown onto the supply carts, but usually they were simply rolled off to the side of the road. Maybe they were the lucky ones.

One night, after they'd been walking for a few days, a skeleton of a man approached her, torn rags barely covering his body. "I was at your wedding," he said. He talked about Lazar. It seemed they had been friends.

The man's words floated in the air, as if they were in a foreign language, just meaningless sounds, with nothing to anchor themselves to in this new world.

"Too bad about what happened to him," he said.

"What happened?" Esther asked. "All I know is that he went to claim his brother's body."

"He never made it," the man said. "He was killed on the way there. We were ambushed by Roman soldiers. Only two of us managed to escape."

"You *saw* him killed?" Esther asked. So there had been a witness to her husband's death after all. "I'm no longer an agunah." A bitter laugh escaped her lips. "I'm free."

CHAPTER LXXII

THEY WALKED OVER HILLS, THROUGH FORESTS AND FIELDS. THEY slept on the hard ground. Their first stop was Caesarea, where they learned that Titus was holding games to celebrate his victory over the Jews. *Games.* How could God reward people like this, who turned abominations into entertainment?

Everyone knew about the murderous spectacles the Romans loved. People told stories of gladiators fighting until death and women torn to bits by tigers. The more the blood flowed, the more the crowd roared. Esther had seen enough blood to last a lifetime.

When they arrived at the port, they were told to wash in the sea. Surely, Esther told herself, the Romans wouldn't bother to let them bathe if they were going to be killed. Ships were moored off a wide pier that jutted out into a massive basin formed by the seawalls. Sailors and merchants hurried along, slaves rolled barrels and heaved crates, and fisherman repaired their nets.

Esther stood in awe of the busy port and the beauty of the ocean's infinite blueness. Still holding Matti's hand and their shoes, she took a few tentative steps into the swash, letting the warm mud seep through her toes and the water lap around her legs. Matti dropped her hand to scoop up the water and fling it into the air. The gesture was so playful, so innocent that it brought tears to her eyes. Even here, even now, Matti was still a child seeing the sea for the first time. She scrubbed herself, using the mud to scrape off the dirt that had turned her skin black. She hated the filth. She had gotten used to the gnawing hunger in her gut but not the dirt beneath her fingernails and her grimy feet. She used to dream of food. Lately she dreamed of baths: the warm bath in her house that she'd dip into before the *mikveh*. She tried to clean Matti's face, but he wouldn't stand still; he was jumping up in the water, chasing the small waves rolling onto the shore. She looked at him in amazement. She felt a glimmer of something—if not exactly hope, then possibility. She looked from Matti's face—the face of a young boy once more—to the horizon.

How could God *not* be here? Who else could have created something so big, stretching out in all directions as far as the eye could see? The words of the creation story came to her: *Now the earth was formless and empty, darkness was over the surface of the deep, and the Spirit of God was hovering over the waters.* The ocean's vastness made her feel small and more insignificant than a speck of dust or a single grain of sand, yet still a part of it all, and again, for the first time in a long, long time, she felt His presence.

That afternoon, hundreds of captives, white with terror, were picked out and ordered to strip naked. Hands tied, they were loaded onto carts. The soldiers laughed and said they were fortunate; they'd get to see the famous amphitheater. As they rolled away, one of the captives stuck his head through the spokes of the big wheel and broke his own neck.

The rest of the captives, including Esther and Matti, were rounded up and led toward a waiting ship. From there, they sailed to Alexandria, where there were more selections, and more games. Then on to Ostia, where they were put onto barges and pulled up the Tiber to Rome. From the more than two thousand captives who'd started the march a month ago, only a few hundred were still alive.

CHAPTER LXXIII

ESTHER KNEW WHAT WAS COMING. SINCE THEIR ARRIVAL IN ROME TWO weeks before, they had been treated better. Not like people, perhaps, but at least like valuable animals. The guards made them smear themselves with resin from the terebinth tree to make their skin supple, and fed them double rations to fatten them up. For the first time in years, she wasn't hungry. They even got real bread; it was so hard that she could barely chew it, and her mouth was full of grit from all the sand in the flour. Still, she relished the feel of food in her mouth.

For a few hours a day, they were allowed outside into a large pen. The men were shackled at the ankle, but the women and children were not. Matti and another little boy played in the dirt, making marks with sticks. Esther savored the sight; maybe Matti didn't know the fate that awaited them. But every so often, he looked up with an anxious expression.

When he saw Esther, the worry in his face disappeared and he turned back to his game. But then he'd look up again, with that wild fear in his eyes, to make sure she was close. Matti was eleven now, but looked much younger. She felt ancient, an old woman at nineteen. She prayed they'd be sold together, although she knew that was unlikely.

People talked, they speculated, they prayed. Esther hadn't talked to Matti about what could happen; she didn't want to scare him. That night, she whispered to him, "Remember, God will take care of you."

"I don't want God. I want you," he said.

She looked into his eyes, so defenseless and trusting. She was overwhelmed by a sense of helplessness. Should she arm him with faith—however false—or the truth? Tears stung her eyes. "Yes, I promise. I promise I'll . . ." *I'll what?* It didn't matter; he seemed satisfied. Whatever she had said, it was enough. She wished she could believe in herself as much as he did.

He lay his head in her lap. Esther wished Miriam were there too. She smiled, imagining Miriam telling her to stop feeling sorry for herself, telling her that a living dog was better than a dead lion. Esther missed her so much that she could feel the longing in her chest. She missed searching for angels together; she missed the way Miriam's long, bony fingers used to rub her feet at night; and she missed the way Miriam would look at her with those half-moon eyes. She even missed Miriam's constant countenance of irritation and condescension. She knew that Miriam's scowl had been merely a mask for a love too timid to announce itself.

The next morning the guards set up long iron troughs filled with brackish water. As Esther washed herself, she thought of the baths back home: their colorful mosaics; the clear, flowing spring water; the floral frescoes on the barrel-vaulted ceiling. She closed her eyes so that she could see only the memories.

In a little while, they would be put onto the auction block.

CHAPTER LXXIV

ESTHER AND MATTI, ALONG WITH EIGHT OTHER CAPTIVES, WERE chained together at the ankle. After walking slowly because of the heavy iron fetters, they reached the market, a large public square bordered by colonnades.

She heard fragments of conversations as they walked through the crowd:

"Don't go to that dealer. He sold me a defective one and wouldn't take him back."

"They're all swindlers."

"I would never buy a freeborn slave."

"Egyptian boys make the best pets."

Rows of men, women, and children stood on wooden platforms set up all along the perimeter of the square. The atmosphere was festive, and the crowd boisterous. She found herself thinking of the treading in Jerusalem. People milled around, shouted greetings to friends, drank, ate, and inspected the slaves.

The dealer's assistant, a young man with a self-important expression on his oily face, prodded her with a stick. One of the other captives told her to say she had a trade. Otherwise she'd end up in a brothel. Esther didn't know the word for "healer" in Latin. She said she knew plants that could make you feel better. She pretended to hold a bowl and mix. The assistant wrote something on a wooden sign and draped it around her neck. He marked her feet with white chalk, signifying her status as a new slave, and pushed her toward the stage, behind the men and women already crammed together there. She clutched Matti's hand.

"The price of slaves has plummeted," the dealer bellowed. "Only six, seven hundred *sestertii*. Can you afford *not* to get one?"

From her perch, Esther looked out at the mob. Newly purchased slaves were led through the crowd. One looked like Zahara, but Esther couldn't be sure.

In the meantime, several customers had climbed up to inspect the captives.

"You've only got Jews?" one asked.

"A fresh batch," the dealer answered.

"Jews don't make good slaves. They're unwilling to submit; everyone knows that."

"You just have to break them in."

"Hey, this one has his tongue cut out!"

"That's not a defect; it's an advantage!" the dealer said, laughing like a hyena.

A buyer approached. Long strands of sparse hair on the side of the man's head were combed over a bald scalp, and a round belly strained the fabric of his toga. Small squinty eyes studied her and Matti.

The dealer greeted him, "Proculus, how good to see you again!"

The man barely glanced at the dealer. "The last one you sold me had an eye infection, and the one before that was a thief."

"I got a new shipment. Let's see if we can do better this time."

The dealer made her strip. The man wanted to not only inspect, but also handle, every part of her body.

Lift your arms. Bend over.

"Did she give birth yet?" Proculus asked. "How often does she bleed? I want to breed her."

While his fingers prodded and probed, she stared ahead with

steely eyes. Her body was a commodity, something to be bought and sold. She didn't belong to herself anymore; she hadn't for a while. But her soul was hers, and hers alone.

Proculus scrutinized Matti and licked his lips.

"He's soft and ripe," said the dealer. "He can sing at your parties."

"They're not brother and sister, are they?" Proculus asked.

"Of course not."

"I never buy family. That's asking for trouble."

The dealer put his hand over his heart. "I swear."

They argued over the price, and money changed hands.

"Sold!"

Proculus wrapped a rope around Esther's and Matti's necks and led them off the stage, through the crowd, and to his cart.

Esther whispered, "Don't ever let him know I'm your sister."

"I'm scared," Matti said.

Me too. She squeezed his hand.

PART THIRTEEN

SEPTEMBER 70 CE
ELUL 3830

The slave is a living tool.

Aristotle, *Nicomachean Ethics* 8.11

A household of slaves always needs clothing and food. You have to fill so many bellies of the greediest creatures, and buy clothes and guard against their very thieving hands, and make use of the services of those who weep and those who hate you.

Seneca, *An Essay on Peace of Mind* 8.8

CHAPTER LXXV

THERE WERE NINE OTHER SLAVES IN THE HOUSE: A DOORMAN, A COOK, a launderer, a gardener, a man who delivered letters, and four others who tended the animals and carried the litter when Proculus or his wife, Valeria, went out. Valeria had a face as long as a camel's; wide nostrils that expanded even more when she spoke; and thick, leathery lips. Her black hair was piled high on her head. She inspected Esther with a calculating intensity, starting with her hair and slowly moving her eyes downward.

"Turn around," Valeria said, making a circle with her finger. Then she glared at her husband. "*This* is what you brought me?"

"The slave dealer said she's a hairdresser."

"Dealers lie as easily as they breathe. And this one?" Valeria pointed to Matti.

"A replacement for the last boy. He'll work in the kitchen."

Valeria studied Matti, then said, "And somewhere else too, I suppose."

As her meaning sunk in, Esther felt a cramp in her stomach.

"How could you have bought Jews?" Valeria continued. "They make terrible slaves; they're too rebellious."

"But they're cheap. They cost half of what they used to. Good for us that they were stupid enough to rebel."

He's right, Esther thought as she stood staring at the floor. *If only we'd known how much we had to lose . . . All those passionate*

305

speeches about throwing off the chains of oppression and fighting for our dignity. For what? So we could end up in real chains?

"You can train them." Proculus repeated what the dealer had said. "It won't take long to break them in." He strode off, followed by two male slaves bearing his wine purchases.

That night, Esther and Matti found a spot by the kitchen fire and lay down. But the cook, a sour slave woman with rotten teeth, kicked Esther and made them move. They squeezed into a grimy alcove under the back stairs, next to the woodpile. As long as they didn't sit up, they could fit. Most of the slaves slept upstairs in the loft above the kitchen, or down in the cellar, but Esther was afraid to join them. This was better, she thought, even if there were spiders crawling up their legs.

Esther concentrated on her breath, riding it in and out. This feeble stream of air was the only thing separating her from death. It didn't seem like very much. She wrapped herself around Matti's sleeping form.

CHAPTER LXXVI

EVERY DAY, VALERIA HIT HER. THAT WAS THE TRAINING. FOR NOT coming fast enough; for being dishonest, greedy, or lazy; for looking at her when she spoke; and for not looking at her when she spoke. It was for her own good, Valeria said.

"Ancilla, come here!" Valeria used the Latin word for "slave-maid." "Ancilla, draw my bath!" "Ancilla, undress me!" "Ancilla, clean the birdcage!" Even her name was gone. She was no longer Esther. She was Ancilla, girl-slave; and Matti was Puer, boy-slave.

Esther combed Valeria's hair and massaged her feet. She helped in the kitchen and served the food. Matti emptied the cesspit toilet by hand and spread the contents on the household garden, swept the hearth, and fetched water from the fountain. In the afternoons, he worked in the kitchen. When they woke before dawn, they did it all over again.

They didn't have enough workers, Valeria said. Her beloved slave, who had been with her since Valeria had been a girl, had gotten the shakes. They couldn't sell her, so they'd done what they had to do; they couldn't have kept feeding her. Esther wondered what that meant. She was too scared to ask.

Valeria actually looked sad while she talked about her old slave, but quickly returned to character, becoming increasingly angry. The old slave, Valeria said, was the only one who had known how to dress Valeria, apply her face paint, and curl her hair. "You were supposed to take her place, but you can't even comb my hair properly," she said to Esther. When Esther accidentally pulled her hair too hard, Valeria stabbed her with a hairpin.

In spite of the beatings, Esther felt a sense of relief. Proculus hadn't touched Matti. Matti spent more and more time in the kitchen, where he was out of the master's sight. With its copper pots hanging from the ceiling, the small, dark room looked like a cave with bats dangling from their feet. The cook, Coqua, often hit him with a large spoon, but Matti said it didn't hurt as much as he pretended it did.

Coqua prepared the food on metal grates set over embers on the raised stone counter. To light the embers, she struck a piece of steel against a fragment of quartz and caught the spark on a slice of a fibrous mushroom. She blew until the heat made holes in the mushroom, and then used the mushroom to light the straw. She had to keep blowing while she added the wood. When Matti saw her struggling to catch the spark, he blew with her. The next day, he lit the embers himself. After that, Matti took over the job of lighting the coals in the morning, and Coqua let him take more scraps.

"He's a fast learner," Coqua told Esther. "Better than the last one."

"What happened to him?" Esther asked.

"He got older."

Esther raised her eyebrows.

"His voice dropped," Coqua explained. "He got hair on his rosebud. The master likes them young. He wanted to get the boy fixed, but he waited too long."

Esther swallowed but it didn't help; what was stuck in her throat wouldn't go away. Matti was not out of danger.

—◊—

Later that day, when Matti was cleaning the columns in the peristylium, Esther spotted Proculus behind a statue, watching him. She wiped her sweaty palms on her tunic. Then she called out, "Puer! The cook wants you in the kitchen. Immediately!"

The next few weeks went by in a blur. There used to be a past and a future, an order to the week, a countdown until the Sabbath. No more. Maybe God still had His day of rest, but they didn't.

One morning, Valeria commanded Esther to arrange her hair. When Esther reached for the comb on the dressing table, she knocked over a bottle of rose oil. It shattered on the floor. Valeria punched Esther on the chin. Esther's head snapped back, and she fell to the floor, dazed. She moaned and rubbed her chin; the pain was excruciating.

"Get up!" Valeria screamed.

She whimpered and rolled to her side.

"Get up, I said!" Valeria kicked her in the stomach.

Esther eased herself up. A shard of alabaster was stuck in the fleshy part of her palm, and blood dripped down. Esther yanked the shard out.

"Can't you do anything right?" Valeria shouted.

"I'm sorry. I—"

"Quiet! How dare you address me?" Valeria inhaled deeply, as though to calm herself. "You slaves break things, you lie, and you steal. And then after we put so much work into training you, you get sick and die."

Esther hobbled away. Her body, already covered with purple welts, cuts, and scratches from Valeria's previous attacks, throbbed with each step. Her arms were dotted with burns from the scalding water that splashed onto her as she filled Valeria's bath, and with the lashes she'd received for the water not being hot enough, or for being too hot. Sometimes she thought she deserved the punishment. It dulled the pain of the wounds inside: the memory of Miriam's outstretched arms; the aching loss of her parents, Yehuda, and Shimon; and her guilt about not being able to protect Matti. When her body hurt as much as her soul, she was in equilibrium.

Before Esther closed her eyes that night, she said to Matti, "I'm Esther Bat Hanan, daughter of a Temple Priest. You're Mathia Ben Hanan. Our mother was Sarah. We had two brothers, Yehuda and Shimon." She used to make up stories for Matti, but no longer. She wanted him to remember his own story. She was terrified that they'd forget the names of their family, maybe even their own; that one day, their past would be gone, and she would be Ancilla and he would be Puer.

She recited the prayer *"Shema Israel, Hear O Israel, the Lord our God, the Lord is One."*

She made Matti say it too. When they finished, he asked, "Do you ever think sometimes that maybe it's not real? We'll go home and everyone will be there again?"

If her heart could have torn, it would have.

CHAPTER LXXVII

THE FOLLOWING NIGHT, AFTER ESTHER LIT VALERIA'S FIREPLACE, Proculus called her. His bedroom door was ajar. He called again, this time louder. "Ancilla!"

Esther pushed the door and it creaked open, gradually revealing the master's bedchamber. She swallowed, and took a tentative step forward, as if she weren't sure her foot would meet ground. Proculus lay on a high bed with carvings of cats on each of its four posts and an ornate curved headboard. His robe was open.

"You, girl, come here."

She didn't dare look at him.

"Bring the boy," he ordered.

"The boy?" she repeated numbly.

His face got redder and redder. "Why are you standing there like a statue?" he shouted. "Go, now!

She ran to Matti and told him to hide under the pile of harnesses in the barn. Then she went back.

"I couldn't find him," she said breathlessly. "He was covered in shit from cleaning the cesspool, so the other slaves made him sleep outside. I looked everywhere, even in the animal pens and stable."

Her heart pounded in her ears as she stood perfectly still. She kept her eyes lowered.

"Get out!" Proculus yelled. Then he began cursing.

The next morning, she snuck out to the kitchen garden. She had saved Matti the night before, but she wouldn't be able to use the same excuse twice. She scanned the plants in the garden. No henbane, nightshade, or mandrake—all plants she was familiar with from back home—but there was poppy. The cook used the seeds as seasoning; Esther would use the milk.

She poured a few drops of poppy milk—and a bit of honey to disguise the flavor—into Proculus's wine before dinner. Her mother had said that the right amount would induce sleep, but too much could kill. She hoped she'd guessed right. If Proculus died, she and Matti could be sold. And more than likely, they wouldn't be sold together.

By the time Proculus had finished eating his meal, his pupils had shrunk to small dots, and then his head fell backward. He was asleep. The servants carried him to his bed. For tonight, at least, her brother would not be harmed.

As Esther was clearing the table, Valeria barked, "Ancilla, come here!"

Esther held her breath as she turned around. Could Valeria know?

Valeria seemed to appraise her. "Tomorrow you'll go with Coqua to the market."

Esther exhaled. She too was safe.

For now.

CHAPTER LXXVIII

They left before dawn. They had to, Coqua said, if they wanted to get the best pick of the fishmonger's catch. Usually one of the male slaves accompanied her to carry the purchases, but today the men were all busy preparing the house for an upcoming dinner party. Esther pulled a ragged shawl tighter around her shoulders.

The scent of the pine trees infused the fog with a smell that transported Esther to the family estate. She closed her eyes and inhaled deeply, and for a few seconds was back in that spot where she and Miriam used to pick daisies, between the oak and carob trees, behind the olive press.

She opened her eyes. The sun's rays, peeking through the fog, slowly illuminated the terra-cotta rooftops and the bronze tiles of the temples and imperial buildings—a sight as different from the canopy of green in the Jerusalem hills as could be. Esther didn't know where to look first. As much as she hated Rome, she wanted to see more. Coqua snapped at her to hurry. They had to be back in time to prepare the main course, jellyfish stuffed with sea urchins.

Coqua expertly wound through one piazza after another and past apartment buildings that—even though they were almost all new, built after the city's fire a few years before—were already covered with lewd graffiti. Esther was astounded at the buildings' size, some four and five stories high, with hundreds of tenants. She wanted to remember everything, so she could tell Matti.

Esther sidestepped the puddles of urine and excrement thrown from the buildings, and ducked below the lines of laundry strung between them, flapping in the wind. She walked around people sleeping on the streets, whole families surrounded by piles of belongings.

Finally they reached the market, entering through a monumental arch crowned by a large statue of a woman.

"Who's that?" Esther asked, craning her neck to look.

"Livia, wife of the first Emperor Augustus. Says it right there on the gate. Can't you read?" Coqua asked.

Esther could read, although she was pretty sure Coqua could not. Esther had been staring at the statue and hadn't noticed the writing. The statue had an angry face, like Valeria's.

The streets near the market were already packed with early-morning buyers like themselves and people on their way to work. An ordinary day in Rome was as congested as Jerusalem on the most holy days, when the city was teeming with pilgrims.

Just inside the gate, the herb seller was setting up baskets of rosemary, sage, mint, and juniper. Boys hawked cabbage, asparagus, and onions. Stalls overflowing with produce lined the streets. One stall sold birds: flamingos, thrushes, cranes, and parakeets. The next stall displayed slabs of blood-red meat dangling from hooks, with halos of flies around the rabbits' and pigs' heads.

Esther inhaled a spicy aroma. Her mouth watered, but she wrinkled her nose when she saw the suckling pig roasting over a low flame. Next to it stood a table piled high with sow teats and pig jowls.

Slaves and a few freedmen crowded into the narrow streets, pushing to get their pick of the choicest produce. She was astounded that so many slaves were wandering around not only unguarded but with purses full of *sestertii,* shopping for their masters. There were only a few women in the market, mainly assisting their shopkeeper husbands. A young juggler reminded Esther of those long-ago days when the boys she knew had thrown balls into the air instead of stones and spears.

After a protracted performance—with Coqua accusing the fishmonger of selling spoiled goods, and dickering over each coin as if her life depended on it—the cook bought what she needed for the dinner. When Coqua turned her back, the fishmonger made an obscene gesture, sticking his thumb through the fingers of his fist.

A plan was beginning to take shape in Esther's mind. If she and Matti could get back here, they could slip into the crowd, and flee. But to where? They wore the rags of slaves, and as soon as they spoke, their accents would give them away. It would be easy to spot them as runaways.

In the meantime, she had to keep Matti safe from Proculus. Trailing a few feet behind Coqua, Esther searched the side of the road for more plants she could use. She thought she spotted some hellebore but wasn't sure. It looked like the kind with the black roots, but it didn't matter. White hellebore purged up, and black hellebore purged down; either kind would do. As she reached for the purple flowers, she felt her mother's presence: *Look to the east when you pick it, and make sure there are no eagles overhead.* Esther quickly scanned the sky, pulled the plants, and then ran to catch up with Coqua.

CHAPTER LXXIX

THE NIGHT AFTER THE BANQUET, PROCULUS AGAIN CALLED TO HER AS she left Valeria's room.

"Prepare the boy," he barked. Esther's heart sank. All afternoon, she had waited for Coqua to leave the kitchen so she could boil the hellebore roots. Finally Coqua had gone outside, and Esther had boiled the leaves and poured the cinnamon-scented water into a small bottle. She had slipped some of it into Proculus's wine, but maybe it hadn't been enough.

Esther stood just outside his door and looked at him: his smug expression; his thick, scraggly eyebrows; cold, glinting eyes; and the dark stubble on his chin.

"Take me instead," she said, walking closer.

"I don't want a filthy, bloody hole," he snapped.

Just then, a male slave walked past her into the room, carrying a pile of blankets. "Get the boy," Proculus commanded him. "Oil him and rouge his lips."

Valeria was calling her again. "Ancilla! Come here!"

Esther bit the inside of her cheek, fighting the urge to run to Matti. They had kept their relationship a secret. If she tried to stop Proculus now, he might guess. As punishment, he might sell one of them. She couldn't take a chance. Besides, she knew she couldn't stop him; she'd only make it worse. She staggered back, her feet dragging along the floor as if they were filled with lead. How could she feel so heavy, yet be so empty at the same time? Every day that she lived as a slave, a little more of her disappeared. Soon she would be all hollowed out, merely a ghost.

After filling the brazier in Valeria's room, she returned to the alcove. She found herself whispering to her mother, "I'm sorry I let you down. I tried to keep him safe . . . I'm sorry . . . I'm so sorry."

When Matti came back, he told her what had happened. He had gotten into bed with Proculus. Matti had been so nervous, he couldn't stop shaking, but just when he'd feared the worst, Proculus had groaned and cursed as the hellebore had torn through him. He'd yelled for Matti to bring him the chamber pot.

Esther and Matti laughed so hard, there were tears in their eyes. She couldn't remember the last time either of them had laughed.

But in the morning, Proculus said he would sell the cook if it happened again; her food was making him sick. Coqua wasn't exactly kind, but Esther didn't want her to be sold. Esther would have to go back to the poppy milk.

CHAPTER LXXX

Esther was dressing Valeria for the baths. Her mistress was very particular about her clothes, even when she was only going to a place where she would be taking them off. Esther adjusted the hem of Valeria's stola so that it flowed freely. She tied one ribbon around Valeria's waist, and another just below Valeria's breasts. When Esther finished arranging the gown, she draped a shawl over Valeria's head. She couldn't help rubbing the soft wool between her fingers.

Miriam would have liked this shawl, Esther thought, with its colorful embroidery and intricate border. It wasn't like the cloth back home. *Back home.* The home that was no longer there.

Esther walked behind Valeria's litter through the winding streets. It was a steep climb and her legs ached, but she didn't care. She was glad to be out of the domus, Proculus's house, even if the stench of the rotting garbage on the side of the road and the smell from the public latrines made her gag. The water from the ever present fountains and basins left a slippery, smelly sludge on the streets.

Figurines of erect phalluses were prominently displayed wherever she looked. There was even a cluster of bronze phalluses hanging over the front door of a house, and they chimed in the wind. The family kissed and rubbed them, just like she used to kiss the mezuzah on the doorpost of her house. She would never understand Roman customs.

The sweet fragrance of the flower stalls signaled that one of the city's many temples was nearby. Each one was dedicated to a different god. As she passed the temple, Esther peered between the massive columns of the imposing building. Inside were rows of brightly painted statues, and piles of flowers on the floor. The first time she'd walked past one of the temples, she'd looked at the ground and tried not to inhale the scent of the burning myrrh. But after a while, she'd allowed herself a quick peek and then a longer look, until ultimately she stared directly inside, challenging God to show His displeasure. His silence didn't surprise her.

Esther smelled the fumes before she saw the bathhouse. The boilers burned wood continuously, and filled the sky with plumes of dark smoke. Like the taverns, the baths were always crowded. Maybe the Romans didn't need to work because there were so many slaves. Coqua said that most Romans worked only until midday, and then spent the afternoon in leisure.

Valeria went inside first, dropping two coins into a wooden strongbox at the entrance. Esther followed, and was greeted by a blast of humidity. Heat radiated from the floor and walls. Statues of painted marble stared from their niches in the walls, which were decorated with colorful sea scenes. Esther's robe stuck to her skin, and her throat was parched. As soon as Valeria went into the bath, she would take a drink from the fountain.

They entered the dressing room, with its large mosaic of Triton in the middle of the floor, and the large glass windows. Valeria sat on a bench against the wall and lifted her leg for Esther to untie her sandals. She waited for Esther to undress her, like a small child. Naked men and women strolled by. Esther was shocked. A sign at the door said it was the women's hour, but apparently no one enforced the rule.

Esther wrapped a thin cloth around her mistress's waist and slipped clogs onto her feet. Valeria refused to use the cloakroom—too many thieves, she claimed—so Esther had to carry her clothes, following her from room to room. Valeria said she usually skipped the sudatorium, where nude women playing ball worked up a sweat. Valeria preferred instead to go straight to the hot baths of the tepidarium. Depending on who was there—and how juicy the gossip of the day was—she would either stay or go for a swim in the cool waters of the frigidarium. Finally she went to the unctuarium, where she was massaged with oils, scraped with strigils, and anointed with perfume. The scent of perfumed oils and sweat hung in the air, and the swell of conversation rose and fell in waves. Vendors walked through the rooms bearing platters of delicacies, making Esther's mouth water. She wouldn't have eaten the oysters, but she would have liked a fresh roll.

To her astonishment, Valeria gave her a coin to buy lupini beans from one of the vendors. Esther ate a few right away, relishing the feel of the beans in her mouth: the pop of the skin and the crush of the meaty seed between her teeth. They were delicious, but she forced herself to stop. She wanted to save the rest for Matti.

As she waited with the rest of the slaves in the back of the room, she thought of the baths in Jerusalem, where people went for purification, not pleasure. In Jerusalem, people had prayed and studied. In Rome, people went to the baths, had lavish feasts, and had all-night orgies.

She thought of Yehuda and his friends arguing over the finer points of the law, and the young men here, arguing over whose penis was longer, or whose slave was better in bed. Rome was as sinful as she'd always heard. But so what? Their cities flourished, their bathhouses were full, their plates overflowed, and their appetites—all their appetites, from high to low—were sated. Meanwhile, her Jerusalem—*holy* Jerusalem—was in ruins. Her people were scattered and enslaved. The city of God was no more, while this den of iniquity flourished.

CHAPTER LXXXI

INSTEAD OF GOING STRAIGHT HOME, VALERIA ANNOUNCED THAT THEY were going to the Transtiberim to see a sought-after Jewish sorceress who, Valeria had learned from a woman in the baths, knew a secret for ensuring a male birth. Esther didn't know which surprised her more, that Valeria would consult a Jew, or that she was trying to get pregnant.

"Jews know magic, right?" Valeria asked.

"Everyone knows that Jews' magic is the most potent," Esther said, trying to sound assured. What she didn't say was that magic wouldn't work if your husband had sex with the slaves instead of with his wife.

They left the bathhouse. The slaves carried Valeria's litter on their shoulders, and Esther followed. They walked past the Theater of Pompeius, with its small monument marking the spot of Julius Caesar's murder; past ancient brick temples and gleaming new ones; past the Circus Flaminius, where posters announced upcoming chariot races; and past the new library in the Porticus Octaviae.

Finally they reached the Fabricius Bridge. It was packed with donkey carts and porters weighed down with heavy baskets. Rows of small, pastel-colored boats moored to the docks below bobbed in the Tiber.

The bridge led them to the Transtiberim, an island of rickety tenements and exotically dressed foreigners. As they made their way onto the island, the crowd thinned. It was a relief not to be touched or pushed. Echoes of languages and dialects Esther had never heard swirled around her, along with the familiar Greek, Aramaic, and Latin.

People pushed handcarts laden with bolts of cloth, wine jars, baskets of food, and even dead bodies. A noisy thrum blanketed it all: the clopping of the mules on the stone-paved streets; the clucks of chickens; the shouts of the merchants. Through the parted curtains of the litter, Esther could see Valeria holding a handkerchief over her nose.

It seemed as though all of Rome's foreigners had been dumped here. Esther was astonished to even see Jews with their fringed garments walking freely. She studied their faces, hoping to see someone she knew. There were mezuzahs affixed to doorposts, synagogues with red doors, and lintels with crudely carved Jewish symbols of menorahs and lulavs.

Arriving at an alleyway too narrow for the litter to enter, Valeria stepped out. She continued on foot until they reached a statue at the end of the street. It was the god Priapus holding a sickle. Someone had placed a small wreath on the statue's erect phallus, and there were notes attached to its head and chest. Valeria rubbed the statue's phallus, and then turned right.

After passing two houses, they reached a green door adorned with paintings of fantastical animals. Valeria pushed it open. The porters waited outside as Esther followed Valeria into a dark hallway that led into a courtyard lined with small huts. The courtyard was crisscrossed with clotheslines and littered with metal tubs and piles of straw. Valeria looked around, then strode toward the hut with a partially opened purple curtain.

Esther staggered backward, mouth agape, when she saw the sorceress, dressed in a crimson robe and a yellow turban wrapped high on her head. The woman remained impassive, although her eyes, rimmed with black kohl, darted almost imperceptibly. She welcomed them in with an exaggerated smile. When she raised her chin, Esther saw the mole.

Zahara studiously avoided looking at Esther while she listened to Valeria's request. She asked questions about Valeria's anatomy, and that of Proculus. Just when Esther was sure that Valeria would explode into an impatient tirade, Zahara began assembling ingredients in a stone mortar: the eggshell of a crow, a dried flower with a blackish color, some viscous plant juice, and a purplish powder. She ground them into a paste, scraped it all into a jar, and said solemnly, "The God of Abraham is the most powerful for bringing sons. But for this to work, a Jewish girl must mix it with honey. Then you must put it on your pudenda—inside and out."

Zahara scrawled some Aramaic words on a piece of leather. "Put this under the bed where you will lie with your man, and make sure to lie on your right side when he enters you. You have to whisper 'I say to you, womb: open and receive the seed of Proculus. I adjure you by the name of Sabaoth, Arbathio, Tapheiao, Michael, Zuriel, and Gabriel to bring his seed into my womb, and let it be a male.'"

Valeria scowled. Zahara quickly added, "But if you can't remember all that, just say, 'I adjure you by the name of Abraham and all the other great and wondrous names on this amulet.'"

Zahara turned toward a shelf of colored liquids and reached for the one on the end. She uncorked the top. Esther instantly identified the fragrance: persimmon of Jerusalem. She breathed deeply.

"Put a drop of this perfume behind each ear and under your left armpit," Zahara said. "And one last thing—" She plucked two leaves from a thick philodendron. "When it's still night, urinate on these. If they are green in the morning, you'll have a son. But if they're brown, your womb is empty, and you must do everything again the next night."

Zahara closed her eyes and held out her open palms as though she were trying to catch something in the air. "I feel something," she said dramatically. "I feel the presence of a Jewish slave."

Valeria nodded vigorously and pointed to Esther.

"I must speak to her by myself," Zahara said, "to verify that she is trustworthy. Give me a few minutes alone with this slave so I can look into her soul, and see if she is capable of completing the task."

As soon as Valeria left, Zahara opened her arms, and Esther flew in. Pressed against Zahara's soft bosom and enveloped by her strong arms, Esther felt as though she had arrived at a place as close to home as she would ever get. She wanted to stay like this forever.

"We don't have much time," Zahara said, releasing Esther. "Are you all right?"

Esther didn't trust herself to speak without crying. She looked around in amazement. "How—how did you . . . ," she stammered.

"Don't let this fool you," Zahara said. "My master owns the building. He sells cures and potions too. When he realized that he could make more money from me if I were on my own, he set me up here. He keeps what I earn, but I have a peculium, my own savings. I always put a bit to the side, to buy my freedom."

Esther looked at Zahara like a drowning person who has spotted a piece of driftwood. She had so much to tell her, and so much to ask.

Zahara grabbed her hands and squeezed. "Come see me again . . . whenever you can."

She called for Valeria. "You are fortunate," Zahara said. "This slave is well versed in mixing potions, and she is pure. Keep her close."

Finding Zahara had cracked open Esther's world and let in a

sliver of light, brilliant and blinding, the way light is when everything else is dark. She thought of the words from those Passover feasts, so long ago.

My people were slaves before, and then they were free.

Since her capture, the shackles had moved from her legs to her spirit. She had to throw them off. She had to get Matti away from Proculus. She would make a plan. She would learn the city; she would devise an escape route. She would need to gain Valeria's trust, so her mistress would send her on errands by herself, like she sent Coqua.

If Esther could get back to the Jewish quarter with Matti, Zahara would help them. She would use that sliver of light, no matter how faint, to guide her.

That night, Esther and Matti huddled together in their sleeping nook and ate the rest of the beans, chewing as slowly as they could. They licked their fingers, savoring the last of the salty, garlicky flavor.

CHAPTER LXXXII

It was only a week later that Esther had her chance. Proculus and Valeria were gone for the day, visiting family outside the city.

"I'm going to the fountain," Coqua said. "The pots had better sparkle by the time I get back."

Esther knew Coqua wouldn't rush back. The fountain behind the domus was a favorite meeting place, along with the *popina,* the tavern next to it, for the slaves of the neighboring households. Slave owners were rarely seen there, and few carts traveled down the narrow lane. Even though the city's aqueduct and the private rain cisterns fed the domus's spouting sculptures, watered the gardens, and flushed the latrines, Valeria and Proculus would drink only fountain water. The other water, they said, had too much sand in it. Fetching water was Coqua's excuse to get out of the domus and socialize. If she had wanted to get the water quickly, she would have sent Matti. After accompanying Coqua to the *popina* the week before, Esther finally understood why Coqua haggled over every last coin in the market. She must have managed to nab a few without Valeria noticing. The *popina* served anyone with money. Cups were shared, and freedmen drank alongside slaves, gravediggers, goat-skin sellers, prostitutes, and musicians.

"Let's go," Esther whispered to Matti, grabbing his hand.

"Where?" Alarm flared in his eyes.

"Quiet! Follow me." They left through the back door, carrying pails so it would look like they were on their way to the fountain.

Esther prayed they wouldn't see Coqua or any of the other house slaves. When they'd passed the fountain, they flung the pails down and broke into a run. They raced through a warren of lanes and back alleys until they reached a wide, crowded thoroughfare. Fear and exhilaration rushed through her; she felt like she was falling through the air. There was no turning back now.

They stopped running but continued to walk briskly, like slaves on an errand. Only free people walked at a leisurely pace. They navigated around a cart carrying timber, and two slaves hauling cooking gear. As Esther stepped over clumps of donkey dung, she heard the notes of a flute. A funeral procession was coming toward them. Incense filled the air. Along with the other pedestrians, they stepped out of the way. Shutters slammed in the buildings. No one, it seemed, wanted to get too close, lest they become contaminated. Esther and Matti watched a man in front shouting commands, masked actors walking in circles, and slaves carrying a funeral bier. Musicians played, and singers brought up the rear. Instinctively Esther pulled Matti into the procession. There was so much noise, and there were so many mourners—clearly hired ones, by the theatrics and howling—that no one would pay them any attention. They would hide in plain view.

They joined in the wailing. It felt right, cathartic even, to scream and cry out.

They continued in the procession until they neared the market. In the distance, Esther spotted the statue of Livia. Her heart leapt; she could find the bridge from here.

PART FOURTEEN

OCTOBER 70 CE
TISHREI 3831

I have run away. Capture me. When you have returned
me to my master . . . you will receive a gold coin.

Latin inscription on a slave collar:
Corpus Inscriptionum Latinarum 15.7194

One must not depend on miracles.

Babylonian Talmud, *Shabbat* 32a

CHAPTER LXXXIII

ESTHER'S HANDS PARTED THE PURPLE CURTAIN. ZAHARA SNATCHED her turban from the counter and looked up. When she saw them, her face registered confusion. "Where's your owner?" she asked.

"We ran away," Esther said, stepping inside. Matti stood stiffly by Esther's side.

Zahara continued to stare, seemingly speechless.

"You . . . you said to come back," Esther said haltingly. "I thought we'd be safe here."

"You're not *safe,*" Zahara said, lowering her voice to a whisper. "You're far from safe." She led them into the courtyard, her eyes darting around. "Come, we need to hurry—before anyone sees you." She pulled them into a stable next to her hut, bolted the bottom half of the door, and swung closed the top half. The air was foul, and the ground muddy. It took a few seconds for Esther's vision to adjust to the sudden darkness.

Zahara's eyes narrowed, and she pointed a finger. "Do you know what they do to runaways? Have you ever seen it? I have! The owners don't get bloody themselves, of course. They bring in *professional* torturers who come with their own equipment—racks they use to stretch and separate your limbs, and boiling pitch to throw onto your back! If you survive, you'll get branded or fettered with iron collars."

Esther's face fell. This wasn't the reception she had expected.

"Your owner will offer a reward. Soon—before you can turn

around—the public criers will be shouting out your descriptions. Buildings will be plastered with notices about you. Bounty hunters will be on the lookout in every neighborhood."

Esther's mouth went dry.

Zahara wasn't finished. "Catching runaways is a sport. Soldiers, officials, regular folk, even other slaves . . . soon they'll all be searching. You and Matti are stolen property—no matter that you stole yourselves. You have to get out of here—and fast."

"I thought you could help us," Esther said plaintively.

"Do you know what happens to people who harbor fugitives?" Zahara demanded.

"What should we do?"

"A young girl and a boy . . ." Zahara shook her head slowly. "You'll never survive on your own."

Esther felt like the world was collapsing and she was being buried under the rubble. She slumped down on a pile of straw. She hadn't had time to make a plan; she'd only thought about getting here, not about what could happen to Zahara, or where they would go afterward.

"Stay here," Zahara said, her face softening. "I'll be back soon."

"Where are you going?" Esther asked, sitting up.

"I have to work."

"Don't go! You're right, we shouldn't have come. We don't want to put you in danger. By now, Proculus will know we ran away. He'll be looking." Esther stood up and swiped at the yellow straw clinging to her tunic. "Do you have any old clothes you can spare, maybe a few coins?"

Zahara laid a hand on her arm. "Sit. You'll be safe here. I'll be back soon. But if you hear anyone, hide under the straw."

Esther and Matti huddled in the corner, their backs against the wall. Esther clutched her knees and dropped her head.

"Let's say the Shema," Esther whispered.

"I don't want to."

Esther could sense Matti's body stiffening. He had never refused to pray with her before.

"It's a waste of time," he grumbled. "God doesn't hear."

"He always hears," Esther insisted, surprising herself with her own conviction.

"Then He doesn't answer," Matti said.

"How can you say that? We're here, aren't we?"

"For now, but what if she reports us?"

The thought had entered her mind too. But the memory of Zahara bringing food to their house during the siege pushed it aside. "She'll do the right thing," Esther said.

Matti didn't look convinced. "For her, or for us? Maybe she wants to collect a reward. If we go back now, no one will have noticed that we left."

Esther squeezed her temples. "Go back? After we finally escaped?"

"You heard what she said," Matti said. "There's a net closing around us, even though we can't see it."

Esther had been sure that coming to Zahara was a good idea. But Zahara's description of what happened to runaways, and Matti's doubts, chipped away at her conviction. They waited for Zahara to come back. Esther's mood darkened as the minutes crawled by, second by slow second.

Footsteps!

They crouched under the straw, clinging to each other. Esther squeezed Matti tighter.

"It's me," Zahara said as she opened the door and quickly latched it behind her.

Esther jumped up. Zahara held out some hard biscuits, salted fish, and wine. "Last week, a client told me about a wealthy freedman who was making inquiries about slaves from Jerusalem. I didn't think anything of it until"—she hesitated, looking Esther right in the eyes—"until she said that his hand was scarred."

Esther fell back against the rough wall of the stable. "Tiberius?" she said faintly, almost afraid to give voice to the hope.

"It could be, but we can't be sure. I asked my client to find out where he lives."

Esther felt almost giddy with relief.

Zahara continued, "The woman comes to me every week for her fortune. But, listen, you can't wait here; my neighbors will sniff you out right away. It's not safe."

"Where should we go?"

"Either back to your master or hide out in the street until I find Tiberius—assuming it really is him."

"That could take days!" Esther said, trying to stay calm. "Those are both bad choices."

"I know, but sometimes that's all we get."

Just as Esther and Matti stepped inside the back door, Valeria called. Esther released Matti's hand. "Stay here," she commanded him in a whisper. She went through the dark hallway leading to the atrium.

Valeria was waiting. "Where were you?"

"Feeding the dormice." The rodents were kept in terra-cotta jars in the garden. "Coqua told me to give them chestnuts and water. We're fattening them up for next week's banquet." Esther clasped her hands to keep them from shaking.

"You didn't meet the litter when we returned."

"I didn't hear you come back." Esther realized her voice was higher than usual.

For a long moment, Valeria was silent. Finally she said, "I never really trusted you."

Each nerve in Esther's body felt taut, like a string about to snap. She needed to stay calm, to *think*.

Valeria continued to glare at her. "Everyone says that Jews are cunning. I know you enticed my husband. Maybe you're the one who put a spell on me so I wasn't able to fall pregnant. Who knows what you and that charlatan really talked about? I was a fool to consult her."

Esther wanted to claw at Valeria's face, but not a muscle twitched in her slave-mask. "Oh no, mistress," she said, in what she hoped was a convincing tone. "I would never do anything to harm you or the master."

Matti appeared in the doorway.

"Where's *he* been?" Valeria asked.

Esther turned to Matti, as if she had just noticed him. "He was helping Coqua, shelling peas."

"You two look alike," Valeria said, looking from one to the other. She squinted. "The round shape of your faces . . . the way your noses turn up at the end."

"That's because we're both Jewish," Esther said quickly. "My people don't have noble noses, like yours—long and strong like the beaks of eagles." Then, for good measure, she added, "For a people born to rule."

At that, Valeria seemed to uncoil. She looked around the room. "The couch cushions are in disarray and the silver needs polishing. Get to work!"

CHAPTER LXXXIV

Esther squatted in her usual position in the corner, ready to serve her masters as they ate.

"I've been offered an interesting business proposition," Proculus said, dropping an oyster into his mouth and slurping noisily.

Valeria stroked the dog sitting in her lap, a Maltese with a silky white coat and feathery tail. "Really," she murmured, with little apparent interest.

"I was approached by a freedman, one of the biggest grain traders in Rome," Proculus said.

"I certainly hope you're not thinking of working with an ex-slave!" Valeria wrinkled her nose in disgust. "Trade is sordid. What if people thought *you* were one of them, a common merchant with insatiable greed?"

"No one will know. The deal will be completed in two days, and we'll be left with enough money to put marble floors down in the country villa."

"Yes, go on," Valeria said quickly, now regarding her husband with an eager expression.

"Obviously," Proculus said with an exaggerated slowness, clearly enjoying Valeria's attention, "Rome needs a steady supply of grain. Without imported grain, there'd be famine. Even the government is involved, buying and distributing the grain." He took a swig of wine, then set down his empty wine goblet. Esther refilled it.

"It's a once-in-a-lifetime deal," Proculus said. "I don't have to put up any money, just sign my name. The freedman needs some-one of equestrian rank to guarantee a payment to the ship's captain. There's no risk because the ship has already made the journey from Alexandria and is safely docked in the port of Puteoli."

"I don't understand," Valeria said, dangling a piece of meat from her plate over the dog's open mouth. "If the ship's already here, what do you need to guarantee?"

"The captain's payment. He won't release the grain until he gets paid, but the buyer won't hand over any money until the grain is de-livered and in his warehouse. Apparently the captain finally agreed to accept a document signed by someone of equestrian rank—like me—guaranteeing his payment." Proculus looked pleased with him-self. "The freedman will pay the captain when he sells the grain, and I'll get a hefty share of the profits without putting up any money."

"But why is this freedman coming to you?" Valeria asked. "Surely he has other investors."

"He does, but they're all nobles, mostly senators. He won't name them; he said he has to be discreet because legally senators are not allowed to do business. Aristocrats are supposed to make their money from their land; they're not supposed to sully their fam-ily name with commerce." Proculus laughed. "But profits smell just as good to them as to the rest of us." He swallowed another oyster. "The deal is foolproof."

Esther had only been half listening to the conversation. The de-tails of Proculus's new business deal didn't interest her; her stomach did. She couldn't take her eyes off the meat Valeria fed to her dog.

"I'm taking the boy to the castrator next week," Proculus said. "There's a new one in town; they say he's a real artist."

Esther snapped to attention, placing a hand on the wall to steady herself.

"So soon?" Valeria asked. "His voice hasn't dropped."

"That's the best time."

Valeria grunted.

Proculus pasted a smile onto his face. "They say the urine of a eunuch is potent. It can rekindle the flames of desire and cure infertility."

"Well, then," Valeria said pointedly, "I guess we should do it soon."

Proculus pounded his glass on the table for another refill.

Esther jumped up.

As Esther cleared the table after the meal, she dropped the wine pitcher. It smashed on the floor, shattering into small pieces. Luckily, the pitcher was empty and Valeria and Proculus had already left the dining room. Without a word, Coqua handed Esther a broom. Normally Coqua would have hit her for such a serious infraction. Coqua must have also heard what they'd said about Matti. Esther stared at the broken shards on the floor, her thoughts racing. There was no time now for Zahara to track Tiberius down; they couldn't wait to be rescued. She'd have to get Matti away from here—soon.

CHAPTER LXXXV

ALL ESTHER COULD THINK ABOUT WAS HOW THEY'D ESCAPE. AS SHE swept the entrance hall the next day, she tried to make a plan. She looked up just as Proculus stormed in, followed by Valeria, shaking her fist in the air.

"You said there was no risk!" Valeria yelled at Proculus's back.

Proculus turned to face her. "The grain was ruined," he said. "The shipping agent had added dirt and barley to bulk it up, and the buyer wouldn't take it."

"So it wasn't a foolproof opportunity after all, was it?" Valeria sneered. "It was an opportunity to prove who's a fool!"

"How was I supposed to know? There were senators in the deal too."

"You *think* there were senators in the deal. You only know what that freedman told you. He played you! How much do you owe?"

"Fifty thousand *sestertii*," he said under his breath. "His man-slave said he'll be here soon to collect."

Valeria closed her eyes and threw back her head. "You *are* a fool!"

The door chimes sounded. Proculus and Valeria froze, their eyes shifting around nervously. Proculus said, "He's here."

The doorman opened the door. Tiberius strode in wearing a scarlet cloak fastened with a jeweled clasp, draped over a white tunic. It was all Esther could do to stay still and not run into his arms.

Zahara had found him! It hadn't occurred to her that Tiberius was the freedman who'd set Proculus up. Tiberius's jaw clenched when he saw her, but he looked away. If he didn't want to reveal that he knew her, she wouldn't either. Every muscle in her body tensed. She gripped the broomstick so tightly that her fingernails dug into the wood. It had been six months since Esther had last seen him, but it felt like six years.

"A most unfortunate turn of events, Proculus," Tiberius said smoothly. "Most unfortunate. Some of these agents are not trustworthy. It happens." He shook his head ruefully.

Red-faced, Proculus stepped forward like he was about to throttle Tiberius. "You said there was no risk. You said—"

"Whoa . . . ," Tiberius said as he held up both palms. "You know there's no such thing as *no* risk."

This seemed to enrage Proculus further.

"You signed a legal document," Tiberius said. "I could get the urban praetor to enforce it." He paused and smiled. "But if we involve the judicial magistrate, you know what might happen. . . ."

"What?" Valeria demanded.

"A public auction of your property—if you don't pay, that is." Valeria paled.

"However," Tiberius continued, "I'm willing to settle this amicably, without the courts or public embarrassment. I'm willing to take something else of value in lieu of the payment."

"Like what?" Proculus said.

Tiberius made a show of looking around. "I don't see any valuable art here. Sculpture? Jewelry? I'm a collector of fine things."

Proculus and Valeria looked at each other with blank expressions.

Tiberius reached for Esther and pulled her toward him. "Here's something that's nice to look at. I'll take her."

"Wh-what?" Valeria sputtered. "You can't just come in here and take our property."

"Oh, but I can, my dear lady. And this is all I see that you have of value around here. Not worth fifty thousand *sestertii,* though." Esther shot him a sharp look.

Tiberius sighed as though he were trying to decide what to do. "But truly, I have enough slaves. Maybe I *could* be persuaded to take another one. Do you have a pretty boy somewhere?"

Proculus glared at Tiberius. "No, I don't."

Tiberius raised an eyebrow. "I find that hard to believe."

"I have a strong stable man from Dacia you can have."

Tiberius drew himself up and flung out his arms. "How dare you try to bargain with me?" he shouted. "You should be grateful I'm willing to cancel this contract with a symbolic payment of only two slaves. I could take all of them—and your house too!"

Valeria held Proculus back like she was restraining a wild dog. She turned to the doorman. "Get Puer," she commanded.

Tiberius crossed his arms over his chest and waited. When the doorman came back with Matti, Tiberius said, "I'll take these slaves now and send over a bill of sale for you to sign. As you know, this transfer of property requires both of our signatures."

Proculus knocked his knuckles together as he gave Tiberius an angry stare.

Tiberius smiled. "I'm sure you'd like to settle this behind the scenes. No need to see the magistrate."

"You think that because you have money, you're one of us?" Proculus asked. "I was born here. I took my first breath right here on the Aventine Hill, and you were brought over in chains. You freedmen are ruining Rome."

Tiberius stared back. "I may never be a Roman citizen in your eyes, but in the eyes of the court, I am. And that's all that matters. Good day."

CHAPTER LXXXVI

ESTHER SQUEEZED MATTI'S HAND TO REASSURE HIM AS THEY FOL-
lowed Tiberius out of the domus. He untied two mules, which had
been tied to a post.

She had so many questions for Tiberius: how he'd found them,
why he'd concocted such an elaborate ruse to get them, where he
was taking them, and what would happen now. She waited for him
to speak first. His eyes bore into her with an intensity that made her
shudder.

"Are you . . . all right?" he asked in a hoarse whisper.

She nodded, waiting for him to say more. But his lips were set
in an angry line, and he seemed in a hurry to get them away as soon
as possible. He helped her and Matti mount one of the mules, and
he rode the other. The streets were crowded with people and carts;
the clatter of the mules' hooves and the creaking of the large wooden
wheels on the stone road made it impossible to talk.

After a while, the sounds of the city faded away, but Tiberius
was still silent. He led them up the gentle slope of the wide, paved
Alta Semita. Lush gardens peeked from behind the exterior walls
of the houses. The understated aura of the neighborhood spoke
loudly. This was where the very rich must live. She knew that few
people could afford this kind of quiet. Even the air seemed different:
fresher and cooler. Matti looked around, wide-eyed.

They turned into a clean side street, and then into another street
wide enough for two litters to pass. They stopped in front of a house

with high wooden double doors. She and Matti exchanged glances. A doorman opened the doors, and they entered a tall, light-filled vestibule with a black-and-white mosaic floor. The cedar planks of the raftered roof infused the air with a sweet woody fragrance.

Tiberius strode into an atrium that opened to the sky. Esther stared at the dwarf trees with small orange buds, and rows of roses and junipers. Birds hopped between a painted marble statue of entwined nymphs and a running fountain. A stream wound through a row of tall oleander and laurel shrubs.

Colorful doors opened to other rooms. She looked around in wonder.

"A bankrupt senator with an old Republican name needed money," Tiberius said with a shrug. "I bought it a year ago. It's fine for now, but I won't stay in Rome forever. I have a villa in Campania; that's where I want to be."

It looked more than "fine for now," but Esther didn't say anything.

Servants scurried about, casting curious glances in her direction. They didn't look like the slaves in Proculus's house. Tiberius gave his cloak to a short bald man who nodded and asked if he should prepare lunch. There was a tattoo on his neck, but he didn't have a slave's demeanor. He even smiled when he walked away. When Tiberius's back was turned, Matti pulled on Esther's arm and whispered, "I'm hungry." Tiberius spun around and called the servant back. "Give the boy something to eat."

Matti looked to Esther for permission. She nodded, and Matti left, without a backward glance. Tiberius told Esther to wait in the atrium; he wanted to send the bill of sale over to Proculus as soon as possible. Her stomach growled. She was hungry too, but had been too embarrassed to say so.

She hadn't expected to feel so awkward around Tiberius. She'd expected him to talk more, to tell her what he'd been doing, and ask about her. But he'd spoken few words. When Tiberius returned, he said Matti had eaten and fallen asleep. She followed Tiberius into a large dining room, where plates were laid out on the table—plates of bread, olives, fruit, stuffed pheasant, and boiled vegetables arranged to resemble a hare. Couches, with small three-legged tables in front of each one, faced each other. Tiberius sat down. Esther assumed he must have been expecting company. Uncertain, she stood, waiting for him to tell her where to go. When he didn't, she went to the corner and squatted.

He slammed his fist on the table, then stood up and walked toward her, his eyes blazing. "What have they done to you, my proud Aster?" He grabbed her shoulders and pulled her up.

She cowered and shielded her face with her arm. He seemed surprised by her reaction and quickly let her go, stepping away. He motioned for her to sit on one of the couches. Esther lowered herself stiffly, bracing herself with both hands. Reddening, she squirmed under his intense gaze. She couldn't remember when she'd last sat on a chair with cushions. She hadn't reclined on a couch in a dining room since those long-ago Passover seders in Jerusalem.

A different servant set down a platter piled high with grapes, quince, and pomegranates. Her mouth watered.

"Eat," Tiberius commanded.

Esther didn't know what to eat first. She grabbed a cluster of grapes and began stuffing them into her mouth. She could hardly chew. She wanted to swallow faster, so she could put more into her mouth. The sweet juice of the grapes burst in her mouth and tickled her tongue.

She stopped abruptly and grabbed her side. A pain shot through her stomach.

He smiled. Was he laughing at her?

Esther rearranged her face in a slave-mask and stopped chewing. Tiberius said, "Go on. Eat your fill," and she did.

"Come, you must be exhausted," Tiberius said after the meal. She followed him through the house. He opened a door. "This is your room."

There was a dresser and an empty bed. "Where's Matti?"

"In that room," he said, pointing to a closed door at the end of the hallway.

When Tiberius left, she went to Matti's room.

She had to lie on her side to fit into Matti's narrow bed. She'd never slept on a cloud before; even the mattresses at home had been filled with straw or wool, not feathers. She rested her head against Matti and put her hand on his back. She needed to touch him, to tether herself to something familiar, to reassure herself that this—*all of this*—was real, reassure herself that they wouldn't wake up and be back on the hard, cold floor in Proculus's kitchen. She knew they were safe with Tiberius, but something felt wrong; he seemed different. Besides, the papers weren't signed yet. Maybe Proculus would change his mind; she couldn't sink into the clouds just yet.

CHAPTER LXXXVII

Esther saw Tiberius leave the house early the next morning. There were shadows under his eyes and a hard edge to his face. He dipped his head slightly when he saw her, then quickly looked away.

Since their arrival the day before, Esther had had a simmering sense of unease. Tiberius had treated them like guests instead of slaves. Yet he had hardly spoken to them. She didn't understand his silence, and she didn't trust it. Maybe he regretted bringing them here. His home too made her apprehensive. Everywhere she looked, something was meant to look like something else, as if there were an art to hiding reality. The vegetables at dinner had been arranged to look like a hare; the legs of the tables were shaped like horse legs; and frescoes of fake doors and windows adorned the walls.

Felix, the bald slave, offered them breakfast. She took some of the bread and cheese from the table and after the meal hid it in her room, behind the dresser. Then she and Matti wandered around, unsure what to do or where to go. They found themselves in the atrium, where they tried to count the small red birds perched in the trees. One flitted across the garden and disappeared behind the fountain.

"I wonder why they don't fly away," Esther said, looking up at the square opening in the roof, open to the sky.

"Why would they?" Matti said. "It's nice here."

Esther sat on a bench in the garden while Matti studied the beetles in the hollow of an old tree. He was fascinated by them.

Tiberius returned midafternoon. He sat down next to Esther. "Proculus signed the bill of sale," he said.

We're safe. Her shoulders dropped and she let out a long breath. *But not free.* "Now we're legally your slaves."

Tiberius looked down, clearly uncomfortable. He shook his head but didn't say anything.

"Then what am I?" she demanded. "What am I?" She bit her lip, trying to keep her voice from shaking.

"You're my friend," he mumbled.

"How can I be your friend *and* your property?"

Tiberius didn't answer. She turned away from him.

Matti came running over, his hands cupped together. "Do you want to see? I caught some beetles. You should see the color of their backs."

Closing one eye, Esther bent down and looked into his hands. "I think," she said, lifting her head, "you should let them go."

That night, Matti said he wanted to sleep by himself, the bed was too small for both of them. Esther tried to hide her surprise. *It's fine,* she told herself as she walked to her room. Unlike her, he felt secure here. *Let him be happy.*

When she got to her room, she saw the food that she'd hidden earlier behind the dresser now sitting on a plate. There was another plate next to it with fresh bread. *Maybe it will be all right,* she told herself.

CHAPTER LXXXVIII

IT FELT STRANGE TO SLEEP ALONE, TO HEAR SILENCE INSTEAD OF Matti's rhythmic breathing. She didn't think she'd be able to fall asleep. She decided to wait for a while, then check on him.

But she must have fallen asleep, because when she opened her eyes, Tiberius was standing in the doorway. He didn't say anything; he just stood still with that inscrutable expression of his. She didn't know how long he'd been there, watching her. But it was night, and she knew what men wanted at night. Why else would he be in her room?

She got out of bed and walked toward him. Silently she pulled her tunic over her head. She unwrapped her loincloth and let it fall to the ground.

She stood naked and looked down.

Placing his finger under her chin, he tilted her gaze to meet his. She averted her eyes.

"Look at me," he said.

Slowly she raised her eyes. "This is what you want, isn't it?" she said. "You bought me."

Tiberius picked up her tunic and held it out. "Cover yourself," he said, looking away. "I don't want you like this."

He walked out of the room.

—◊—

The light streaming through the window woke her. Esther took a few tentative steps out of her room and looked around. Why had she goaded Tiberius the night before? She was angry that they were still slaves and now belonged to him. And his aloofness and perpetual scowl troubled her. He didn't seem happy that they were there, and he had made no effort to really talk to her.

She didn't know what she had expected. She hadn't had time, really, to expect anything. Yet he *had* brought them here, fed them, let them sit at a table again, and sleep in a bed.

She needed to apologize.

As she made her way to the dining room, she overheard Tiberius talking to Felix. Tiberius said he was going to see a slave dealer who traded in Jewish captives, and he was taking Esther and Matti with him.

Esther felt the ground spinning. She had been right; he did regret his purchase. And now he wanted to get rid of them. The words from the night before came back to her.

I don't want you.

No! They would not be sold again. There was no time to make a plan. She called for Matti. "Come on! We have to leave!"

He shook his head. "Leave? Why?"

"I don't have time to explain. Tiberius is going to sell us!"

Matti crossed his arms over his chest. "I don't believe you."

She pulled his arm angrily and yanked him behind her. "Matti, you must believe me! I'll explain on the way. Hurry up!"

At least this time they weren't wearing slave rags. There had been new tunics in their rooms. Maybe they'd blend in to the crowds.

Felix was in a side room, talking to the gardener. His back was turned. She and Matti snuck past him, taking light, quiet steps. She opened the front door, and they stepped out into the fresh morning air. She tried to remember the route they'd traveled when Tiberius had brought them here. Had they come from the left, or the right? She remembered wide clean streets, but that was all. A starling peeked through the branches of a tree across the street, then warbled and made a high-pitched trill. It seemed to look directly at her, then flew away. *It must be a good omen,* she decided. Holding Matti's hand tightly, she followed the bird.

CHAPTER LXXXIX

AN HOUR LATER, THEY WERE LOST. SHE WAS HUNGRY AND TIRED. THE strap on her sandal had broken, and she had a blister where she had tied it back together. She and Matti sat on the ground next to a small fountain. There were people all around, but no one looked at them. She put her head in her hands. If only . . .

If only she had taken the bread and cheese from her room . . .

If only she had tried harder to find the landmarks she knew . . .

If only she knew how to get back to Zahara . . .

When she lifted her head, she saw Tiberius standing behind the fountain, his hands folded over his chest. Waiting. When their eyes met, he walked toward her.

"Why did you run away?" Tiberius asked.

Tears glistened in her eyes. "What choice did I have? We're not going on the block again, ever."

"What are you talking about?"

Esther stood up. "You told Felix that you were taking us to a slave dealer. I heard you."

"You thought I was going to *sell* you?"

She looked down at her hands. "Last night you said you didn't want me."

Tiberius looked bewildered. "Do you have any idea how hard I searched for you? I went to every slave market from Sicily to Pompeii, from Rome to Luca. I spoke with all the *mangones,* every filthy, depraved slave trader who had Jewish captives for sale. I even had my old friends in the ministry check the tax records in Rome for any tax paid on a Jewish slave who fit your description or Matti's. I asked every Jew I found if they knew you. I even went to the amphitheater games"—he shuddered and spat to the side—"to see if you had been selected. I knew that it was hopeless, that you were probably dead, and if by some miracle you'd survived, you could have been sold anywhere, in any province of the empire. But I couldn't stop looking, because then I would have had to accept that I would never see you again."

She flushed. His gaze was so intense that she had to look away. Clearly she'd panicked; they shouldn't have run away. But there was still something she didn't understand. "Why were you so angry when you found us?"

"I wasn't angry at *you*."

He wasn't making sense.

"I was angry at myself for not finding you sooner. I was angry that I hadn't been able to protect you. I was worried Proculus wouldn't sign the papers."

"If you didn't want to sell us, why were you going to the slave dealer?"

"I'm trying to buy Zahara, but her owner won't sell. She makes a lot of money for him. I thought I'd have better luck if I got the slave trader to negotiate for me. And afterward, I wanted to take you to see her."

After so long starving for kindness, Esther hadn't been able to recognize it standing right before her.

CHAPTER XC

THE FOLLOWING MORNING, TIBERIUS SAID HE NEEDED TO TAKE Esther somewhere, and take care of something. She was curious, but he refused to say more.

They walked to the Forum Iulium, with the equestrian statue of Julius Caesar towering over the crowds and the massive temple to Venus. The forum was bustling with toga-clad men. Esther followed Tiberius through a gleaming white portico, and through two wooden doors. They entered a large hall decorated with frescoes of port scenes on the walls and a tall ceiling tiled in bright colors. Busts of Apollo and Mars filled the wall niches.

The magistrate sat behind a table covered with fragments of parchment, abacuses, quills, jars of ink, waxed tablets, and seals. Clerks carrying scrolls and boxes scurried in and out of the hall. Tiberius held her hand tightly, the way, she thought, one holds a child. He seemed jumpy. What were they doing here?

The magistrate demanded to see the bill of sale.

Bill of sale? What was happening? She swung around to Tiberius. He didn't look at her, but he squeezed her hand and pulled a parchment from inside his cloak. The magistrate looked it over and said, "Are you certain she is only nineteen years old?"

Tiberius nodded. The magistrate continued, "Then you can't liberate her yet. She's too young. Thirty is the minimum age set by the Lex Aelia Sentia in the time of the Divine Augustus—"

"But there is an exception, as the honorable praetor knows," Tiberius said, cutting him off. "I intend to make this woman my wife."

Her knees went weak. Tiberius pressed his thumb into her palm, as if he were sending her a message. He continued to look at the magistrate.

"Hmm," the magistrate said, rubbing his chin. "If marriage is a codicil to this manumission, I will have to convene a council to approve this exception to the law."

Tiberius flashed an ingratiating smile. "Perhaps the worthy praetor will not have to do that." He jingled his coin purse. "She won't run away."

The magistrate looked at the purse and licked his lips. "I trust your word as an honorable Roman citizen. Let's get started." He picked up a thin twisted branch without leaves. "This rod is called the *vindicta*," he said, tapping her on the head with the smooth end. "And with its touch, you are free from slavery."

Esther remained motionless, even though she felt light-headed. Through her fog, she heard the magistrate mumble their names, the date, and some official-sounding words as he filled in the blanks on a long scroll already covered with Latin writing. He confirmed the clerks' names as witnesses, and signed his own name at the bottom. He showed Tiberius where to sign, took the document back, looked it over, and then handed it to Tiberius. Tiberius gave it to Esther and whispered, "I'll liberate Matti too, as soon as the law permits."

"Congratulations, Claudia Aster," the magistrate said. "You are now a free Roman woman, a legal citizen, and a member of the *populus Romanus*, with all the privileges, responsibilities, and restrictions that entail for a *libertina*."

He shuffled beads up and down on the abacus and said, "Five percent of the sale price would be . . ."

Tiberius didn't wait for the calculation. He counted out several silver and gold coins and handed them to the magistrate, who looked pleased.

With one hand on Esther's back, Tiberius gently pushed her, guiding her from the hall. She had to tell herself to put one foot in front of the other. As she stepped back into the forum, she felt the sun bathe her in light, as if she were entering the world anew. Her name was Claudia Aster. She was free.

She had grown so used to her cage that she'd hardly noticed it. Especially since she'd been with Tiberius. But now that he'd unlocked it and opened the door, she had an unobstructed view of the sky. It looked different without the bars.

She owed her freedom to a man she'd once hated. She had hated him for being Roman, and for putting her father in danger. But it hadn't really been Tiberius whom she had hated, any more than it had been Joseph whom she had loved.

"Am I really free, or am I your wife?" she asked, looking up at him.

He dropped his gaze. "You're free. I had to say we're getting married so I could manumit you. I'm not . . . It was just for the magistrate."

Of course. His kindness was overwhelming, but it didn't change what he had said the night before. He didn't want her. Not as his slave, but certainly not as his wife. She was surprised to find that she felt a flicker of disappointment.

CHAPTER XCI

THE DAYS WENT BY QUICKLY. MATTI ATTACHED HIMSELF TO FELIX, AND was soon busy pruning the shrubs in the atrium and working in the outside garden. Esther found things to do too, but she still asked Tiberius's permission for everything: Could she walk outside? Could she read the scrolls in the library? She found *The Iliad* and *The Odyssey,* works of philosophy, histories of Greece and Rome, and even love poems. She couldn't read Latin, but she could decipher the names: Virgil, Ovid, and Catullus.

And she was excited beyond anything she could have imagined to discover that she could still read Greek. At first, she struggled, but gradually the marks on the page faded and she saw letters instead, and then whole words, and finally those fell away to reveal mythological creatures and jealous men and virtuous, beautiful women and raging gods and storms and mountains and seas. When she read, she couldn't hear the paralyzing prattle of her own mind. She was elsewhere. She read urgently and violently, demanding that the stories take her away again and again.

Matti wanted to learn to read too. In the afternoons, they sat together with a scroll. He was making progress, but he lost interest quickly. When he tired of reading, Matti asked Esther to tell him stories. Tiberius liked to listen too; he especially liked the Purim story with Queen Esther. Esther treasured those moments.

Tiberius didn't seem like someone who would read for pleasure or, like her, for sustenance. The longer she stayed in his house, the more she learned about him. He read poetry and drew pictures, but he loved pork and games of chance. He was still an enigma. She looked up from the scroll. He was watching her—again. She squirmed under his scrutiny. "What are you looking at?"

He came closer. "The specks of gold in your eyes, like the sun is shining right through them. The curve of your neck, the way the tips of your eyelashes curl, the pale down on your upper lip—"

She turned away. She had gotten used to being unseen. A good slave was invisible.

"I want to draw you. I'm looking for the lines and the light." He paused. "And the shadows. The shadows are a part of you too."

That night, she examined herself in the mirror. She didn't see any lines or any light. But her slave-mask was gone. For the first time in a very long while, she recognized the face staring back.

CHAPTER XCII

It was a cold night. The swifts in the chimney made a high-pitched buzz, and the wind rattled the window.

"I have something to tell you," Tiberius said as they sat in the dining room.

Esther looked up, curious.

"I owed you money from the shipment with your father, two talent-weights of gold. But it's not two anymore."

She wasn't surprised. She knew he sometimes gambled, and she'd seen what had happened to Shimon. Besides, she hadn't really expected Tiberius to keep the money for her for so long. "You bought us from Proculus," she said, "and for that I'm more grateful than you'll ever know. All you've shown me is kindness, even though I haven't always shown you the same." She looked around the room. "You bought this house, where we now have refuge; you bought the library, where we can read; you—"

"Aster," he interrupted, laying a hand on her arm.

"No, it's all right. I want you to know that I don't care where the money's gone."

"I never spent one denarius of your money."

She stared at him, blinking. "But you said it's not two talents anymore."

"That's right." A faint smile tugged at the corner of his mouth. "It's five."

"Five?" she echoed, not sure she'd heard correctly.

"I invested it."

She was speechless. It was a fortune. If it was true . . .

"But . . . why didn't you tell me when you rescued us from Proculus?" she asked.

"I was going to, but I . . . I didn't want you to leave. At first, I told myself that you needed to get your strength back. You were both emaciated when I found you. And then I kept stalling, since I feared that as soon as you had your freedom and the money, you'd leave. That you wouldn't have any reason to stay." He lifted his eyes shyly.

She let the meaning of his words sink in. He wanted her with him. To stay.

She heard Miriam whisper in her ear: *What you think you know isn't always so.*

CHAPTER XCIII

IN THE MIDDLE OF THE NIGHT, ESTHER BOLTED UPRIGHT IN HER BED. She was screaming in her sleep. Tiberius rushed into her room. He must have heard her shouting. He took her hands and held them firmly. "Shh. . . . It's a nightmare."

She was suffocating; she felt as if someone were pressing on her chest, holding her down. She fought for breath, screaming and shaking her head wildly as she tried to throw him off. The soldier was on top of her. Proculus was laughing.

Get off me! Get off me!

Tiberius held her tightly until she could catch the air again and the room stopped spinning. He lit the oil lamp, and she opened her eyes. There were no soldiers, no Proculus; only Tiberius. Their heads were so close together, she could smell his hair. Like rain in a pine forest.

"You won't feel like this forever," he said. "I know." He stroked her hair and began to talk. At first, he spoke haltingly, as if the words were so heavy, he could hardly carry them. He told her stories that couldn't be told in the day or to her face, about how, after he was captured, he had to sleep on the floor, tied to the bed of a soldier who raped him at night. When he tried to escape back to his mother, the soldier whipped him so savagely that he couldn't walk for weeks. To this day, he couldn't touch a strap made from ox hide.

She thought of Matti.

"Pallas, my boss in the treasury, made me do things too. At first,

I just had to walk on his back or massage him, but then . . ." His words trailed off. The hurt look on his face returned.

The room was so still, she could hear his ragged breath.

Esther leaned toward him and their cheeks touched. The rough stubble of his face rubbed against her. They stayed that way, unmoving.

"All the money I made couldn't erase my shame," he said. "But I wanted money anyway. I still do." He told her how people respected successful freedmen, even though they hated them. After he was freed, he saved enough money—and skimmed enough from the treasury receipts—to buy his mother's freedom. She hadn't always been kind, but she'd been all he had.

He started to get up.

Esther touched his hand; she didn't want him to go. "I think I might love you," she said.

"Love," Tiberius said slowly, as if he were savoring the word in his mouth, reluctant to swallow it. He sat back down. "Would that be so terrible?" His face wore a half smile that couldn't mask the sadness behind it.

"It's wrong," Esther said, her voice shaking. "You're a Roman and I'm a Jew."

"I'm a man and you're a woman." He stroked her hair, gently. His hands traced the scars on her arms, and he trailed his fingers up to her bare shoulder, where her tunic had slipped off. She felt his warm breath on her neck. Then his lips. He kissed her lightly, carefully, and slowly. His mouth on her flesh filled her with an exquisite sensation. She felt herself burning up while she kept herself perfectly still.

He pulled himself away. "Not yet," he said, lifting the edge of her tunic and draping it back over her shoulder.

And then he left.

PART FIFTEEN

NOVEMBER 70 CE
HESHVAN 3831

And the king said to her, "What do you wish, Queen Esther? What is your request? It shall be given to you—up to half the kingdom!

Esther 5:3

CHAPTER XCIV

A WEEK LATER, THEY SAT TOGETHER IN THE LIBRARY. MATTI AND Tiberius were playing a game, moving small pebbles on a stone slab. Tiberius was quiet as he studied the arrangement of the pebbles. He moved one, then looked up.

Finally he spoke. "Some Jews in Rome are going to incriminate Joseph—Josephus—in a plot against the emperor. They hate him as much as I do."

"He's in the emperor's inner circle now," Esther said. "You told me that yourself."

"That's why it will give me such satisfaction to see him beheaded, when Emperor Vespasian thinks Josephus has betrayed him."

"And what if their plot fails? Something could go wrong. If you're involved, you could be the one who ends up with the executioner."

"I can finally taste revenge," he said. The veins in his temple pulsed.

"What really happened between you?" Esther asked.

"He wanted information. Stupidly, I fell into his trap. I told him that Poppaea, Emperor Nero's wife, was having an affair, and the paternity of her baby was in doubt. Joseph told Poppaea what I'd said. As a reward—for naming me as the source of the palace gossip—Poppaea convinced Nero to pardon the Jewish priests who'd been jailed in Rome. I had to flee for my life."

"So why did you tell him?"

"I guess . . . I wanted to impress him with my knowledge of the court gossip." He paused, looking down. "I wanted a friend. He treated me differently than the Romans. Like I had never been a slave."

Esther sat back in her chair. "And then you came to Jerusalem?"

Tiberius nodded. "I knew Joseph would eventually go back. Plus, the Temple coffers were overflowing, and the priests were purchasing cloth, spices, and building materials as fast as we could supply them. I wanted in on those deals."

Esther grabbed his hand, surprised at her own daring. "It's too dangerous," Esther said. "Stay out of it."

"You don't understand," Tiberius said.

"I do. He betrayed me too. But, don't do it . . . please. I'm not protecting Joseph," she said, grimacing. Even his name in her mouth was loathsome. "I can't lose you. I've lost too many already."

CHAPTER XCV

THAT NIGHT, AFTER MATTI WENT TO SLEEP, TIBERIUS WALKED INTO the library, where Esther was standing next to the shelves. "I have to ask you something, something that I could ask only once you were free and could answer truthfully. You've always told me the truth, and you're the only woman who never wanted anything from me except"—he smiled wistfully—"except for me to stay away from you and your family."

Esther smiled too, remembering.

"I trust you," he continued, "and I can't live without you. I love you. You said you . . . that you might love me too." He dropped his voice to a whisper. "Will you marry me?"

She thought of the young girl she had once been, Esther Bat Hanan, daughter of a priest. And she thought about Tiberius. He hadn't been born a Roman, but he was one. He was a member of the tribe that had destroyed her city and her Temple, and banished her people. But he was also the man who had taught her again how to live without fear, the man she could never stop thinking about, no matter how hard she tried. Esther Bat Hanan would never have married a Roman. But that girl, who'd danced in the vineyard and tried to catch rainbows in her father's office, was gone. In her place was a woman named Claudia Aster. A woman who already loved a man who was the enemy, like her biblical ancestors Naomi and Boaz had loved Ruth, from the tribe of the despised Moabites.

Looking into Tiberius's face, filled with such yearning, she realized that what she felt *was* love. She wanted to tell him this. She wanted to tell him about the textures, tones, and hues that hadn't existed before. But it was complicated.

She was still putting her thoughts in order when he jumped in. "I'm sorry for asking. I don't blame you. You're free now and you have money; you don't have to marry me. You don't want another chain around your neck." He turned away, perhaps so she wouldn't be able to see the disappointment on his face.

"Wait," she said, beginning to laugh. He looked back. "I've been making plans all my life," she said, "and none of them worked out like I expected. This is the last thing I would ever have planned." She drew a deep breath. "Yes."

Tiberius's face lit up.

"But," Esther added quickly, "there's one condition."

"Anything, up to half my kingdom."

Esther smiled. He'd remembered the king's words from the Purim story she had told him. "Promise me that you won't join the plot against Josephus. He'll get what he deserves. You could be killed. And I can't live without you."

He looked down and rubbed his temples, his expression betraying the battle in his heart.

After a pause, he nodded.

"Then yes," Esther said, beaming. "Yes. Claudia Aster says 'yes' to Tiberius Claudius Masculus."

He grinned, and moved closer, putting his hand on her waist, but then his eyes turned serious again and he took a step back. Esther touched his arm, surprising herself with her boldness.

Tiberius stood perfectly still, as if her hand were a butterfly that might fly away at any moment. He looked into her face, his eyes asking a question. She answered with a dip of her head. He bent to kiss her, slowly and tentatively, his lips surprisingly soft as they met hers. His heat infused her with an unfamiliar warmth. He pulled her close, and she wrapped her arms around his shoulders.

She felt something she'd learned not to take for granted; she felt safe and loved.

CHAPTER XCVI

ESTHER AND TIBERIUS WERE ON THEIR WAY TO VISIT THEIR OLD FRIEND in the Jewish quarter. Even though Zahara was free now, thanks to Tiberius, she still lived and worked there. She liked it, she'd said, and had turned down their numerous offers to have her move in with them.

As they passed a store selling scrolls and writing utensils, Esther paused.

"Wait. I want to buy Matti a wax tablet so he can practice his script." She was eager to look at the scrolls too. Maybe she'd find another Greek novel. Her Latin had improved greatly, but she still preferred the language of her father's lessons. It made her feel closer to him.

"I'll wait here," Tiberius said.

The door screeched on its hinges as Esther pushed it open. An earthy, spicy smell greeted her, a welcome relief from the foul street odors. Stacks of flat papyrus sheets, reed pens, and jars of ink were strewn over a table in the middle of the small room. The shelves overflowed with scrolls and wax tablets.

A kindly-looking man with fuzzy white hair looked up from his writing. "I think you're in the wrong place," he said, his gaze taking in her elegant stola, which draped to the floor in the latest Roman fashion. "Surely you're looking for someone who writes Greek or Latin? I'm a Jewish scribe."

"I don't need a scribe. I came to buy a wax tablet."

The scribe pointed to a stack of tablets in different sizes.

"I'm Jewish too," Esther said, surprising herself. She didn't know why she wanted him to know that.

The scribe narrowed his eyes in a dubious expression. "What's your name?"

"Claudia Aster . . . but I used to be Esther Bat Hanan."

He nodded, as if she had just told him her whole life's story. "I thought I detected an accent. Well, if a myrtle lives among the willows and acts like a willow, it's still a myrtle." He looked pleased with himself. "Come closer, Esther. I have something you might like to see."

He reached for a small scroll on a shelf, untied the flax ribbon, and unrolled the scroll in the opposite direction from the Greek and Latin texts she'd read in Tiberius's library. The scroll was in Hebrew, written from right to left.

As she stared at the lines and curves of the ink strokes, her breath quickened. The letters were intimately familiar. They seemed to fly off the scroll, summoning everyone she had lost.

She closed her eyes, wanting to prolong the moment. She felt as if she could leave the store, walk past the bridge to the Temple, past Yohanan the sandal-maker, and Babatha, who sold the softest, juiciest dates in town. She'd avoid the dip in the road where it flooded every winter. She'd walk through the gate to the courtyard; Miriam would be spinning; Matti would be feeding the goats; Yehuda and Shimon would be arguing; her mother would be mixing her potions; and her father would be in his study. They'd all be there, waiting for her.

She opened her eyes. "Where did you get it?" she asked softly, touching the papyrus with her fingertips.

"Someone rescued it from the flames of Jerusalem."

She cleared her throat and began reciting the *Megillah.*

The scribe smiled and chanted a few lines with her.

"How much is it?" Esther asked.

"I'm sorry; it's not for sale."

It wasn't as beautiful as the *Megillah* her family had owned. But she didn't care. She wanted it. "I want something that survived."

"You have something. Yourself. Like Queen Esther, you survived."

Yes, I did. But how can I be happy when I think about all the others who didn't?

She stared at the scroll. "I wonder what happened to Esther after the story ends. No one talks about that. She had to stay with the king in his palace. She couldn't go home."

"She must have made a new home," the man said.

Wasn't home where you were from? How could she make a new home? The words of the psalms came to her, and she said, *"How can we sing the songs of the Lord in a strange land? If I forget you, O Jerusalem, let my right hand wither."*

"You won't forget," the scribe said.

Esther shrugged. "Maybe it doesn't matter. What's there to remember anyway? It's all gone. Even the Temple."

"Let me tell you something: once before—a long, long time ago—the people of Jerusalem were defeated. The first Temple, the one King Solomon built, was destroyed. The people were taken captive to Babylon. Do you know what the prophet Jeremiah told them?"

Esther shook her head.

"Build houses and settle down; plant gardens and eat the fruit. Marry and have sons and daughters." He paused, then continued, "In other words, live. Live . . . and remember."

He was right. She would live and she would remember—her family, her beloved city, and the stories of her people.

Then she had an idea, something that would help her remember. "I'd like to commission you to write a scroll. Would you make a *Megillah* for me?"

He smiled. "Of course."

Esther tucked the wax tablet under her arm as she left the scribe. She smiled when she saw Tiberius. Maybe she would teach him to read Hebrew, like her father had taught her. Maybe she would teach their sons one day—or their daughter.

Maybe, someday, someone would remember her too.

AUTHOR'S NOTE

—◆—

During the ten years I worked on this book, I immersed myself in research on the first century. I worked closely with one of the world's premier experts of this period, Professor Jonathan Price of Tel Aviv University. Under his guidance, I consulted with leading scholars and archaeologists on a wide range of topics, including first-century magic, marital customs, clothing, food, and even children's games. I read stacks of books, conference proceedings (including one about first-century garbage dumps!), and doctoral dissertations. I spent hours in museums studying Roman and Jewish artifacts. I spent days and weeks exploring excavations in Jerusalem. I walked that beautiful city in the morning and afternoon, in every season, to see where the light fell and how the rain sounded as it hit the ancient stones. Even though there was much I had to imagine, I wanted to make sure that what happened in the story could actually have happened, at least from a historical perspective.

My main characters, Esther, Tiberius, and Joseph/Josephus, were real people, as were the leaders on both sides: the Jewish king, Agrippa; the Roman governor, Florus; the emperors Nero, Vespasian, and Titus; and the rebels Eliezer and Menachem. Some of the Temple priests and Jerusalem merchants who make cameo appearances were also real people. The fictitious characters have Jewish and Roman names from that time. I felt a tremendous obligation to Esther and Tiberius to tell their story as accurately as possible.

Of these characters, historians know the most about Joseph/ Josephus because he wrote an autobiography as well as a detailed account of the revolt and his role in it. Although we know that his writings contain exaggerations and inaccuracies, they still provide an invaluable eyewitness report. They were my primary source for the chronology and the people, just as they are the primary source for professional historians writing about this time.

Born into one of Jerusalem's most distinguished families, Josephus became the commander of the Jewish forces in Galilee when war broke out in 66 CE. After his defeat, he was imprisoned in the main Roman camp through the siege of Jerusalem. He survived by serving as a translator and adviser, and by his own account, lost his passion for Jewish independence. He began urging his fellow rebels to make peace. While still in the Roman camp, Josephus was granted Roman citizenship. After the war, he lived a comfortable life in Rome, supported by a stipend from the imperial family, and even enjoyed a close relationship with the Roman emperor Titus.

Was he a traitor, as Esther and many of her contemporaries believed, or a realist who tried to save his people from annihilation? The debate continues to this day.

We know far less about Esther and Tiberius. The little we do know comes from a two-thousand-year-old gravestone discovered in southern Italy, now on display at the new Museum of Italian Judaism and the Shoah in Ferrara, Italy. The ancient inscription reads:

Claudia Aster, captive from Jerusalem. Tiberius Claudius Masculus, freedman of the Emperor, took care [to set up the epitaph]. I ask you, make sure that you take care that no one casts down my inscription contrary to the law. She lived 25 years.

While the stone doesn't reveal much, archeologists and historians have inferred quite a lot from its few words. The most significant facts are that Claudia Aster was taken prisoner during the conquest of Jerusalem in the first century and ended her life as a freed slave in Italy. Although she could have been a priest's daughter or a poor farm girl, or anything in between, her unusual name hints at an upper-class birth. Aster is the Latinization of Esther, an aristocratic Hebrew name from this period.

In all likelihood, Esther was captured during the great siege of Jerusalem in 70 CE. In ancient times, a war captive immediately became a slave, regardless of his or her prior status. Esther would have spent time in the Roman camp, together with the thousands of other captives, and suffered greatly. Afterward, she would likely have been abused until she was finally purchased by Tiberius. Physical and sexual abuse was the grim reality for a foreign-born slave girl.

Esther's relationship with Josephus was a product of my imagination, but it is nonetheless possible since Josephus was a prominent figure in Jewish Jerusalem. The two would also have been in the Roman army camp at the same time. The incident in Chapter XXIV when Josephus is allowed to save fifty friends and family is based on his written account.

Since Esther ended up in Italy, she most likely was marched with the other captives down to Caesarea, the main port of Judea, and put aboard a ship. We know (again from Josephus) about the games with gladiators, slaves, and wild animals that Titus staged along the way. Esther probably was part of those, too, if only as a witness. Once she survived the perilous trip to Italy, she would have been sold there, probably as a household slave.

Tiberius was not necessarily her first owner, but he was her last, since he freed her and gave her his name, Claudius. Scholars presume that Tiberius loved her, since there would have been no other reason for him to free her and erect a gravestone. Roman law forbade manumission of slaves below the age of thirty. There were, however, certain exceptions; marriage is the only one that could apply to Esther and Tiberius.

It is noteworthy, too, that Tiberius had been a slave himself. His middle name, Claudius, reveals that he was an ex-slave of either the Roman emperor Claudius or the Roman emperor Nero. In my view, Tiberius's background might have made him sensitive to Esther's trauma. In those days, many freedmen, especially those who had risen through the ranks of the imperial bureaucracy, became quite influential and wealthy. These men were resented by the old guard in Rome. Tiberius was at least rich enough to buy Esther, but he would likely have had other slaves as well.

According to the epigraph on her tombstone, Esther lived to be twenty-five years. Her age suggests that she died in childbirth. Tiberius begs future generations to take care of her final resting place.

Using the history I read, as well as conversations I had with experts, I tried to tell the truest story I could. But this is fiction, and there's much we can never know. The only thing we do know for sure is that these two people weren't supposed to find each other, but they did. A story of struggle for freedom and love is as relevant today as it was two thousand years ago. History is not a dry record of events; it's a portal to the human soul, one that connects us to all the people who lived before. I hope Esther's story inspires you, as it did me, to go through the door that history opens and explore how the past and present are connected.

HISTORICAL NOTE

—◊—

The war that engulfed Esther's life and altered it forever was a world-changing event that overwhelmed tens of thousands, maybe hundreds of thousands of lives, transformed Judaism permanently and contributed to Christianity's eventual emergence as a world religion. The war is conventionally called the Jewish War because from the Roman perspective, that is what it was: the Jews who lived in Judea and the Galilee, an area roughly the size of the modern state of Israel (without the extreme southern portions), rose up in rebellion against the Roman Empire, under whose rule they had lived uneasily for more than a century. The Jews would have called it the Roman War; today it is commonly called the Great Revolt.

In the first century CE, the Romans ruled a vast empire of conquered lands, stretching from Britain to Mesopotamia, from Germany to North Africa. The Romans dominated all lands and peoples around the Mediterranean Sea. In Rome, they called the Mediterranean "Our Sea." Their power was based on the most efficient and successful army the world had ever seen. Unimaginable wealth poured into Rome from the many provinces into which this empire was organized. Roman power and influence extended far beyond the most distant provinces of their realm. Roman merchants traded along regular routes extending all the way to China.

Within their enormous realm, the Romans ruled over hundreds of different peoples and religions. Unlike other empires in history, the Romans generally did not impose their religion or social norms on their subjects, and they presented themselves as tolerant and accepting rulers. In many but not all cases, this was true.

The Jews living in Judea were among the Romans' least cooperative subjects. The Romans conquered the region in 63 BCE, using the conflict within the family of Jewish kings known as the Hasmoneans as a pretext for intervening in the region. The Hasmoneans were allowed to continue ruling for a while, under Roman supervision, and after their demise the Romans continued to control the area, either by proxy or direct rule. The Jews never regained full political independence or full control of their lives—until the rebellion.

Roman rule brought certain benefits, such as peacekeeping forces within each province and across the empire; a thriving economy; good roads; security on land and sea; urban amenities such as water and sewage systems, and entertainment complexes; and relative freedom in local politics and religion. These benefits were touted by the Romans themselves as the results of universal peace and enlightened governance. Yet many subjects, including the Jews, chafed under the frequent abuses and financial burdens of Roman rule, which were added to heavy financial demands of the Jews' religion, such as agricultural tithes and obligations to the Temple in Jerusalem. Roman taxes and other interference in people's lives by the provincial administration also served as constant, irritating reminders that foreigners, not God's appointed rulers, ruled over land promised to Jewish sovereignty. Moreover, during the sixty years leading up to the war, Rome, contrary to its policy in other parts of its empire, installed in Judea a series of governors who, with malice or through ignorance, offended Jewish sensibilities and in some instances directly provoked the population. As Josephus, the main historian of the war, wrote about Florus, the last Roman procurator, or local governor, of Judea: "Fleecing individuals seemed a small matter to him: he stripped whole cities, brought ruin on entire populations, and nearly went so far as to proclaim throughout the country that all were permitted to rob and pillage, on condition that he himself got part of the take."[1]

The sixty years before the rebellion were, moreover, a time of spreading messianic fervor, an expectation, based in Scripture, that according to God's plan the last world empire—Rome—would soon fall and be replaced by the sovereignty of the Children of Israel, who would preside over a world of everlasting peace and justice. The leader to emerge would be God's anointed one, or the Messiah. This was proven through a variety of biblical verses, and the visions of the End of Time differed in other ways as well, but almost all included a cataclysmic battle between the forces of Good and Evil, with the eventual triumph of the Good (i.e., Israel), or the favored faction within Israel. An important conceptual difference was the question of whether the Jews should begin the final battle, which God would join, or wait for God himself to begin it. In the decades before the Jewish rebellion, many messianic figures arose in Judea, claiming to be the anointed one or announcing his imminent arrival. Some attracted very large groups of believers. Some but not all were militant and preached armed uprising. One of these militant groups, which was also messianic, was called Sicarii, or "knife-men." They specialized in assassinating their perceived enemies in the Jewish leadership. Another group called itself the Zealots, who were mostly priests inspired by the biblical figure Pinchas; they claimed that they would submit to no ruler but God. The followers of Jesus of Nazareth were a relatively small group that few people at that time would have predicted would be the founders of a great world religion.

It was this unshakable faith in God's plan and purpose that the Jews, people of a tiny nation, took into battle against the mighty Roman Empire. They were emboldened further by a selective historical memory. They recalled the recent victories of the Maccabees

[1] Josephus, *The Jewish War* 2.278.

(aka the Hasmoneans, the heroes of the Hanukkah story), whose revolt against the powerful Syrian-Greek empire in the second century BCE was astonishingly successful. They also saw a sign of God's favor in the retreat of Sennacherib, the powerful and megalo-maniacal Assyrian king who failed in his siege of Jerusalem in the eighth century BCE; that distant victory was vividly recalled as if recent and immediately relevant.

The question of war with Rome in the first century CE and how to interpret God's purpose bitterly divided the Jewish population in Judea. This conflict played out not only between rival revolutionary groups but also along class lines, since the wealthy Jewish upper class, consisting of high priests, wealthy priests, and other aristocrats, earned protection of their personal interests by cooperating with Roman rule. Yet even they lost patience as the abuses by Roman governors worsened, and many of them joined the rebellion. It should not be forgotten that educated Jewish aristocrats could be as pious and devoted to God's promises as the simplest peasants.

The war broke out in 66 CE, after Florus's most grotesque offense, a series of attacks on the population in Jerusalem, drove many Jews, including priests and lay aristocrats, to desperation, and a group of radical priests in the Temple stopped the sacrifices on behalf of the Roman emperor, Nero. Nero sent his governor of Syria, Cestius Gallus, to crush the incipient revolt. After a successful sweep through the Galilee and along the coast, Cestius laid siege to Jerusalem, but for reasons not fully understood, he suddenly fled from the city, his forces being trapped and cut to pieces in the Beth Horon pass, near the city. That incident indicated that war was on: the Romans would return in full force to avenge Cestius and crush the rebellion in their ruthless, methodical manner.

After Cestius's stunning defeat, the elated Jews founded an independent government in Jerusalem and organized the defense of their new state. They proclaimed "Jerusalem the Holy" and "The Freedom of Zion" on their new coins. The first government was led by members of the old ruling class, priests and wealthy lay leaders. Joseph ben Mattitiyahu, who would become the historian Josephus, was appointed governor and military commander of the Galilee. That meant that Joseph would be the first to confront the Roman army, for the Romans mustered forces and planned the invasion from Syria, in the north. By his own account, Joseph did the best he could in spring 67 CE, when the large Roman force, commanded by the general Vespasian, attacked Galilee, as expected. But God's intervention did not come, and without that, no one, including a small Jewish army armed with faith and impromptu weapons, could hold out against the Roman military machine. Galilee fell, Joseph was captured, and the Roman army continued to roll over all areas of Jewish habitation and resistance, eventually occupying the entire province and drawing a ring around Jerusalem.

The failure of Jewish defense, growing messianic expectations, class resentment, and a power struggle led to a coup d'état in Jerusalem in the winter of 67 to 68 CE. The leaders were forcefully removed from power, many were executed, and a new, more radical regime was installed. This new government was an uneasy coalition of militant groups and individuals who cooperated in seizing power but soon fell into conflict with each other. For nearly three years, the Jews in Jerusalem and elsewhere wore themselves out with constant civil war. Many were killed, and in the unceasing turf wars in Jerusalem, most of the food hoarded in anticipation of the Roman siege was burned. This internal conflict continued even as the Romans abandoned the war against the Jewish rebels for nearly two years as their own civil war over the emperorship raged throughout the empire, ending in Vespasian's proclamation as the new emperor in 69 CE. Four Roman legions, under command of the general Titus, the son of Vespasian, arrived in Jerusalem in the spring of 70 CE and laid siege to a city already exhausted by famine and civil conflict, beginning on the first day of Passover.

The siege of Jerusalem was unusually long and bitter, owing to the city's strong defenses—the Romans had to break through three walls—and the fierce tenacity of the Jewish defenders, which impressed even the Romans. The Romans overpowered the Jewish defenses with superior technology and superior numbers: against each wall, they built, at great expense, ramps and mounds, upon which they rolled up battering rams, catapults, and towers filled with slingers and archers. Inside the city, great suffering prevailed: people died not only from Roman missiles and swords and the ongoing Jewish civil war, which resumed during every pause in the Roman assault, but also from a cruel famine, a result of the destruction of the hoarded food. The famine became especially intense when a Roman siege wall built around the city cut off all chances to smuggle in food.

The city's defenses finally collapsed when the Romans, who had gained a foothold in the porticoes on the Temple Mount, were able to set fire to the Temple itself, in the hot month of August, traditionally on the date of 9 Av in the Hebrew calendar. We can only imagine the emotions of the Jewish defenders as they watched their holy Temple go up in flames. Josephus, an eyewitness to the calamity, wrote that "one would have thought that the Temple Mount was boiling over from its roots, since it was on all sides one mass of flame, but the river of blood was more abundant than the flames."[2] Many killed themselves. The Romans systematically destroyed the Temple Mount and burned much of the city. Thousands—including

---

[2] Josephus, *The Jewish War* 6.275.

Esther—were taken into captivity and sold throughout the empire. Many of the captives perished in the violent Roman games in amphitheaters in provinces and cities far from home.

There were scattered mopping-up operations, including one in Masada, the holdout fortress in the Judean Desert, but with the fall and destruction of Jerusalem and its Temple, the rebellion was effectively crushed. The year after the Destruction, the Romans celebrated their triumph in Rome, as depicted on the Arch of Titus, still standing in the Roman Forum. Judaism was forever changed. From a Temple-based religion, it became a religion based in the synagogue and study-house, where prayer and study replaced sacrifice as the main ritual focus. For many, messianic expectation did not die, but was encouraged by the Temple's destruction. Just sixty years after the Destruction, another religious-political leader who many thought was the Messiah, named Bar Kochba, led another rebellion against Rome, which ended in another crushing, massively bloody defeat. After that, most Jews did not lose their faith in the truth of Scripture, but revised their calculation of God's purpose and their expected role in it. Being barred from Jerusalem, a substantial Jewish population under a new rabbinic leadership established itself in the Galilee. Much of Jewish life in the following centuries, centered on the synagogue, was lived in creative tension with non-Jewish culture in cities and settlements throughout the Roman Empire and beyond.

Jonathan J. Price,
Fred and Helen Lessing Professor of Ancient History
Departments of History and Classics
Tel Aviv University

ACKNOWLEDGMENTS

—◊—

The idea for *Rebel Daughter* was sparked by a conversation with Professor Jonathan Price, who at the time was researching inscriptions of the ancient world. Without his inspiration and guidance, I would never have written this book.

Many other scholars took the time to speak with me and guide me to relevant source material, including Professor Joshua Schwartz of Bar-Ilan University and Professor Lee Levine of Hebrew University. I would also like to thank Naomi Schacter of the National Library of Israel.

My friends Cathy Raff, Elisa Moed, David Greenberg, Michelle Orelle, Stefanie Raker, Natalie Barkan, Alison Leigh Cowan, Judith Weill, Joel Rosenfeld, Lainie Cogan, and Ruthie Sobel read early drafts and made valuable suggestions. My brother Mark Banov provided important comments. I'm also grateful to Renee Atlas, Beth Lieberman, and Leslie Wells, for their in-depth critiques.

My agents Deborah Harris and Rena Rossner of the Deborah Harris Agency in Jerusalem are world-class and a pleasure to work with.

My editor, Beverly Horowitz, had unerring instincts about what worked in the manuscript and what needed revision. I would also like to thank her team, including Emily Harburg and Rebecca Gudelis, for their comments and help, as well as Design, Managing Editorial, Copyediting, and Production: Shameiza Ally, Kenneth Crossland, Denise DeGenarro, Colleen Fellingham, Regina Flath, and Tamar Schwartz. As a first-time novelist, I was extremely fortunate to have had the chance to learn from the best.

And last, I would like to thank my family. Spending time with my fictional creations was exciting and challenging, but it was nothing compared to time spent with my real ones: Dov, Matan, Danya and Jennie. Yadin, my partner in raising them—and in everything else I've done for the past forty years—was supportive from the very beginning. He never had any doubts that this book would find its readers, and deserves way more credit than I usually give him.

ABOUT THE AUTHOR

—◊—

Lori Banov Kaufmann was a strategy consultant for high-tech companies before she became a writer. She has an AB from Princeton University and an MBA from the Harvard Business School. When she learned about the discovery of the first-century tombstone, she wanted to know more. She was captivated by the ancient love story the stone revealed, which served as the inspiration for this book. *Rebel Daughter* is her debut novel. Lori Banov Kaufmann lives in Israel with her husband and four adult children.

lorikaufmann.com